READERS TALK ABOUT RICHARD EVANS

Richard Evans' first book, *Deceit*, is a five-star thriller that brings the Australian political process to life. — *GOODREADS*

I absolutely loved it, couldn't put it down. I would love to see your book become a movie. — *IAN S., MELBOURNE*

Rich in ideas and provokes much thought about our parliamentary process, abuses of power, corruption, and the need, at times, for ordinary people to step up and take a stand in the name of honour and professional integrity. — *NADINE D., EDITOR*

'The Kill Bill has such a fascinating concept at its heart and you brought the characters to life brilliantly.' — *C.dB, EDITOR*

This is an outstanding debut from Evans, and this terrific read comes highly recommended.' — *GOODREADS*

From former Federal MP Richard Evans comes this exceptional political thriller debut, which serves as the first part of his Democracy trilogy.' — *CANBERRA WEEKLY*

I adored Gordon O'Brien. Straight as an arrow amongst those who are only in things for themselves, I couldn't help but cheer him on as he was like a dog with a bone, searching out the truth' — *BJ'S BOOK BLOG*

Just finished reading *Deceit* and it was gripping; I could not put it down. It was brilliant. I just loved the book and can't wait to read *Duplicity*.' — *FORMER CLERK OF VICTORIAN LEGISLATIVE COUNCIL*

I thoroughly enjoyed the book and did not want to put the book down, but neither did I want the story to end! Congratulations! — *TRINITY MARKETING*

THE KILL BILL

THE PERSONAL IS POLITICAL

RICHARD EVANS

852 PRESS

852

PRESS

First published in 2021 by 852 Press,
an imprint of Corven Pty. Limited
Suite 208, 5-11 Cole Street, Williamstown Victoria 3016 Australia
www.852Press.com

10 9 8 7 6 5 4 3 2 1

National Library of Australia Cataloguing-in-Publication entry:

Author: Evans, Richard
Title: The Kill Bill / by Richard Evans
ISBN: 978-0-6489328-3-3 (paperback)
ISBN: 978-0-6489328-4-0 (ebook)
ISBN: 978-0-6489328-5-7 (hardcover)
Australian fiction.

A catalogue record for this book is available from the National Library of Australia

Cover Design: Working Type, www.workingtype.com.au
Internal design: Working Type

*For my mother Rena
I remember and will never forget.*

The majority of deaths in Australia, like other developed countries, occur among older people. Sixty-six per cent of deaths registered in Australia are among people aged 75 or over.

Let us all hope they each died with dignity.

CHAPTER

1

These were the tiresome moments. Resolving the angst of sinners. Lending an ear to wearisome stories about unthinkable breaches of canon law. Having to discipline reckless priests and miscreant clergy for tedious sins, some literally caught with their pants down, was not what he coveted. Unprecedented sacrifice for the sake of church and community led him to a life of devotion, but he expected he was above this demeaning suppression of ambition. His aspiration for higher office knew full well the dark politics of the church, and without these moments, counselling others, he would never achieve what he lusted after.

Cardinal Rosseau scheduled these dreary sessions once a month, dedicating most of the day to attending sinners before dispensing virtuous opinion and teachings.

As the most senior cardinal in the Vatican, many within the papal conclave thought him unfortunate not to have been elected Holy Father three years earlier. He petitioned his colleagues spiritedly for elevation after the unexpected death of the pontiff, but the prevailing chorus from religious media and influential social media trolls persuaded the Catholic Church to contemplate that the time was right for the elevation of a black Pope. It just wasn't foreseen that the new Pope would emerge from the United States of America, indeed, Las Vegas.

So now the cardinal dispensed pastoral guidance every month with as much enthusiasm as he could muster, which wasn't much.

Rosseau's office in the Vatican was seldom visited by fawning VIP guests, and tourists never stepped foot across the threshold. His private apartment on the second floor was a short distance along a darkened stone corridor from the Sistine Chapel. A nearby secluded private chapel allowed him to pursue spiritual renewal with silent prayer and daily communion with the Lord, hoping, as always, for acceptance and love.

Over the years, whilst remaining dedicated to the fidelity of the liturgy and spiritual readings, it was becoming an increasing observation among residents within the Vatican that the cardinal, with advancing age, was grumpier, often seeking greater penance for his lack of enthusiasm. Now, during his many moments of reflection, he considered that a new, much younger pontiff meant that his ambition to have divinity bestowed upon him by his peers was long gone. He now often mused if he had wasted too many years with far too many sacrifices.

'How many more do we have?' Rosseau sighed as he slunk back into his leather chair, resting his head into a hand.

'Just two more, Your Eminence.'

'Some parish charity gone down the gurgler, has it?' The cardinal waved languidly, his other hand now wiping his brow with the tips of his fingers. 'Or a grimy farmer's wife pregnant from an immaculate conception?'

'We have one last priest and a bishop for you.' The cardinal's secretary, Bishop Aitken, itemised from his folder as he attended by the door.

'I wager I know why the priest is here.'

'It could very well have been as you suspect, but thankfully, not yet.'

'What's the goose gone and done?' Rosseau sighed, then almost snarled, 'Can't these disciples ever control primal urges?'

'This one has admitted viewing inappropriate material on the internet and downloading images.'

'What is wrong with these people?' Rosseau spat the words. 'Don't they know that the sin of smut is the vilest impulse for their celibacy?'

'This case is more complicated, I'm afraid,' a sullen Aitken replied.

Rosseau glared at the bishop, but Aitken had averted his eyes. 'What's he done?'

'It has to do with children, Your Eminence.'

'How young?'

'Just teenage boys.'

'Just?' Rosseau snapped. 'Just? Is this what we now call it?'

'Sorry, Your Eminence.' Aitken bowed, seeking forgiveness.

'I would have thought our recruitment process would have been more rigorous by now and picked up on these pathetic morons before they had any position in the church.'

'He used a parish computer to download ten files. The security system in the network picked it up. He was interviewed and we have no further evidence of him acting upon his urges.'

'He has groomed no one?'

'No, Your Eminence.'

'Are you sure? Have we checked with the parish committee?'

'Yes, Your Eminence.'

'Why is he here to see me?'

'He has confessed and repented,' Aitken responded. 'His progress reports are complimentary, and the archbishop believes he is worth saving.'

'Send him to me to sort him out… is that it?'

'Yes, Your Eminence.' Aitken glanced at the cardinal and faked a smile. 'You do have a reputation for saving souls.'

Rosseau returned the gaze, pursed his lips, then squeezed a thin smile. 'Where is the bishop from?'

Aitken referred to his notes. 'He has travelled from Toulouse. It's a personal matter, apparently.'

'My family is from Toulouse.' Rosseau's eyes narrowed. 'I had better see the priest first.'

Aitken bowed and stepped away to the anteroom, leaving the cardinal to ponder why a bishop might have travelled to Rome seeking an audience. The room was darkening as the gloomy light from the small window retreated, casting shadows and colours across the room, turning his scarlet cassock into cherry blood red.

A gentle knock at the door interrupted his thoughts. Bishop Aitken was tracked into the room by a nervous priest dressed in a fitted full black cassock with a rope cincture. He came before the cardinal, waiting with his head down. Rosseau let him remain in this position for some time before he proffered his right hand. The anxious priest took it, raising it to his lips, kissing the enormous sapphire.

'They tell me you want to be a buggerer of boys; is this correct?'

The priest remained bowing and whispered, 'No, Your Eminence.'

'They tell me you watch repulsive films of boys.' The priest did not respond. 'What am I to do with you?'

After a short wait, there was still no response from the priest.

'I'm tempted to excommunicate you from the church and have you exposed to the police for your malevolent ways.'

'Your Eminence, I seek your forgiveness, nothing more. I ask you to do unto me whatever you see fit as retribution for my wanton and craven acts of selfishness.'

The cardinal gazed at the priest who dropped to his knees with his hands clasped outstretched before him, head still bowed.

'Yeah, nice one,' Rosseau replied with a disdainful flick of his hand. 'You talk a good line, but do you walk the path toward true repentance? Am I to believe you are not so youthfully challenged that you will not weaken to your urges and transgress again?'

The priest began sniffling, his hands stretched above his head toward the cardinal. 'Your Eminence, forgive me and punish me as you must.'

Rosseau glanced to Aitken, who shrugged, mouth pouted, head bobbing.

'Stand up and collect yourself,' Rosseau demanded. The priest raised himself to his sandalled feet. 'Look at me. Begin to live the life of a true disciple and do not cower on your knees from the truth.'

The priest glanced up into the cardinal's eyes, wiping his cheeks with the back of his hands. 'Yes, Your Eminence.'

Rosseau clasped his hands, elbows resting on the soft arms of his chair and holding his chin and mouth; he evaluated the young man. 'You need to understand duty and honour to forsake your selfish needs, do you understand?' The priest gnawed at his lower lip and nodded. 'To cast you out of the church is not punishment. It seems to me, that for you to learn from your guilt, you must apply yourself to seeking forgiveness so you may serve the community. Have you sought forgiveness?'

'With my every word.'

'Then seek it now.'

The priest glanced askew at the cardinal, wondering what he should do. Rosseau nodded encouragement, roll-waving his hand for him to speak the words they have taught him.

The priest cleared his throat, raised his hands and said, 'O Lord, Jesus Christ, Redeemer and Saviour, forgive my sins, just as You forgave Peter's denial and those who crucified You. Count not my transgressions, but my tears of repentance. Remember not my iniquities, but more especially, my sorrow for the offences I have committed against You. I long to be true to Your Word and pray that You will love me and come to make Your dwelling place within me. I promise to give You praise and glory in love and in service all the days of my life.'

As the priest lowered his hands, Rosseau said, 'I'm going to take away your access to the internet which is a continuing tool of Satan for the disruption of our message. I'm going to send you to a place where any sign of you weakening to your nauseating urges will be reprimanded in the most horrendous ways… trust me.'

Rosseau glared with intent at the priest to reinforce his words.

'I'm sending you to Egypt to work with my friends at the Coptic Church at the Cathedral of Our Lady of Egypt in Cairo. I want you to discover from them an understanding of the injustices against Catholics within a Muslim country. They have only rudimentary internet networks, so your need to satisfy your lust will in time diminish. I expect your tenure to be no less than three years.'

The priest at first did not respond, his jaw tightening, teeth grinding as he stewed on what he had just heard. He grasped that his wickedness was being punished most severely, which could lead to a death sentence. 'I am thankful, Your Eminence.'

'You won't be thankful in three years; I can assure you.'

The priest bowed and was led from the room by Aitken. Rosseau gazed out to the darkening sky, his knuckle stroking his lips as he reflected on his forgiveness and what he had commanded the young priest to do. Politics and culture toward Christians in Egypt meant it would not be easy for the assigned young man, but forgiveness was not always honey and roses.

'Bishop Berneux, Your Eminence.' Aitken announced the next meeting then withdrew, after predetermining what the conversation would cover. Berneux strode toward the cardinal, who idly waved his right hand, which was taken, and a quick kiss placed upon his ring.

'Please make yourself comfortable. What brings you to seek an audience?'

The bishop noticed a wooden chair to the side and took the seat. 'I need to talk to you about your mother.'

'What about her?'

'She is close to death, Your Eminence, and I'm seeking your instruction.'

'What instruction do you need?'

'It's a little dark in here; would you mind if I switch on a lamp?'

'If you must.' Rosseau was losing patience.

The bishop stretched up to a lamp on a shelf above him, located the switch and flicked it on.

'That's much better. I'll be able to see my papers now.' He opened the leather binder on his lap, withdrawing two sheets of crisp typewritten paper and referring to one before speaking. 'As you are the oldest child, under French law you have the authority of procuration to make decisions on behalf of your mother.'

'I've not had anything to do with my mother for over twenty years. Can't my sisters provide whatever it is you need?'

'Not on an issue like this.' The bishop tightened his tone. 'You are the titular head of your family, and this decision is yours.'

'I do not regard my family with any sense of benevolence, so whatever it is you want me to do, I'm reluctant to submit.'

'This is unfortunate, Your Eminence; however, I must insist you consider this important issue and perhaps provide me with a sense of compassionate direction.'

'You insist,' barked Rosseau. 'You insist? What is it you insist I do?'

The bishop held up an apologetic hand. 'Please pardon my enthusiasm, Your Eminence; this has been an issue for your mother for some time and it needs resolution.'

'I won't have anything to do with her estate. My selfish, money-hungry sisters are welcome to it all; I want nothing.'

'This has nothing to do with your mother's estate.'

'What is it then? Stop dilly-dallying... spell it out.'

The bishop lowered his voice. 'I am sad to advise you that your mother has moved into a hospice and is under palliative care.'

'What's the problem?'

'We can make her comfortable and pain free. Eventually, under God's will, she will pass.'

'Then what is it you want me to do?'

'We need your instructions on how to manage the palliative care.'

'What does that mean?'

'We wonder if we should allow her to pass in her own time under continuous sleep sedation, or does the family prefer her to reach an end sooner?'

'Oh, for heaven's sake, Berneux tell me what you want!'

'Do you want us to hasten her death?'

Rosseau turned away, trailing a hand across his face, stroking, then cupping his chin. She meant nothing to him. He had loathed his childhood and the extreme beatings he and his sisters had shared, always by the hand or leather strap of his mother. Any excuse to punish him, she took it. She blamed him for his father's sins and was a constant reminder of devious criminal acts and abhorrent behaviour with the girls. The cardinal never forgave her for the absence of love in his childhood, and it enticed him to the church, which welcomed him with sympathetic open arms.

'It's acceptable, Morris, to be saddened on these occasions when we are confronted with decisions we thought we would never have to take.' The bishop leaned forward, reaching out to comfort the cardinal.

Rosseau almost choked on the words as he forced them out. 'What is your name?'

'You can call me Jean-Paul; I am here to care for you during this time of judgment.'

Rosseau didn't move, almost growling, said, 'Jean-Paul, if you ever disrespect me or my position by referring to me by any means other than my title, I will ensure that your appointment in Toulouse will end and you will be thrown on the scrap heap of inconsequence within the church.' He swung around, brushing away the bishop's hand. 'Do we understand each other?'

The bishop sat back in his chair, alarmed by the savagery of the delivery. 'I was just trying to support you.'

'Are we clear?' Rosseau demanded.

'Yes, Your Eminence.'

'How long will it take naturally?'

'Probably two months, maybe longer.'

'And if you hastened the deed?

'A week or two, maybe less.'

Rosseau paused for a moment, then locked eyes with the bishop and said, 'End it as soon as you can.'

'I need you to sign this release.'

Rosseau snatched the paper, scanned it, then moved to his desk, removing the cap of his Mont Blanc and signing the document before proffering it to the bishop.

'I do not want to hear from you again.' He pushed a button on his desk as the bishop placed the document in his satchel. Aitken entered, ready to usher Berneux from the room.

The bishop stopped by the door, turned and said, 'Peace be with you, Your Eminence. May you find what you are searching for.'

Rosseau did not acknowledge him, moving to the window to watch the last of the day, musing on his meeting. He hadn't been prepared to think about his family, having pushed them from his consciousness many years earlier. His mother was not a saint and did not deserve a moment's thought, ever.

After seeing the bishop from the building and thanking him for his patience, Bishop Aitken returned, sidling into the office, hesitant, a little unsure of his cardinal's mood.

'Eminence?' Aitken murmured. 'Can I speak with you for a moment?'

Rosseau turned and smiled, returning to his armchair. 'Sure, Bruce. What is it?'

'Are you feeling all right?'

'I'm fine; what do you have for me?'

'These decisions are always hard; do you want to talk about it?'

'No, I'm fine; can we move on, please?'

Aitken wasn't persuaded. He had known and respected Rosseau for many years for his clarity of interpretation of the scriptures, facilitating a modern narrative to the social teachings of the church, yet keeping the moral sanctity of canonical scripture. The cardinal often advised his followers that the magisterium of the church should prevail, yet it was he who coveted that authority.

'The Holy Father has requested you meet with him this evening,' Aitken said. 'I will delay dinner until your return.'

'That will not happen,' the cardinal smiled, crossing his legs and feeling more relaxed. 'The great man can wait. I shall have dinner at the normal time, thank you. I will visit him after. Perhaps you may care to join me. I have a nice Bordeaux which may tempt you.' Aitken hesitated. 'Oh, come on, Bruce, relax; it's not every day I share a meal with my staff. Perhaps you can guide me through my suffering.'

'It would be my pleasure, Your Eminence.'

CHAPTER

2

At eight, the cardinal ambled through the darkened corridors of the Vatican to the pontiff's office. The tourists were long gone, and he observed no one as he strolled past the chapel. The masterpieces didn't distract him; they never did anymore, he'd stopped being captivated by the history and reverence of the building and its aging chattels many years ago.

Rosseau knocked on the large wooden door. Not waiting for a response, he stepped into the vast room. The pontiff was at his desk at the very far end reading papers, and he glanced up as the cardinal crossed the various woven rugs covering the black-and-white checkered marble floor, passing the formal international visitor greeting precinct and its presentation table. As the cardinal reached the wooden table desk, the Pope sat back in his chair, almost hard up against the wall.

'Dressed in scarlet? No need for such formality.'

'I wear it when conducting visitations. It seems to influence the people who come seeking advice.'

'Nothing like power dressing.' The Pope smiled, gesturing for the cardinal to sit.

Rosseau struggled to grip the heavy chair to shift it, but soon settled, waiting for the Holy Father to outline why he was attending.

'Thank you for coming, although I expected you earlier.'

'I have a busy diary.'

'Yes, don't we all?' The pontiff steepled his fingers and rested his chin on his thumbs, examining the cardinal. 'Why is it we are yet to find a role for you here in the Vatican?'

'I want the job as president.'

'It's not available.'

'Then I'll wait.'

'Not good enough to do other, shall we suggest, lowly tasks?'

Rosseau glared at the pontiff, then said, 'It was a close race between us; I think your skin colour got you over the line, but don't think for one moment that I will agree to your elevation.'

'I'm not asking you to be a servant to me. I'm asking what job you would like to do while you're waiting.' The Pope smiled again.

'I'm happy doing what I'm doing right now.'

'Which, I'm advised, is nothing… other than of course your busy diary, once a month.' Rosseau's jaw flickered for a moment as the Pope studied him. 'You don't like me, do you?'

Rosseau accepted the offer. 'It's not you, Holy Father; it's more your flashy Vegas ways.'

'I may have been born there, but I escaped sin city as hastily as I could. I embraced none of that culture.'

Rosseau didn't respond straight away. He displayed a Vegas poker player's face. 'If you say so. It's just the manner in which you dress, speak, and move that unsettles us, and this new period of enlightenment you insist upon, is, how shall we say, challenging.'

'Unsettling? That's the perfect word, because, that's exactly what I'm hoping. We need to change the management culture around here, and I suspect I know how to change it.'

'Sometimes change is stressful, Your Holiness. The Lord was a man of change, but he brought us together. Perhaps you may wish to consider this proposition.'

The Pope smiled as he reflected on the rebuke.

'I have a job for you I would like you to consider. It's important for the church, and if you are successful, it could see you reach the reward you desire.'

'What is it?' Rosseau was sceptical.

'It's a political campaign we need to win. Are you interested?'

'I could be. What's it about?'

'No doubt you know the brand is under threat.'

'Why do you insist on calling the Catholic Church a brand?' Rosseau sighed, repositioning himself in the chair. 'This is what I'm talking about.'

'It's the reason they elected me over you… not because of my skin colour, but the modern world strategies I bring to the job.'

'Two thousand years of development and we are being commercialised into a marketing strategy. No wonder they're leaving us.'

'They are leaving us because we trashed our reputation. We are not relevant to young people. The traditions and conservatism we espouse are no longer heard within the social media tsunami drowning our voices.'

'They are leaving us because we don't fight for justice any more. They consider us out of touch.'

'Exactly. We are on the same page.'

'I wouldn't have thought so,' Rosseau sneered. 'The only book I read is our bible.'

'You see? That's the reason you lost the vote. You are far too set in your ways.'

'Reading the scripture is too set in my ways?' Rosseau seethed.

'We all follow the scripture, and we bow to its tenets. Of course we do, but we don't have to do it in a tone that is so depressing. You need to get more joy in your life, Morris.'

Rosseau tightened his jaw and over bit his bottom lip, gnawing at it, trying to stop himself from saying something he would later regret. 'Yes, Your Holiness.'

After an uncomfortable pause, the Pope continued, 'We have a serious challenge in Australia.'

'Oh yes? What have those reprobates done now?'

'They are about to legislate life and death decisions into national law, not as it now stands in regional state law.'

'Why should we be concerned?'

'They are about to formalise euthanasia into law by use of a referendum.'

'Letting the people speak is something we would support, surely?'

'We all love democracy, but only when we know the result. I have no issue with politicians enacting law, because they can amend it at a later time,' the Pope said. 'If the law results from a referendum, then it would become impossible to change the will of the people.'

'I understand the euthanasia debate, but why is this action in Australia any different from Europe?'

'It's because they are undermining the Catholic teachings of the sanctity of life, enabling the killing of people at the end of life.'

'This is the argument we used in Europe. We lost that debate; why now, why Australia?'

'We need to make a stand. We need to stop this trend away from Christian teachings, and we need a government to send a powerful message to western and developing worlds it is wrong to enact laws on morals and ethics. The church retains this responsibility, not government.'

'We are losing this debate, just as we lost the abortion debate.'

'That's the point; if we can get a government to retreat on legislating this part of life, then perhaps we can reignite debates about other life and death issues. We just need a win.'

'What's the government's position?'

'They are all over the place. No clear leadership. We have an opportunity to influence a result our way. I think you're the man to do it for us.'

'The archbishop out there… is he not capable?'

'Useless, has little influence.'

Rosseau thought through the pontiff's argument and considered whether there was an opportunity for him. 'If we win?'

'You could get what you want.'

'If we lose?'

'Then we are all in deep doo-doo… including me.'

Rosseau pursed his lips, smirking behind his hand. The campaign was a win–win for him, no matter what he achieved.

'When would you like me to start?'

'The parliament is in recess for a few weeks, so get out there as soon as you can. I'm expecting that they will bring the legislation forward once they resume parliament.'

CHAPTER

3

'I warned you not to do it.' The treasurer was barely inside the prime minister's office. 'Now we have the greatest stuff up in legislative history. What the hell are we going to do?'

Nancy Pasco didn't respond, bemused by the manner in which her treasurer was shifting blame to her. 'Good morning, Parker. When did you get in?'

'Last night.' Osborne sat frustrated, dumping his thick wad of papers on her desk. 'PM, I can promise you my community leaders are seething about the result from this damn plebiscite debacle.' He slapped the wooden arm of the chair. 'It's the role of the parliament to make laws, not the damn community. They told us not to do it, but of course, you knew better and did it, anyway.'

'Ease up, Ozzie… it was a cabinet decision.' The unacknowledged attorney general, Charles Stevedore, joined the conversation from his seat on the nearby sofa.

Osborne swivelled in his chair, surprised to see him. 'This will kill us at the next election, Charlie, you know that.'

'We have our troubles, but this issue is not a major one.'

'Just explain that weird opinion to me. Have you not seen today's polls?'

'No different from the last two years,' sighed Pasco. 'At least the preferred prime minister didn't fall any further.' She chuckled nervously.

'Nancy, for heaven's sake; it's not a joke.'

'Settle down will you, Ozzie, please?' Stevedore implored. 'Raving about the past will not affect the future. The question we need to resolve is… what are we to do about it?'

'Given the result, do we need to do anything?' Pasco suggested.

'You are kidding, right?' Osborne returned his attention to the prime minister. 'Fifty-three percent in favour of overriding the states. We have to follow through.'

'You're right; we weren't expecting that result.' The prime minister stood, joining Stevedore on another nearby sofa, kicking off her heels and stretching her stockinged feet onto the marble coffee table. 'Anyone want a drink?'

Stevedore shrugged a no. 'Prime Minister, this is the time to make a decision. Do we push this through or not?'

'What do you think, Charles?' Pasco placed an arm on the back of the lounge, combing her fingers through her hair, clearing it from her face.

'Parker is right, we are now obligated to bring legislation to the parliament; if we don't, then democratic principles are trashed. We need to legislate a referendum and amend section 51. To ensure the absolute majority in the parliament, we should spell out what the new euthanasia law. If we get the referendum up, we will need to campaign hard to get a Yes vote over the line.'

'It will be called Mission Impossible… Rogue Parliament,' laughed Osborne. He then sighed. 'Stuff me; we're screwed.'

'I'm not so sure,' Stevedore advised. 'Although a small majority voted for the plebiscite, the question was ambiguous. I reckon voters will change their minds and support the new law.'

'Ambiguous? That's a good one,' chided Osborne, as he then emphasised each word by blocking a headline with his outstretched hand. 'Should the federal government have the power to make Life and Death laws? It was a total disaster.'

'Yes, but we never put a law to them. This was the trouble, I suspect.'

'Ya think?'

'I think it's time for a drink,' Pasco said, moving to the cocktail cabinet. 'I'm having a wine, anyone?'

'Not for me, thanks,' Stevedore replied, as Osborne gaped, shaking his head. 'The really interesting point to consider on this opportunity...'

'Opportunity?' Osborne snorted.

'It's life and death. Perhaps, we can nationalise the abortion laws.'

'Interesting.' Pasco polished off a half glass of chardonnay before refilling it, returning to the lounge with the bottle.

Osborne shook his head again, checking his watch to register that it was not yet eleven. As the prime minister passed by, he glanced at Stevedore, who was also observing the prime minister, raising an eyebrow at his colleague.

'Let me get this straight.' Osborne leaned forward, elbows on his knees. 'If we are making federal life and death laws, why don't we address capital punishment?'

'We can,' Stevedore responded. 'If that's the murky policy pit we want to venture down.'

Osborne shook his head. 'We kill them before they're born; we kill them when they're too old; and, if they stuff up during their miserable lives, we kill them as well... un-fucking-believable.'

'He's not recommending that,' Pasco scoffed. 'Are you, Charles? '

'It's an option; that's all I'm saying.'

Osborne sat back, crossing his legs. 'Don't say it too damn loud, otherwise we're gone.'

'What's your recommendation?' Pasco asked Stevedore.

'I suspect it will be a hard road to achieve a Yes vote in a majority of states.'

'It may be in our best interests if we don't get it done,' the prime minister replied, taking a large gulp of wine.

'You campaigned for the Yes vote on the plebiscite; you can't back down now,' Osborne insisted.

'I'm not backing down, but if we delayed by process, then that's not my fault.'

'Of course the media will see it as your fault,' snapped Osborne.

'This will not be my fault if it fails, I can assure you,' Pasco smirked, taking another mouthful of wine.

'Whose fault will it be?' Osborne demanded.

'You two, as much as me.' Pasco drained her glass, pushing it back onto the table. 'I'm not going down alone on this, I can assure you.'

'It has to pass the party room first,' Stevedore interrupted. 'Then the parliament, then the referendum. Any of those steps could fail to obtain a majority.'

'Which is why I say, it might be easier to go soft on the legislation,' Pasco said, as she waved a newly poured glass, spilling a little on the carpet.

'The PM's right, Ozzie. This is not a first order issue.'

'Let me make my position very clear.' Osborne moved to leave, picking up his bundle of papers. 'I will not nail my colours to the mast of this doomed ship unless you, Prime Minister, give it your full support.'

'Parker,' Stevedore stood to address him. 'We're all in this together. We can't afford to have a gossamer thread of difference between our public comments and the manner in which we negotiate this through the parliament.'

'Yeah, right,' sighed Osborne, as he brushed past his fellow leadership contender. 'Just make sure the admiral is on the bridge in a fit state, will you?'

'That was interesting,' said the prime minister, as she finished the bottle. 'What do you think we should do, Charles? Run hard or just jog it through the process?'

'I have my reasons for running hard.'

'I also have my own reasons,' Pasco said. 'Get started on it, please; but don't treat it as a priority.'

'It's listed for the first session back in three weeks.'

'Get it ready, but feel assured, if it has holes that delay it, I won't be too annoyed.'

CHAPTER
4

Osborne tracked the blue-grey carpet back to his office, considering political opportunities; he determined he had delayed his career ambition far too long; he was the prime minister in waiting, but believed he had waited long enough. Loyalty had its political advantages, but now it was time to step forward. He would provide the nation with a new leadership model, not one based on an early morning bottle of wine.

'Kaitlyn,' he barked as he entered the foyer of his office, ignoring the smiling staffer at the reception desk. As he crashed through his office door, tossing his wad of papers onto a side meeting table, Kaitlyn May marched into the room from another door with pad in hand, pen in hair. 'What do you think I should do?'

'I think you should tell me what your dilemma is.'

'Do you think we have the numbers to challenge, or would you recommend we wait until the PM falls flat on her face when the referendum fails?'

'What referendum?'

'The Kill Bill.'

'Don't call it that,' May hushed him.

'I can to you.'

'Not even to me. Walls have ears; you should know that by now.'

Osborne walked around his desk, flopping into the chair. 'The euthanasia legislation.'

'What's got you into this mood?'

'I just left Pasco's office. Another uninspiring meeting. She has no idea.'

'She does have a tight hold on the numbers.'

'This bill might loosen her grip.' Osborne dragged his chair into the desk. 'Is any of this urgent?' he asked, waving at his in-tray.

'No. Tell me about the meeting?'

'Charlie was there.' Osborne reflected for a few moments. 'Good ole Charlie, he hasn't been the same since his wife died.' He squeezed his hands in front of him, then glared at May. 'If there was a leadership spill, do you think he would put his hand up?'

'He might, but I wouldn't have thought so. Australians will not elect a widower.'

'Ouch, that's harsh,' Osborne winced. 'I don't trust the bastard though.'

'You don't trust anyone.'

'Not true,' Osborne smirked. 'I trust you.'

'What did the three of you decide?'

'We're developing legislation to amend section 51 and allow the feds to control life and death matters.'

'Just euthanasia, right?'

Osborne smiled, waggling his finger at May. 'You're a brilliant girl, aren't you?' May twisted a querying face. 'This is the exact point Charlie made. We could go the whole hog and roll in abortion and… believe it or not, he suggested capital punishment.'

'You all agreed?'

'Kind of… she would have agreed to anything after polishing off a bottle.'

'Then wait until the referendum fails; she will be toast in the electorate.'

'What do I do if she doesn't push for the bill? She implied she might not,' Osborne queried.

'Then you must encourage her to support it. She will go down in a screaming heap, and voila, they elect you prime minister, unopposed.'

'She wants Charlie and me beside her.'

'You are, and you will be… when the critical time comes, you are in the shadows.'

'You're not only smart, you're also devious, aren't you?'

'That's why I'm here.'

'Hmm, and I thought it was for your coffee.'

'I'll get you one, but you had better get yourself ready, you have a flight to Sydney in ninety minutes.'

'Why am I going to Sydney?'

'Don't worry, you'll be back for dinner with your anonymous colleagues. The archbishop has requested you to visit this afternoon.'

'What does that pathetic moron want?'

'He wants to put a proposition to you.'

'Interesting. Why doesn't he come here? Perhaps he can come to dinner?'

'He insisted on Sydney; he didn't say why. I'll get your coffee. Just plough your way through your tray. Nothing major, mostly signatures.'

'Thanks, Kait.' Osborne dragged over his tray as she left and began working his way through the pile of files, signing where showed by yellow tabs.

CHAPTER

5

The chauffeured commonwealth-plated white limousine swung into the drive of St Mary's Cathedral just before the two thirty scheduled meeting. It stopped close to the gothic cathedral, a staff member waiting by the door of the residence to usher Osborne in for his meeting with Archbishop Moran. The treasurer followed through the dark hallways into an office, where Moran stood in expectation. Osborne noticed another clergyman sitting in a lounge chair, a distinctive pectoral cross resting on his chest.

'Excellency, nice to meet with you again.' Osborne offered his hand.

'Mr Osborne, I'm so pleased you could come at such brief notice,' Moran said, taking his hand and weakly shaking it before dropping it and waving to his guest. 'Allow me to introduce you to His Eminence, Cardinal Rosseau, recently arrived from the Vatican.'

Osborne swung to greet the cardinal who didn't respond, so he bowed.

'Pleased to meet you. What brings you to our fine city?'

Moran ushered Osborne to a seat before the cardinal could reply, so Rosseau waited for everyone to settle down.

'I am here to speak to leaders of the government regarding legislation that has been mooted for debate.'

Osborne snickered a little. 'Straight down to business. I like it.'

'The cardinal is here for a week or two,' offered Moran. 'He has meetings scheduled with the Bishops Council and will meet with various government leaders, both state and federal.'

'Have you been to Australia before?'

'No, but I am looking forward to learning more about your country. I also want to see a koala bear.'

'They're not really bears.'

'What are they?'

'Marsupials.'

'Not sure I know what that means. The archbishop has promised me a trip to the zoo where I can meet such a creature.'

'Should be fun.' Osborne changed the discussion. 'You mentioned you wanted to discuss legislation.'

'Yes. It's to do with this euthanasia law your government is proposing.'

'What do you want to know about it?'

'Why?' Rosseau said, gazing at Osborne. 'Why is your government wanting to legislate this despicable idea of medical homicide?'

Osborne's head dropped sideways, face winced, eyebrows raised, lips pursed. He then shrugged, opening up his hands. 'Well, I wouldn't frame it in those terms.'

'What terms are more appropriate?' Rosseau snapped. 'Assisted suicide? Or perhaps we can call it assisted dying?'

'We are trying to assist the terminally ill to receive palliative care humanely.'

'So, if death is foreseeable, killing a patient is okay, as it reduces the burden on the community?'

Osborne didn't respond. He glanced at the cardinal, then flicked a glance to Moran, then looked back to the cardinal. 'I take it the church will not be supporting the legislation?'

'Why are you doing it?' Rosseau persisted.

'The community has voted to enact federal law to deal with life and death matters. We have some states with this legislation, and we believe bringing the nation under one consistent law will resolve the tragic occurrence of folks locating to another state to access the service.'

'Access to assisted medical homicide, you mean?'

'That is an extreme framing of what the government is trying to do. Words are important in this debate, and those you chose are highly provocative.'

'Do you think it morally, or indeed, spiritually prudent for the government to sanction death?'

Osborne shifted in his chair, uncomfortable with the language. 'It may never be enacted.'

'If that is the case, why bring it forward?'

'The community has told us this is what they want.'

'Fifty-three percent? Hardly a decisive decision.'

'A democratic decision,' Osborne said. 'The prime minister wants to move forward.'

'Then it's time for a new prime minister.'

The statement took aback Osborne, raising his eyebrows and shaking his head. 'The church does not have that kind influence any more.' He checked his watch, noting that he had twenty minutes. 'Decisions about who leads this country are made by the party room and not influenced by anyone. I find it troubling that a clergyman from Rome would suggest we overthrow the Australian prime minister.'

Rosseau regrouped. 'I was not suggesting a coup, my friend. It should not be just one person who is deciding.'

'Why am I here, John?' Osborne asked, now gazing at Moran.

Moran cleared his throat, then leaned forward. 'I recommended your name to His Eminence when he asked who the most influential person in the government might be.'

'I wanted to learn your view and whether you support the bill,' Rosseau added.

Osborne considered both men using his political face, his bland expression blurring his true thoughts and the anxiety he was feeling.

'We want the bill killed and we think you are the best person to ensure that it is,' Moran suggested.

'That is not as easy as you may think,' Osborne retorted. He had strategised about the politics of the issue during the forty-minute flight to Sydney. 'I'm now of the view that if we don't bring it forward to a vote, the progressive left will keep fighting to have the government legislate, then it becomes an election issue.'

'Why not just stop it dead right now?' Rosseau demanded, his tone sharper.

'Of course, that can be done, but the beast will grow another head,' Osborne grumbled. 'To kill it properly, we need the Australian public to vote it down at a referendum.'

'You support us?' Moran asked.

'I support the government getting reelected. This matter is not a significant election issue for us,' Osborne said. 'My preference would have been that we should never have brought it up, but now that we have, we must deal with it.'

'My preference is that it doesn't go to a vote,' Rosseau responded.

'Politics is never that easy,' Osborne advised.

'Wouldn't it just be easier to get rid of the prime minister?'

'Play our cards right, and we may achieve both outcomes,' said Osborne, with a cheeky grin. 'If we defeat the referendum, then its political sponsor will also be vanquished.'

'If the prime minister is smart, she should kill it dead and not bring it to a vote,' Moran suggested.

Osborne nodded his head in agreement. 'This is why you need to put pressure on her. Bully her and she will legislate to spite you.'

'Why would she do that? She may end up supporting our view,' Rosseau said.

'She hates you.'

Rosseau thought about the comment. 'Us, or all Christians?'

'She is a devout atheist. She comes from a science background and reckons we base all religions on some kind of voodoo.' Osborne smiled at the body language of the clergymen. 'The more you push a religious position, the more stubborn she will become, which I predict will be to your advantage, as she will make mistakes.'

Rosseau ran a finger through his lips as he gazed at Osborne. 'You consider pushing someone away masks your exact wishes?'

'Politics 101, Your Eminence. Never disclose your true intent,' Osborne smiled. 'If you want euthanasia legislation crushed forever, then drive the prime minister to endorse it. It goes to a referendum, then gets voted down, forever. You get what you want, and perhaps I get what I want.'

'What do you want, my son?' Rosseau smiled.

'To be elected prime minister, of course.' Osborne stood, readying himself to leave. Rosseau also rose, extending his hand. 'Let us work together to get what we want; we shall be in touch with you. Most revealing.'

Osborne took his hand and shook it. 'What's your name?'

'Morris.'

'Well, Morris, if you can drive the prime minister to a decision to stage the referendum, then I can assure you, using John's words, that I will kill the bill.'

'I'm very pleased we have met; I have learnt much from this brief meeting and hope to talk to you again.'

'Oh, I'm sure we will.' Osborne turned to the archbishop. 'John, anytime, always a pleasure.' He then walked off through the building, into the waiting car for his return flight.

'Interesting man, that one,' Moran said, after closing the door.

'Yes,' Rosseau replied. 'And, I suspect, one never to be trusted.'

CHAPTER

6

'How's that cup of tea travelling, Julia?' Charlie Stevedore didn't enjoy calling to his staff, but he'd been waiting a while for his tea and chocolate biscuit and was feeling a little needy. He wouldn't have described himself as pedantic, but a cuppa helped refresh his day.

'Sorry, boss. I'd forgotten all about it.' His long-time senior policy officer, Julia Smethers, placed the Wedgwood cup and saucer of steaming tea before him with two chocolate biscuits and a folded napkin on a matching plate. She stood back, straightening her thick auburn hair.

'The PM has been chasing you, and there is a request from the Dennis Sadler Drive Show to appear this afternoon.'

'We can forget that sod, Sadler. The last time I was on his show, he carved me up and left me hanging like a stale carcass full of flies.'

'He only wants to talk about the referendum; well, at least that's what his producer said.'

'That's what they say to get you sucked into appearing on the programme, then they smash you with questions about something else, like leadership. I hate them, especially Sadler.'

'If you ever want the top job, then I suspect you may have to change your attitude.'

'Those days are long gone.' Stevedore picked up his cup with two hands, blew, then sipped his tea. 'Ah, that's the best one yet.'

'You say that every day.'

'I mean it every day.' Stevedore smiled as Smethers bit her lip, perplexed, watching him. 'Trust me; I'm from the government.'

'Your daughter wants to have dinner with you.'

'Did she say why?'

'I think she wants to talk to you about the referendum.'

'Everyone wants to talk about the referendum.'

'For some people it's a life and death issue,' Smethers joked.

'Smartie pants. Can you book a table at the European for me? Outside if you can… make it for seven.'

'Done. I'll let her know. Do you want to meet her there?'

'Yes, let's do that.' Stevedore took another mouthful, replaced the cup, then took a generous bite of a Tim Tam and fell back into his chair. 'What does the PM want?' he asked, chomping the chocolate biscuit.

'She wants to hook up with you as soon as we can.'

'Let me guess, it's to do with the referendum.'

'They didn't say, so I thought I'd connect you in thirty minutes. Before then, I just need you to concentrate on reading, then releasing that first section of the discussion paper; we are waiting for it.'

'This one?' Stevedore stretched to a stapled bunch of papers at the edge of his desk. 'Is this the suggested explanatory memorandum?'

'Sort of; it's only the first draft. We just want to get something out to the troops as some are getting anxious and want to see what you're planning, especially the Christians.'

'Not sure that's a sensible thing to do until we're ready. The party works together on social issues like this, but a few ambitious members are prone to leak contentious policy.'

'No one will leak it because no one will ever see the full final draft.'

Stevedore glanced at her. 'Do you think that's wise?'

'We need to do something strategic to control the narrative during the public debate, because at the moment we are losing.'

'You don't think the Yes vote will get up?'

'No, and if it's going to go down, I don't want it reflecting on you, frankly.' The staffer began moving away, ending the conversation. 'I'll get the PM on the line once you're done with that, so finish your tea whilst you're reading.'

'Thanks, Julia.' Stevedore smiled, acknowledging her significant support and sage advice over the decade. He relied on her often contrarian view and laser-like advice to assist him with the politics of issues.

As he read through the document, occasionally sipping his tea, he became even more convinced that the idea of a federal law overriding differing state laws was the best outcome to manage the contentious issue of euthanasia. He believed Australia, with its vast land mass, could not be administered by a central government needing the support of a federated system keeping states' rights sacrosanct. The states usually managed euthanasia and other moral issues, but he questioned why citizens received various standards of rights depending on the state they lived in. Desperate folks could access end-of-life treatment in some states, but not others, and this is fundamentally unjust.

He was the chief law officer with the obligation of drawing up acceptable euthanasia law. As a practising Catholic, sanctioned death conflicted him, but he yielded to his responsibility for providing fair laws for all citizens, no matter where they lived.

As he finished the various documents with coloured tabs showing where he was to sign or place an initial, he shifted them to a tray behind him. Smethers entered, advising that the prime minister's office was on the line.

'I just need to connect your Zoom with the PM's office, so if you could excuse me for a moment,' she said, as she stepped around to his side of the desk, studying the computer screen and leaning over him to use the mouse. 'I won't be a moment.'

Stevedore pushed his chair back from the desk and stood aside to give her room. Smethers tugged the vacated chair to her, without losing sight of the screen activity, and sat on its edge as she began tapping the keyboard.

'There we go,' she said, as she stood to leave the room.

'Shouldn't you be listening to this?' Stevedore asked as he came back to his seat.

'I will if you think I should.'

Stevedore nodded and waved to a chair. 'Do you reckon she'll have someone listening?' he quizzed, smiling. 'She probably has a team of twenty behind the screen, all taking notes. You know how she is.'

'She trusts no one, and it's the same attitude with everyone from her office.'

'In politics that can be a good thing,' Stevedore said.

'She brings this poor perception on herself. She is having a terrible time in the media, my mum can't stand her.'

'Perhaps I should take advice from your mum.'

'She thinks you're okay but adores Osborne.'

'I suspect your mum needn't worry; there is no urgent need to switch leaders.' Stevedore rushed a finger to his lips, silencing Smethers as he now watched on screen the prime minister get into position for the call.

'Hello, Charles, are you there?' Pasco squinted, searching for something on her screen.

'Yes, Prime Minister. Can you see me okay?' Stevedore could see her fiddling with papers and her mouse. 'I see you and hear you okay.'

A staffer appeared behind the prime minister, leaned over and touched the keyboard, bringing an immediate smile to her face. 'Oh, there you are. Technology is a marvellous thing, isn't it? Here I am in Canberra and there you are in Melbourne. What's the day like down there?'

'It's great, Prime Minister.' Stevedore didn't want to waste time chatting, an increasing habit of the prime minister. 'I need to cover a few things about the referendum bill. Is there anything else you want to talk about?'

'Nothing I can't defer until the cabinet meeting. How is the development of the bill going?'

'To be honest with you…'

Pasco interrupted. 'Yes please, be honest with me Charles, always good policy.' She smirked, chuffed with her own joke.

'Yes, well.' Stevedore noticed her dark cherry-red lips, the dead giveaway of a wine drinker. 'I remain unclear on how you want me to manage the bill; what's on the table and what's not?'

'What's troubling you?'

'As agreed, I'm drawing up legislation to enact the referendum to amend the constitution,' Stevedore said. 'I think it imperative we have the new bill for national euthanasia law public so voters can consider it during the referendum debate.'

'Is that wise?' The prime minister slunk back into her chair, rocking it. 'We may never need the bill if the referendum doesn't get up. Australians don't change their constitution that often.'

'The plebiscite gave us the authority, and if we don't have the accompanying bill, then I expect that constitutional change will not be approved.'

Pasco shrugged. 'Well, we gave it our best shot. The electorate can't complain about the democratic process. It would be their decision not to vote Yes.'

'Is that fair?'

'To who? To the government? It will certainly get us out of being blamed for any failure of the referendum,' Pasco said.

'I don't agree, Prime Minister,' Stevedore said, sparking Pasco to sit back into her desk. 'If you don't campaign hard enough for a Yes vote, explaining the new laws, then you may be seen as causing the loss.'

'I think to do something like this is fraught with danger, frankly. Overriding state laws is never popular.' Sitting straighter, Pasco clasped her hands in front of her. 'My preference is for the referendum to fail.'

'I get the internal politics, PM, but I think we should provide the electorate with what the comprehensive bill will mean. If the Yes vote got up, we would avoid last-minute lobbying from the usual suspects, such as the churches.'

'Why would you want to do all that work just to have it possibly fail?'

'It's my role and duty as attorney general to provide the community with a clear understanding of what they are voting for with the referendum.'

'They are voting for euthanasia.'

'Correction, Prime Minister; they will vote to change section 51 of the constitution, this is the point.' Stevedore scrawled his fingers through his hair. 'This is why the enabling legislation must be debated as part of the Yes campaign.'

'I see, but won't that put the punters offside if they don't understand it?'

'Which may provide you the outcome you want. I'm obliged to put the proposed law to the public and debate it during the referendum campaign, so they can understand what they are voting for.'

'What is the proposed question for the referendum?'

'Just a second, I have it here,' said Stevedore, opening a levered arch folder to the appropriate page. 'It is proposed to alter the constitution so as to allow the Commonwealth Parliament to accept power to make laws with respect to life and death. Do you approve the proposed amendment?'

'Read it again,' Pasco said as she scribbled. Stevedore obliged, but this time more slowly. Pasco studied it for a few moments after she had finished writing. 'Are you sure you want to frame it as life and death?'

'Yes, it allows us to override any state laws which are contrary to the mood of the country.'

'Won't this frighten them a bit?'

'They have already given us approval with the plebiscite,' Stevedore said. 'If my legislation only enacts euthanasia laws, then they should not be so concerned.'

The prime minister reached out of screen, bringing a glass of red wine into view, and took a sip. 'But this could mean we can enact legislation on abortion.'

'And capital punishment.'

'Christ, Charles, are you sure about this?' Pasco took another sip.

'This may affect us at the next election.'

'We have no plans to enact on either issue, only euthanasia. I will reassure the community that those debates will never come again.'

'They could, in say, fifty years.'

'All the better for the federal government to have control and not have the states doing their own thing.'

Pasco drained her glass and considered the question again. 'Charles, I remain in two minds about this; my preference is that the Yes vote doesn't get up. I don't support the federal government sticking its nose into state issues.'

'We are one country, Prime Minister, and we can't just let the states do their own thing on these matters.'

'When will you have the first draft?'

'I should have it ready for the next meeting of cabinet.'

'What are your colleagues saying?'

'That it's a waste of time,' Stevedore said. 'I must advise you, some members are framing it in the context of a leadership test if the government is embarrassed by the result.'

'Who's doing that? No, wait… don't tell me, my treasurer Parker Osborne will say it's all about leadership.' Pasco shook her head and smirked. 'Am I right?'

'Well, unexpectedly, you're not. Parker has said nothing to me about leadership.'

'He's always up to something. Always moaning, and briefing against me, trying to undermine me.'

'He supports you, PM; we all do.'

'Yeah, right.' Pasco wasn't convinced. 'Okay, Charles; wonderful work. Let me know when you have a final draft of the legislation, will you?'

'One last issue, PM.'

'I have another meeting at the Lodge.' Pasco glanced up past the screen. 'Be quick.'

'Do you want me on the front foot with the media on this?'

'What, as the government's voice?' She glanced up again, seeking something, then checked back to the screen. 'That would be good of you, Charles. Okay, got to run. See you.' She pushed a button, but it did nothing to the screen or the audio. She glanced up again. 'What do you think?'

A male voice responded, 'If you want it to run dead and return a No vote then he is our guy. With Stevedore trying to sell it, it'll never get up.'

Pasco stood up, her head now out of shot. 'Do you think he'll challenge?'

'He hasn't got the gonads to challenge you, boss.'

'I suppose you're right,' she said, moving away from the screen.

Stevedore punched a few keys, exiting the call, then smiled at Smethers, sitting opposite with a bemused look on her freckled face, and said, 'Poor old Nancy just doesn't get the hang of how to manage technology, does she?'

'She's hopeless in more ways than one.'

He frowned. 'Just be careful who you say that to.'

'Nice to know they value you in her office.'

Stevedore leaned back in his chair, swivelled and put a foot up on the desk, hands clasped behind his head. 'I think I might do Sadler's show now, what do you reckon?'

'Put it this way, in the eyes of the PM, you can't do any worse than you're doing now,' joked Smethers, preparing to leave the office. 'I'll prepare speaking points and get you on later today, maybe after the four o'clock news, just enough time for the television news if it becomes controversial.'

'And another tea?'

CHAPTER

7

Cardinal Rosseau was joined by the prime minister soon after he sat down at an outside table, under a trellis of lush vines providing shade from the sticky Canberra sun. The table was set for an early afternoon tea, with starched white tablecloth, flowers and matching Wedgwood-designed accouchements. A broad brimmed, black straw hat created more shade, but the heavy black cassock was turning his body into an uncomfortable furnace. He had already poured an iced water and was greedily drinking as Pasco sat with him.

'Your Eminence,' Pasco smiled. 'Are you comfortable here or would you prefer to move inside? They say it will warm up later, but it's perfect right now before the sun comes over. Would you like some tea? I have sandwiches coming.'

'I'm happy with the water at the moment.'

Pasco poured herself a cup, splashed in milk, then sat back, stirring her cup with a teaspoon of sugar. 'What brings you to Australia, and what did you want to talk with me about?'

'The Holy Father has asked me to visit and counsel you of his concerns regarding the matter your government is about to legislate.'

'The Pope sent you to talk to me?' The prime minister placed her cup back on the table. 'I'm not sure whether to be complimented or worried.'

'Oh, I shouldn't be worried.' Rosseau paused as he studied her. 'At least not yet.'

Pasco responded as he expected, bristling, 'What does that mean?'

'What it means, Prime Minister, is that we are serious in our endeavours to persuade your government not to proceed with the referendum and enact the euthanasia legislation.'

'The public have told us to get on with it. I'm not sure a church in Rome should be trying to override the will of the Australian people.'

Rosseau contemplated her response before saying, 'It is not for the church to involve itself in the proper administration of government within one country or another; rather, we would prefer being consulted on issues legislating moral standards.'

Pasco took another sip of tea as an attendant placed a stand of delicately cut sandwiches on the table, and she waved the cardinal forward to partake. 'I would think the church would have an important voice on any issue that affects parishioners, but with no greater influence than any other religion or special interest group.'

Rosseau picked up a cloth serviette from the table and wiped his forehead and neck, then his hands. 'I do not propose that you amend your process to suit the Holy Father's will; these are matters only for you to consider. What I am saying is that there are consequences for every decision we make.' He reached for his iced water and took another hefty mouthful, touching his lips with the serviette as he replaced the clinking glass.

'To be frank with you, I remain in two minds about the legislation.' Pasco gazed out into the gardens and across the lawns. 'I share your view about the change in the manner we treat life and death, but we already have state governments legislating, all with different standards, and this concerns me more than the moral argument.'

The response surprised Rosseau, as they had advised him that the prime minister was set in her ways and determined to push legislation through. He dabbed his face before saying, 'Once you legislate for these matters, then the influence of the community on standards and managing right or wrong becomes problematic.'

'Perhaps, but the community is already rejecting the influence of the churches.'

'Consequences.' Rosseau wiped the back of his neck. 'Once you begin to undermine the church and question its relevance, then the consequence is that it can no longer contribute to society as it does.'

'No one goes to church.' Pasco smiled at him. 'Science has questioned all of your teachings, and governments have led the way in enacting laws that were once deemed the absolute prerogative of canon law.'

'That may be, but once we are destroyed by science and government, who will build the hospitals, the schools, the universities, the aged care? Who will provide the administration of social consciousness, and who will be there to provide the community comfort?'

'Government paid social workers,' the prime minister joked.

'As I think you will agree, not the answer for community well-being.'

'Euthanasia is not the end of the world.'

Rosseau shook his head at the unguarded comment. 'Once we diminish the sanctity of life, we step into a world that allows institutionalised homicide.'

'That is a too provocative word for this debate,' Pasco said.

'We are crossing an ethical threshold where there will be lives we honour in the community, and then, there will be lives the government believes will be better off ended.'

Pasco took a deep breath, turned away and pushed a call button on the table. An attendant appeared. 'Could I have a glass of wine please, Rennie? Your Eminence, an apéritif?'

'Too early for me, thank you.' Rosseau waved a feeble no.

'Safeguards will be provided at every step of the way to protect the vulnerable.'

'This is what is so weak in the argument by the advocates, you cannot protect the poor, the vulnerable or the depressed. They say they act with compassion, but no law or process can provide full protection.' Rosseau took off his hat and began waving it in front of his face. 'If medical practitioners are prepared to bend the law now, there will be some who will bend the laws in the new system, exposing the vulnerable.'

'It won't happen…' Pasco smiled when Rennie placed the glass of chilled white wine before her; she snatched at it too hastily, spilling a little. 'I'll make sure it won't.'

'What happens when you're no longer here?' Rosseau continued waving his hat. 'Once termination of life legislation is enacted, we cross the ethical threshold. Once it is law, then it is just a simple matter of liberalising the conditions governing the law.'

'We will have strict conditions.' Pasco took another mouthful, then another, placing the empty glass back on the table.

'Politicians know that pressure will grow to liberalise laws further, based on the human rights notion that people are being discriminated against and denied their rights.' Rosseau sat forward toward the prime minster, wanting to stress the point. 'In other countries, this has already happened, and liberalisation of euthanasia laws becomes irresistible.'

'What do you think I should do?' Pasco pushed the call button again.

'I think you should defer the move to the referendum,' Rosseau encouraged. 'If that is not possible then campaign for a No vote.'

'If I were to do that, it would finish me as prime minister.'

'If you don't, then you are finished anyway.' Rosseau stood before her. 'It's your decision, but there are always consequences.'

'Is that some sort of veiled threat?' Pasco pushed the button again.

'Not at all, Prime Minister,' Rosseau smiled as he secured his hat. 'I do not veil my threats. Thank you for your time.'

Pasco watched as the cardinal left, being shown to the door by an attendant. His car was waiting, a priest in front, and he dived straight into the back seat. 'Damn, it's hot.' The chauffer cranked up the air-conditioning as he headed for the airport.

Rennie brought another chilled glass of wine and a tall glass of iced water, placing them in front of Pasco. 'It's hot, Prime Minister.

Perhaps water to refresh you?'

Pasco smiled. 'You know fish shit in water, don't you Rennie?'

The knock at the door was first ignored, then as it became insistent and louder, it forced Doug Ferguson to peel himself off the couch and meet whoever wanted to disturb him. A sticky day teaching had him stripped down to his underwear for a comfortable nap and recover from the tedium of raucous students. Grabbing a sarong, wrapping it around his waist and tying it off, sliding the knot to his hip, he scooted to stop the racket. The banging was much louder now.

'All right. I hear you,' he howled as he came to the front door. 'Geezus, give it a break, will you?' He unlocked, then opened the door to two students on his front step. 'What the hell do you want?'

'Nice to see you, Teach,' said the first one as she brushed past. Ferguson squinted at the second girl. 'Who are you?'

'I'm her sister, sorry. She said we would only be a few minutes.'

'You had better come in then.' As the girl went inside, Ferguson stepped out, scanning the neighbourhood and searching for any nosey-parkers before closing the door. He followed the girl into the lounge and saw her sister helping herself to a drink of soda from the refrigerator. 'Are you right? Why don't you make yourself at home?'

'Oh, come on, Teach, you know you like it.'

Ferguson moved to the kitchen bench, taking a stool. 'What are you doing here?'

'This is my little sister Bree. She's at senior school next year, and she'll be in your class. I thought, like, I'd bring her over to check you out.'

'Why?'

'Maybe she can take my place.'

'No one could replace you, Rosie.' Ferguson combed his fingers through his hair. 'Now, what do you really want?'

'Put your bag down, Bree, and take a seat. We're gonna be awhile.'

Ferguson shook his head, disappointed by the interruption. 'I have things to do. What do you want?'

'Ooh, you're snarky today.' Rosie took the stool next to him.

'I haven't got time for this crap. What do you want?'

'I want a couple of bags.'

'Rack off. You're still into me for five hundred from the last deal.'

Rosie swung her arms around his neck. 'Oh, come on, Dougie, please.'

'No, rack off.' Ferguson brushed her away.

Rosie straightened. 'So, if I give you what I owe you, we can deal today?'

'I want what you owe me, then we can talk.'

Rosie stepped off the stool, standing between her sister and Ferguson. She then raised her uniform, holding it with her hands on her hips, her navy-blue cotton shorties not leaving much to his imagination. 'Is this worth five hundred?'

'I want cash.'

'Then take it out of the bank.'

Ferguson examined what was before him. She smiled and wriggled her hips, nodding reassurance as he considered her waist. He stretched out his hand and tugged at the elastic, peering into her underwear. He saw a bundle of notes and gently dropped in two fingers, withdrawing them.

Rosie squirmed and giggled as he flicked her; she then dropped her skirt and returned to the stool. 'Debt cleared. Now two bags, thank you very much.'

Ferguson smirked as he placed the five notes on the bench. 'What's going to happen to your clients when you go to Uni next year?'

'Bree will take over school, and I'll establish a new market,' she said. 'You keep supplying the ganja and I'll keep buying from you.'

Ferguson swung off his stool, moving to the kitchen door and stepping out into an enclosed, attached garage. He pulled a soup tin from a top shelf and fiddled inside, withdrawing a small key. Then he went to a tool chest, unlocked it, and dragged a shelf out to reveal six half kilo bags of marijuana. He plucked out two, returning to the kitchen and dropping the wrapped drug in front of Rosie.

'That's a grand, thanks.'

'I don't have it with me.'

'What a surprise.' Ferguson snatched them back. 'Nothing more in the bank?'

'I have plenty to give, but I'm only taking deposits.' Rosie smirked. 'Would you like to make a deposit?' she giggled.

'I want at least five if you want to do the deal.'

'Crumbs, you're a hard arse,' Rosie said. 'Okay, I'll give you five, but only if we blow a fatty with Bree.'

Ferguson glanced over to his future student and likely client. More athletic than Rosie, blonde longer hair in trusses, she was taller, but seemed not as worldly wise as her sister. 'Sure.' He plucked a plastic packet from the fruit bowl and tossed it to Rosie. 'Roll one and I'll get us a wine. Fancy a wine, Bree?'

'Just a small one thanks, Mr Ferguson.'

Thirty minutes later, Bree was stretched out in the lounge chair, blowing smoke rings from a second reefer whilst her sister was on the couch making out with her English teacher. Ferguson came up for air and reached for a splash of wine, leaving Rosie panting face down into a cushion on the couch. He fumbled with his sarong as he ambled into the bedroom, taking from his side table a small pack of white powder.

As he prepared four lines on a glossy magazine cover, he called Rosie. She left her sister, pushed open the door and saw Ferguson sitting on the edge of the foot of the bed with the magazine resting on his lap. As she came in and knelt on the floor, he sniffed two lines, leaving the other two for her. She didn't hesitate to take the offered rolled note and sniff in the powder.

He couldn't remember who initiated their first date. He didn't really care, but he enjoyed advancing their activities every time she came for a deal. Although sixteen years younger, she applied many talents. They ignored the obvious risk, enjoying time together.

Ferguson's phone shrill disturbed them awake, and he slid off the bed to answer, finding it in the lounge. 'This is Doug.'

'Dougie, how are ya, man?'

'Who's this?'

'What do ya mean, who's this?' The cheer went from the call. 'This is Rikki Ortega, ya dickhead.'

'Sorry, I didn't recognise your voice.'

'Might be 'cause youse's avoidin' me.'

'Not avoiding, Rikki, just not hearing you.'

'Dude, where's me money?'

'Why are you ringing me? That wasn't our deal.'

'I don't see ya no more. Where's me money?'

'I told you, by the end of the month.'

'Guess what dude? It's the end of the fuckin' month.'

Ferguson started pacing, worried by the tone. 'I can have ten for you by the end of the week.'

'No can-do, shit for brains. I want all twenty.'

'I can give you ten, then the other ten in a fortnight.' Ortega was silent.

'I promise you ten by the end of the week,' Ferguson insisted.

'No good, Dougie.'

'It's the best I can do.'

'Ya see, dip-fuckin'-stick, it don't work that way. Ya pay when ya buy. Cash on delivery, man. Ya know that.'

'Rikki, I'm sorry, but most of my clients are kids and I'm running credit.'

'Not me problem man. Ya pay up, else I lose face and me operation falls apart. Youse'll take advantage, then someone else will. Ya know what I mean?'

'Yeah, I get it,' Ferguson assured him. 'I can have ten for you by the end of the week and the other ten the following week… will that do?'

'Nah, no it won't,' Ortega said. 'Do ya want me to come hurt ya, is that what ya want?'

Ferguson gulped, then squeaked out, 'No.' He cleared his throat.

'Tell ya what I'm gonna do, Dougie. Instead of comin' round and slittin' ya throat, I'm gonna give youse 'til ten to get me five, then I'll take another five tomoz, then ya deliver ten before the end of the week. How does that sound?'

'Will you take a cheque?'

'What the fuck? Are ya havin' a go, ya dead-set moron?'

'No, Rikki, but that's the only way I can get money to you tonight. The banks are closed.'

Ortega thought through the offer. 'Okay, I'm a reasonable man. I can help out a friend when he needs it.' Ferguson blew out. 'I want a cheque for ten before ten,' Ortega laughed. 'Get it? Ten before ten, geez, I'm hilarious.' He paused for a moment. 'Then if the cheque bounces, I'm comin' to see youse, and cut a finger off every day I don't get the twenty, are we clear?'

Ferguson gnawed his bottom lip, cupping the back of his neck.

'Are we clear, Dougie?'

'Crystal.'

'I'll call at 9.50. I'll be in Yarraville, and let me warn youse, ya better be within ten minutes otherwise I'm comin' for ya.' The phone cut out.

Ferguson tossed his phone to the bench, skittling it along the marble.

'You okay, Mr Ferguson?' Bree was collecting her bag.

Ferguson glanced up, his mind racing. 'What?'

'Are you okay? You're looking a little white.'

'What's going on?' Rosie bounced into the room, coming over to the bench to pick up her stash.

'I was just saying Mr Ferguson appears pale.'

'Yeah, you do, Dougie. Might be an idea to get some water into you.'

She took the two packages, tossing them to Bree, who secured them in her bag. She tugged five notes from her shirt pocket and flung them on the others.

'That was so good, Dougie.'

She wrapped her arms around his neck, dragging him onto her mouth. Ferguson pushed back onto the bench to steady himself, leering with a smirk as she left.

Bree slung her bag over her shoulder, stepping over to Ferguson.

'I'm looking forward to classes starting next year, sir.'

She cupped his neck, moving in to kiss him, and he snatched her close. When she needed to draw a breath, she stood back and admired him.

'I reckon you and me are going to have fun, Mr Ferguson, see ya.'

She bounced off to join her sister waiting in the hallway, both hooting and chortling as they slammed the front door.

Stevedore waited for the news to finish, then for an advertisement break to complete. A producer came over the line. 'Just one more commercial, Minister, and you'll be with Dennis. Good luck.'

He thought the comment odd, so stood rather than relaxing in his chair; perhaps this would not be the walk in the park he was expecting. He then heard the change in tone and knew he was now with the king of Sydney talkback radio, drive time announcer Dennis Sadler. He cleared his throat, took a sip of water and listened.

'Welcome back. It's ten past five on this beautiful Sydney afternoon. Nothing better than a sunny day in Sydney. I can see plenty of yachts out on the harbour, and the view of Circular Quay from my window is magnificent. You wouldn't be dead for quids, listeners, would you? Well, it seems the federal government wants to change all of that. Listeners, there are two things you can be certain of in life… death and taxes. The government already has you fair and square by the short and curlies with taxes, now they want to enact laws so they can come and kill you. Listen to this; it's unbelievable. The federal government, led by a woman who commands little respect, has announced that they will put to the people a referendum to allow assisted homicide. That's right, they want to change the laws of this land to allow others to decide when you die.'

Sadler paused for an exquisite moment to allow his statement to rile a listener or two enough to hit the telephones.

'Now, I say, governments should get out of our pockets and get out of our way. We don't need them in our house, we don't need them in our beds with their laws, and we don't need them telling us when to die. This is what the future will be like. if you fall into an unhealthy state and don't have enough insurance, and you become a burden, well, the government says it will be okay for someone to come along and assist you to say goodbye.'

Another pause.

'Now, I call that murder. What do you call it, Charles Stevedore?'

Stevedore, provoked by the question, began pacing around his desk, stretching the cord as he went. 'Good afternoon, Dennis, and good afternoon to your listeners.'

'Yes, yes, stop dithering and give us something no politician is capable of providing, an answer.'

'I can assure your listeners the government is not planning to provide laws that will allow, as you call it, assisted homicide, and it's a little provocative to even use terms like that when talking about the terminally ill.'

'So, you aren't bringing in new laws to kill people? Oh, I'm sorry, I thought that's what our prime minister said the other day?'

'What the prime minister confirmed is that the government is moving to a referendum to amend the constitution to allow the federal government to control laws relating to life and death.'

'So, I'm right, you are introducing a Kill Bill.'

'No, and again, that is a provocative, irresponsible statement, and incorrect. As you may know, some states already have enacted euthanasia laws, and what we are asking the community to do is to standardise those laws across Australia so everyone in need can get fair access to quality palliative care.'

'Why do we need a referendum? We've already had the biggest waste of money plebiscite on this issue already. Why can't you just get on with it and do it? Why do we even need to vote again?'

'This democratic process has been transparent. On such a sensitive moral issue, it is incumbent upon government to provide access and information so the people of Australia can make a fair decision. That's what the prime minister has instructed me to do.'

'So, it's Daffy Duck's fault?'

'I don't understand; who's Daffy Duck?'

'Who else but the prime minister? So let me ask you this, Minister. You say you want to standardise the laws across this vast country on life and death, so does that mean abortion laws are next?'

'Dennis, I don't think you should refer to the prime minister in such terms… but let me say this in response.' Stevedore snatched up his speaker's notes to quote lines. 'The plebiscite was in the majority for us to take control of life and death laws, so that is what we are doing… taking control. This requires a referendum to amend the constitution. If the Yes vote is successful, we will enact euthanasia laws with very strict conditions imposed, providing direction for those delivering palliative care, and it will not create, as you wrongfully suggest, a market where it will be easy to access this form of care.'

'What, you think killing people is a form of care?'

'No… I…'

'Well, you heard it here, listeners, straight from the nation's chief law officer's mouth. We will soon have euthanasia laws, and the government considers this to be a form of care. Let's go to the callers. John from Werrington, what's your view?'

Stevedore responded, 'I didn't say that. You know I didn't…' The line was dead, the interview concluded. 'Hello?' With no response, he tossed the phone back into the cradle. 'I knew I should never go on his programme.'

'He has the biggest listening audience in Sydney with a syndication to other cities and regions, so he speaks to our voters,' Smethers said, standing nearby.

'Those voters won't be ours for long if he keeps taking grotesque shots at us like that.' Stevedore flopped back in his chair. 'He was really abusive of the prime minister; can we do something about it?'

'Like what?'

'I'm the attorney general; surely there is a law we can use to shut him up?'

'He has been on her back since she was elected. He is, however, all lovey-dovey on his weekly spot with the treasurer.'

'Parker is from Sydney, maybe that's why. They're all weird in Sydney.'

'What's next?' Smethers asked.

'We just need to make sure we have very clear and protective legislation in place for the referendum debate. We don't need folks getting scared the government is coming to kill them.'

'I'll make sure we consult again with the experts, doctors, and aged care professionals. Should we be consulting with the churches?'

He sighed. 'We should, but I reckon it'll be a waste of time.'

'I'll put the word out that we are prepared to listen if they want to have any input.' She turned and strode from the office. 'I'll get you a tea.'

Stevedore swung his seat so he could look across the bay toward Williamstown. The late afternoon light highlighted the small peninsula where he once lived, and he sighed as he reexamined the motives he had for remaining in politics. There was seldom a win or good news.

J ulia Smethers carried in a cup of tea for her boss, who was gazing out of his office window over the city of Melbourne. He could see his beloved Williamstown, a bayside village settled centuries ago on a small peninsula with stunning views back over the city. He had moved out of the suburb when he first married, and never felt the yearning to return, but was delighted his daughter had settled in a townhouse development at the end of the train line.

'The prime minister would like a word,' Smethers interrupted. 'Are you free to take the call?'

'Is it about the Sadler Show?'

'Not sure; they didn't say.'

'Get her on the line. Let's hope she's switched on.'

'Let's confirm 6.30, which gives you twenty minutes to clear your tray.' She pointed to a stack of papers in his in-tray.

'What would I do without you, Jules?'

'You wouldn't be sitting here, I can assure you.' She needed him doing his job, because if he didn't, then she would lose hers. Who was going to employ a fifty-year-old political apparatchik with a large mortgage?

Stevedore moved back to his desk, hauling the tray over, working through documents and reading briefings notes. He signed correspondence where required, hardly looking at the content of letters before scrawling his signature. As he read, he sipped his tea, and when done he placed the tray on the edge of his desk.

He leaned back in his chair, rocking, continuing to sip his tea. As he waited, he glanced about his office at the various knick-knacks he had collected during years as a government minister. Gifts from dignitaries, smiling photographs with international leaders; he liked the photo with the Pope when he had visited the Vatican before the pontiff's death. He contemplated whether his sacrifice of service to the parliament was worth the effort. His telephone buzzed, Smethers announcing the prime minister was on line four.

'Prime Minister, how has your afternoon been?'

'I read the transcript from the Sadler Show; what were you thinking?'

'You know what he's like.' Stevedore bent forward, pulling a drawer open, thrusting a foot on it, then rocking back into his chair.

'You got off easy, if it was me he would have butchered, then eaten me,' Pasco said.

'That's why we advise you to stop appearing on his show. You'll never win.' Stevedore curled the cord around his finger. 'The government still needs a presence… his audience are our voters.'

'He's Osborne's man, I'm sure of it.'

'That's a long bow you're drawing there, Nancy.' Stevedore sighed at her anxiety, pondering how many wines she must have slipped in to allow her guard down. 'He supports you; we all do.'

'Not sure about that. Say, listen, did you know there was a Vatican emissary in town?'

He screwed his face into a 'not-a-clue' expression. 'Who did they send, a cardinal?'

'Cardinal Rosseau, who seems to have no position in the Vatican other than running an unlucky second with the conclave.'

'Is he here to argue against the bill?' Stevedore suspected that the Catholic Church would oppose the legislation, but it surprised him they had sent someone so senior from Rome.

'He gave me a tongue lashing this afternoon, and he didn't hold back, even expressing an implied threat.'

Stevedore sat to attention. 'A threat? What sort of threat?'

'He said if the government doesn't drop this whole idea of a referendum, then my leadership is on the line. Consequences, he said, and he said it a few times.'

'Was Archbishop Moran there?'

'Only the cardinal, and he didn't waste too many words with argument, I can tell you. He told me it was legislated murder, and once we cross the line, there is no going back.'

'What was your response?'

'I had a glass of wine.'

He scoffed. 'No, really, what was your response?'

'It's interesting,' Pasco sighed. 'I would never do what the church would have me do, but he made a valid point.'

'Which is what, exactly?' Stevedore rubbed his temple. 'I thought you were strong on doing this?'

'I think we should have the referendum, but I'm not sure I should support the Yes vote.'

'You are kidding me? Surely, you're joking? You can't flip flop like this, Prime Minister.' Stevedore stood leaning against his desk, again curling a finger. 'You have given me a clear direction to prepare legislation and now you're changing the government's position?'

'What I'm saying is that I remain undecided about it,' Pasco said in her staccato tone. 'I'm obligated to bring on the referendum, but we don't need to campaign for a Yes, do we?' She was hoping Stevedore would agree.

'Prime Minister, I need your definitive instruction… do I campaign hard for a Yes vote, or are you asking me to back off?' Stevedore waited for an answer, but only heard soft panting. 'Prime Minister?'

'What do you want me to do?' Pasco asked, exasperated.

'I want you to go hard with the campaign and win the Yes vote.'

'Prime Minister Howard didn't campaign for the Yes vote with the republic referendum. This is similar.'

Stevedore didn't answer, but then said, 'I suppose there are similarities in process with the government promising a referendum. Howard promised the republic convention, then a referendum, but he never supported the idea of a republic, he campaigned against it. You support euthanasia; you can't now campaign for a No vote.'

Pasco didn't respond, but then murmured, 'Is your attitude toward a Yes vote because of Stephie?'

Stevedore felt angst rush through him at the mention of her name; his throat tightened, and he coughed to clear it, then said, 'It has nothing to do with her.'

'Are you sure?'

'Prime Minister, I would prefer you leave it.' He rocked back. 'Let's move on.'

'Charles, I understand you have personal circumstance with this issue, but it should not cloud your thinking.'

'It doesn't, my support for the legislation has nothing to do with her.'

'I understand if you want to step away.'

'Don't be ridiculous,' Stevedore said. 'Can we move on, please?' He waited for a response. 'What do you want me to do?'

'Let's be very clear on this for you.' Pasco elevated her tone, frustrated her compassion had been rejected. 'I want you to run dead. Get the referendum bill drafted, but do not draft legislation for a euthanasia bill; we won't be using it during the campaign and we will campaign for a No vote.'

Stevedore didn't respond for a moment, thinking through what he had been advised. 'This could affect your hold on the leadership, you know that, don't you?'

'You're the second person to say that to me today, except that the other party was arguing the opposite position. It seems I can't win, no matter what I do.'

'I'm just letting you know that this decision to run dead will be problematic for you.'

'Thinking of taking me out, Charles?' Pasco mocked. 'I always assumed you might give it a go.'

'Nancy, you're being ridiculous. I have zero ambition for leadership, and indeed, I'm contemplating leaving parliament after the next election.'

Pasco ignored the proposition. 'Just do what I ask, then you can do whatever you would like.'

The line went dead. Stevedore loosened his grip on the handset, dangling it from his thumb. 'Yes, Prime Minister.' He dropped it back in the cradle as Smethers entered the office.

'What's the news?'

He squirmed his face. 'She wants us to run dead, get the referendum legislation tabled and then campaign against it so that we get a No vote.'

'You're kidding?'

'I wish I was… she asked me if my judgment was impaired because of Stephanie.' Stevedore examined her face for a sign. 'Is she right?'

'No one should have to go through what she went through, but this is not about you, it's about doing what's right.'

'So, a politician's personal circumstance should never affect their vote on any legislation, is that what you're telling me?'

'It's the right thing to do, Charlie. Stephanie or no Stephanie, you know that.'

'The prime minister wants to have a different conversation.'

'What's your instructions, Minister?'

Stevedore steepled his fingers in front of his face at his desk. He then wrung his hands, saying, 'Let's go hard and see what happens.' He grinned. 'Anyway, she probably won't remember our conversation in the morning.'

Smethers left the room, and Stevedore glanced at a framed photograph of his wife. 'Am I doing the right thing, Steph?' He walked over to the photo, gazing into her blue eyes. 'Could I have done more?' He felt his eyes well. 'I won't let you down this time.'

CHAPTER

11

Trams in Melbourne's central business district were free, so Stevedore, running late for his dinner date with his daughter, hopped on one at a stop along Bourke Street. A variety of passengers were spread throughout the double carriage. He grabbed a seat by a door, gazing out the window as the tram whooshed through the city. The bulk of the passengers exited at Swanston Street and replaced by an assortment of travellers heading home.

Stevedore jumped off at Spring Street and strode around the corner to the European, the elegant restaurant opposite the Victorian Parliament and next door to the Princess Theatre. On a balmy night the theatre crowd was out, and he hoped Julia had secured a table outside. He smiled when he spotted his daughter, Vikki, already waiting with a large glass of white wine, scrolling through her phone on an outside table.

'Hello, darling.' Stevedore hugged his smiling daughter and kissed her cheek. 'I'm sorry I'm late. Have you been waiting long?'

'No, just got here. I've ordered a bottle of Hugel Pinot Gris. Would you like to share it, or would you prefer a red?' Vikki signalled to a waiter to attend.

'No, a white will be fine.' Stevedore sat facing the street, his back to the parading pedestrians as they filed past, gawking at diners. 'You look terrific. How was your day?'

Vikki asked the waiter for a glass before answering. 'Aargh, it was just the usual nonsense. I have a case I'm going to lose because my client is a nutcase.'

'I warned you about days like this if you went into criminal law.'

'I know, but it pays well.'

'What, criminals paying you from proceeds of their crimes?'

The question annoyed Vikki. 'It's my job. I enjoy it, and sometimes I get the innocent off.'

'It's an irony.'

'What is?'

'The chief law officer's daughter working to defeat the prosecution of people breaking the law.'

'Yes, well, someone has to do it. I guess that would be me.' Vikki shook her head, trying to convince her smiling father to give up the conversation. 'How was your day?'

'Oh same-ole, same-ole.' Stevedore took a sip of wine, placing his glass on the table. 'The prime minister has asked me to do the nation a disservice.'

'What?' Vikki almost guffawed. 'Will I be defending you in court soon, breaching your own laws?'

'Who knows? No, wait. She hasn't asked me to break the law.'

'Phew, thank heavens. Not sure how I would plead with you as my client.'

'Always not guilty, gorgeous,' he laughed, changing the subject. 'Now what do you feel like eating?'

'I haven't eaten today, so I'm starved. What do you recommend?'

'Let's have an antipasto variety and the chateaubriand.'

'Hmm, sounds delicious, but I would like a couple of oysters as well.'

'Then let's get a half dozen and a small tasting plate.'

Stevedore glanced around, catching the eye of the waiter standing by the door who ducked and weaved through the pedestrian traffic to the table. Stevedore liked the fifty-minute preparation time for the briand, as it meant he could chat, and he asked for a refill of his glass.

'Now, tell me, why are you wanting to see me?'

Vikki hesitated, unnoticed by her father, who seemed more interested in the passing parade of theatre goers waiting to gain entry to the show next door.

'Crumbs, the punters are out tonight,' he said.

'I'm told it's a great show.'

'I saw it about twenty years ago with your mother. It was terrific.'

Vikki paused to sip her wine, then asked, 'Tell me, father dearest, what did the PM want you to do?'

'Oh, not much.' He was still glancing sideways at the theatre crowd. 'Why is it most theatre goers are female?'

'Stop avoiding the question.'

'Yes, counsellor.' He turned and smiled at his daughter. He was about to respond when the waiter arrived, placing the oysters and antipasto on the now crowded marble-topped table. The waiter returned with a small plate each and cutlery. When he left, Stevedore raised his glass and toasted his daughter. 'Here's to a lovely dinner.' He smiled, looking over the top of his proffered glass. Vikki smiled too, dropping her fork onto the plate and raising her glass, and they clinked.

'Love you, Daddy.'

'I love you, sweetheart. Enjoy the oysters; they look great.'

'Stop avoiding the question,' Vikki insisted. 'What does the PM want you to do?'

Stevedore fell silent for a few moments, collecting his thoughts, and slid an oyster from its shell. 'She wants me to go slow on the euthanasia bill.'

He sat up, glancing about him to check if anyone may have been listening, as he placed the overturned shell back onto the tray. 'She wants me to prepare the referendum legislation and then sponsor a No vote.'

'By doing what, exactly?'

'Not preparing comprehensive euthanasia legislation for scrutiny prior to the referendum.'

Vikki hiked her eyebrows in surprise, before asking, 'How do you feel about that?'

'I'm a little disappointed in a couple of ways.' Stevedore scooped up a shell and slurped in another oyster, swallowing it whole, the salty taste recalling images of childhood swimming, just like Pavlov's dog. 'First, the plebiscite, although not providing a conclusive mandate, was still a majority which means we must initiate a referendum. Second, if we prepare the referendum and then support a No vote, the government will be seen as irrational, impacting our chances of retaining government at the next election.' He repeated his oyster slurping method. 'I see a leadership challenge if we do what she wants.' Once he had swallowed, he replaced the shell on the plate. 'They're superb, get stuck in.'

He waved encouragement to his daughter, who took up an oyster. 'Anyway, third, I don't think it would thrill your mum.'

Vikki swallowed the oyster and tossed the shell onto the empty serving tray, following it with a sip of wine. She smiled at her father, but it never reached her eyes. 'I hate politics, and in particular I hate politicians. Why can't you ever do what you say you're going to do?'

'You hate me?'

'You know what I mean. It's the system you have to work in.' Vikki took another sip. 'The prime minister is the one who pushed for the plebiscite. If I recall, it was you who advised her not to go down that path.'

'We all have to compromise, I suppose.'

'What a bitch.'

'Sshh.' He scolded his daughter, glancing about for big ears that might be listening.

'I won't be quiet on this.'

'This is not the time nor the place, honey.'

'You have done everything you were asked to do, acting against your better judgment. And now she wants to screw you again.'

'It's a harsh world, sometimes.'

'No, that's bullshit. You deserve better than her.'

He gawked about again, then tried to pacify his daughter. 'She has a tough job and has to call it as she sees it.'

'It's a wonder she can see anything these days.'

'Victoria, you can't say things like that,' Stevedore pleaded, peeking over his shoulder.

'She likes a drink… well, doesn't she?'

'Look, will you stop this nonsense?' He held up a hand to her.

Vikki pushed back from the table, crossed her arms and legs and considered the news. 'I'm not happy about this, about how this affects you, but more so, what we promised Mum.'

Stevedore grimaced, tightened his lips and gnawed at the bottom one, trying to hold his emotions. 'It's, ah… it's not about your mother.'

'It is to me, and I know it is to you.'

Stevedore dabbed at his eyes with his napkin and took a mouthful of water. He cleared his throat and said, 'I'm a minister in the government. My job is to do what is best for my country and its people. I have responsibilities to my cabinet colleagues, and what the prime minister wants, it is my job to deliver.'

The waiter came and cleared the table. Vikki waited, swinging her leg. 'We promised Mum we would do whatever it took to end the same suffering we had to face for other families in similar circumstances. She wanted them to bring dignity to the end of a life of a loved one. Not suffering through bureaucratic nonsense, as she did.'

Stevedore didn't respond; he glanced down, a little saddened as he reflected on his daughter's words. The images of the debilitating death from motor neurone disease were still with him. The two promises he made to his wife were proving a little problematic, as they were out of his hands.

Vikki was still married to the man Steph never trusted; and the government might never enact euthanasia laws.

They said nothing as the waiter delivered their meal, which now seemed ambitious. 'Vikki, I'm sorry, but I must do as requested by the prime minister. I know this disappoints you, but let me assure you, I will campaign for a Yes vote.'

Vikki weakened as she watched her father. She stretched out a hand, and he clasped it. 'Dad, I know this is not about you. I know it's your job and you have to do as directed. I know that.' She paused for a moment. 'I know you will try to do the right thing by the country, and by Mum.'

'I love you, honey.'

Vikki squeezed his hand and smiled. 'Now, let's get this beautiful meat into us and talk about how you are going to challenge the prime minister for leadership.'

Stevedore guffawed as he once again glanced about to check who might be listening. He continued to chuckle as his wide-eyed daughter nodded encouragement. 'Let's eat first and then we can talk about the future.'

They worked their way through the prepared meat, the accompanying garlic mash and sautéed mushrooms, chatting about the weather, life in Williamstown, reflections on childhood, and their careers. Once done, the table was cleared; they declined dessert and settled in with coffee and a liqueur.

'So, Daddy, what's your thinking about becoming a grandfather?'

He didn't respond straight away. He stared across the table at his beaming daughter, trying to formulate the right words. 'Whatever you want to do in your life has always been fine with me.'

Vikki chuckled, then said, 'You don't seem overwhelmed with enthusiasm.'

Stevedore altered his dark tone. 'Of course, I'm happy for you. Nothing would give me greater pleasure than being a granddad.'

Vikki wasn't convinced. 'But?'

'No buts. If this is something you want to do, then I support you,' he smiled. 'Your mum would have been thrilled.'

'But?'

Stevedore sniffed and smiled.

'Why do I get the feeling you are dying to say something about this?'

'Honey.' He shrugged and shook his head. 'There's nothing. When are you planning to have a baby?'

'We decided a few weeks ago.'

'Should you be drinking? You might be pregnant now.'

'You know how the birds and bees thing works, don't you?' Vikki sassed her father. 'Since we made the decision, we have only done it once, maybe twice.'

Stevedore skewed a face. 'Ewe, too much information.'

'We're both busy doing our jobs and living life.' Vikki swirled, then smelled her cognac. 'I want to take a break from the law and this is the perfect opportunity.'

'Finally, an admission that the morons are getting you down.'

'It's not that so much.' Vikki took a sip and swallowed, responding to the pungent taste with a face. 'I'm just tired of druggies dealing with kids. It's not healthy for me when I have families on my mind.'

He sat back and considered what to say, then suggested, 'Why not come and work for me?'

'What as, your tea lady?'

'No,' he smiled. 'I've been thinking about asking you for a while. I need a good policy officer with frontline experience. I think you have the background and training to do well. You're certainly very capable.'

Vikki took another sip of cognac; this time it didn't trouble her, and she thought through the idea. 'I'm about to have a baby. How will that work?'

'I won't need you until after the next election, so you'll be ready by then to return to the workplace. We will work around care for the baby; perhaps we can set you up at home for a few days a week.'

'I'll have to think about it… but my first reaction is positive,' Vikki smiled.

'That's great.' Stevedore crossed his arms, satisfied he might help his daughter into a new career. 'So, tell me, how is your husband?'

Vikki gazed at her father, swirled the last of her cognac, then washed it down, followed by the remains of her espresso. 'You know? That's the first time you've mentioned him in the three hours I've been here.'

He squirmed, avoiding her fierce gaze. 'Oh, is it? Surely we talked about him, given the many things we have spoken about.'

'Nope, not a word.' Vikki peered at her father, bemused by his avoidance of her gaze. 'You don't like him, do you?'

'I have never said that,' Stevedore said.

'You don't have to, it's obvious,' Vikki snapped. 'Both you and Mum never warmed to him.'

He shrugged, glancing back to the crowd now leaving the theatre. 'Whatever.'

'Come on, Dad, speak your truth.'

Stevedore returned her gaze and considered his next move. Say nothing and go home was the best course of action. He smiled and waved to the waiter to indicate he wanted the bill. 'I don't think my view is important, because it's your relationship and it has nothing to do with me.'

'Always the friggin' politician.'

He returned her gaze, then accepted her invitation. 'You're right, I don't like him, never have. I don't trust him, and I think he's dodgy.'

Vikki shook her head, tapping her fingers on the table. 'Well, that's interesting.'

He hadn't finished. 'I think you could have done better, and your mother and I feel he hasn't done the right thing by you. There's something shifty about him, and I just don't trust him.'

'Say what you really think.' Vikki started collecting her things, making ready to head home.

'Well, you asked.'

'Yes, I did, and I'm shocked and sorry I did. Perhaps I'll have to rethink your job offer.'

'Oh, come on, Victoria; don't be like that.'

Vikki stood. 'It's pretty simple, Dad. I'm part of a couple, and if you want me, then my husband is part of the package.'

'Where are you going? Sit down, this is crazy.'

'I have a train to catch, plus, I have run out of words to say.' She bent down and kissed him on the forehead. 'Love you, see you.'

Stevedore didn't reply, but watched her stride off. He kept watching, hoping she would glance back so he could give her a wave, but she dashed off to catch the green pedestrian light at Bourke Street. He admired her sudden dash along the footpath in those ridiculous high heels she insisted on wearing, making it just in time to cross the busy street. When he lost sight of her, he tossed his credit card on the tray. As he sat and waited for the account, his phone pinged a text.

Just made the train. Thanks for dinner. Love you heaps. XX

CHAPTER

12

The men were waiting around an oval board room table in St Mary's College by the cathedral in Sydney. Curtains drawn, it was dark, as only a standard lamp in one corner was switched on. Some men worked phones; others wondered why they were there.

They knew each other from working together in the federal parliament. Some were politicians, others influential staff members. All were devout Catholics.

They had been invited to meet with the archbishop of Sydney; no other information was available. When the archbishop requested something done, then a way was found to make it happen. Each of them assumed they were assembled to listen to a setback the church wanted handled. They had responded in the past and no doubt they would respond again now, and in the future.

Brethren of sorts, although they preferred not to be associated with labels.

They attended the best Catholic schools, some graduated from Catholic universities and a small number had been in the seminary once upon a time, when they were idealistic and their ambition was to serve their god. Now they waited in the darkened room, as if in silent prayer. They had left three chairs vacant at the centre of the table, by the door.

Around ten minutes after they were ushered in, the heavy wooden door swung open. The archbishop entered, followed by Cardinal Rosseau and treasurer Parker Osborne. It was no surprise Osborne had attended, as they considered him their leader, holding the most senior position in the government. Eyes were attracted to the unknown charismatic man, dressed in black cassock, scarlet zucchetto and tasselled fascia.

'Gentlemen,' the archbishop greeted them. 'Please remain seated,' he said as some rose. 'Allow me to introduce Cardinal Rosseau. His Eminence is the Holy Father's emissary and has been asked to visit Australia to reinforce the position of the Vatican in relation to the proposed referendum and subsequent euthanasia laws. Would you care to say a few words, Your Eminence?'

Rosseau stood, and as he crossed himself, said, 'In the name of the Father, and of the Son and of the Holy Spirit. Amen.' Rosseau waited for those seated to cross themselves and respond Amen. 'Lord, we are meeting this evening to conduct matters of important business. Guide our hearts and our minds in the spirit of fairness, right thought and speech. Impart Your supreme wisdom upon our deliberations so that our affairs may reach a successful conclusion. Thank you for being our source of guidance this evening. Amen.'

Rosseau crossed himself again, then sat with a broad smile. 'Gosh, it's hot in Australia. No one said to me I should come prepared for such hot and sticky weather. I don't know how you can put up with it.' The men relaxed, many smiling, glancing at each other. 'The Holy Father has sent me to speak with you, and others, about this troubling legislation that will enable assisted suicide. Stopping this legislation is top of mind for him and for other leaders in the church. I know it is of vital importance to the archbishop.' Moran nodded. 'I wanted to meet you this evening so we can have an initial discussion as to what strategies are available to mitigate this dreadful legislation.'

A voice from the end of the table said, 'We have already lost the fight; the plebiscite killed our influence.'

Osborne sat forward in his chair next to the cardinal. 'It was a mistake, that is for sure, but since it was a majority...'

'A minuscule majority,' another voice interrupted.

Osborne glanced at the speaker before continuing. 'A majority have directed the government to put forward a referendum. If it is then voted down, I believe it will resolve the issue. If we don't have a vote at a referendum, there will always be voices, such as the Greens, seeking to mandate the policy. I consider we should support the referendum being established, and then campaign for the No vote.'

Archbishop Moran seemed surprised. 'What happens if the Yes vote gets up?'

Rosseau took back control. 'There are five non-negotiables for voting Catholics… same-sex marriage, embryonic stem cell research, human cloning and the big two, abortion and euthanasia.'

'We have lost the marriage debate, but we must never forgo fighting for the sanctity of human life. Once we lose that, then the apocalypse is upon us.'

'I'm not sure we would face the gates of hell if we were to pass a bill which brought dignity for the terminally ill,' a voice from the table suggested.

'Any attempt to end life is a mortal sin causing spiritual death of the soul, and therefore a separation from God. Murder is a grave matter. Ending life, no matter at which stage of life the victim may be, is murder. Therefore, euthanasia is legislated murder,' Rosseau said.

The room hushed, the men flicking glances at each other, troubled by the provocative language.

After an uncomfortable pause the treasurer offered, 'What I think the Cardinal is saying, is this… we must protect life, and having government condone the taking of life provides the first step in the breaking down of community ethical values.' Osborne glanced about the room.

Moran glanced at Rosseau, then nodded a light acknowledgement, knowing they had the right man to lead the Catholic assault.

'The question then becomes, what are we to do about it?' Osborne asked.

'I visited your prime minister today,' Rosseau said. 'An interesting woman, but I noticed she had what seemed a significant burden on her shoulders.'

'She may lose us the next election,' someone said.

'It's not that. I just felt she needs to embrace a faith, and it seems she has little trust, or indeed support, from those around her.'

'Pasco doesn't attract confidence in what she does, and her behaviour is erratic,' Osborne offered. 'She needs a break; she deserves it.'

The politicians understood what he meant.

The group discussed options for the next few hours, including making a leadership challenge against the prime minister. They considered moving against the attorney general, forcing his resignation and replacing him with one of their own; this idea died when they were staggered to learn that the attorney general was a Catholic. All concurred that they needed to control the debate, and all agreed with Osborne's notion that the issue be killed by the referendum once and for all. A few talked about the benefits of attacking abortion laws if the Yes vote won; no one linked capital punishment to the debate.

Osborne waved goodbye to his colleagues at ten o'clock and was pulled back from departing by the cardinal. 'Parker, I should like a private word.'

The men retired to a secluded chamber within the archbishop's residence next door. Osborne was ushered to sit in one of the soft leather chairs. 'Would you like a drink? I'm going to have an Irish whiskey.' Rosseau moved to the side cabinet and unscrewed a half empty bottle of eighteen-year-old Tullamore Dew, splashing a generous amount into a crystal glass, before proffering it to Osborne.

'Okay, you've convinced me,' chuckled Osborne.

Rosseau splashed another generous shot into a glass, then poured two waters from a jug, bringing the four glasses on a silver tray to a small wooden side table between the chairs. 'Cheers.'

'Here's to your next meeting with the PM.' Osborne offered his glass for a clink, swirled then sniffed the single malt before sipping a taste.

'Irish whiskey is always best taken straight with a little water on the side, just in case the smooth taste requires a little encouragement going down, don't you agree?' Rosseau said.

'I don't touch the stuff. I tend to reflux when I drink it, so I always have a mixer.'

'Then you only ever drink Scotch whisky, which is overrated when compared to Irish,' Rosseau said.

'You seem to be a bit of an expert.'

'I once visited Irish Whiskey Corner in Dublin. Toured the fascinating place, and as we finished the tour, they gave us a taste test. I had my misgivings, as you could imagine, given it was barely eleven in the morning.'

'I've heard of this. What was it like?' Osborne asked.

'Amazing. On the smell test alone, you would never drink bourbon whisky, so I don't. The taste test was much the same, Irish far superior on the palate to Scotch. Then they gave us a variety of whiskeys to sample, and I must say, I love a good Tullamore Dew.' Rosseau was holding the glass up to the light, studying the whiskey's colour.

After a few moments, still gazing at the whiskey, he said, 'I think you will make a fine prime minister, Parker.' He dropped his hand to the arm of the chair and gazed at Osborne. 'What do we have to do to get you there?'

Osborne was a little stunned by the comment, returning the cardinal's gaze then taking a sip, expecting reflux but getting none. He cleared his throat before saying, 'I know I will, and I must confess, given we are sitting here peacefully,' he smiled at the scene, 'I want the job within a month, before we present the referendum. If I'm prime minister, then I will ensure it is a No vote, believe me.'

Rosseau smiled, impressed with the confidence of the politician. 'Then what must we do to make that happen?'

'As I said recently, you must do all in your power to get the prime minister not to stage the referendum. By doing so, she will push for the referendum to not side with the church and then campaign for the Yes vote. Your suggestion of the Pope calling her was terrific. Would he do it?'

'I want what you want.' The cardinal sipped his whiskey. 'My leader is no different to yours, except he's supposed to have the job for life. I don't have your benefits of time or elections.'

'You sneaky little shit, Morris.' Osborne took another sip and smiled at the cardinal before adding, 'You want to be Pope?'

'We are similar and we want the same things. If I help you, perhaps you can help me?'

'What can a lowly politician like me do? The Holy Father is second only to God. I don't even know where to begin,' Osborne smirked.

'You must set the scene for him to be involved. If the vote appears lost, then he might speak to the prime minister. If he does that, and they see her to be dealing with him and goes on to lose the vote as leader, I can leverage that information and get what I want.'

'You're not Italian, are you?' Osborne asked. Rosseau shrugged and shook his head no. 'I thought all the princes of Machiavellian politics were supposed to be Italian.'

'We Catholic princes are the most conniving in the world. I just want to serve as their spiritual king.' Rosseau smiled, his glass pressed against his jaw. 'If I can embroil the Vegas flunky into this crisis, then I may use it against him. What did you say the other day? Get them to think the opposite of what your actions are and never expose your real interests.'

'Huh,' Osborne smiled, before raising his glass to toast again. 'Here's to us getting what we want.' They clinked their glasses and took a generous mouthful. 'What about another, Morris?'

It was a slow dinner, the kind Ferguson loved sharing with his girlfriend. The night sky still had remnants of a sunset highlighting the city of Melbourne, across Hobson's Bay from Williamstown. The blue-grey towering buildings, windows lit, provided a rippling reflection on the water, and were a favourite backdrop for the couple when they came to Pelicans, on Gem pier. Ferguson cuddled a glass of wine into his shoulder as he admired the view.

'What are you thinking, darling?' Bronte Mariner said, holding his hand and studying him.

Ferguson gazed back at her, placing his glass on the table after taking a sip. 'I was just admiring the view and thinking what a wonderful place this is.'

'I love it, and the marinara was to usual standards.'

'I love we have these times together, it's so clumsy at work.'

'I agree; it's hard, given our roles.'

'Your role, you mean,' Ferguson smiled. 'What was that email you sent around today? It's got the staff room going crazy.'

'I just think we're getting slack registering absentees. I've had a directive from the department saying that we must tighten up, so if kids are missing after lunch, they require us to inform their parents.'

'I can't disclose anything specific.' Ferguson withdrew his hand. 'Several of your staff are not happy.'

'Too bad. If they don't like it, they know what they can do.'

'They say screw the principal.' Ferguson waved his arm. 'Then I think, yeah, I am.'

'Does anyone know, do you think?'

'Not likely. I don't care.'

'What, you don't care about us?'

'I didn't say that, Bronte; don't be so provocative.'

She smirked, paused, then took a sip. 'When are we going to fix this?'

'I didn't realise we had anything to fix.' Ferguson sat back in his chair.

'You see? This is what I hate.'

'What do you hate, gorgeous?' Ferguson pushed a hand against the table. 'Something not going well for you with us?'

Mariner flopped back in her chair. 'You just don't want to acknowledge us. You just want me to remain your dirty secret.'

'That's not true.'

'You only want me for sex.'

Ferguson leered at her. 'You do it so well.'

'I want more than a quick grope or pash in a cupboard. I want you to stay a night, instead of rushing home.'

'You know I hate doing that.'

'Do you? Then why don't you man up and do something about it?'

'I want to, you know I do,' Ferguson leaned back into the table. 'It's not that easy.'

'How hard can it be? Just tell her.'

'I don't want to be left with nothing.'

'I have money.' She held out her hand. Ferguson squeezed it.

'Yeah, well, I don't.'

'Does it matter?'

'It matters to me. I own less than half the house, and I won't get any of it, if I pull the pin.'

'What the hell?' Mariner snatched her hand away. 'You value money ahead of me?'

Ferguson didn't know what to say, studying his fuming boss. 'I have a few debts and I won't be able to clear them if I leave her.'

'How much?'

'Twenty.'

'Twenty what… dollars?' She couldn't believe what he was saying.

Ferguson joked. 'I wish.' He gazed at her, taking a nervous sip of water. 'No, it's twenty thousand.'

Mariner flopped back in her chair, coarsing fingers through her long tresses. 'Who do you owe this amount to, the bank?'

'No… it's Ortega.'

She dropped her hands to the table, mouth agape. 'You owe money to Rikki Ortega?'

'It's not what you think.'

Mariner sat back, crossing her arms. 'Why would you borrow money from that foul-mouthed moron?'

'You see? This is the problem, I didn't borrow money from him.'

'Why do you owe him money?'

'I love you, Bront.' Ferguson tried to change the subject, but she was having none of it.

'Don't shit me, Doug… why do you owe that lowlife money?'

'I don't want to talk about it,' Ferguson snapped.

'What the hell?' Mariner almost stood. 'You tell me you can't leave your wife because you need money. Then you tell me you owe it to a criminal, and now you won't say why,' she said. 'If you expect us to be together, then you need to share with me right now why you owe money to Ortega. Otherwise it's over, and I'm leaving right now. So, make a decision.'

'I can't.' Ferguson said, his eyes welling as he gazed at Mariner.

They sat glaring at each other. A waiter arrived before stepping away, assessing that it was the wrong time to ask a question. Ferguson picked up his wine and drained it, wiping his lips, then his eyes, with his white napkin.

'My mind is going crazy and I'm worried,' Ferguson said.

She held out her hands, seeking to hold Ferguson's. 'I love you, Doug, and whatever it is, then we can do this together.'

'I'm not so sure you will want to.'

'Is it drugs?'

Ferguson didn't answer, his eyes welling again as he gnawed his bottom lip, trying hard to control his loosening emotions.

'Is it?'

'Yes.' He felt relief admitting it.

'You've been getting the lines from him?'

'Yes.'

'You moron!' Bronte still searched for Ferguson's hands. 'If you owe him twenty grand, does that mean you're dealing?'

He felt as if he was in confession. 'Yes.'

'How much do you plan to make?'

'One twenty.'

Mariner turned away, calling over the waiter. 'Could I get an espresso, please?'

'I'll have a latte, thanks.'

The waiter left.

'Are you supplying Rosie Chandler?'

'You know about Rosie?'

'She does weed, right?'

'Shit, I don't deal hard stuff with kids. I have standards.'

Ferguson was serious, but Mariner howled an enormous guffaw, continuing to laugh for a few moments and only calming when the coffee arrived.

'You don't sell to the kids. That's a good one.'

'It's true.'

'How did you get involved in this?'

'I used Ortega for coke supply. You know coke, the stuff that gets you going?'

'Yeah, all right, leave it.'

'Anyway, he suggested I sell for him. He told me one of his clients was jailed and his client list was available. He said it would be easy money. It was at first. Then I just started trusting people and my debtors list went up. Now I don't have cash to pay for the last deal. Most owe me within thirty days.'

'You're running a debtors list like a business? Are you nuts?' Mariner tapped her head with a finger. 'This is a COD business. You don't give credit. Does Chandler owe you?'

'She's into me for five hundred.'

'What's the biggest debt?'

'Five grand.'

'You are so dumb.' She shook her head in disbelief. 'How much stock do you have?'

'I have around twenty-five on credit and around a hundred in street value.'

'No wonder you're a teacher. You have no idea about running a business.'

Ferguson pushed out a hand. Mariner squeezed it.

'I just need to clear Ortega in the next few days.'

Mariner glared at him, working through options, then after a while said, 'Okay, this is the deal.' Ferguson glanced up. 'I'll give you the twenty, and in return, I want thirty.' His mouth opened as his jaw dropped. 'But, it's conditional.' A smile brushed over her lips.

'What do you want?'

'I want the ten. I want you to stop dealing once you sell the stock, and I want you to tell your wife you're leaving.'

'I need ten tonight.'

'Christ, Doug, you're screwed, aren't you?'

'He said he'll take a cheque.'

'Bullshit,' Mariner exclaimed.

'That's what I promised him, otherwise he reckons he'll start cutting off my fingers.'

'I can have twenty for you tomorrow. Will that be okay?'

'You're kidding me?'

'I love you, Doug, and no lowlife creep is going to hurt my man.'

'You give me twenty tomorrow and I give you thirty?'

'And, you stop dealing.'

'I can do that.'

'And, you tell your wife, otherwise no deal tomorrow.'

Ferguson couldn't believe his luck. They resolved his troubles. All he had to do was trust his girlfriend.

'And one last thing.'

'What's that, gorgeous?' asked Ferguson, feeling good as he took a mouthful of coffee.

'I want you to stop seeing that slag, Rosie Chandler.' Ferguson almost spat his coffee. 'I saw her coming out of your place a few months ago and figured she was getting private tuition. I wondered why her marks had seen a slight improvement, and when I saw her skip away from your door, I suspected she might be teacher's pet.'

'I-I-I-I,' Ferguson stumbled for a response.

'Say nothing; nothing to explain,' Mariner continued. 'Just know this, I have your balls in my hand, and if you fuck me over, I will squeeze them so hard you'll wish you didn't have any.' She smiled. 'Understand this, my love. I will have no hesitation reporting you to the police and the department over your indecent dealing with a student. You will never work again, and you'll go to jail.'

'She was… um… she came onto me.'

'No doubt; but that's no excuse.' Mariner relaxed. 'I reckon it's hot a student wants to screw my man, especially a nice-looking slag like Chandler, but you end it, and you end it now. Are we clear?' Ferguson was glancing down and didn't respond. 'Are we clear?'

'Crystal.'

'Now take me home and do rude things to me until my sins soak the sheets.'

As they reached the steps outside, Ferguson's phone shrilled.

'Hey dude, got me money?'

'I'll have twenty in cash tomorrow lunchtime.' Mariner nodded when he sought clarification.

'That's not the deal, cocksucker.'

'Twenty cash tomorrow is what I offer.' Bronte punched her hand, encouraging him to go harder. 'Take it or leave it.'

'What say I come to ya house right now and take a toe?'

'If you do, I call the police.'

'Fuck ya! I want me money.'

'You'll have it at lunchtime, make it one o'clock.'

'I want it now,' Ortega screamed into the phone, forcing Ferguson to pull it away.

Mariner bounced back up the steps, snuggling under Ferguson's arm, kneading the front of his trousers. He smiled and said, 'Listen here, Rikki, I'll have your money at one. That is the full twenty, as agreed. So, either I see you then, or I don't.'

'Man, if youse was in front of me right now, I'd be squeezin' the friggin' life out of ya.'

'You'd have to wait in line. See you tomorrow.'

CHAPTER

14

Ortega couldn't believe what he just heard, and when the phone went dead, he almost tossed it against the wall. He stormed back into the hotel bar to tell his cronies about what they might have to do tomorrow to get his money.

'What's up, boss? Is he coming?' Mickey Cole, a spindly kid, asked.

Ortega walked past the table to the bar and ordered a pint of beer before returning, taking a mouthful as he did, careful not to spill beer on his shirt.

'The cocksucker put me off 'til tomorrow.'

'He's got balls,' grunted Tommy Haslam.

'Why the hell say that?' Ortega was tempted to take a swipe. 'He reckons he'll have it, if he doesn't, then he's dead.'

The three teenagers swapped peeks. 'Boss, when ya say dead, ya don't mean dead, do ya?'

'What's the friggin' point talkin' tough if we never follow through?'

'Yeah, but it means twenty years in the can,' Rocky Galatea said.

'He can't take advantage,' snapped Ortega, then gulped a large mouthful of beer. 'If this gets out, we're rooted.'

'We get the money tomorrow, yeah?' Cole asked.

'That's what the prick said,' Ortega replied.

'That'll be good,' Haslam smiled. 'So, we get paid tomoz.'

'Youse'll get paid when I get the money,' Ortega snarled.

The others took up their beers and sipped, avoiding the boss' eyes.

Mates at school, they were attracted to the big-noting Ortega, who got them into petty crime, pinching things like bikes and lawn mowers and selling them on eBay. They knew adult prison would be bad for young blokes and gave the game away once they turned eighteen. *"They do nothing to juvies. It's when you're an adult that things change"* was Ortega's tenet, so they trusted and followed him.

According to local police, they were reckless teenagers with petty crime offences. They weren't pillars of society and could cause a skirmish or two, but they avoided police attention. Ortega used them to build his school kids' network, some as young as ten, who seemed the most cashed up.

Ortega drained his glass and stood. 'I'll pick youse up in the mornin'. Stay outta trouble.'

'No wuckin' furries, boss,' laughed Cole. 'We'll finish these and catch a train home. What're ya doin'?'

'I'm going to get my cock sucked.'

'Lucky bastard,' smiled Galatea. 'Can I watch?'

'Ya like watchin', don't ya?'

'Don't mind,' Galatea smiled.

'Go get ya own. See youse tomorrow at eleven. Bring ya fightin' gear.'

'You think there'll be trouble?' Haslam asked.

'We have to teach him a lesson, so I s'pect youse'll kick the shit out of him.'

'No worries, boss,' Haslam said as Ortega left, then turned to the others. 'Let's finish up here and go catch porn at home.'

'Sounds good to me, got any booze?' Cole said.

'Got a jar of Daniels.'

'Is that enough?' Galatea asked.

'Should be. We need clear heads tomoz,' Haslam replied, finishing his beer, hitching up his grubby jeans and strolling to the door. The others did the same, Cole scooping up the change left on the table.

The hotel was just a short walk from the station; a train swooshed in as they walked onto the platform. They skipped into the first carriage, walking through the train, checking for security officers. It was full with shift workers making their way home, students after a late class and others who were entertaining themselves, not wanting to drive home.

They passed a group of girls in the second carriage, and when they could walk no further, they agreed to go back and have a chat.

'Who knows, Rocky, you might get lucky,' Cole said.

'I bet they get off at Newport,' said Galatea.

'Then you had better talk fast,' mocked Cole.

The girls were chatting, and the gang squeezed past them to sit. Cole sat against the window, with Galatea on the aisle and Haslam across the aisle, blocking any escape route.

'Say girls, been out tonight, have ya?' Galatea asked as he sat down. They ignored the question.

Cole gazed at a dark-haired girl, and when she glanced at him, he smiled. She averted her eyes, but then glimpsed back. He was still smiling. 'Hi, girls, my name is Mickey. Where ya heading?'

No one responded. Cole swung his leg up onto the seat sideways next to Galatea. 'You wanna take me number and maybe we can hook up, maybe go to the movies?'

The train pulled into Spotswood and passengers got off. Within thirty seconds it was moving again.

Cole continued. 'Are you girls interested in some weed or maybe something stronger?' The girls peeped at each other, giggling behind their hands.

'Oh, so you want some gear?'

'No thanks,' said a girl on the aisle, as she got up moving to the door, the other two following. The boys stood and tailed them, standing close. Cole flicked the dark-haired girl's hair from her face and she cringed away, bumping into a man standing by the door. Haslam stepped up behind one and ran his hand over her butt, squeezing it hard. The girl panicked, stepping away and pushing into another waiting passenger.

'Why don't you leave them alone? They're not interested in what you might have for sale, and they're not buying your suave sophistication.'

The boys gawked around to see a business woman eyeing them.

'What's it to ya, lady?' demanded Cole.

'Who friggin' asked ya?' Haslam demanded.

'Crumbs, what a potty mouth you have. No wonder your diary is full of dates from girls who can't resist your charm.'

The girls sniggered, and Haslam pushed the girl he had manhandled away, moving to confront the woman. 'Who the fuck are you?'

Now the carriage passengers were paying attention, and a big guy from five seats away stood and moved to the door between the girls and the gang as the train swished into Newport station. The doors opened, and the girls ran from it, followed by other passengers, including the big guy. A soldier shouldering a heavy duffle bag got on, brushing past the boys and sitting behind the woman.

'You're friggin' lucky this train has witnesses,' snarled Cole, joining Haslam and confronting her.

'And a camera too, dipstick.' The woman pointed out the CCTV camera. 'You aren't that smart, are you?'

'Smarter than you,' said Cole, his hands forming fists.

'Is that all you have? That's the great rejoinder that makes me quiver with fear, that you are smarter than me?'

It struck Cole dumb. Galatea now joined his friends, standing over the woman and saying, 'Yeah? I bet we 'ave more money, smartarse.'

'I'm betting you got all of your loot from criminal activity.' The boys didn't respond. 'Yeah, thought so. What, selling drugs to your friends at school?'

'So, what?' Cole demanded.

'Jail will sort you boys out,' the woman smiled.

'I think we should sort you out,' sneered Haslam, as he hovered, glaring into her face.

'Why don't you boys go sit down and behave yourself?' The soldier joined the conversation.

'Why don't you go fuck yourself?' Cole retorted.

'Interesting,' replied the soldier. 'Are you getting your aspirations mixed up with your capability?'

'Why don't ya mind ya own business, baby killer?' Haslam chirped as he stood in a defensive position, gazing at the soldier.

The soldier stood. 'This is now my business,' he said with intent. 'Go into another carriage or I will be forced to deal with you.'

'What, three of us?' Galatea cackled as the boys fanned out. 'You wanna take on three of us?'

'I have skills,' the soldier shrugged. 'I'm just suggesting one more time that you move on.'

Haslam seemed the bravest and rushed with a round arm right to the soldier who was paying attention to Galatea. The soldier blocked the incoming danger, stepped to his right, and with a swift punch to the pit of the stomach rendered Haslam useless and struggling for air. The soldier grabbed him as he staggered, helping him to a seat to recover.

'Now, boys, I would like you to please reconsider your current position and move along to another carriage if you don't mind.'

Cole and Galatea stood ready, but the quick neutralisation of their friend changed their minds. They picked up Haslam, still struggling to bring his gasping under control, and moved off toward the front of the train, the soldier watching them go.

As he turned to resume his seat, the woman smiled and said, 'Thank you. That was very chivalrous of you.'

'Always keen to protect and serve, ma'am.'

'Are you coming home?'

'No, ma'am. I'm about to begin speciality installation of equipment on a vessel in the defence dockyards.'

'Oh, you do intelligence work?'

'Can't say, ma'am, but I'll be in Williamstown for three months. I arrived from Sydney a few hours back, caught the train, but ended up at the end of the line in Werribee, twenty minutes away, so I had to backtrack on the return trip to. What was it called, Newport? So, I'm heading for Williamstown. They have assigned me serviced quarters at a Quest Apartments, do you know it?'

'Yes, I do. It's a lovely spot, right on the water.'

The train pulled into North Williamstown, and the woman changed seats to talk with the soldier.

Meanwhile, the boys struggled to an almost empty carriage, setting down their friend, who was gaining some coherence.

'That bitch… so smug. I'd still like to have a crack,' Cole fumed.

'That ain't gonna happen,' Haslam said, rocking and stretching to relieve the discomfort and get his breathing under control.

'Let's forget it and go watch movies,' suggested Galatea.

The boys sat for a moment, thinking about events and what they had planned. Then Cole suggested, 'Hey, those girls may have been goin' to catch a bus. What say we get the car and go lookin' for them?'

'Nah, a waste of time.' Galatea shook his head.

'We could use me brother's car and hike back to Newport, just to check.'

'You ain't got a licence, Coley,' Haslam reminded him.

'Hasn't stopped us in the past.'

'Nah, they'll never go with us,' Galatea said.

'I'll get me knife when I get his keys,' Cole said.

'I'm in,' Haslam said, with a leery smile.

'Why are you suddenly game?' Galatea asked.

'If you felt that slut's arse then ya know why.'

The train was leaving Williamstown Beach station, and they prepared themselves for the quick dash to the housing commission tower next to the train tracks. Once the train stopped at Williamstown, they pressed the button to open the doors, bursting onto the platform, through the station's building, and off along the path to the twelve-storey flats nearby.

The woman saw them dash off, thankful they had lost interest in her.

'Where are you going?' the soldier asked.

'I have a townhouse almost opposite the dockyards. Just around the corner from where you're staying.'

'Then you won't mind if I check out the area, so I know where to go in the morning.'

'Sure, tag along. I'll point out some things that might interest you along the way.'

The soldier slung his duffle bag and walked politely behind as they swiped their transport cards for payment. Then they walked together along Ann Street. When they got to the historical Stag's Head Hotel, a small corner bar that had opened around two hundred years earlier, the woman stopped.

'The least I can do is buy you a drink. I'm going to have a wine. Would you care to join me?'

'Well, ma'am, it's been a long night, but if you're sure, then I would love to have a beer.'

'That being the case, you had better tell me your name.'

'Sergeant John Peters, ma'am.'

'Well, Sergeant John Peters, my name is Victoria Stevedore.' She held out her hand. 'Pleased to meet you.'

'Pleasure to meet you, ma'am.'

Vikki and John chatted about various local sights and where to go for coffee or a quick meal. She showed him on her phone where the shopping district for groceries was.

'I notice you have a wedding ring, husband not worried where you are?'

'He's out late on Tuesdays, some scouting thing he's involved in. I must admit I know little about it, and he gets home around one in the morning. He works hard in the community; too hard, I think.'

'Is he a politician?'

Vikki chuckled. 'No, he isn't, but my father is. I was just having dinner with him in the city.'

'He must be proud of you.'

'Why do you say that?' Vikki asked.

'Most fathers are proud of their daughters, and it seems to me you are quite successful. I would imagine you are fearless in what you do.

I would guess a lawyer, because you seemed to know how to handle those boys.'

'What are you, a spy?' Vikki laughed.

'If I told you, I would have to kill you,' said John, smiling over his glass before taking another mouthful.

'I'm a defence lawyer and deal with scum like those kids all the time.'

'Do you enjoy it?'

'Not really, but it pays well.' Vikki yawned. 'Oh, sorry; I'm crashing fast, so I'd better go.'

'I think I might have another beer before closing, if you don't mind.'

'That's fine. I only live around the corner in the next street.' Vikki stood and held out her hand. John stood to attention and took it, then leaned in for a peck on the cheek, which she welcomed. 'Thanks once again for your bravery,' she smiled, squeezing his hand.

'Perhaps let's catch up for a coffee in Nelson Place on the weekend?'

'That'll be great.'

'Here's my number.' Peters scribbled on a coaster. 'Call me on Saturday. Drag your husband along, it'll be fun.'

Vikki stepped away and out through the door with a last wave and smile, thinking she wouldn't be asking her husband to join her. She had enjoyed meeting the soldier and skipped along with confidence, keeping her smile and putting her music plugs into her ears. She paid little attention to the dirty sedan with one headlight turning into Ann Street from Nelson Place.

CHAPTER

15

The boys had hammered the car back to Newport and over the railway flyover, squealing left into the bus station. There was a crowd of twenty folks waiting for buses, but no girls.

'Let's cruise around for a bit. They may be walking,' Haslam said.

The boys roamed the streets around Newport Station for a few minutes, searching for three young girls walking by themselves, but found no one other than a man taking a dog for a late-night walk. Out of luck, they decided to cruise home, get into the Jack Daniels and watch a few movies. They drove to the end of North Road, turning into the Strand, where the affluence of the suburb expressed itself with enormous houses commanding million-dollar views across the Hobson's Bay back to the city. It was their favourite racetrack.

'Give it some juice, Mickey,' Haslam cried from the back seat, windows down, wind whipping his long lank hair.

Cole planted his foot, and the old V8 cranked up the speed. They sped past a pier restaurant and mooring facility, then the scout hall, only slowing as they manoeuvred the roundabout, and squealed the car into Nelson Place, rounding the next roundabout, blasting past the police station, honking the horn and yelling obscenities.

They soon cruised into Ann Street and gunned up the slight rise. As they surged past Aitken Street, Cole pointed to a woman walking the street in a short black dress and a light black coat.

'That's the bitch from the train.' Cole braked, spinning the car and turning off the headlights, then cruising thirty metres behind her.

'Where? I don't believe it,' Haslam said, searching the street, following Cole's pointing finger.

'Let's take her,' said Cole, transforming his boyish excitement into a focused criminal.

'What are we gonna do?' Galatea asked.

'We're gonna screw her,' said Cole, wheezing like a rabid dog. 'Tommy, will ya be right to get her? Ya can help, Rocky boy.'

Vikki turned onto Aitken Street, oblivious to the darkness lurking behind her. She appeared to be sending someone a text while she walked.

Cole shouted, 'Now!' as he gunned the car closer to her.

Haslam jumped from the car as Vikki struggled to find her house keys deep in her bag. He punched her hard to the side of the head, knocking her to the pavement. He then kicked her in the stomach, hoping to stifle any screams. Picking her up by the hair, he punched her again, breaking her nose. Galatea rushed over to help, collecting her legs while Haslam held her in a headlock, tight around her throat.

Vikki fought hard, bucking, screaming and scratching at anything she could reach with her flaying arms. Galatea dragged her legs into the back seat of the car, but she clung onto the roof and the door, arching herself back out and kicking out, striking Galatea with her stiletto and dazing him. She managed an almighty scream, and a light appeared from a window on the first floor opposite. Haslam glanced up and saw a curtain move.

'Christ, get her in, will ya?' Haslam shouted. 'I'm losing me grip. Vikki bit into his arm and he yelled as he tried to break her grip.

Cole leaned over the front seat and punched her in her pelvic region with all the force he could muster. He weakened her, allowing Haslam to bundle her in, grab her bag and pile in on top of her. Once in, Cole gunned the engine and sped off to the end of the street, squealed into Kanowna, past the Prince of Wales hotel, then right into Battery

Road, heading for the Time-Ball Tower. Haslam flipped her over and punched the screaming woman again in the face, splitting her lip.

Vikki weakened further, sobbing, holding her hands and arms to protect herself. 'Please don't hurt me, please don't hurt me.'

'Shut the fuck up.' Haslam slapped her in the face.

Galatea scooped up her bag and slid over the front seat, making himself comfortable, searching through its contents. Cole began banging the steering wheel as they passed the tower, speeding along the coast, ignoring the speed humps, which made the journey even more exciting.

'Where shall we take her?' asked Cole as he peeked back at Haslam, who was now rubbing his hands over the dazed woman, squeezing her breasts.

'She's a beauty,' he said. 'I think I'll do her now.'

'Ya dun wanna wait?' Cole shouted, slowing as he got to the football ground at the end of the peninsula.

'Pass me ya knife,' Haslam said, as he tried to pull at her frock. He positioned himself so he faced her as she lay across the back seat. 'Tonight is ya lucky night, sweetheart.'

He took the knife, ripping his way from the hem of the dress to the neckline. The knife was sharp for the job, and it took him no time at all. He peeled back the dress to expose her underwear.

'Oh man, look at this,' Haslam said.

Cole slowed and the boys in front craned over the back to see the semi-naked woman sprawled across the back seat, trying to cover her black lingerie.

'Come on, Tommy, hurry up, we all wanna go,' Galatea growled.

'Rocky, we call this foreplay. The girls love it, apparently. Calm down, would ya?'

Galatea returned to his treasure, finding a wallet and opening it to reveal credit cards. 'Hey, she's got cards, we can get fuel, and maybe the bottle shop at the Rifle is still open.'

Haslam slipped the knife through the bra straps and then sliced through the centre at the cups. He brushed the cups away and then squeezed her breasts before slurping and biting hard.

Vikki groaned in pain. 'Don't hurt me, please don't hurt me.'

'Honey, we're not gonna hurt ya,' Haslam said, as he ran the tip of the knife down her body until he reached her panties. He then sliced each side, snatching the remnants from her, tossing the small piece of cloth over to the front seat.

Galatea grasped at them and took a deep breath of the fabric.

'Just do what ya told and youse'll be okay. Christ, ya friggin' beautiful.' Haslam ran his hands over her stomach and down her legs to her knees, forcing them open.

'Shit man, don't fall in love,' shouted Cole, as he watched in the rearview mirror. 'Just screw her and get it done, will ya?'

Haslam unbuckled his belt and wriggled his jeans down. He then positioned himself over her and tried pushing into her. 'Christ, she's tight.'

'Spit on it,' Galatea said, watching from the front.

Haslam withdrew, then shoved back; then again withdrew, then pushed back. 'There, that's better.' As he thrust into her, he shoved the tip of his knife into her nose. 'Now you just lay there and enjoy it, bitch.'

Vikki lay and absorbed the punishment, her mouth bloodied, her body numb. She could only squint through one eye. She did not feel the boy turning away as he panted to a finish, attempting to kiss her.

'You ain't the man I thought ya were,' shouted Galatea, as he scrutinized his mate rolling away after less than a minute. 'Let me have a go.' He leaned over the seat, shoving Haslam back as he hitched his jeans, and swapped seats.

Cole glanced at Haslam as he dropped into the front. 'How was it?'

'Silk, man, pure silk.'

Cole gunned the car into Bayview Street, heading for the Rifle Club hotel and the servo across the road. Galatea had tugged his trackie–daks down and shoved the woman's knees up to give him more room. 'Please don't hurt me,' she whimpered. 'I'll do whatever you want. Please don't hurt me.'

'Shut up, bitch,' hollered Galatea, as he thumped her face, splitting her eyebrow with his gold ring, oozing blood into her hair. He then crushed into her, snorting like a bear until he rolled away as the car slowed to enter the drive-through of the hotel. Haslam got out, rearranging his jeans and sauntering into the liquor store. He collected two bottles of Jack Daniels and a bottle of Johnny Walker, confirming the total amount didn't go beyond the hundred-dollar pay-wave limit.

Cole watched Haslam with his window open, checking for any pedestrian traffic.

Galatea sat in back, leaning over the woman.

'Where shall we go to treat you, Mickey?' smiled Galatea. 'And I don't mean Maccas.'

Cole gazed into the mirror. 'I know the exact place. Nice and quiet, and we can have a party. We'll get petrol and maybe snacks then settle in for a good night,' he sneered. 'She any good?'

'You'll love it.'

Vikki struggled to lift her head. There was a dull sense of sound, she could hear muffled voices. She ached as she wriggled, tugging her sliced dress and summer coat over her. She sensed she was alone, squinting about as she raised her head, hair matted with blood and sticking to her face. The front seat was empty. Voices and laughter came from the back of the car, at the petrol cap. She twisted from her back to her side, leaning on an elbow, careful to remain out of sight.

'Where ya reckon we should take her?' Galatea asked, pumping the fuel.

'Why don't we go to your place, Mickey?' Haslam asked. 'I want another go, on a cot this time.'

'Don't be fuckin' stupid,' Cole snapped. 'Too dangerous. Nah, let's take her to Altona. I know the exact place. Nice an' quiet.'

Vikki could only squint through one eye, the other split, swollen and closed. A waft of air from the door, left ajar, brushed a tuft of her hair. She raised her head to the level of the window, straining to identify her surroundings. She recognised the 7/11 servo at North Williamstown station, the end of the retail district. She assumed she had one chance; she had to act now.

Her plan was to tumble from the car, screaming and running to the attendant; he would sound the alarm and call triple zero. Vikki trembled as she prepared to jump, waiting for when the men would be unguarded and relaxed. She heard the pump hose being replaced, and the cap screwed in with raucous laughter.

It was time.

She coiled, grabbing the edge of the seat and preparing her feet. She strained to see if the men had moved and shoved the door further open. Heart pumping, she lunged, thrusting open the door, grabbing the handle and dragging herself from the car, screaming. As she struggled to get out, a foot slipped on the drive shaft hump and she tumbled to the cement driveway.

She recovered and ran shrieking toward the front of the car as Cole charged around the rear, grasping, trying to grab her. He bounced off the corner of the car as he lunged toward her and fell on the driveway. She was now rounding the front and could see the attendant with a customer.

She screamed again, but the attendant didn't respond.

Haslam came at her, almost intercepting her dash as she spun away, charging past the petrol pumps, sliced clothes flapping like a cape. The door to the shop and safety was just five metres away, and she screamed, hoping the doors would open as she got to them. They did, just as Galatea came stumbling out, grabbing her in a headlock, twisting and silencing her before stomping back to the car. The other two now with him. He bundled her back into the car. Cole glanced over his shoulder to see if the attendant was paying attention. He seemed engrossed in a magazine, ear plugs blaring, with no idea what was happening.

'Let me go,' Vikki screamed. 'Help me! Let me go!'

The railway boom gates begun operation, the pinging bells drowning out her screams. They rammed her back into the car. Galatea dived in after her. Sitting up, he tossed several quick jabs into her head and then a driving thump into her stomach.

'Shut up, bitch.' Galatea sat on her legs, examining the now silent woman. 'Keep ya friggin' mouth closed and no one'll hurt ya.'

'Leave her,' said Cole as he gawked back. 'I haven't had a go yet. She won't be worth squat if ya keep hittin' her.'

'She'll be okay. Just drive.'

Cole gunned the engine, the car cruising past the shop and out on to Kororoit Creek Road. He opened up the throttle, pushing it for a fast getaway. Past the school and the rifle range estate, past the oversized fuel storage tanks; then he slowed before the train fly-over, turning into Racecourse Road, which led to the old Williamstown horse racing track, now open foreshore land. The road was dark as the boys cruised across the causeway, stopping at a parking cutaway.

'Party time, boys,' Cole declared, turning off the engine and clambering out. The air was crisp with a trace of sulphur from the nearby petrochemical plant. He stood listening for any citizens out walking. Haslam followed, as did Galatea, locking the door by Vikki's head. 'Let's take her out to the centre of the paddock, away from the walking track, in case a snoopy someone comes along.'

Haslam searched around for any noise or lights. The soft hum of the plant was the only sound. He then pointed to several lights over to his right. 'What're they?'

'It's a scout camp. They use it sometimes for outdoor training,' said Cole, as he went to the boot of the car and hauled out the three bottles of alcohol. 'Let's get the bitch and go party. I fancy a root.'

Galatea opened up the back door, dragging the woman from the car by her legs.

He didn't bother protecting her head as it thumped into the gravel. He then grabbed a handful of hair and heaved her up. She wriggled but didn't resist. The boys moved to the wire fence and Galatea dumped her over, bending and picking up her legs, flipping them like a rag-doll. The gang moved another hundred metres from the road before stopping.

'Any snakes around?' Galatea asked.

'Heaps,' Cole replied. 'Tigers everywhere. I used to come catch 'em when I was a kid.'

'Should we be worried?' Haslam asked. 'Nah, Rocky would've scared them off.'

The boys stomped their way around a small area, flattening the long grass; when they sat down, they couldn't be seen. The woman collapsed. They screwed the tops off their bottles and clinked the necks before taking a mouthful.

'Ow, geez, it burns,' Haslam said, rubbing his chest. Galatea glanced at Cole. 'You gonna root her?'

'Okay, okay, give us a minute, would ya?' Cole took another slug of bourbon, screwing the top back and tossing the bottle aside. Then he crawled over to the woman. He brushed aside the clothing, rubbing his hand across her, grabbing her roughly. 'My turn, baby. How do ya wan' it, hips or lips, bitch?'

Cole rolled her over, flipping up material, hauling her to her knees. He dropped his jeans and spat on his hand, rubbing himself ready. The woman's head was face down in the dirt, hips high. He positioned himself behind, prodding himself until he found what he was looking for, then thrust hard.

'Oh man, that feels good.' Cole gripped her hips, heaving them back as he thrust hard, screaming 'Ye-hah!' He slapped her, shoving harder and faster until done. He fell back, tossing her prone hips aside. 'That was great, who's next?'

'She ripe for a blowie?' Galatea asked.

'Still breathin', so yeah,' Cole laughed.

The boys swigged more alcohol, cracking jokes. Galatea kicked off his trackie-daks and sat down near the woman's head. 'Hey, Tommy, why don't we have a threesome? You take her while I do her mouth.'

Haslam moved over to her, lugging her hips prone again. He dropped his jeans to his ankles, then dribbled bourbon over her from back to front. He then squatted to his haunches over her prone hips, tugged open her buttocks and spat on her, then forced himself upon her. 'She's tight.'

'Virgin arse bandit, ya reckon?' Cole laughed.

'Hey, wait for me,' said Galatea, as he jerked up her head, dropping her jaw. He lowered her mouth. 'Okay, let's go.'

The two boys then pummelled her, squealing like rodeo riders. Galatea, gripping her hair, forcing himself in, choking her as she grunted for breath, with Haslam bouncing up and down as if on a bucking horse.

Haslam finished and fell away. Before Galatea finished, the woman threw up in his lap. 'Fuck me, what a bitch,' he cried, as he squirmed, wriggling away. The others laughed, watching him try to shake off the vomit and wash himself with his bourbon.

'That's hot watchin' youse. I'm horny for another go.' Cole was squeezing himself, walking over to the woman and kicking her over onto her back. 'She's one hot momma, check out those tits.' He dropped his jeans, kneeling between her legs and lifting them, placing one on his shoulder. He lowered himself, shoving her legs up and back. He then thumped into her.

When he was done he stood, kicking the woman in the ribs, and before buttoning his jeans, asked, 'Youse done?'

'Yeah,' said Haslam. 'Can't get it up and sore.'

'What about you, Rocky?'

'Nah, she put me off, chuckin' up.'

'Great, cos I've been dying for a piss.' Cole emptied himself; the others laughed, joining him.

Vikki stirred. She supposed it was raining and rolled onto her stomach, inching herself away.

Galatea guarded her, and as she lifted her head, he kicked it hard. 'Where do ya think ya goin', bitch?' he yelled into her bloodied ear.

'What do ya think we should do with her, Mickey?' Haslam asked.

'We can't dump her,' Cole replied.

'Ya reckon she'll remember us?'

'Not after that beatin',' Cole said.

'I don't wanna take her to Willy,' Galatea said. 'Too many chances bein' seen.'

'Leave the bitch,' Cole said. 'Snakes can have her.'

'Ya reckon she knows us?' Haslam asked.

'Nah, she don't know us.' Cole kicked her in the ribs; she didn't respond. 'Bitch.'

'Why not do her now?' Gateau suggested. Haslam sneered. 'That's murder, dumb arse.'

'So?'

'Done for murder means jail time, dickhead.'

'No one's gonna chop anyone,' Cole interrupted. 'She won't remember if she spends the night here. Let's leave her.'

Haslam took a slug of bourbon and dragged a rumpled cigarette pack from his pocket. 'I smoke after a good root.' The others took a stick, waiting for his lighter. He patted his jeans. 'Nah, I ain't got a light.'

'Fuck me, you're friggin' useless.' Cole tugged a book of matches from his pocket. 'We did well, boys, what d'ya reckon?' Cole held the lit match to the others.

'Yeah, we did,' Haslam agreed.

'Hey, you guys, what do you think you're doing?' A group of torches were bouncing toward them from the scout camp.

'Geezus!' cried Cole, dropping the matches. 'Let's get out of here.'

The boys ran off as torch lights spread out, some following, others going to the party scene. With a whoosh, the dry grass burst into flames, spreading rapidly, distracting the chasing torches to veer back to the party site to help extinguish the blaze.

Panting on return to the car, the boys gunned it, speeding off and hoping no one had seen their number.

The men with torches were now losing control of the fire, being pushed back as it fanned toward the scout camp.

'Wait up,' a man yelled. 'There's someone in there.'

Two men ran through the fire line and over the burnt grass to find a disfigured woman, barely alive.

Charlie Stevedore loved this time of day, out on his large terraced balcony, another clear sky welcoming the rising sun above the roof shapes to the east. The air was crisp and smelt clean. He treasured the chance for a mug of sweet tea, skimming the morning newspapers delivered early. They had purchased the fifth level penthouse in East Melbourne when his wife Stephanie was first diagnosed with motor neuron disease. He understood MND was a killer, and it would only be a matter of time before his beloved wife would pass. He purchased the apartment because it was next door to St Vincent's private hospital, allowing immediate care when she needed it. No matter how much she deteriorated, Stephie remained cheerful, but would have terminated her suffering earlier, coveting death with dignity.

Stevedore preferred to remain in the apartment, even with its horrible memories, as it was opposite Fitzroy Gardens and allowed him an amiable stroll to work. He enjoyed relaxing during his walk, reflecting on the many good times he had spent sharing the gardens with Stephie.

He finished his tea, picking up the hose to spray the shrubbery his wife had planted.

He sprayed the olives, lemon and pear trellises, and the assorted plants in large tubs that provided an oasis on the terrace. As he finished winding the hose back to its hanger, he glanced across the horizon and marvelled at the rising sun. Orange and yellow streaks were building in the eastern sky, and the nearby suburbs were visible as dark silhouettes. He filled his lungs and considered how lucky he was to enjoy these moments. He scooped up his newspapers, tossing them on the dining table, and placed his mug on the kitchen bench. It was time to shower and begin another day of arduous politics, no doubt placating an anxious prime minister.

He undertook to call Parker Osborne before he left for the office, otherwise he might not get a connection during their busy day. Dinner with his daughter and a fidgety sleep had reinforced the idea that he would ignore the prime minister and not do as she wanted; he was unequivocal that he would campaign for a Yes vote. Stephanie would have wanted him to as he had promised, even if it meant ending his political career. Euthanasia was an important dignity and human right to allow the terminally ill, and the treatment should be available to families to end the suffering of a loved one. He was clear on what he must do, whatever the consequences would be for himself.

As he dropped his thick robe on the bed, the security buzzer echoed throughout the apartment. Stevedore noted the time, thinking that 6.30 was early to be calling on him.

When he got to the security unit, he didn't recognise the two suited men waiting.

'Good morning. Can I help you?'

'Minister, my name is Commander Hanrahan, my colleague and I are from the federal police.' Both men displayed their credentials to the camera. 'If you have a moment, we would like to have a chat with you.'

'Sure, come on up.' Stevedore pushed the door release and watched as the two men entered the lobby. He then dashed to his bedroom and pulled on his running suit. It was not unusual for federal police to seek his advice, but not at this early hour, so he suspected the visit must be important. He slipped on a pair of loafers, scurrying to the front door and opening it as the elevator door released and both men filed out. He shook hands as they entered his apartment.

'Can I offer you a tea?'

'Sir, not at this time. Would you like to take a seat?'

The tone was ominous, reinforcing his impression that their reason for coming must be important. He took a stool by the kitchen bench.

'What's up?'

'Minister, we have tragic news.' Stevedore thought of Nancy Pasco. 'It leads us to believe that a serious assault was carried out on your daughter, Victoria, last night.'

Stevedore gasped, a hand cupping his mouth.

'She is in Alfred Hospital in their specialist burns unit.'

'What happened?'

'We are uncertain. The local boys have little information at this stage of the investigation, but we are monitoring progress and we will assist should they request it.'

'Is she all right?'

'She's on the critical list in intensive care, in an induced coma.'

Stevedore didn't speak; he couldn't. His jaw gaped to say something, but nothing came out; colour drained from his face and his eyes welled, spilling over his cheeks.

'We are yet to formally identify her, sir; we would like you to accompany us to the hospital, so we can complete that.'

He shook his head. 'How do you know it's her?'

'She had no possessions or identification with her at all when she was found. They helicoptered her to hospital, and when the medical staff searched through the remnants of her burnt clothes, they found a beer coaster with a name and number on it.'

'Are you sure it's Vikki?' Stevedore was wiping his eyes with a kitchen cloth.

'The name was John Peters, so we rang his number. He met her on the train to Williamstown last night. He last saw her heading for home.'

'Then how do you know it's her?' He was sceptical, looking for answers.

'We don't, unless we get a positive ID. That's the reason we would like you to attend. We tried her home, but no one answered, so we now need your help, sir.'

'Surely this is a mistake.'

'Minister, we have a woman in a bad way, and the only connection we have is from this Sergeant Peters chap, which points to your daughter. We just need you to come and determine one way or another if it is her.'

'How bad is it?'

'Bad enough, sir. She has burns to almost sixty percent of her body, ranging from first to fourth degree burns.'

'Fourth degree? I thought it only ever went to third?'

'You and me both, Minister.' Hanrahan said.

The men didn't move. They gazed at each other, the other police officer bowing his head, evading all eye contact. Stevedore glared at Hanrahan, taking in what he was told, then started shaking his head. His bottom lip quivered; he was losing control of his emotions. His eyes flowed, nose dribbling as his jaw stretched wide as if ready to scream; no noise came, just a shuddering of his body. Hanrahan moved closer, ready to catch the minister, who appeared in a grip of a spasm.

A deafening howl of a guttural wail scared the police officers as Stevedore fell from the stool to the floor.

'Quick, Billy, a glass of water,' Hanrahan directed his colleague as he jumped to the attorney general's aid.

Stevedore clawed at him, wailing like a banshee, sobbing through tears.

Hanrahan sat beside him, hugging a father learning of a monstrous crime against his daughter. He held him tight, rocking, comforting, waiting for him to recover, taking the glass offered from Billy as he calmed. Hanrahan passed the water to Stevedore, who greedily drank. Billy took the glass for a refill.

Stevedore pushed away, trying to stand; he used the wooden stool to lift himself, Hanrahan assisting. He sat at the bench, gratefully accepting the offered water and swallowing another huge mouthful.

After a while Hanrahan asked, 'Would you like to take a shower, minister? Change, perhaps?'

'Are you nuts?' A tear-streaked Stevedore faced the police inspector. 'Sorry.' He held up a hand, apologetic. 'I think we should go now. Let me just collect my things.'

He swept up his phone, wallet and keys and began walking to the door.

Hanrahan and his colleague followed. It wasn't until they were in the car that Stevedore spoke. 'What time was she taken to hospital?'

Hanrahan turned from the front seat as Billy drove. 'She was caught up in a brush fire out in some wasteland in Altona.'

'What was she doing in Altona?'

'We are yet to piece that together, sir. Anyway, a group of men from a management training session at a nearby campsite were roused around midnight by suspicious noises and carry-on and went to investigate. When they approached, a group of kids ran off, leaving a brush fire that rapidly spread, pushing them back. A couple of plucky blokes ran through the fire as they thought someone was lying in it. They found the woman, possibly your daughter. They called emergency and fire unit, advising the ambos they may need air support. The coppers have been on it ever since.'

'Did it take long?'

'The paramedics diagnosed pretty quickly, calling in the chopper. The fireys were able to put the grass fire out before the chopper arrived, and the coppers sealed off the area. We have her arriving at the Alfred emergency at 2.47.'

'I'm uncertain, but I think she left me after dinner in the city at around ten.'

'If you identify her, we'll go through that process, sir, so let's just get through the first step then worry about further questions.'

Stevedore gazed out of the window as they crossed the Yarra River at Punt Road Bridge before hammering up the hill. They engaged their flashing light without the siren to clear the road of early morning commuters, arriving at Alfred Hospital within fifteen minutes, parking in an emergency vehicle bay.

The police officers had prepared the medical staff for an impeding identification and were shown to the intensive care unit on the sixth floor. They were given masks, hoods for their hair and gowns so they could enter the suite. They used an alcohol hand sanitizer, conscious of contamination, then entered the viewing room. The police officers placed themselves either side of Stevedore and walked to a window that further separated the ward from contamination.

They approached the window; the patient was lying with a multitude of tubes hanging about her. A large tube attached to a flexible metal arm hung above her face; from this they inserted a small plastic tube in her mouth, presumably to her lungs. They draped her in light cloth sheets, covering her body. The only indicator confirming she was alive were the monitors flicking rhythmic charts and numbers and a beeping noise.

'Is it her?' Hanrahan whispered.

Stevedore moved closer, reaching his fingertips to the window to steady himself. All that was visible was the woman's face swathed with tubes, matted hair pushed back behind her head with dirt, grass and blood still clinging to it. He searched for a clue. Her face was swollen, eyes black and red, puffy and split. He could see nothing he recognised.

He shook his head. 'I'm not sure.'

'Take your time,' Hanrahan murmured close to him.

Stevedore examined the face again. The split nose, the teeth, but there were too many tubes blocking an unobstructed view. He studied her hair again. Could that grubby mop be the bouncing brunette he saw last night? It now seemed a different colour. Then he noticed her ear, paying particular attention to a dark mark on her neck.

'Can someone lift her ear?'

Hanrahan waved the nurse to lift her ear, and there it was. She had got it when her mother died. A bold red heart in a black outline. He had told her she was silly, and she told him it was none of his business.

'Is it Victoria?'

Stevedore was struggling and answering weakened him. 'It's her,' he sobbed. 'It's my darling baby.' He reached out his other hand in a tight fist, knuckling the window. 'Vikki,' he whimpered.

CHAPTER

18

Walsh Bay was tucked away from the tourist precinct of the Rocks, on the other side of the Dawes Point peninsula linking Sydney Harbour Bridge with Darling Harbour. Once known as a backwater collecting rubbish and rats, it now was a trendy, expensive place to live. Unkind cynics opined it had changed little.

Dennis Sadler bought into Walsh Bay off the plan. Saving a small fortune on stamp duty, the four-million-dollar price tag complemented his celebrity status. He had the highest rating radio show in Sydney and was second only to a breakfast show in Melbourne for the national honours. His publicity seduced him and welcomed the notoriety he gained over twenty years. Politicians often queued to get airtime because his audience were voters who would change their vote if Dennis told them to. Now he was a powerful voice in Australian politics. If he favoured you, then your career was on the stellar highway, but if he despised you, then nothing could save you.

Sadler enjoyed entertaining at his nearby café, Pier 8, often asking the current treasurer to join him so he could espouse economic ideas and encourage reform.

Treasurers were the next in line for promotion to prime minister, so Sadler worked his influence on the snotty-nosed morons, as he was often heard to say, before they reached the nation's highest political honour. Although he had once considered a political career, he believed it a step down in status; and why should he go through the stress and agony of public humiliation when he enjoyed flaying politicians at every opportunity?

Sadler's current enthusiast was Parker Osborne, the rakish, troublesome politician from Sydney's north shore. He was just a little too ambitious, and Sadler was yet to groom him to meet his needs for future influence.

'You must enjoy it here,' Osborne said, as he gazed over the harbour.

They were sitting in Sadler's reserved table down back, away from the entrance and the kitchen clatter, with a panoramic view of the harbour. Generous tips for the maître d' and staff, including the chefs, ensured they always favored him. His ego needed to be fussed over, and Sadler didn't care what the price was.

'It's boring viewing it every day, but I must say, I much prefer this view to the crumby hole I used to live in with my parents. Gawd, those were the days. When a good smack around the ears was considered love.' Sadler wiped his thin lips with a napkin, then folded it neatly on his plate, showing he was finished.

A waiter was soon at the table, laying a crisp napkin across his lap and clearing his plate. Osborne continued tucking into the shakshouka, enjoying the Arabic flavours. The waiter returned, pouring a steaming cup of peppermint tea for Sadler, placing the teapot within reach. He then presented a thinly sliced, toasted seven-grain sourdough before him, cut to order in quarters with lashings of butter and small dabs of vegemite.

'You'll have to excuse my little foibles, Parker. I just have this thing about vegemite,' Sadler laughed, embarrassed at being exposed. This was the covert routine he employed at every first date. 'I think it might have come from my humble upbringing. I always like to finish breakfast with a slice.'

'No, go right ahead.' Osborne shovelled the last of his meal into his mouth, glancing at the celebrity, wondering if it was all an act for his benefit, or if the man was weird.

'I'm pleased you accepted my invitation. I know we've spoken many times on the programme, but this is the first time I think we've had a social outing.'

Osborne thought for a moment. 'I recall we were across the harbour at Kirribilli House once. You were mouthing off about government policy, and I remember you didn't have many kind things to say about the government.'

'I have nothing kind to say about the government, someone needs to keep you on your toes.'

'How do you think we're travelling?'

'Whilst you keep that horrible woman as your leader, you are doomed. Doomed never to sit on the government benches again for at least ten, maybe fifteen years.'

'That's harsh, Dennis.' Osborne was never timid under political threat.

'Not really.' Sadler tapped his lips with the napkin. 'I have been saying for longer than a year now that the prime minister is out of her depth. As a junior minister she might be fine, but as the leader of the country, well, we could do better.'

'What do you expect us to do, get rid of her?' Osborne glanced about to check if anyone might have been listening.

'What's the worst thing that can happen? You go to the election with her and you lose. You go to the election with someone else, and you might win. It seems obvious to me.'

'Who would you say would make a fine prime minister?' Osborne glared at him as Sadler appeared to be daydreaming, gazing outside, sipping on his peppermint tea.

Without returning Osborne's gaze, Sadler asked, 'Who would you put forward?'

He thought for a moment before responding. 'I think Charlie Stevedore offers something.'

Sadler glanced at Osborne and smiled. 'That's rubbish, Parker, and you know it. There is only one person who can and should be prime minister, and it's not Charles Stevedore.'

Osborne demurred, not wanting to provide Sadler the opportunity to confirm his ambition.

'Only treasurers become prime minister. You're the treasurer, so it is up to you to rid the nation of this pathetic woman and bring back decency and prestige to the role of prime minister.'

'I have no plans.'

'Then get some, son; because, let me tell you what will happen if you don't.' Sadler sipped another taste of tea. 'If I take a dislike to you, then you will never be able to lead this country, ever.'

'What do I give in return?'

'I want nothing from you, son. I just want what's best for the country.' Sadler flashed his capped teeth.

Osborne gazed across the table, collecting his thoughts. 'I have a plan,' he said, with a little reluctance. Sadler raised an eyebrow and smirked. 'The church wants the same as you.'

'Which church?' Sadler demanded. 'Tell me, it's not the fiddlers. Rome burns, and they still fiddle.'

'That was Nero.'

'Same thing.' Sadler wiped his mouth, tossing the napkin on the table. 'They have no authority, no credibility to speak on any issue. They have let down a lot of followers, all over the world.'

'They've sent a cardinal from Rome.'

'Geezus, they must be worried.'

'They're worried about the euthanasia legislation.'

'It's a state government issue, and the feds should not be getting involved. Stay out of it, I say.'

'We are obligated to initiate a referendum to amend section 51 of the constitution, that's the plan. The referendum is lost, and the prime minister has no alternative other than to resign.'

'Is that it?' Sadler guffawed. 'Is that the Machiavellian plan for a leadership change? Maybe I was wrong about you.'

Osborne, now unsettled, squirmed in his chair and leaned into the table. 'The prime minister does not want the referendum.'

Sadler tossed back his head and laughed. 'Then I'm backing the wrong horse.'

'No, listen,' Osborne snapped. Sadler recovered, sneering a smile. 'To kill this issue dead, once and for all, we need a No vote. What we don't need is the prime minister going soft on the idea of a referendum and never putting the issue to a vote.'

'So, what? Let me tell you, Parker, there had better be a solution to this mess, otherwise I'm going in guns blazing and I don't care about the body count.'

'No, listen… please, Dennis.' Osborne leaned in even further. 'I'm convinced the referendum will be a resounding No vote. Especially when the churches and advocates for the negative speak up. Advocates such as yourself. If it is a No, then she is gone.'

'Just because I think the feds should not be doing this, doesn't mean I won't support the Yes case. You see, I use moral issues like this to bring my politicians to heel. So, don't rely on me.'

Osborne studied Sadler, wondering if he was a supporter of good government or just a celebrity seeking to stay out front of a fawning audience. 'The way I read it, if the Catholics put pressure on the prime minister not to go ahead with the referendum, she will go with it to spite them. She hates them and will do whatever she can to humiliate them.'

Sadler sat back in his chair, picking at his teeth with a thumbnail. 'Why doesn't she tax them?'

Osborne sighed. 'I would if I could. Their response is to warn me they would seek government rebates for the use of services they provide the community, like hospitals and schools. Or if pushed, they would close them down.'

'Rule number one: never get between the church and a bucket of money. Rule number two: always back self-interest if it is running because you know they try harder. The church always tries too hard to get what it wants. Rule number three: never trust Romans at any level, especially the higher you go.'

Osborne continued his plan. 'If they push her hard enough, she will approve the referendum, and snap…' he clicked his fingers, 'her leadership is doomed.'

'What happens if she supports the No vote?' Osborne didn't respond. 'She doesn't need to support a Yes case; she just needs to move the referendum forward.'

Osborne sucked his teeth as he considered the proposition, then said, 'She wouldn't do it.'

'Howard did.'

'I suppose I need the church to campaign harder and force her to support the Yes vote.'

Sadler didn't reply, gazing out the window, watching a yacht sail by. 'There's just one problem with your plan.'

Osborne wasn't convinced. 'What might that be?'

'What happens if she then wins the referendum?' Sadler smiled, gawking at the treasurer.

'She won't,' was all Osborne could muster.

'You need more than that, lad.'

'No matter the result, the Catholics will be furious, and they hold the votes in the party room.'

'Wouldn't it be better to take the leadership off her prior to the referendum?' Sadler queried.

Osborne paused, reflecting on the proposition. 'Why do you say so?'

'If you take her on before the vote, the result of the referendum would not affect the new leader. They would argue it was all Pasco's idea.'

'How can we justify an early leadership spill?'

'Create something that embarrasses her. You're close to everything, surely you can give me something that exposes her? Misappropriation of funds, misuse of a government plane. Something personal might going on in her life. Is she screwing anyone? Or maybe she is doing a shady deal with someone, like a foundation or a company? You'll need to find something.'

Osborne nodded his head, checking over his shoulder. 'Maybe I could. What do I do then? Just give it to you?'

Sadler leaned into the table, sliding his hand across and patting Osborne's. 'Parker, ole son, I would do anything, say anything, to get rid of her. She's an atrocious embarrassment to the office she holds, a total policy flake,' he croaked. 'I want her gone… the sooner the better.'

Osborne did not remove his hand from under Sadler's.

'What do you want?'

Sadler leered as he moved closer, waiting for the secret. 'What do you mean, Parker my son?'

'When I become prime minister, what do you want?'

'Nothing,' Sadler smirked, then slunk back. 'Of course, the odd dinner invitation to Kirribilli when the world comes calling would be appreciated,' he smiled. 'I have grand plans for you, my boy, so don't let me down when your country needs you.'

Osborne sat back, checked his watch and speculated whether he would regret dealing with Sadler. 'As it happens, the prime minister has asked me to join her at Kirribilli this morning and I must be going. Thanks so much for the invitation; I hope we can do it again.'

Sadler stood, extending his hand. Osborne took it and was surprised it wasn't a bone crushing attempt at asserting power. Rather, it was a soft, polite shake as Sadler tugged him close. 'Get me reliable information and I'll guarantee you your leadership spill.'

Osborne thought about the conversation as he crossed the harbour bridge en route to the prime minister's Sydney residence. Sadler's words had created a level of anxiety that concerned him; maybe he was ill prepared to lead the country if he needed to rely on a radio commentator for party room votes. Sadler was his tool to use, but the manner in which he had demanded action wanting nothing in return was troublesome, somewhat chilling, considering the web of deceit and patronage it could lead to. Osborne was keen to take the prime minister's job, but was not willing to be a puppet for people like Dennis Sadler.

The white commonwealth car made its way through Kirribilli's security, crunching to a stop on the pebbled drive at the front door. Osborne collected his bag from the boot with the assistance of the government chauffer and entered the house. It had been converted to a residence upstairs, with a functioning office for five staff downstairs.

They led him to a meeting room with a central wooden table and eight surrounding chairs. He withdrew the files he needed and positioned himself at the centre of the table, facing the door, expecting the prime minister to sit opposite. It wasn't a boardroom, more like a dual-purpose dining room with rigid wooden chairs.

After ten minutes, a little annoyed with the persistent disrespect the prime minister had for other people's time, Osborne scanned through his notes, reinforcing his discussion points. The door was flung open and Pasco rushed in, followed by two attentive advisers, all taking a seat opposite Osborne.

'Sorry for the delay, Parker. I've just had some disturbing news from Melbourne.'

Osborne didn't want to listen to another excuse and continued to check his notes.

'It seems Charles Stevedore has had distressing news, his daughter is a victim of assault.'

Osborne glanced up. 'Is she all right?'

'Intensive care with severe burns to most of her body.'

'What happened?'

'No one knows. The feds are working with the local police and keeping me informed. Charles is at the hospital.'

'Have you spoken to him?' Osborne registered that this could be an end to any rivalry.

'Not yet.'

'What will happen to the referendum legislation?'

Pasco didn't respond, but a growing smile crept across her lips. 'I suspect he may have more important things to worry about at the moment.'

'That should not stop us from moving forward.'

Pasco shook her head. 'Government will always move forward. I'm a little confused by your lack of sensitivity for a colleague.'

Osborne appreciated he should deflect the conversation away from the news. 'Prime Minister, I can grasp Victoria is in good medical hands. They will work hard to care for her. I also understand that Charlie is probably very emotional and I'll call him once done here, but there is nothing you or I can say or do, which will change the current circumstances. Now as tragic as this news is, we have a duty to continue to complete our work.'

'This is why the electorate doesn't like you, Parker, you provide them no empathy in times of need.'

'You may think that, but others don't.'

The prime minister smiled at her rival. 'You want to have this conversation now?'

'I have time.'

Pasco indicated to the staffers to leave, and they scooped up files, closing the door behind them. Pasco waited and then said, 'Why is it you continue to make these subtle, but obvious remarks about your leadership ambitions?'

'I'm not sure I implied anything of the sort,' Osborne said.

'Parker, your ambition is not contagious. I suspect you still don't have the numbers, otherwise, like a little kid, you would jump up and down demanding a leadership spill.'

'You misunderstand me, Prime Minister. I'm supportive of your leadership.'

'Crap,' Pasco sneered, studying her colleague, then said. 'How did your meeting with Sadler go?'

The question rattled Osborne. 'We discussed economics and taxes.'

'Sadler never talks about policy, he only ever spruiks populism. Why do you think he has it in for me?'

'Oh, let me see, maybe he thinks your government makes critical policy mistakes, like running this plebiscite nonsense which now has us hurting in the polls.'

'You know damn well we were forced into it. If your Catholic mates had kept their mouths closed, the Greens and other liberal wankers would not have grown so vocal.'

Osborne snorted. 'So, it's my fault.'

'The trick now is this… what do we do about it?'

Osborne saw an opening. 'I can assure you this, after being embarrassed by your plebiscite result, you have no option but to withdraw the legislation.'

'That is actually my plan. I've told Charles to slow everything down.'

Osborne felt anxious; this was not the response he hoped for. 'It's a good plan and will restore the government's focus on economic matters, rejecting this constant haranguing of guilt and privilege that is with us.'

'You would support me?'

'Prime Minister, I always support you, no matter how many times you stuff up.'

Neither of them spoke, and an uneasy silence continued as they stared into each other's eyes. Not a flicker of emotion passed across their faces. The prime minister weakened first, laughing out loud; Osborne responded with a broad smile.

'There'll be time for you, Parker, but not now.'

'That being the case, then let's hope you win the next election.'

'We win the election; I'll transition to you within twelve months.'

Osborne wasn't expecting the declaration and gnawed at his bottom lip. 'Write it down, and sign it.'

Pasco didn't reply, considering her options. She then flicked open her leather compendium, and on a pad with an embossed gold crest of the coat of arms on every sheet, she wrote out her promise and dated it, before signing it, tearing it from the pad and flicking it across to Osborne. He took it and read it, then folded it and placed it in his jacket.

'I can assure you, Prime Minister, that I will do all I can to support you and will not undermine you. I will support your decision on deferring the referendum and I encourage you to remain true to your beliefs.'

The prime minister didn't believe a word of it.

CHAPTER

20

Charlie Stevedore had difficulty getting comfortable on one of the rigid chairs in the tiny waiting room outside the critical care unit. He was sore from sitting, his mind skittering through endless possibilities. A federal police officer assigned to watch over him sat opposite, flicking through his phone.

It was too soon to be stressing about another vulnerable loved one, waiting for harsh news in a sterile room. Five years was a long time to rebuild a future, but his wife's harrowing death lingered every day. He stood, stretching out his stiffness, hoping the soreness would leave. He moved around the room, but it wasn't big enough, so he walked out into the corridor. Through various windows he could see patients hooked up to medical equipment; this was assisting with their care and ensuring their survival, judging from the flickering lights. He wondered where their loved ones might be, questioning if he should do something more productive.

When he reached the ward's reception, a young doctor, talking to a clerk, was distracted by his approach. She finished receiving information before turning to Stevedore.

'Sir, are you Victoria Stevedore's father?'

'Yes, Charlie Stevedore.' He held out his hand. 'Are you my daughter's doctor?'

'Chinh Nguyen. Pleased to meet you,' she smiled, accepting his hand. 'I've been meaning to talk to you about your daughter. Would you like to have a coffee with me? Do you have the time?'

Stevedore nodded. 'Will you be able to update me on my daughter's condition?'

'Most certainly,' Nguyen said. 'I would like to talk about the next few hours and what it might mean for you and your daughter.'

'Let me talk to my security.' Stevedore went back to the police officer and advised him to have a break as he was about to meet with medical staff, then he followed the young doctor to the elevator.

They travelled to the ground floor and found a table at an almost empty Alf's Café. An attendant took their order, referring to Doctor Nguyen in an almost reverential tone, and they settled into an isolated table.

'Mr Stevedore…'

'Charlie, please.'

Nguyen smiled and started again. 'From my experience, it is always realistic to tell family members what they can expect when their loved one is in the ICU.'

He nodded, giving permission to the doctor to tell him straight.

'Your daughter has significant burns to sixty-five percent of her body, ranging from two degrees to four. You're probably familiar with three-degree burns, but new medical burns theory has added fourth degree burns. This means that the damage has gone beyond skin and into muscle tissue.'

Stevedore winced. 'What does this mean?'

'Your daughter is in an induced coma as we stabilise her. Her breathing patterns seem regular and her respiratory system appears functional considering the trauma she must have been through; other vital signs are promising. We are yet to complete a full examination, given her condition, and her current state limits opportunity for scans. We have yet to detect disability in any of her limbs and her chest cavity seems okay, although we won't know until we x-ray her. Her eyes and ears seem functional, although she sustained significant abusive trauma, but we will know more once the damage moderates. We're monitoring her through ECG, but this does not record her clinical reaction to her condition and the trauma she has been through. As I said, we are yet to x-ray for other conditions or injuries she may have, but we have recorded no evidence of internal organ damage from the tests completed so far. We have her on fluid resuscitation, and her urinary output is normal, which is a good sign. We also have inserted a nasogastric tube to provide immediate feeding that will decrease the potential for intestine dysfunction. This means we are on track to stabilise her.'

The coffees arrived, allowing Stevedore to sit back. He glanced away to collect his thoughts, then turned back and asked, 'What happens now?'

'We wait for evaluations from surgeons and other medical team experts, but we are likely to begin surgical debridement within thirty-six hours. Our goal is to remove necrotic tissue. We remain wary of circumferential burns which may limit recovery movement in her joints such as her wrists. We need to close the wounds as soon as we can, and this may mean grafting, possibly cadaver skin grafting. These techniques are above my pay grade, so we need the experts to tell us what will happen and when.'

Stevedore swallowed hard. 'Prognosis?'

'Uncertain at this stage. Once we have the wounds closed, we will be in a better position to determine patient outcome. Whilst her core body temperature remains below thirty-four degrees, we can't operate. We're hoping to recover temperature within the next few hours. She has encouraging cardiovascular signs, which means surgery is probable. The dangers of course are many, including increased pain and how she will cope with that in the short and long term. We expect increased bleeding, and how we manage this is important, as we need to ensure she is hemodynamically stable. Then, of course, we will have potential issues of infection.'

Stevedore took a sip of his coffee, trying to regulate his anxiety, which was shoving him toward a rising need for an emotional meltdown. 'Survival?'

Nguyen said nothing for a moment; she picked up her coffee with both hands and held it to her lips, gazing over the top of her cup. 'There are never any guarantees, but we are hopeful for full recovery. She appears strong and, in the past, we have had full recovery in similar cases.' She took a sip of coffee, then another, before replacing her cup on the saucer.

Stevedore shivered, his head internalising the information. 'Is that the best you can do?'

The doctor shifted in her seat. 'I can only tell you from my analysis.'

'Which is?'

'We will know with greater certainty within forty-eight hours.'

Stevedore gazed at her. 'Are you suggesting she may not pull through?'

'No, I'm not saying that.' Nguyen was forceful in her reply. 'We don't know the full extent of her injuries. We have made assumptions, so until we can fully scan her and complete our tests, we don't know. As I said, we have achieved full recovery in similar cases.'

'Better than fifty-fifty?'

'Perhaps.' Nguyen glanced down into her coffee, avoiding Stevedore's stare. 'I remain confident of full recovery, but we will know more once we complete the tests.'

The news stunned Stevedore. The doctor was confident at first, but then she wasn't. They taught doctors to be truthful, so perhaps it was as bad as she alluded. She had said all vital signs were good, but Victoria remained on a respirator. He turned away, smudging a tear across his cheek.

Nguyen wanted to change the subject. 'What do you for a job, Mr Stevedore?'

'What? Me, oh I'm a lawyer.'

She smiled at the response, relieved to be on a different topic. 'Oh, neat. What do you specialise in?'

'Actually, I'm a little more than a lawyer.' Stevedore felt embarrassed at not having said what he did when first asked.

'Are you a judge?'

'No, I'm the federal attorney general.'

'A politician?'

Stevedore smiled, self-conscious. 'Yes.'

'Oh, so that's the reason for the police and the shenanigans regarding Victoria.' Nguyen leaned back in her chair. 'Wow, you're the first politician I have ever spoken to.'

'Really? That surprises me.'

'Yeah, I don't get out much, and after I finish here, I'm too depressed to do anything else.'

'Why do it? You're young. You can do anything you want.'

'I love intensive care. The life and death decisions we're required to make every day are a terrific challenge.' She sat forward and picked up her coffee. 'Are you the politician that has been talking about euthanasia on the news?'

'I suppose so.'

'I thought you were familiar.' Nguyen grinned, as if meeting a celebrity. 'Do you think we need euthanasia laws?'

'You're the doctor, you tell me.'

'I think the current system works fine. We don't need more laws; it's way too risky.'

'In what way?'

'I've seen it here… folks fighting over a loved one, whether to let them die with dignity or prolong their life.'

'Why wouldn't you want a law to protect you?'

She drained her cup and made ready to move. 'I don't need protection; the patient does.'

They returned to the ward, chatting about politics and whether the prime minister was good enough to win the next election. Stevedore confided it might be difficult; Nguyen reassured him that Pasco had the right stuff. As they reentered the ward, she advised him that the specialist would be in later and Stevedore might wish to talk to her once further tests were completed. He thanked her for her candid remarks and moved back to the waiting room. Hanrahan was there.

'We attended your daughter's address, and no one was home; the number you gave us for your son-in-law was switched off, we can't track it either.'

'That's a surprise; you don't think he had anything to do with this assault, do you?'

'All options are open until we piece together further evidence. We have requested CCTV from the train she travelled home on; hopefully, we can find evidence from cameras around her home.'

'Have you spoken to the chap who gave you her number?'

'He's coming in this afternoon; apparently, he is a decorated intelligence sergeant on assignment at the dockyards.'

'There have been plenty of heroes who were criminals.'

'We appreciate that, sir, and we are taking all evidence we find on face value.'

'Where the hell can that moron be?'

'Not a great fan of your daughter's husband, Minister?'

'He's a dud as far as I'm concerned. He was a druggie and I reckon he still is. Vikki was involved at one stage, but she was strong enough to get away. She wised up and I suspect it's doubtful he is smart enough to do the same. But hey, what can you do, you support your kid's decisions, don't you?'

'Don't have children, sir.'

Stevedore drew in his lips and tightened his face.

'Do you want to stay here, or can we take you home?' Hanrahan asked.

'I should stay here.'

'My recommendation is that you come back in a few hours. Try to get some rest and be ready for any decisions you may have to make.'

'What decisions?'

Hanrahan baulked at the question. 'I'm just saying, it might be a good time to take a break for a few hours and come back this afternoon.'

Stevedore rejected the idea, stepping away from the police officer, but then turned back, saying, 'Are you able to take me to my office?'

'Yes, sir, if you're sure?'

'You're probably right; there is little I can do here, stuck in this room, so I may as well go clear my desk.'

Fifty minutes later Stevedore was walking into his office, calling for Julia Smethers, ignoring the gasps of surprise from concerned staff.

'Is everything okay? How's Vikki?' said Smethers, scampering into the office and closing the door.

Stevedore was rocking back and forward in his chair, gazing out the window, over to Williamstown.

'Where are we with the legislation?'

'Don't worry about any of that; there are more important things to consider.'

'Like what?'

'The prime minister would like a word. Osborne has called you, and the media are sniffing around. The police have provided us a briefing, and I've advised the staff to say nothing to anyone.'

Stevedore was resting his face in one of his hands. He swung his chair to face her. 'You're a brilliant girl, Julia. Thank you.'

'How's Vikki? Is she okay?'

Stevedore glanced up, trying to say something, but the words wouldn't come. He crumbled, shuddering a sob and putting the palms of his thumbs into his eyes to stop the tears. It didn't work, and he swivelled his chair back to the window.

CHAPTER

21

Osborne's white chauffeured car swung into St Mary's, crunching to a stop on the pebbled parking area. Still chuffed from his meeting with the prime minister, he thought it prudent to advise Cardinal Rosseau of developments, prior to heading to a formal lunch with colleagues supporting his covert strategy to rid the country of the prime minister.

They advised the treasurer the cardinal was enjoying the late morning sun in a small grotto by the rose garden. Rejecting the cassocked guide, he set off to find him. Roses were blooming, their scent pure as he walked the small path through the variety of colours. He discovered the cardinal sitting on an aged wooden bench, reading a folded newspaper.

'Good morning, Morris,' Osborne called to the unsuspecting cardinal. 'Can I have a word? I have delightful news for you.'

Rosseau glanced up, smiled and beckoned Osborne to join him on the bench, shifting to make room and placing the paper beside him. 'I've just been reading about you.'

'Oh, yes? What did you learn?'

'Surely you've read it? It's in the national newspaper.'

'Let me tell you a secret.' Osborne sat after shaking the cardinal's extended hand. 'I don't read the newspapers. They corrupt your mind with their political spin. I'd rather not have the angst.'

'That surprises me; I would have thought an ambitious man like yourself would be right across every word written about him.'

'Yeah, nah. I'd rather make the news than read it.'

Rosseau examined his visitor for a moment.

'Ego has many forms, and I don't doubt you have more than the average political ego.'

'If ego means ambition, then I have that in spades,' Osborne said, then smiled. 'I don't need to feed it.'

'The article says you would make a fine prime minister, and government members should make it happen. The journalist implied that the prime minister was a vapid and vanquished shell. His thesis was that for the sake of the country it needs a change at the top.'

'Interesting.' A smiling Osborne felt satisfied, knowing that the background briefing he had provided the journalist two days earlier would be talked about around water coolers today. He shifted the conversation. 'I have news from the prime minister which could mean your trip to Australia will be a raging success.'

Rosseau stroked his chin as he waited for the news.

'The prime minister has assured me she will not bring on the referendum legislation.'

Rosseau turned and faced Osborne. 'You believe her?'

Osborne turned away toward the cathedral and watched a bird swoop over the roof. 'No. No, I don't.'

'You politicians amaze me,' snorted Rosseau. 'None of you can be trusted, and what's worse… you don't trust each other.'

Osborne looked over his shoulder toward Rosseau as he rested his elbows on his knees. 'Your mob of cardinals all trust each other, do they?'

Rosseau smiled, nodding. 'You have a point.'

After a moment of silence, Osborne jerked the prime minister's note from inside his jacket, passing it to the cardinal. 'This might surprise you.'

Rosseau took the paper, unfolding it and scanning the crest before reading it. 'Congratulations.'

'It means nothing, it's only a piece of paper.' Osborne gazed out into the garden. 'What it means, though, is that her intent and my ambition have been acknowledged, and to mollify me she made a promise.'

'This is a good thing for you though, surely?'

'For me, yes. For the prime minister, I'm not so sure.'

'How is this not helpful to her by keeping you to the promise?'

'Because, I can use it now to recruit supporters. I will tell them she has agreed to me taking over the leadership, but we cannot afford to wait.'

'But you must, this is your agreement.'

Osborne chuckled. 'Do you understand politics at all? The power, and the glory that comes with power? It's what drives most of us, and if we achieve it, no matter the level, it sates what lies within.'

Rosseau studied Osborne. 'You don't do it because you want to serve?'

Osborne reeled back, feigning objection. 'Morris, please. It's only ever about power.'

Rosseau refolded the note, passed it back and sighed.

'If only it were that easy in the church.'

'Not based on merit?'

Rosseau laughed. 'Not likely, it's total patronage, and who knows more than someone else.'

'Pope Caspian not there on merit?' Osborne shared a broad grin.

'Hardly.' Rosseau stood, agitated. He moved to a nearby bush, cupping a rose with his fingers and bending to smell it, before pulling it from its stem and tossing it into the bed. 'He made promises and now he isn't delivering.'

'Just like the prime minister,' Osborne mused.

'The big difference is that you can get rid of your leader, we cannot.'

'You have before, Benedict retired.'

'Old age. Jean Paul should have gone much earlier, before he died. I can say to you there have been others who were just not up to it, just like this one.'

'One or two?'

Rosseau turned to Osborne, frowning. 'What?'

'Was it Jean Paul one or two who was too old?'

'It was two. One only lasted thirty-three days before they killed him.'

'Wait up!' Osborne stood. 'You're not a conspiracy man… are you?'

'We were in trouble back then, more than we are now; folks didn't like the new order. So…' Rosseau shrugged. 'It's possible.'

'Machiavellian conspiracies exist everywhere there is a lust for power. If you want to get rid of the Holy Father, then it is possible… hemlock, perhaps?' Osborne laughed at the joke.

'These are issues that should not be joked about.'

Osborne glanced at Rosseau, seizing his gaze. 'Anything is possible, you just have to want it bad enough.'

Rosseau ignored him. 'Come, let's have a cup of tea. Do you have time for lunch?'

'No, I have another meeting at one.' Osborne checked his watch, then suggested, 'As I'm about to dispatch my prime minister, there are things you can do now to rid yourself of your man.'

Rosseau considered the comment for a moment, then turned to walk back to the cathedral. 'There is nothing that can be done; this is foolish talk.'

The men strolled through the garden, stopping to admire a rose before reaching an outside patio set up for tea, close to the archbishop's open cantilevered doors. As they settled in for the refreshment, the conversation came back to the referendum.

'You think the prime minister will reject the idea of a referendum, even though the people want it?' Rosseau asked as he sipped his tea.

'She thinks she wants to stop it, but to ensure we end all debate forever, we need to go to a vote.'

'You already have her commitment.' Rosseau raised his eyebrows, shaking his head. 'Why do you still want a vote?'

'Two reasons. As I've said before, I want to end the issue, that's one. I also reckon, if you demand she does not bring the referendum on, she will approve it out of spite to you.'

'The second?'

'I want to challenge for the leadership before the vote.'

Rosseau smiled and shook his head again. 'You have a written agreement you will be the next leader, why do it now?'

'If she stays leader, she may not win the next election. If we don't win, then I won't hang around.'

Rosseau leaned forward and poured himself another tea, picked up the saucer and sat back, considering the treasurer who watched him in return. 'How will you bring on a challenge?'

'The only way to bring down the queen is to execute her when you can.'

'What makes you think you can?'

'I have information on her. Personal information about her fitness to do the job, and I have a confederate willing to dish the dirt.'

Rosseau turned away and thought about the comment. 'It's dirty, this play for power, isn't it?'

'Morris, if you want the top job then you use whatever means it takes to get it done.' Osborne tapped his fingertips together as he leaned on the rickety wooden table. 'If you had something on your man, would you use it? Tell me you would?'

Rosseau took a deep breath, then exhaled noisily. 'I have nothing on him, unfortunately.'

'But if you did, would you use it?' Rosseau didn't respond. 'I take it from your silence the answer is yes.' Osborne smiled and stood ready to leave. 'Thanks for the tea; let's talk again before you meet with the prime minister.'

It surprised Rosseau as he stood, taking the outstretched hand of the treasurer.

'When am I supposed to meet with the prime minister?'

'Within the next few days, I would expect.'

'You expect?' Rosseau squeezed his hand tighter. 'Be careful with the manner in which you speak, young man.'

Osborne bowed. 'Eminence, with all due respect, we want to achieve the same thing. Let me do the politics… you do the religion.'

CHAPTER
22

It was forty-five minutes until Cardinal Paas needed to arise for early prayer before commencing his daily routine. The time zone differences with Australia were tricky to manage, and he wanted to be sure he was on call for his supervisor, Cardinal Rosseau. The illuminated digital clock appeared brighter this morning as he lay on his back, gazing at the ceiling. He hadn't heard from Rosseau for a couple of days and worried if he needed to be completing an assignment. Rosseau was demanding, as he wanted everything concluded accurately and urgently, and this stressed Paas.

The appointment to Rosseau's staff was an opportunity for him to progress in the Curia. A cardinal deacon was the lowest rung on the promotion ladder within the Vatican, but he was pleased he was being mentored by Rosseau, even though his life with him was perplexing.

After trying one last time to snatch a few moments of sleep, he considered it a waste and decided that he would be better answering emails. Once he threw his quilt off, it reminded him that the privilege of working in the Vatican did not extend to central heating. He pulled on a pair of fleecy workout pants and a college sweater, wrapped a scarf about his neck and put on a beanie. The romance of living in Rome had left him years earlier.

Once he had tugged on his woollen slippers, he shuffled into his other room, sparse of furniture but for a desk where he managed his lonely after-hours work, with a large-screen computer waiting for his gentle touch. He tapped in a password and the screen lit the room. As he waited for his email account to download recent mailings, he thought about Rosseau and how warm he must be feeling right now, enjoying a lunch in the sun of Sydney.

Paas checked his private Rosseau email account, feeling a twinge of anxiety to find no waiting message or direction in his inbox. He considered sending a message, but knew Rosseau wouldn't appreciate the intrusion, so he would have to wait until the cardinal deemed it worthy to communicate.

Rosseau was a rigid man, but Paas overlooked his nerve-wracking idiosyncrasies, believing he should stick with him to help progress his career. Paas considered Rosseau should have been voted the Bishop of Rome by the conclave, as he was the much better candidate, and now assumed that working with him would be to his benefit.

The cardinal blew into his icy hands as he flicked the mouse to open the business email account that was used to manage all Rosseau's communication and contacts. Heavy demand meant he spent too much time responding to petty requests, and he wished he could delegate this menial task to a priest, but Rosseau demanded that he administer it all. Sixty new emails had appeared since midnight, when he last worked through the list, and he began categorizing them into four email files; do it, defer it, delegate it, dump it. Once he had them categorised, he would then start with the do it file.

Paas clicked and dragged emails after making a judgment based on the subject line and initial greeting. He was almost done when he clicked on an email that came from a Hotmail account marked *vaticanscandal@hotmail.com*. He opened the email and read the contents. *"We need to talk, else this gross pig goes viral."* There was an accompanying link.

He considered the message, wondering if it was an attempt at spam sent to cause disruption if he opened the link. Wary of unidentified links within emails and protective of digital security for the cardinal, he dumped it. After categorizing the few remaining emails, he pushed back from the desk, heading to his kitchenette to brew a mug of tea, and perhaps chew on a piece of left-over dinner pizza. It didn't look appealing, so he binned it, cutting a thin slice of pane casareccia and tossing it under the grill before yanking his larder box from the overhead cabinet.

He poured the steaming water into his earl grey bagged pot before placing cheese and a few slices of meat onto a plate, placing the warm pane on top and transferring his breakfast to his table with its single rudimentary chair. He wiped soft cheese onto the pane, along with a slice of salami, taking a substantial bite and sitting reflecting on his day. As he appreciated his breakfast, he glanced over at the computer. He took another bite, then wandered over to his desk, clicking onto the trash folder and reopening the dumped file.

He wasted little time clicking the link, then waiting for it to connect. A digital video presented, then engaged. The production was poor quality, and the dim lighting made it difficult to recognise what was going on. The video seemed to have recorded from a device sitting on a shelf or bureau in a darkened room. Against the far wall, above a bed, was a framed stereotype print of the Virgin Mary. After a few moments, the image changed, with someone in a white cassock and mitre swaying into view. Their back was to the camera as they made evocative, sensuous moves. They then turned to face the camera with the mitre ribbons falling across the face and revealing an adolescent male, possibly a teenager. As he continued his sensual twirls and whirls, he raised the hem of the cassock until the video revealed his excitement.

The boy moved closer to the device, reaching out and adjusting it so its vision was straighter, more parallel to the floor. As he was adjusting the camera, a thick male arm came across his chest, the hand caressing down his body. The boy twisted to face the man, raising his arms to rest on the man's shoulders, then lowering him from sight.

Paas remained mesmerised by what he was viewing, not knowing what to think or why he had been sent the link. The boy glanced back at the device and winked, then gazed down at the man as he moved away. He tossed off the mitre, shucking the cassock over his head as he reached the bed, lying back, his willing partner now in view. The boy rested on an elbow, his other hand gripping the tight knotted hair, encouraging faster movements. The man lifted the youth's leg, draping it over his shoulder as he pleasured him. The boy collapsed back, his foot over the man's back, in a red slipper.

23

The sound of Dennis Sadler's syndicated drive time programme was unobtrusive as Charlie Stevedore slid into the back seat of the commonwealth car. The icy leather chilled him, sending a shiver through his back as his driver welcomed him and requested the destination. He asked to be taken to his residence, so he could freshen up before heading to the hospital. As he sank into the seat, pushing his head back on the rest, he ignored the radio until he heard a comment that pricked his attention.

'This prime minister is the worst in my living memory. Not only does she not understand the fundamentals of the economy, she also is an embarrassment internationally. I have said this before, and I'll say it again… it is time her ministerial colleagues grew hairy balls and challenged her leadership.'

'Do you want me to turn this off, minister?' Guy, his long-term driver, asked.

'No, I'm listening to it.' The driver increased the volume. 'Thanks.'

'Listeners, it seems to me, we have a rudderless government at the moment. We have a prime minister stultified by this idea of the Kill Bill legislation. You will recall, I spoke to the attorney general yesterday, confirming that he has little idea… or if he does, he is keeping quiet on the marching orders of the prime minister. This is not good enough, quite frankly, and it is my view that for the sake of the country, we need a change in leadership.'

Sadler slowed his tone and seemed closer to the microphone.

'We need a change of narrative from this government, and I just don't think the prime minister is up to it to lead us from this malaise. How long do we have to wait to rid ourselves of this prime minister? Surely, we don't have to wait until the next election, in which on current form, with Nancy Pasco as leader, the opposition will blitz the government. We will then be rid of the worst example of a politician I have ever had the misfortune to deal with.

'But don't be too keen to achieve that scenario, because it could go from bad to much worse. If we get rid of Pasco at the next election, that will mean we'll have the other mob in power. They are hopeless, far worse than Pasco's government. It's time for Nancy Pasco to go. I know it and I'm convinced we have to make a stand.'

Sadler slowed his diatribe, pausing for a moment. 'Now I know we all love social media… the kids are always on their phones, so I know if we start a social media campaign on Twitter and Instagram we can motivate the cowards in cabinet to step up to the challenge and change the prime minister for the sake of the nation. So, I'm suggesting we all use hashtag *sackPasco* and share our comments. If we get the hashtag trending, maybe the politicians will listen and take action. It's worked in the past, so there is no reason it can't work right now. Let's show this miserable prime minister we don't want her anymore. Let's demand she either resigns or is sacked. She can do the honourable thing and resign; but if she doesn't, let it be on her head when she gets sacked.'

Stevedore's phone buzzed, and Guy turned the radio off.

'Hello,' he said.

'Charlie? It's your mate, Parker.'

'Hey Ozzie, what's up?'

'Mate, I was told about your daughter. I'm terribly sorry. Is she okay?'

'Not sure, mate.' Stevedore didn't want to talk about it. 'We'll know more over the next forty-eight hours.'

'It's dreadful and I'm mortified by it all. Is there anything I can do for you?'

'No, thanks, mate.' Stevedore trailed his fingers across his cheek. 'I appreciate it.'

'Anything. Just let me know and I'll make it happen.'

Stevedore smiled, releasing a little snort. 'I know you're ambitious, Ozzie, but having the ear of God on call for your friends… I wasn't expecting such influence,' he said, gazing out the window.

'You know what I mean. If you want me to cover for you, I'm happy to do so.'

Stevedore sighed, then said, 'The office has everything under control.'

'We're moving forward with the referendum?'

Stevedore tapped the end of his nose. 'Those are my instructions.'

'Humph, that surprises me. I spoke with Nancy this morning. She advised me she was going soft on the whole idea.'

'She instructed me to slow it down, but only that… not to drop it.'

'If your office is under control, then so be it,' Osborne said, then switched the chat. 'Are you taking a few days off?'

'Not sure; everything is uncertain.'

'Don't suppose you've been listening to Sadler this afternoon?'

'Just heard a little, right now.'

'He's bagging Nancy big time, calling for her sacking.'

'Is that something you want?'

'Ease up, Charlie. I'm no different to you, ambitious and talented. But I support the leader until she decides otherwise.'

'Yeah, I bet you do.'

'Don't be like that.' Osborne reframed the discussion. 'Do you think this campaign has any legs? If it does, how do we stop it?'

'The day we listen to moron shock jocks like Sadler is the day we should call it quits and retire.'

'Shock jocks have dragged down prime ministers before.'

'Maybe, but they have little influence these days.'

'Not so sure about that, comrade.' Osborne prepared to move on. 'Take care and lots of love for Victoria.'

'Thanks, Ozzie.' Stevedore dropped the hand holding the phone to his lap without clicking off.

After refreshing and changing, Stevedore was at the hospital before six. As he entered the ICU, he asked at reception if his daughter had had any visitors during the day, wondering if her husband had surfaced. There had been none.

'Is Doctor Nguyen on duty?'

'She has left for the evening, sir. Doctor Rogers is the duty specialist tonight; would you like to speak to him?'

'Doctor Nguyen had mentioned that a specialist would see me tonight. Is that Doctor Rogers?'

'That would be Professor Thompson; she is due in shortly to speak with you. Would you care to wait in her office?'

'Show me the way.'

'Six doors down on the left.' The receptionist pointed along the corridor.

'I'll just look in to my daughter first, if you don't mind.'

Stevedore walked into ICU and entered the sealed viewing room. Vikki was now in a different position in the ward. More equipment was being used, and a nurse in a sterile protective gown was recording data. He couldn't see much, so he placed the palm of his hand momentarily on the chilled glass screen, then moved off.

The professor's office was a little different from what he expected. It wasn't clinical, as one would imagine, but was more like a charming home office with various knick-knacks and mementos on shelves and bureaus. The framed photos on the wall included smiling faces, and they attracted Stevedore to one with a beaming Nancy Pasco presenting an award to a tall, elegant woman.

'Minister, good evening. I'm Vera Thompson.'

The sudden declaration startled Stevedore, and he straightened, knocking a trophy which bumped a book, tumbling it to the floor.

He didn't know what to do. Shake the outstretched hand or pick up the book?

'Sorry, clumsy me.' Stevedore replaced the book and took the professor's hand. 'Charles Stevedore; pleased to meet you.'

The professor was embarrassed for him. 'Please have a seat.'

'Thank you.' As the professor skirted the desk to take a seat, Stevedore said, 'I note you have met the prime minister.'

'Yes, one of my better hair days, that one.' The professor glanced over at the framed photo.

Stevedore grinned. 'Like today, I suspect.'

'That's very kind of you, Minister, but I'm not sure you're allowed to say things like that these days.'

Embarrassed again, Stevedore responded, 'I'm sorry. That was inappropriate of me and I apologise.'

'Gotcha!' Thompson laughed. 'Men are hopeless these days. They never know what to say. In my case, Minister, if you want to give me a compliment, then by all means, fire away.'

'Sorry?' Stevedore felt flushed, a little anxious at the unexpected levity. He wiped his forehead with the tips of his fingers, pushing his head against them. 'I'm confused. Are we not here to talk about my daughter?'

'Yes, of course we are. Please excuse my bedside manner.' Thompson flipped open a file. 'I'm of the view that no matter the crisis, a friendly laugh helps.'

'I don't get the connection,' Stevedore replied, bewildered. 'I don't see this as a laughing matter.'

'Your daughter's condition isn't humorous, of course, but we should ease all-encompassing stressful moments.' Thompson took her cue, straightened and glanced at the file. 'We have conducted further tests on Victoria today, forensic swab collections and other evidence taken by police. We then x-rayed her and found no bone or organ damage. Given the head trauma she suffered, there is no skull damage, although she has significant tissue damage around eye sockets and nose.' Thompson glanced up. 'Are you okay? Do you want me to go on?'

Stevedore was sitting forward, elbows on his knees, face cupped in his hands. 'Yes, it's okay.' He sat back and glanced at the professor. 'Just don't crack any more jokes.'

Thompson smirked, referring to her file. 'We're having difficulty in recovering her respiratory system, and we have placed her on a ventilator to help breathing. Whilst it remains shallow, we are loath to begin surgery.' Thompson glanced up again, pausing for a moment and returning Stevedore's gaze. 'Indeed, I'm sorry to advise you Victoria cannot breathe independently, as her condition has deteriorated since this morning.'

'What does that mean?'

'She is on life support until we can stabilise her.'

'And?'

'We can't operate until she has a functioning respiratory system.'

Stevedore crossed his legs, sitting as erect as he could, his hands fisting then gripping the arms of the chair. He gazed at the ceiling, hoping for the rushing feeling to pass.

'It is my view that whilst her breathing is not functioning to capacity, which could be caused by her lungs responding to the blunt trauma, her heart is not responding to respiratory levels we need for surgery. We will continue to monitor her over the next few hours; when she recovers, we can decide about operating.'

'Do you need to operate?'

'We need to address wound debridement and closure. We also need to support post burn hypermetabolic response and control potential infection, so we need to operate soon.'

'If you don't, what happens?'

'Her respiratory system will continue to struggle to improve and she is in danger of infection. Combine those two and we may lose her.'

Stevedore cleared his throat as his eyes welled. He struggled to speak. 'Is she close to death?'

'We'll have a better idea within the next forty-eight hours. Once she stabilises, we can go to surgery.'

'How significant? How long would the surgery be?'

'It depends on the technique we use to debride the wounds.'

'What do you mean?'

'We can use traditional grafting, but I suspect we will need to rethink this method. The body is a terrific source for repairing tissue, but unless we do it right, there may be substantial scarring. Using traditional techniques may lead to significant disfiguring.'

'What does it matter, so long as she survives?'

The professor moderated her tone to explain. 'Burn patients struggle more with post-surgery treatment and their healing process. Many are psychologically damaged and regret surviving the incident. I'm pleased to say that recent advances have improved treatment options. We may have to use different methods for your daughter.'

'She is on life support now, right?'

Thompson nodded.

'If she were off the ventilator, would she survive?'

Thompson considered the question. 'At the moment, she would not survive for long without support,' she said, then sat up into the desk before adding, 'I stress… at the moment.'

'Wow.' Stevedore whispered, cupping his hands behind his head, leaning back in the chair and gazing at the ceiling. 'Are you telling me, my daughter is clinging to life?'

'She is strong, but yes, she is in peril, and I stress, at the moment.'

'But if we turned the machines off, she would die?' Stevedore dropped his arms, sitting upright.

'I'm confident we won't need to do that,' Thompson said, studying the minister. 'It'll be a fight and she'll need full support, but I'm confident we can have her up and about within a few months and then she can start rehab.'

Stevedore eyed the professor, thinking through the options, pursing his lips and twisting his face. 'With great respect to your abilities and skills, Professor, what rating would you give her at the moment… ten being survival?'

'Three.'

'Geezus.' Stevedore dropped his head, squeezing a thumb and

forefinger into his eyes, rubbing and squeezing the bridge of his nose.

'Mr Stevedore, I don't want to give up on Victoria. I'll be working hard to ensure she recovers, but I need your support, as the quality of the recovery must be worth the acute pain of survival.'

'How? What do you want me to do?'

'I would like you to give me permission to use radical skin grafting techniques. If we can graft within ten days, then scarring will be limited and this will aid her recovery.'

'Why do you need my permission?'

'The technique has not completed clinical trials and we need family approval.'

'Why? Surely we can't be using made up science?'

'The technique of tissue engineering is one with proven success; it's just difficult to get clinical trials as we deal with emergency patients like your daughter. If we did it the normal way, we wouldn't get access to skin cells for twenty-one days, earliest. With this technique we can graft in five, maybe earlier.'

'Do whatever you can to save her.'

'This is a wonderful decision, many families don't want to try with the worst possible result.'

'What? They let them die?'

'In many intensive care emergency cases, this is the decision made by the closest relatives after weighing up various competing interests.'

The professor's comment confused Stevedore, raising his hands. 'What competing interests could a family have in not wanting a loved one to live?'

'Age and finance are the most common. The older the patient, the more likely the family will not proceed with treatment. Once folks know the cost, they become nervous, shall we say?'

'Family want their loved one to die?'

'Let's put it this way; when a patient's prognosis is not encouraging, there is an undercurrent of bias toward allowing the patient to die rather than operate.'

'Does this happen often?'

'If quality of life is no guarantee, it is more common than rare these days.'

'How do you manage the ethics around that?'

'We ensure the patient is comfortable and pain-free, and let nature take its course.'

'You don't intervene?'

'We give the best advice, then it's up to the family to decide… we follow their direction.'

Stevedore gazed at the professor as he considered the information. 'If we changed the law, would you manage end of life differently?'

'Probably. If we're directed to provide end-of-life services, rather than wait, we would provide the same result, but earlier and perhaps in a more dignified way.'

'If I understand you correctly, you could save a patient, but if the family says no and asks for an end-of-life procedure, you will respond?'

'Yes.' The professor did not drop her gaze, and after a moment she added, 'We hold life sacred here, Minister, but unless we have support from loved ones, we cannot protect patients.'

Stevedore glanced away, nodding as he considered the information. 'Interesting.'

'I realise this is rather confronting, but we are nowhere near that stage with your daughter. She is in expert hands, and although we have challenges before us, we remain confident we can stabilize her. We just need to get through the next forty-eight hours without significant change to her condition and begin debridement.'

'Do whatever you have to do to ensure she survives. Do I need to sign anything?'

'We don't need to do any of that just yet.' Thompson glanced down at her file, then back at the minister, gnawing her bottom lip. 'There is something else to advise you.'

'Can there be anything worse than what you have already said?'

'Your daughter is two months pregnant.'

CHAPTER
24

Doug Ferguson didn't know what to do. He had failed to meet Ortega and had avoided his many calls. Beside him in a small leather purse rested twenty thousand dollars, bundled together in two tight packs of fifty-dollar notes. He had visited the bank with Bronte at eleven and was due to meet Ortega at one. He missed the meeting and now sat in his car, wondering how to get through the rest of the day without incident.

He pushed the door open with his foot and swung out, leaning back to pick up the purse. He locked the car, dropping the bag into the boot before heading into the building, not looking forward to what he was about to see.

The elevator doors opened, and he stepped out almost into the path of Charlie Stevedore, walking past after his meeting with Professor Thompson.

'Where the hell have you been?'

'Hello to you too, Charlie.'

Stevedore brushed past him, heading for the waiting room; Ferguson trailed him, searching for someone at the reception to assist him, seeing no one. As he entered the small room, Stevedore reeled around, almost chesting him.

'Where have you been? Where were you last night?'

'Ease up, Charlie; I'm here to see my wife.' Ferguson didn't show any signs of backing off as they stood almost nose to nose. 'Where is she? How is she?'

'Do you care?' Stevedore moved away.

'Vikki is my wife, and I'm here to support her. Now tell me what's going on.'

'I will, but first tell me where you've been all day. Why weren't you home?'

'I had teacher duty at a student event last night and crashed at a colleague's house.' Ferguson had rehearsed his lines. 'I made a statement to police this afternoon.'

'You couldn't be bothered getting here earlier?'

'What are you suggesting?' Ferguson asked.

'I'm suggesting you haven't been the grieving husband much, have you?'

'You're a prick; you have no reason to say that.'

'How come you only just got here?' Stevedore said.

'The police advised me around midday and I've been giving them a statement most of the afternoon. I left for here once they allowed me to go.'

Stevedore stepped back to the far side of the room. 'Do you know she's pregnant?'

Ferguson didn't respond. He turned away, facing a wall for a few moments before holding on to the slim arm of a chair; he sat down slowly, resting his elbows on his knees, drooping his hands, the weight of his head bowing it below his shoulders.

'By your reaction, I suspect you didn't.'

Ferguson didn't look up. 'How is she?'

'They're expecting to go to surgery, but the next forty-eight hours are the most critical.'

'How do you mean?' Ferguson raised his head to look at Stevedore.

'She's on life support.'

'Oh, shit,' Ferguson dropped his head. 'What do they think?'

'They expect recovery, but the next few days are critical. She could go either way.'

'Seriously?' Ferguson sat up, leaning back in the chair. 'The police told me she was burnt; they didn't tell me she was critical.'

'Yeah, well, she is, and she's going to need our full support. Can I expect it from you?'

'You mean Vikki, don't you?' Ferguson responded. 'You mean Vikki will need my support, don't you? Not you.'

'You know what I mean.'

'Not sure I do,' Ferguson sneered. 'You're hoping I just up and leave, aren't you?'

'It wouldn't surprise me.' Stevedore faced his son-in-law, with his left hand fisted on his hip. 'You've let her down when she relied on you in the past.'

'You of all people should know that's not true.'

'You got her onto drugs.'

'Oh, here we go, same ole line again. When are you going to let it go?'

'When it comes to my daughter, never.'

'This is neither the time nor the place, old man, so why don't you just back off?' snarled Ferguson.

Stevedore gnawed the inside of his grimaced lips as he considered the challenge, then said, 'I have a few things to do. Now you're here, I can go do them, is that okay with you?'

'Might be better if you did.'

Stevedore checked his watch and withdrew from the room, heading for his office.

He pulled his phone from his pocket, flicking through his favourites list, and called Julia Smethers to let her know he was on his way.

Once Stevedore had left, Ferguson went to find a washroom before seeing his wife, emotions crashing through him. He asked the receptionist for directions and was directed toward the appropriate door. He shuffled along the corridor, not bothering to look where he was going, and almost smashed into a gurney with a patient being wheeled to another zone.

When he entered the washroom, he checked under the cubicle doors. The room was vacant, so he moved to a corner of the wash bench, turning away from the door and slipping a cloth pouch from a pocket inside his leather jacket. He dipped his thumb and forefinger into the pouch, removing an object the size of a business card covered in satin cloth. He laid it on the bench, unwrapping it to reveal a thin glass slide used to hold specimens under a microscope, then tugged out a small sealed plastic bag, pouring a generous amount of glistening white powder onto the glass. He used a credit card to work the powder, first into two equal piles, then into straight lines.

Ferguson then hauled a compact bundle of notes from another pocket, tugged out a twenty and rolled it into a tube. Once he had his nose pipe, he sniffed one line into his left nostril, then repeated the same for the right. He sniffed through both nostrils, deep into his lungs as he first squeezed, then wriggled his fingers at the tip of his nose. He tidied up, placing the pouch back into his jacket and left, all complete in a matter of minutes. As he wandered back to the waiting room, the elevator doors popped open; he changed direction, entering the elevator and tapping the ground floor button.

The elevator bounced when it arrived, and as the doors opened, he brushed past waiting passengers, sauntered over to Alf's Café and ordered a latte. He secured a chair by the entrance, scrolling through his phone, checking Facebook and Twitter accounts. When the coffee arrived, he spooned in a sugar, stirring as he read his news feed.

His phone shrilled, startling him as Bronte Mariner's smiling face appeared. He smiled, accepting the call.

'Hello gorgeous.' Ferguson swung in his chair to look out the window.

'Hi darling. How did it go? Is Ortega okay?'

Reality struck Ferguson. 'I didn't get to see him. I still have the money.'

'What?' Bronte exclaimed. 'Why? That was the plan, why didn't you see him?'

'The police were waiting for me when I got home.'

'Oh crumbs.' She whispered. 'Were they there for your drugs?'

'No. Nothing like that, thank goodness.' Ferguson took a sip of coffee. 'No, they wanted to ask me questions about last night.'

'What did you tell them?'

'I was working at a colleague's house and slept on the couch.'

'That's sort of the truth,' Mariner giggled. 'You screwed me on the couch.'

Ferguson changed his tone. 'Vikki has been assaulted.'

'Really? When? By who?'

'They don't know; they think she might have been raped.'

'Do they think it was you?'

'Nah. She's badly injured, burnt, actually.'

'Is she okay?'

'Dunno, I haven't seen her. She's in intensive care. I'm at the Alfred Hospital having a coffee.'

'How badly burnt is she?'

'Dunno.'

'Is she conscious?'

'Dunno.'

'Do they need to operate?'

'Dunno.'

'How long will she be there?'

'Look, Bront, I have no idea. I haven't spoken to anyone yet.'

'What do you want to do?'

'How do you mean?'

'Our deal is you tell her you want a divorce. When will you tell her?'

'As soon as I see her, I suppose.'

'Do you think you should wait until she is okay?'

'I don't know, maybe. What do you think I should do?'

'I think you should come here, and we talk through a plan. This is maybe a good thing for you.'

Ferguson frowned. 'How do you mean?'

'If she's in intensive care, she must be in trouble and may not survive. You know what that'll mean, don't you?'

'We can be together?'

'We are together, Dougie. No, it means you'll have it all. The assets and me.'

'You reckon? I never thought about that.'

'This could be good news. Go get a proper briefing and then come see me.'

'On my way. Love you.'

As he prodded the end call button, the phone rang. 'Where the fuck are ya?'

'Hello, Rikki, what a surprise.'

'We had a deal, and ya welched on it, so I'm comin' to get ya.'

'My wife is in hospital.'

'So, what? I want me money.'

'I have it in the car, but I need to resolve issues here first.'

'How long she in for?'

'Someone injured her last night. I'm at the Alfred now in the ICU.'

'What the fuck is ICU?'

'Intensive care unit.'

'Serious then?'

'Yeah, you could say that.'

Ortega didn't respond for a moment. 'So you're at the hospital now, yeah?'

'I am.'

'And you have the cash with you?'

'As promised, I have it with me.'

Ortega didn't respond.

'Do you want to come pick it up right now?' Ferguson asked.

'What do ya think I am?' Ortega said, then paused for a moment. 'You look after ya, missus. Deliver me the cash tomorrow, otherwise youse'll be sharing the bed next to her. Understand me?'

Ferguson shrugged off a sudden chill. 'I promise you.'

He tapped the phone, finished his coffee and headed back to the ICU, wondering who to talk to about the condition of his wife.

The receptionist at the desk asked for several documents to be completed and signed. When Ferguson asked why, she explained that as the patient's spouse he had a power of attorney to decide about Vikki's care whilst she remained incapable. As he finished signing, the duty doctor approached and led him into an interview room to outline his wife's condition and prognosis.

After a detailed description of the injuries and condition of the patient, Doctor Rogers then set out treatment and all probable outcomes. Ferguson asked for a glass of water to quell growing angst and confusion.

'Will she survive?'

'If we debride within the next few days and surgery is successful.'

'If we do nothing?'

'Then it's only a matter of time.'

'If we turned the machine off?' Ferguson asked, crossing his legs and leaning back in the chair.

'Hours, if not a day, maybe two.'

Ferguson dropped his head, brushing a tear from his cheek.

'I'll leave you to think about all of that and what the next step will be.' Rogers stood, moving toward the door.

'Wait up... what do you mean, what the next step will be?'

'We can't do anything unless you give us the go ahead.'

Ferguson nodded, lowering his eyes, allowing the doctor to leave the room. The information was too much, so he paced the room, before crashing through the door, hurrying to the elevator.

He needed to talk to Bronte.

Cardinal Paas had shared with no one the email or the linked digital recording. He was trying to work out what to make of it. He remained anxious whether the threat was a setup to extort money from the church, or if it embroiled him in a police investigation. The church had tightened up internal communication since the worldwide exposure of sexual assault claims and its poor management since. Everyone, from the local parish priest to the highest levels of the church, was directed to contact the crisis response group if any adverse information came before them. The group was a non-clergy collection of lawyers and hard-nosed negotiators based in New York.

It was too early to call New York as the policy paper directed. He was apprehensive about what might happen. If he failed to report the email as protocol required, then repercussions might stifle his career. He needed advice from his mentor and waited for an appropriate hour to call Cardinal Rosseau in Sydney.

'Tell me, why are you wasting the church's money by calling me? I thought I told you I would contact you if I needed you.'

'Something important has come up, Your Eminence. I need your advice.'

'What can I help you with?' responded Rosseau, concerned by the anxiety in his assistant's voice.

'You received a troublesome email from an obscure Hotmail

account demanding you talk about the contents of the message.'

Rosseau cleared his throat. 'What was the message?'

'It was a video of a young boy having sex with an older man.'

'You should send it to New York and not bother with responding. Get rid of it as soon as you can.'

'This is what the policy advises doing, but...' Paas stalled.

Rosseau waited, then lost patience with the delay. 'What is it?'

'It's a black man.'

This meant nothing to Rosseau. 'And the issue is?'

'They used a mitre and a white cassock.' Paas avoided saying more.

Rosseau thought through the revelation, then understood his assistant's anxiety. 'You think it a religious man, clergy, perhaps?'

'The boy was wearing red slippers.'

Rosseau breathed deep, filling his lungs. He held it and then released it through his nose, trying to calm the sudden knot in his stomach. He ran his hand through his hair, thinking through options but not falling on any.

Paas could hear breathing and probed for a response. 'Eminence?'

'Send it to me from the private account. Delete it and tell no one. If you hear from these people again, let me know, no matter the time. Do you understand?'

'Yes, Your Eminence.' Paas bowed from habit and acquiescence.

'Tell no one,' Rosseau restated. 'No one.'

'Yes, Your Eminence.'

After saying goodbye, Rosseau placed the hand-piece back into the cradle, steepling his fingers against his face. The enthusiasm of discovery was aching to take over, but his response remained muted. He thought through ramifications to the church, should the recording be of the person he presumed it was. He waited an hour before opening his mail account to verify his misgivings, hoping it wasn't who he thought it was, but was a clumsy fraudulent attempt to graft money from the church. It wouldn't be the first time, nor the last. The difference now was the manner in which they could manipulate truth for his own means.

Rosseau stretched out of the chair, shaking off stiffness before moving to a sideboard and pouring himself a generous serve of pre-dinner sweet sherry. He blanched as he swallowed a mouthful, then refilled the glass before returning to his soft leather, high-back chair to reflect on what to do. Was this distressing video a promotional step or a career-ending development?

Doug Ferguson had taken his time driving to Mariner's apartment. The news from the hospital was snowballing through his thoughts, rushing him to a conclusion that life could not get any worse for him right now. A criminal thug was threatening him, his girlfriend was gifting him a stake but demanding unrealistic conditions, he was carrying way too much cash in his car, and he was going to be a father... oh, and his wife was at death's door.

He'd parked his car soon after heading off, deciding as he cruised St Kilda Road that he needed a comforting snort from his drug cache. Now, travelling over the West Gate Bridge, images blurred, encouraging him to slow down and hug the fence line in the Williamstown exit lane. As he drove into Mariner's Spotswood apartment block, he scraped the car, damaging the paintwork.

She opened the door after a gentle knock, and he fell into her arms, crashing her against the wall.

'Wait... wait. Let me close the door first.' Mariner stepped away and locked the door, before scooting around a lunging Ferguson and collapsing onto the couch. 'Would you like wine?' She refreshed her glass from a bottle on the table, leaning back into the cushions, and waved her glass, encouraging him to sit. 'Tell me, how did it go?'

'I'm crushed. The news was not great. I have a decision to make, which I don't want to do.' He staggered to the couch. Mariner shunted him into the lounge chair beside her. 'It's been a wild few days.'

'Did you talk to her?'

Ferguson shook his head. 'I told you she was in the ICU, didn't I?'

'Yeah.'

'She's near death with tubes all over her, so no, I didn't get to talk to her. I didn't even see her.' Ferguson scooped up the bottle, chugging a mouthful.

Mariner watched him. 'Are you sad, or are you pleased?'

Ferguson dropped his head back on the chair, gazing at the ceiling.

She sipped her wine. 'I mean, it's sad what happened to her, and all… but this is good for us. We can plan a future without worrying about what might happen with her.'

Ferguson hadn't moved. He rasped, 'What happens if she survives?'

'If she's at death's door, as you say, then she may not, which means we get the house and any cash she has.'

Ferguson lifted his head, glancing at her. 'She ain't dead yet.'

'A deal is a deal.' She took a generous mouthful of wine. 'I advanced you twenty grand on the proviso you tell wifey she's got to go, which you didn't.'

'Bit hard when I'm bonking you.'

'That's beside the point. The deal is, end it, and then we move forward.'

'I can't just up and leave her when she's in hospital needing support to recover.'

'You could turn the machine off.'

Ferguson licked his lips. 'You mean kill her?'

'No darling, you euthanise her. Let her go with dignity. She wouldn't want to live if she's horribly scarred. No woman would.'

'You're a tough bitch, aren't you?'

'Turn the machine off and your entire life becomes carefree. You won't have to worry about her.'

Ferguson glanced at her. 'I don't know if it's that simple.'

'You're her closest relative, and they'll ask your permission to do any medical procedure. So tell them you want her suffering to end and turn the machine off. Simple.'

'What do I say.'

'Tell them your wife told you about such things and that she would rather die with dignity than suffer extended medical procedure.'

'I don't know about this, sweetheart.'

'Let me tell you what's going to happen.' Mariner sat forward, resting on the edge of the couch. 'You are going to go into the hospital tomorrow, and you're going to tell them your decision is to stop the machines keeping her alive. You then pay Ortega, and within a few months I move in with you, and we live happily ever after.'

Ferguson didn't look convinced.

She moved closer to him, almost squatting on her haunches, and gripped the inside of his thigh, hard.

'Unless you complete that plan tomorrow, then we are over. I will want my money back. Ortega will know where you are, and the police will be told about your drug dealing.'

Ferguson tried to wave her away, but she ignored his protest, moving her hand higher, gripping harder into the meaty flesh.

'You have a choice. Plenty of pain for no fucking gain.' She smiled then released her grip, tickling her fingers. 'Or you can have it all, including moi.'

His grimace curved into a smile. 'You're crazy.'

'No, I just know what I want. That, my precious, is you.' Mariner went down on her knees, moving between Ferguson's legs, stretching up to kiss him. She then dropped away, unbuckling his belt, tugging at the buttons of his jeans.

He didn't resist as his phone buzzed. 'I have to take this,' he said, checking the screen. She didn't stop. 'This is Doug.'

'Where the hell are you?' seethed Charlie Stevedore.

'I'm home getting some sleep. Why?'

'Why aren't you here?'

'They said she was fine, so I left.' Ferguson ran his fingers through Mariner's hair.

'Did you ever think for one moment that Victoria needs you here? She doesn't need an absent husband right now.'

'Charlie, that's not how it worked out. The doctors told me to go home.'

Stevedore paused for a moment, 'There's always two sides to a story, I suppose, and I can assure you, you are a prick in both.'

The phone went dead. Ferguson tossed it aside, returning to more important matters.

CHAPTER

27

Hanrahan parked his rental outside the Williamstown police station. It was sited strategically on the foreshore of Hobson's Bay, allowing the water-police unit a base within the complex. He flashed his credentials and a uniformed officer led him through to a large squad meeting room with an assortment of detectives assembled in front of an over-large whiteboard for a briefing.

A woman waited by the board, tossing a marker up and down. When she saw Hanrahan, she smiled, reaching out her hand. 'Good morning, commander. I'm Paula Caruso, the lead detective on this case; welcome to our meeting.' She turned to her colleagues. 'Guys, this is Commander Hanrahan from the feds. Given the sensitivity of this case, he wants to be across our investigation, so I invited him along for the brief.'

Hanrahan smiled, waved an embarrassed flick of his hand and took a seat to the side. Caruso worked the board, drawing a basic interpretation of the city at the top right corner and a railway line across the board in a curve to bottom centre. She then drew Ann Street, identifying the Stag's Head hotel and Victoria Stevedore's residence. 'This is the journey of the vic.'

'Hey, that ain't bad, transfer and become a police artist,' a colleague laughed at the back.

'A bullshit artist, more likely,' another colleague added.

'Okay, boys. That's enough,' Caruso admonished, glancing at Hanrahan. 'We have her leaving Parliament Station at 9.52, connecting with the Williamstown train at North Melbourne at 10.08.' She jotted details on the board at the various parts of the journey as she spoke. 'We then have three locals, let's call the group Λ, boarding the train at Yarraville at 10.18, causing a bit of a stir.'

'Do we know who they are?' Hanrahan asked.

'We have a copy of CCTV from the train and identified them as locals,' one jokester added. 'Uniforms are attempting to run them down.'

'That's great, Richard. We then have a confrontation between the three lads and the vic,' Caruso continued. 'Sergeant John Peters boards the train at Newport, intervening and calming the scene.'

'I spoke with him yesterday afternoon,' the other jokester said.

'Just hold that thought for a moment please, Dan, I want to finish the trip.' Caruso turned back to the board to add information. 'The train arrives at Williamstown at 10.28 and we then have Peters and the vic...'

Hanrahan interrupted. 'Would you mind if we use her name, please?'

Caruso stopped, glanced back to her guest, squeezed a grin, then continued. 'We have Peters and Ms Stevedore enter the Stags Head to share a drink. She leaves at 11.20 and Peters stays for one last round before the hotel closes. No one at the hotel was a witness to the abduction nor saw any traffic.'

'Do we have CCTV from the street?' Hanrahan asked.

'Uniforms are door knocking as we speak,' Richard Sylvester offered.

'We are yet to confirm, but we suspect they snatched her outside her home in Aitken Street.' Caruso wrote the details on the board. 'We checked the 000 call sheets, and they received a call from a Mrs Camille Dixon, reporting screams in the street at 11.31.'

'I spoke to her last night.' Dan Harris was reading from his notebook. 'Her bedroom overlooks Aitken, and a car screeching to a stop woke her. She then heard what she described as a fight, including loud voices and screaming. When she checked out the window, she only saw tail lights as the car sped off.'

'Sounds like the pickup, did she see a licence number?' Hanrahan glanced over his shoulder.

'She heard at least two male voices and a woman screaming but saw nothing.'

From the bottom right of the board Caruso drew a curved dotted line to the centre, placing an X and labelling it, the crime scene. 'We have eyewitnesses to three men, let's call them group B, running from the scene at 1.05, at the start of the fire.'

'Witnesses are coming in for an interview later this morning,' Sylvester advised. 'Their first response to the uniforms on site was that they heard yelling and went to investigate, then saw the fire. They didn't provide a clear description of the vehicle nor the men at the scene. We'll try to get more. I think there are three coming in.'

'Working backwards, we have a car and a woman screaming at the servo in North Williamstown, at 11.50. CCTV footage is unclear as they are out of range and we only catch lower bodies.'

'I checked the 000 call sheet from the night and we have a Mr Trevor Wheeler registering a fight at the servo. He was walking his dog and observed two men bundling a woman into a car at around the same time as the footage. At first, he thought it was just kids skylarking and having fun, but says the screams became more desperate.' Harris was reading from his notes.

Hanrahan turned and asked, 'Clear descriptions?'

The detective referred to his notes. 'Just basic ages and heights. We don't know enough yet to confirm it was Stevedore.'

'It's in the right time frame after the snatch in Aitken Street to suggest it could be the same group,' Caruso added.

'He also observed that the car was a matt colour. He wasn't sure but thinks it might be grey.'

'Do we have anything else on the trip?' Caruso asked.

'Nothing until the crime scene.' Sylvester read from notes. 'The fire doesn't help much, and it disturbed the site by witnesses and first responders. We identified three separate footprints coming to and leaving the crime scene in the car's direction. We have them matched at where we reckon they parked their car. We found one burnt bottle of Jack Daniels, which is being tested for prints and DNA. It makes sense they could have purchased alcohol, so we plan to hit the bottle shop at the Rifle Club Hotel, opposite the servo at North Williamstown, when it opens later this afternoon.'

'That's good news, Rich,' said Caruso, scribbling notes on the board. 'Has anyone reviewed the status of injuries and forensics?'

'That would be me, boss.' Sandi Moroni joined the discussion. 'I was at the hospital when they extracted samples from Ms Stevedore and reviewed her for injuries likely to have been sustained.'

'Are you comfortable to share the results?'

'Sure.' Moroni flicked open her iPad, swiping several times before settling on her notes. 'Stevedore has been badly burnt and these injuries, coupled with the trauma of assault, mean she remains in a critical condition. The attending surgeon has suggested that unless they operate soon, then their window of opportunity to do so may pass.'

'Is she on life support?' Harris asked.

'She is,' Hanrahan responded.

'This could progress to a homicide; should we get them involved?' Sylvester asked.

'They may want to take over, but let's work on the assumption she survives,' Caruso assured the group. 'Keep going, Sandi.'

'It's been difficult for the medical team to assess her injuries, given the respiratory demands of the patient, but we can determine extensive damage to her skull. Her eye sockets have major contusions and we have evidence of indentation in her brow over her left eye. This shows a ring of some sort from heavy assault. It seems her retina in her left eye is detached. Heavy bruising around her temple region and ears shows a frenzied attack; she has a perforated right ear drum.'

'Do you want water?' Caruso asked.

'No, I'm fine,' Moroni continued. 'Injury to her limbs and skin has been obscured because of burns, but we found on her buttocks two distinct bite marks. Her anus was lacerated, consistent with forced penetration. We have taken swabs to confirm rape. She doesn't have any major skeletal injuries other than her nose and mouth. They did not detect internal bleeding, which is a significant sign and will help with recovery.

'Forensics confirmed semen samples from her vagina, anus, mouth and hair, and although they are still being tested, the initial estimate is two different and quite separate samples.' Moroni closed her device.

'When can we expect their report?' Caruso asked.

'Maybe, later today. I asked them to put some pace on it. If not, no later than tomorrow morning.'

'Thanks, Sandi, That's brilliant.'

'Could I get a copy of the forensics?' Hanrahan asked.

'I'll make sure we get you a copy, Commander.' Caruso responded, then tapped the white board. 'Okay, this is what we know so far, any ideas?'

Hanrahan waited for the others to offer some ideas, but there were none. 'Do you think there is a connection between group A and group B?'

'We have CCTV of group A running from the station; that's the last we see of them. It was another 50 minutes before they took her,' Sylvester offered. 'There could be a link, but what did they do for an hour?'

'You said they were locals. Who are they?' Hanrahan asked, turning to Sylvester.

'They run with a drug pusher, a bloke by the name of Rikki Ortega. He has been on our radar for a long time, but we can't pin anything on him,' Sylvester responded.

'He wasn't on the train though, was he?' Caruso asked.

'It seems to me the liquor store at the hotel may be a key,' Hanrahan offered.

Caruso placed the marker on the white board rail and dragged a chair to face the team. 'I think you're right. And look, group A could be B, but we need to get more information before we assume these guys... what are their names again?'

Harris flicked a page and read the names. 'They are; Michael Cole, Thomas Haslam, and Rocco Galatea. They're just kids. Previous charges have been shoplifting and petty larceny. This would be an enormous step up for them.'

Hanrahan stood to face the team. 'Criminals step up sooner or later.' He walked to the board, studying it. 'I have a feeling you may find it involves these boys, but the key is linking the car to them. If you get any evidence that links them, bring them in. I would like to be informed so I can watch the interview, is that okay?' He glanced at Caruso, who nodded.

'Commander, what do you want us to tell the media?' Sandi Moroni asked.

'This is a sensitive political issue. I would prefer you told them nothing and refer them to me.'

'We can do that, and we'll let you know if we bring them in for questioning.' Caruso stood to see the commander out. 'Richard, can I get you onto the liquor store? Dan, you run after Ortega, and Sandi stay with the forensics while you bring together the witness statements. If this group A are our boys, then we need to nail them tight and their statements need to be rock solid.'

'If group A is not group B, then all this work will be a waste,' offered Sylvester.

'Rich, it's all we have at the moment.'

'Let's eliminate them from our thinking. I reckon that will be the link between the JD bottle and the liquor store. Is the bar code still intact?' Hanrahan shot him a glance.

'Yeah, I think it is, maybe we can check other liquor stores,' Sylvester sounded more optimistic.

'If we can place the bottle at the store and check their CCTV, then we may have clear ID. If that's the case, then I suspect you may have group A in custody tonight.' Hanrahan smiled, leaving. 'You're doing an outstanding job and I thank you for your efforts.'

No one responded as he left. Caruso trailed behind him.

Ortega had perched himself by his pool to get late morning rays, picking up his iPad when he heard the front doorbell ring. He flicked open his security system and saw his young colleagues lingering by the front gate. He released the gate, and they made their way out back of the two-storey house. Ortega had architecturally designed his new residence in exclusive Electra Street, opposite the Freemasons Hall, tearing down the aging colonial house three years earlier. The high-walled property was secure and kept out nosey neighbours, allowing him to do whatever he wanted, so long as he kept the noise down.

'Not at college today, boys?'

'Who needs it?' Rocky Galatea said as he dropped onto a lounge, pulling off his shirt.

'Youse do,' Ortega chuckled. 'What've ya been up ta?'

'Nothin' much, hangin' out,' Mickey Cole replied.

'Where were ya yestie?'

'We didn't get ya call, so we didn't bother, stayed in bed,' Tommy Haslam said.

'Any trouble?' Ortega eyed them. 'Ya know I hate trouble.'

'Nah, we're good,' Cole reassured him. 'Did ya get ya cash?'

'Pickin' it up today.'

'Ya want us to go pick 'im up?' Haslam asked.

'Nah, he's good. His missus is in hospital, so I gave him a coupla days.'

'She havin' a baby or somethin'?' Cole asked.

'Nah,' Ortega scoffed. 'She's a victim of crime. I think Dougie thinks it was me.'

'What happened to her?' Cole joined the laughter.

'She's been done over, real bad.'

Haslam sat next to Galatea, who straightened, pulling his shirt back on. Cole glanced at them, then back at Ortega, before asking, 'Do they know who did it?'

'Nah, don't know any details. She's on life support in the burns unit.'

'Shame, man,' Haslam said, staring out over the pool.

'No worries. It just delayed the cash for a day, is all,' Ortega said.

The boys said nothing as they glanced sneakily at each other.

'What's ya view on all that?' Cole asked.

Ortega swung his head, lifting his sunglasses to see him. 'What d'ya mean?'

'Do ya have a view on the missus gettin' done over?'

'Why would ya ask that?' Ortega asked.

Cole didn't respond. Ortega scanned the other two, his suspicion aroused.

'Youse don't have nuthin' to do with it, did ya?' When he didn't get a response, he jumped to his feet, standing over them. 'Tell me ya didn't do her over?'

'We didn't know who she was,' Cole replied.

Ortega punched him, thumping him to the concrete pool deck. He then turned on the other two, slapping them as they cringed away.

'I told youse to stay outta trouble. Why did ya goin' do this?'

'She was in the street, so we jumped her.' Cole sat up, holding his jaw, a trickle of blood coming from his mouth.

Ortega straddled him, shoving him back, gripping his throat and squeezing tight. 'Ya thought ya'd take a sheila from the street, ya dumb bastard.'

Haslam and Galatea watched, but when Cole began gagging, turning red, they jumped up, dragging Ortega away. As they pulled aside him, Ortega kicked Galatea in the knee, smashing his right fist into his face as he went down. He turned to shrug off Haslam, landing a solid punch to his midriff and dropping him, elbowing him into the pool.

'Youse fuckin' morons.' Ortega stood above them as they struggled to breathe. 'Ya've now got pigs down on us. If they don't know who youse are by now, they soon will.' He prowled around them. 'Whose car?'

'Me brother's,' Cole said.

'Jesus Christ.' Ortega shaped up to deliver a blow and Cole cowered away. 'Have I taught ya nothin'? Don't shit in ya nest. Don't use ya own equipment. What were ya thinkin'?'

The boys didn't respond.

'That's the trouble… ya didn't.' Ortega breathed deeply to calm himself. 'Okay, we need to get youse outta town. Where's the car now?'

'Out front.' Haslam said, regretting it.

'Ya kiddin' me? How dumb are youse pricks?'

'Pretty dumb,' Galatea said.

'You got that right, ya dumb piece of shit.' Ortega glared at them for a few moments, considering options. 'Okay, we take the car out west and torch it.'

'It's me brother's,' Cole said.

'Ya don't get it, do ya?' Ortega stepped over to Cole, grabbing his hair and dragging him from the concrete. 'Ya almost killed the bitch and youse are goin' to jail. If ya get rid of as much evidence as you can, then ya might reduce jail time. Go burn the friggin' thing. Go west until ya find a lonely place, then torch it. Do it today and do it now.'

Haslam crawled from the pool. 'How do we get back?'

'That's your problem. Now get goin'.' Ortega kicked Cole. 'If ya dog me, I'll friggin' kill youse.'

CHAPTER

29

Dennis Sadler liked his peppermint tea before going on air. He never brewed it himself, expecting his producer to provide a steaming cup within moments of him arriving in his office to prepare for the programme. Not a tea bag, but a teapot had to be brewed, and woe betide the producer if it wasn't hot enough. Sadler would then review the programme rundown, querying anything he didn't understand or including topics he wanted to talk about with a large red marker.

His die-hard audience were the Australian battlers who didn't like politicians and hated government. Sadler pandered to them by humiliating politicians who accepted his invitation to appear, continuing the myth of political incompetence. When he did this, his ratings grew.

The prime minister knew it was obligatory to attend the fortnightly grilling.

Advisers prepared her during two rehearsal sessions on the day of her appearance. One session in the morning, the other an hour before going to the studio. Staff asked many challenging questions about policy and government, insisting on a vigorous probe to test her readiness.

Pasco walked into the studio a little after the 4.30 news break, settling in with a cup of tea a producer delivered to her as the traffic report was being read. Sadler then tapped several illuminated buttons for advertisements to broadcast, before holding up a finger to cue the prime minister as he broadcast the show's regular introduction music and announced, 'Welcome back. I'm sitting with the prime minister of Australia, Nancy Pasco. Good afternoon, Prime Minister.'

'Good afternoon, Dennis, and to your listeners,' Pasco smiled.

'Prime Minister, for the last two years we have enjoyed your company we schedule every fortnight our segment for 4.10, it's now 4.40. I want to make a minor point, we are all busy, and I have a job to do, with obligations to sponsors and other guests appearing on the programme; if we agree a time, then I would expect your office to call us if you cannot make it.'

Pasco was taken aback. 'I'm sorry for being late, Dennis, but they held us up at another interview.'

'Yes, but that is fine. You are busy, but common courtesy would not have gone astray. Your staff could have let us know of your delay and perhaps we could have made changes.'

'I believe I am a considerate person…'

'We have had to adjust our programme to accommodate you…'

'If you will allow me to finish, Dennis.'

'We're all busy people, even my listeners.'

'I am also a busy person…'

'As I just said, Prime Minister, we are all busy people.'

'Dennis, if I can just finish. Other commitments delayed me and I am here now.'

'You've had a media commitment with me every fortnight for the past two years at 4.10 and your staff didn't let us know you would be late.'

'Dennis, I'm happy to apologise. I'm sorry. If you would like to ask a question so we can move this interview along onto important national interests, you are welcome to ask it.'

'I have several issues to address with you.'

'Fire away.' Pasco took a sip of her tea, the cup shaking.

Sadler smirked, like a cat ready to pounce, as he plucked up a sheet of notes.

'Why are you killing people?'

Pasco almost snorted the tea. 'This is a preposterous question. I'm not killing people.'

'You said during the euthanasia plebiscite that we should have coordinated euthanasia legislation across Australia. You said you would introduce legislation if the vote was a majority Yes. It was a Yes vote, so now you will legislate to kill people.'

'What I have said in the past is that I will support the will of the people. If they choose to nationalise euthanasia laws allowing death with dignity for those Australians with chronic medical conditions, then I would do as they request.'

'No second thoughts on this one, given the closeness of the result?'

'I am taking advice from those who have a stake in this legislation. Let me remind you, Dennis, I have been consistent with my position. I stated it during the plebiscite campaign. I will do as the people of Australia instruct me on this sensitive issue.'

'Based on what you just said, can you confirm you are pushing ahead with the legislation?'

'Yes, I have instructed the attorney general to prepare legislation for a referendum that will amend the constitution, allowing the federal government to manage life and death issues by overriding state laws. We will release the enabling legislation during the referendum campaign, which will bring euthanasia laws to a consistent standard throughout the nation.'

'No second thoughts and maybe going soft on the idea?'

'I will do what the Australian people want me to do.'

'No change to your announced position?'

Pasco became wary of the repeated question. 'I'm convinced to move forward on this, Dennis, and I am focused on getting the job done.'

'Okay, fair enough. This idea that you stand by your policies and do what's right for the country is something you stake your credibility on, isn't it?'

'I try to do the right thing.'

'Indeed; you have always been a transparent government, haven't you?'

'I try to tell the Australian people the truth.'

'Try or do?'

'I'm not sure what you are asking me.'

'I just wonder if you tell the truth on matters of policy and issues affecting your government, and indeed yourself.'

Pasco swallowed hard, anxious about the question. She brushed a strand of hair from her face. 'I believe I'm honest with the community.'

'Were you honest with the Australian people when you introduced a mining tax?'

'My position has always been clear on this matter, Dennis.' Pasco's throat tightened, her voice staccato. 'Miners quarry minerals from all of us, and should pay for that privilege, given they amass large profits from our natural resources.'

'Why did you not mention that you would introduce this mining tax during the last election campaign?'

'In the election campaign, I talked about sovereignty and the need for mining companies to pay their fair share. I also talked about the urgent need for raising greater revenue. Once elected, I implemented new tax structures for the industry.'

'No, no Prime Minister. You didn't say that.'

'During the campaign, I said we need to protect the sovereignty of our land and its resources. I also said those companies that wish to use it will need to pay their fair share.'

'You gave a policy speech.'

'Get all the statements out and you will see...'

'Prime Minister, people...'

'I said, we need to address the low revenue...'

'Prime Minister...'

'and the mining industry needs to...'

'Prime Minister...'

'restructure their business model to ensure a fair share...'

'PM...'

'That happened during the campaign.'

'PM, PM; this is untruthful. You launched...'

'Dennis,' Pasco scoffed. 'Dennis, check my statements.'

'When you launched the campaign,' Sadler now read from his brief, 'you uttered almost four thousand words in a forty-five minute speech to the party faithful. You did not mention a mining tax once, not once. You said in just one sentence, we need to care for our land.'

'Oh Dennis,' Pasco smirked, trying to lighten the tone. 'It was a thirty-three-day campaign. Are you suggesting the only statement that came from my mouth was my campaign speech at the launch?'

'At the launch, you weren't game to say what your plans were because it would have exposed you.'

'How ridiculous, Dennis, and how deliberate to mislead your listeners with this false idea that I did not tell the truth. I am asking you to consider all my statements during the campaign.'

'You said, specifically, there would be no mining tax.'

'No, that's wrong. I never said such a thing.'

'Oh, really? Then allow me to play this quote from your treasurer.' Sadler pushed a button and Parker Osborne was heard. *"No, it's not in our plans to introduce a mining tax. That is an inaccurate claim made by the leader of the opposition."*

Sadler smiled. 'Your minister said you had no plans.'

'Dennis, any Australian would have known my position on mining companies paying their fair share.'

'Unbelievable.'

Pasco tried to switch the tone. 'Are you suggesting my government is not committed to having our mining companies pay their fair share for extracting the wealth of the nation?'

'You weren't prepared to say it during the campaign launch, so I wonder how many other taxes or policies you didn't talk about you will throw upon the Australian people before the next election.'

'What I can say to your listeners, Dennis, is that the mining levy I announced at the time of the budget will bring greater revenue to the government so that we can provide greater services to the community, such as health and education.'

'The point I make is, you never mentioned it during the election campaign, and earlier you stated you are an accountable, honest and transparent government. Surely, this is an example of deceit and hypocrisy all rolled into one.'

'We are a resource-rich country, Dennis.' Pasco moved closer to the microphone. 'We're going to use those resources to build wealth by exporting them to the world. This decision produces jobs, creating wealth, and that's good for Australia.'

'The point I make, Prime Minister, is about honesty and transparency. You made this decision only after consultation with the Greens; prior to that, you had no intention of introducing a mining tax.'

'It's a royalty, Dennis, and you can play semantics with it if you like, but the facts are these, I have always said the mining industry must pay their fair share for profiting from the nation's resources.'

'If you had been transparent during the election campaign, do you think you would sit here now enjoying the largesse of government and all its political and personal trimmings? If you had told the electorate you would introduce a mining tax, do you think you would have won?'

'This is a ridiculous suggestion. We won the election and we're going about doing the job we need to do to make Australians feel safe and prosperous.'

'Whoa, whoa, whoa.' Sadler threw up his hands. 'If that's true, why then, before the election, listen to this, why then did you say this?' Sadler pushed another button.

"There will be no mining tax under my government."

Sadler sneered at her. 'Why did you say that?'

'During the election campaign, we were open about talking about resources and the need for miners to pay a fair share, and what the mechanisms were to make that happen...'

'Why did you say that?' Sadler repeated, whispering into the microphone.

'There are various mechanisms to ensure a fair share is paid. I was answering a question dealing with all of that…'

'Why did you say that?'

Pasco bit her bottom lip, grimacing. 'Dennis, I don't want to get into any word games. The policy I advocated for the Australian people is a mining royalty mechanism. Ultimately, the price of minerals in the export market will set the amount…'

'Why did you say that, Nancy?' Sadler almost whispered again.

'It's a royalty, and I wanted to be straightforward about it…'

'But, why did you say that?'

'We want to ensure the community gets its fair share of the nation's wealth, which is what I talked about during the election campaign.'

'Why did you say there'll be no mining tax?'

'I've just explained it to you…'

'You rule out a mining tax, you said.'

'and you may not have been listening…'

'I was listening.'

'because you're too busy interrupting, but…'

'No, I didn't interrupt,' Sadler grinned.

'but I've just explained it to you, Dennis.'

'You said you will rule out a mining tax.'

'The Australian people voted, and they voted for my government, and we're getting on with the job by collecting their fair share.'

'The electorate could accept all of that. They wouldn't be as angry as they are now, were it not for the fact that you said there will be no mining tax under your government. You said you rule out a mining tax. Parker Osborne, your treasurer, said it's not possible that you're bringing in a mining tax. And he said it was an inaccurate claim being made by the opposition. What's your response to that?'

'My response to that, Dennis, is this: I speak on a lot of radio shows and I often get told that people who commentate on those radio shows, like you, somehow know what the electorate's thinking.'

Pasco switched to her speaking notes before her. 'I believe the people of Australia agree with my mining royalty, insisting they get a fair share. I have been honest and transparent with the Australian people, and this royalty scheme is the right thing to do. People want us to act on getting their fair share. People want a prosperous future. They want jobs. They don't want to be left behind when the community is growing. That's what I'm going to deliver, and I'll be out there explaining it to the Australian people every day.'

'Just one last point, because you're the prime minister, and I believe you're entitled to be heard, and I've tried to allow that to happen today. I remain concerned about the commitments you gave before the election, but we've covered that ground…'

'What is the point you wish to make?'

'I have a very reliable source, who has never been wrong before with information about your government, or indeed previous governments.'

'This sounds ominous. What is your point?' Pasco glanced into the production room to find her staffer, who shrugged.

'You state you are honest and trustworthy, and you prefer transparency.' Sadler leered over his microphone.

'I stake my reputation on it.'

'I have it on good authority that some in your cabinet do not agree with moving forward on euthanasia referendum. I also know that the Catholic Church has sent an emissary from Rome who you have met to discuss the legislation, and you have made an agreement to not put forward legislation for euthanasia.'

'Dennis, what you have just said to your listeners is untrue. Either you misunderstand what happened during the plebiscite or you are trying to deliberately deceive. We are…'

'I don't deceive.'

'Let's get your listeners the facts then, because what you've just told them is not the truth.'

'You have stated you are going to a referendum. I believe your position may have changed over the last few days.'

'Dennis, are you going to let me give people the truth, or are you going to insist on stating your lie?'

'Will you support the Yes vote?'

Pasco didn't know what to say.

'I have been told by a reliable source you are soft on the referendum, and if the government goes ahead, you will campaign for the No vote. Is that correct?'

'Howard campaigned for a No vote after promising the republic referendum.'

'Beside the point. You support euthanasia. Will you support the referendum?'

'My position is clear.'

'No, you've had a fair go. The truth is what we want to hear.'

'The truth, the truth…'

'Did you make a deal with several ministers you will not bring forward the referendum?'

'the truth, Dennis… I'll finish my sentence, thank you. The truth, Dennis, is that I talk to my cabinet members every day. We have had robust discussion concerning this referendum, but we intend to go forward with it,' Pasco sneered.

'Hang on, facts are facts. I'm just saying your credibility…'

'I'm always truthful, Dennis, unlike others.'

'when your credibility was on the line, you stood up and said there'll be no mining tax. Now you are saying we should believe you about this Kill Bill legislation. It is clear your ministers are briefing against you about an agreement you have struck concerning your leadership.'

'Oh, Dennis, what a load of nonsense. I need to work with people to get things done and I will do that with the referendum.'

'Will you support the Yes campaign?'

Pasco didn't respond.

'Okay. Thank you for your time, and you're always welcome. I enjoy our chats every fortnight. You're welcome to present your views any time.'

'Thank you, Dennis.' Pasco hauled off her headphones, ready to leave, but waited for Sadler to push buttons for an advertisement break. 'That has to be the most reprehensible interview I have ever done.'

'Just doing my job.'

'Is it your job to embarrass the prime minister, admonishing her like she is some sort of schoolgirl?'

'You were late.' Sadler shrugged.

'What's this crap about a deal in cabinet?'

'I'm only asking what has been told to me. Apparently, you have made a deal on your leadership to go soft on the referendum.'

'You don't support the referendum,' Pasco snapped.

'So what? I just want you to tell the truth.' Sadler curled his thin lip into a sneer. 'That's what I want any politician to do, rather than this stupid pollie-speak you all try to use.'

'I'll rethink coming back.'

'Goodo, you do what you want,' Sadler smirked. 'I think you need me more than I need you.'

Pasco swept up her notes, storming from the studio.

Parker Osborne had finished his Melbourne meetings for the day. He had delivered a transactional speech for the Business Council's sponsored lunch at the Park Hyatt, reassuring business leaders about the current state of the economy, an essential role for the federal treasurer. Questions were asked about the government's backflip on the mining tax, but he argued everyone should pay their fair share, and not to do so was against Australian values.

Earlier in the day he had visited the Archbishop of Melbourne to discuss strategy tactics for the referendum and ridding the issue once and for all with an emphatic No vote. The idea of forcing the community to vote at a referendum flummoxed the archbishop when it would be easier to just not have a vote.

'It's all about perceptions,' the treasurer explained. 'If there is no referendum, then the perception will be that the community will still want it. Then all the angry rent-a-crowd will continue marching in the streets, demanding their rights. If there is a No vote, then the issue is dead, if you'll excuse the pun, and will be no longer in the political lexicon.'

After meeting in the city with a major party sponsor, securing election funding commitments, Osborne wandered along Bourke Street to the attorney general's office for a discussion about political strategy, and if he was lucky, a cup of tea. As he passed through the shopping mall, he stopped at the window of a jeweller. A bracelet attracted his eye. He wondered if he should invest in it, as his new girlfriend's birthday was approaching. He thought better of it, considering that she could misinterpret such a generous gesture as some sort of peace offering, or guilt gift for suspicious activities. It was only ever about perceptions.

When he was shown into Stevedore's office, the AG waved him in, gesturing him to sit as the radio blared with the prime minster matching wits with Dennis Sadler. Stevedore was stretched out in casual clothes, his feet on the desk.

'She's getting stick from Sadler.'

'Don't know why she goes on his programme; I keep telling her not to,' Osborne said, sitting in a lounge away from the desk. 'He only ever wants to shove it up her. What's his beef today?'

'Everything… mostly about the leader's honesty.'

Osborne didn't respond and listened to the interview, wincing when Sadler played the quote he made during the campaign. 'Yeah, that was a mistake,' he said to no one in particular.

Stevedore grinned into his hand, resting his head as the prime minister struggled. He chortled when Pasco claimed Sadler was interrupting. 'She's doing okay, but it's almost a blood sport. He's slicing her up.'

The interview was winding up when Sadler advised her of a cabinet leak suggesting the prime minister had made a deal to not bring forward the referendum legislation. When she said she would support the referendum going forward, Stevedore swung his feet off the desk. Osborne glanced over, raising his eyebrows.

As the interview finished, Stevedore gazed over to Osborne and said, 'She told me she was going soft on it, and wanted it dropped.'

'I met with her yesterday and that was the impression I got from her.'

'So why is she now saying something different?'

Osborne shrugged. 'It makes little sense unless she panicked.' His phone buzzed with a text. He pulled it out of his jacket's top pocket, glancing at the message from Sadler.

Get me the information and I'll kill her leadership.

Osborne slipped the phone back into his pocket without replying. 'You don't think she's been got at, do you?'

'I've had other priorities over the last few days, but I wouldn't think so.' Stevedore stood, pacing his office. 'With the plebiscite's poor result, few in cabinet support the referendum.'

'This will send the Catholics over the edge. She may have trouble holding them.'

'Can you corral them?'

'What makes you think I can do that?' Osborne stood.

'Get off the grass, Ozzie. I know very well you're the leader of the brethren.'

'Doesn't mean I control them.'

Stevedore smiled and nodded, before saying, 'If she was going to bin the referendum a few days ago, what changed her mind? Who changed her mind?'

Osborne watched as his colleague paced behind his desk. 'How's Victoria?'

Stevedore stopped, glanced over at Osborne and resumed his seat. 'I'm going back this evening.' He wiped his hand across his face, then brushed it through his hair. 'She's struggling at the moment.'

'I'm sorry to hear that.' Osborne sat at a wooden chair by the desk. 'What's the prognosis?'

'Unless we operate within days, we may lose her.'

'Crumbs, that's awful… sorry.'

'I have this great ethical challenge thrust in front of me.' Stevedore's thumb nailed his front teeth. 'Do I support the medical team knowing the troubles associated with it?'

'What's the alternative?'

'She dies.'

Osborne contemplated his colleague before turning away and gazing out the window. 'That's a terrible decision to make.'

'It's the same one I faced when Stephanie was struggling. Do you hang on, or do you let them go?'

Osborne took a moment, then said, 'I can't tell you what to do, Charlie, but I know you, and I know your values, and I'm certain you'll make the right decision.'

Stevedore turned back to look at his colleague. 'Thanks, Ozzie. I appreciate it.' He glumly smiled. 'Now what do we do about this referendum?'

'We can support her, I suppose, but let's wait until she tells us.'

'Do you support it?' Stevedore asked.

'No, of course I don't. It'll create too much debate in the community, and as we move into an election year, I suspect it will hurt us in the polls.'

'Out of curiosity, why don't you support euthanasia?' Stevedore asked.

'It's all about the sanctity of life for me. It's just too easy these days to make a life and death decision. Look at abortion… I agree that it's the woman's right to do whatever she wants with her body, but there are more considerations once we have conception.'

'Do you think we should include abortion rights in the bill?'

'I think we should include limitations in the bill and not listen to the spurious arguments that get trotted out whenever abortion law is discussed.' Osborne crossed his legs and then his arms. 'I mean, they talk about rape, the health of the mother, the health of the baby, but the C-word is never ever raised by the loud activists and most feminists,' Osborne said.

'C-word?'

'Contraception. The taxpayer supports a hundred thousand abortions on the public purse every year. How many are health and crime related? I reckon its eighty-twenty. Eighty percent is contraception. We kill babies because a sudden pregnancy is unwanted.'

'You don't think choice for the woman is an argument?'

'Of course it is, but choice is at conception, not after,' Osborne said.

'I'm not sure you would get much support for that view.'

Osborne added, 'It involves the man when there's conception, and so is the baby. Yet these two stakeholders are never discussed when we debate abortion policy, and woe betide a male if he ever has the temerity to talk about this issue.'

'It's not a man's issue, surely?'

'You're kidding, right?' Osborne threw his head back, gazing at the ceiling and blowing air out, raspberry style. He then dropped his head back and said, 'How the heck does the woman get pregnant without a man? He should have some rights in this? But current laws exclude him. It's only nine months, for heaven's sake, compared to eighty plus productive years.'

'You are against euthanasia and abortion?' Stevedore suggested.

'I'm for the sanctity of life and the terrible manner in which we now deal with these issues in the community. Loud voices should not dominate important debate.'

Stevedore pondered the treasurer's comment. 'If you were prime minister, what would you do?'

'I wouldn't touch this issue until after the next election and then bring in legislation so the feds control beginning and end-of-life laws. We need to bring back respect for life and stop this creep toward the disposable nature of society by choosing life.'

'Powerful words, Ozzie,' Stevedore said, pausing before asking, 'What's your view on capital punishment?'

'Interesting question.' Osborne steepled his fingers and tapped the tips in front of his face as he considered his answer. 'I'm against it, because I believe it is inhumane. And, just like euthanasia and abortion, I believe in the sanctity of life; although the community may have a justifiable case for a murderer to be executed, the state cannot murder.' He paused, dropping his hands. 'I reckon, we in Australia believe life should be protected and preserved. The thing that keeps us from killing each other is the emotion we have against it. Thou shall not kill.'

'And yet, we are debating euthanasia.'

'Yeah, such irony.' Osborne smirked. 'The greater the sanctity the government gives to life, the greater the feeling of sanctity the individual has for life. So I'm against euthanasia and abortion, as they devalue life.'

'These are strong points you make.' Stevedore reflected on them for a moment. 'So how do we handle the prime minister's change of heart?'

'She needs to own it, so when it fails, her leadership fails, and we'll be rid of her.'

'Not a fan?' Stevedore laughed.

'No,' Osborne scoffed. 'From what I hear, neither are you.'

'What have you heard?' Stevedore was keen to learn more.

'I hear you are building numbers in the party room, so you can make a challenge.'

Stevedore smirked, turning away. Any political ambition he may have harboured literally died in a grass wasteland fire two nights ago.

After the previous night's robust suggestion from Bronte to consider his future with or without her, Doug Ferguson was twitchy in the stomach, anxious how to manage her increasing demands upon him. As he strolled into the hospital, he took a call from Ortega.

'How's the missus?'

'Just walking in now.' The question confused Ferguson. 'I have your money and if you want it, let's meet up later today.'

'All sweet, man,' Ortega said. 'Just let me know what's happenin' with ya missus.'

'Thanks.' Ferguson stopped walking, running his fingers through his hair. 'She's likely to have surgery in the next few days. Hopefully, it'll be all good.'

'Will she survive?'

'I suppose, why do you ask?'

'Just carin' about me family,' Ortega fudged. 'Keep me informed, will ya? I wanna know if anythin' changes.'

'Sure.' Ferguson scratched his face, looking lost.

'Okay then, see ya.'

Ortega ended the call before Ferguson could respond. He stood gazing at his phone, shaking his head, trying to understand and wondering what to do. He slipped the phone into his jeans and made his way to the ICU.

'Ah, Mr Ferguson.' Professor Thompson was leaning on the reception desk reading a document when Ferguson exited the elevator. He stopped, wondering if he had done something wrong. 'Just the man I want to see; we've been trying to contact you. Would you care to step into my office for a brief chat?'

This must have been the unknown number Ferguson had been ignoring all day.

'Who are you?'

'I'm the surgeon who is managing your wife's case.' She held out her hand. 'Vera Thompson.'

Ferguson shook it, flimsily. 'Is her dad here? Can I see my wife first?'

'He was in earlier and I think he was expecting you to be here. He left around 2.30.'

'I was held up.'

'I'm sure you were… at work, were you?'

'No, I was… errmm, doing other stuff.'

'More urgent than spending time here, no doubt. Please come with me, it won't take long.'

Ferguson followed the professor, turning into her office and sitting when instructed. He waited for Thompson to gather the paperwork she needed.

'Mr Ferguson, I have spoken at length with Victoria's father, explaining what needs to happen. He has given permission for us to proceed.' Thompson was yet to refer to her papers. 'He wants to ensure his daughter has the best chance of survival, and the longer we wait, those chances diminish. You understand?'

'Yes, of course.'

The professor glanced down, tugging a document from her papers and placing it in front of Ferguson.

'If you could just sign this approval document, we can then get started on caring for Victoria.'

Ferguson reached for the sheet to examine it. 'What's this for?'

'It is the informed consent form, which is required before we begin any surgery.' Thompson sat back. 'As you are the closest next of kin, it requires us to provide you with as much information as you need to give that consent.'

'If I don't sign?'

Thompson sat forward. 'We cannot operate. Are you thinking about not giving consent?'

'I haven't been advised what it involves, so no, at this stage I do not give consent.'

Thompson stood, circling the desk then taking the seat next to Ferguson. 'What are your concerns? Victoria's father thinks all is okay and has provided consent.'

'He's not the closest next of kin though, is he?'

'No, you have that privilege.' Thompson leaned into him, her hands resting on her legs. 'Do you have any concerns?'

'Yes, I do.'

'About the medical procedure? If that's what you need, I'm happy to step you through the process.'

'I would like that, but that's not it.' Ferguson trembled; he clenched his right hand to stop anxiety cascading through him. 'I'm not sure surgery is what Vikki would have wanted.'

Thompson collapsed back into the chair. 'You know this for certain?'

'She always spoke about not wanting to be a burden. I reckon this might be what she was referring to.'

'You think she would be happy to slip away?' Thompson tried not to expose her scepticism. 'We have a good chance to save her, but we need to act within the next day or two, otherwise we may lose the opportunity.'

'I'll need to think about it.'

'Do you want to talk to her father?'

'Not particularly. I'm sure I already know what he would say,' Ferguson scoffed. 'I know what he would demand. But it's not about him, it's about Vikki.'

'Can I just be reassured that this view is uppermost in your mind as you consider the consent?'

'What are you suggesting?'

'You're yet to visit your wife, Mr Ferguson.' Thompson stood, tracking back to her chair on the other side of the desk. 'You're yet to talk to any medical staff and we are yet to record any calls from you seeking advice on your wife's condition.'

Ferguson, now uncertain how to respond, dropped his head, twirling his thumbs. 'Say what you like, but I love my wife and I want what's best for her.'

'So… give consent.'

'Maybe I will, but I need to think about it.'

'Fair enough.' Thompson flopped back in her chair, rocking it. 'Is there anything I can provide you to help you decide?'

'No, I'm good.' Ferguson gripped the wooden arms of the chair, making ready to leave.

'When do you think you will have your decision?'

'When I've made it.' Ferguson stood and moved to the door.

'Let me know if you need anything?' Thompson said, as the door closed behind him. She then collected her phone, flicking through recent calls and punching the attorney general's name. When Stevedore answered, she advised, 'You may have a problem with Victoria's husband. I suggest you come over as soon as you can.'

After leaving the professor's office, Ferguson asked at the reception desk if he could visit his wife. The nurse directed him to the gowning room, where he changed into sterile clothing, masked himself and placed on a hair cap before stretching on latex surgical gloves. They then led him into the ward by a nurse explaining the machines and their purpose. He examined his wife and didn't recognise her. Her face swollen and bruised, with tubes dropping from her mouth and nose, and from under the cloth cover over her body. The stress of seeing her was too much, and he asked to leave. He changed and advised the staff that he was going to the café for a coffee.

'It's dreadful, I can't stand it.' Ferguson called Mariner as he waited for his latte. 'She is so doped up with tubes running everywhere. A resuscitation machine pumping away next to her and other machines. I can't remember their names. They seem to circulate something through her; I'm not sure what.'

'What did the surgeon say?'

'They want me to sign a consent form.'

'Did you?'

'You told me not to.' Ferguson glanced about to see if anyone was listening. 'I don't think she would survive an operation, anyway.'

'What do the doctors think?'

'They think she might.' Ferguson nodded a thanks as his coffee was placed before him. 'She's such a tough bitch; she might just do that.'

'What are you going to do?'

'I'm going to tell her father that I'm withdrawing consent.'

'What's he likely to do?'

'Thing is, I'm the closest next of kin and it's my decision.'

'They can't override you?'

'Nope. Well, at least that's what I've been told.'

'This is good news, darling, excellent news,' Mariner enthused. 'Just a few more days and then it is over, poor love.'

'Hey guess what? Rikki Ortega rang me.'

'Oh, yes, what did he want? His money, I bet you?'

'Didn't mention it, even though I offered to bring it over tonight.'

'Really?' Mariner's tone changed. 'That's weird. What did he want?'

'He seemed concerned about Vikki. He wanted to know how she was coping.'

'That's strange. Why would he want to know that?'

Neither responded for a few moments as they thought through various notions.

Mariner asked, 'You don't think it involved him, do you?'

'Why?' Ferguson sipped on his now sweetened coffee. 'Because I didn't get his money?'

'He threatened to do something to you.'

'Why ask how she was?' Ferguson asked.

'Maybe he wasn't expecting her to be on life support. The

difference between her breathing, or not, could be twenty years, if it was him.'

'Nah, it wouldn't be him.' Ferguson couldn't imagine it.

'It puts a unique spin on it if she dies, though, doesn't it? Why don't you ring and find out?'

'It's not him,' Ferguson insisted.

'Do what I ask, will you, please? Put it to him and perhaps you might do a deal and get my twenty grand back.'

'It's not him; it can't be.'

'Just do it, will you?' Mariner snapped into the phone, forcing Ferguson to stretch the device from his ear. 'If it is, this will be a perfect moment for us. So, do what I ask.'

'Yes, darling. I'll call him now.' Ferguson relented before changing tack. 'Can I come over?'

'You do what I ask, and you can come all over me, later,' she suggested, then narrowed her tone. 'If you don't, then don't bother.'

Ferguson didn't have a chance to say goodbye, checking the screen to see why there was no response. He dropped the phone to the table, leaning back in the chair. He rubbed his fingers through his hair, grabbed his glass and drained his coffee.

CHAPTER

32

They found the smouldering wreck five kilometres west of the major Melbourne-Geelong freeway. The stench of burning chemicals polluted the air as the two detectives waited for the forensic team to wind up their investigation.

'Why would you burn the car and leave the plates on?' Richard Sylvester asked.

'We're not dealing with the sharpest tools in the box,' his colleague replied.

'You could be right.' Sylvester went to the boot, lifting the still warm lid. 'I just don't get why they would leave all of this gear. Surely it means something to someone?' He tugged clothing and bags aside, searching for nothing in particular.

'It's registered to an Andrew Cole who lives in the houso's tower near Williamstown train station.'

'You reckon he's linked?'

'Bit hard,' Dan Harris smirked. 'He's been in remand for the last few weeks.'

'Why would his brother burn his car?'

'You assume it's his brother; could have been stolen.'

'No one would steal this piece of shit, then burn it.' Sylvester closed the boot, brushing his hands as he stepped back to Harris.

'This is what we know.' Harris started counting off his fingers. 'At least three boys sighted at the servo in a matt-finished car, voila.' He waved his hand like a magician toward the wreck. 'It's registered to Andy Cole. We have his brother on the train accosting the victim.' He grabbed his third finger. 'We believe the car was in the driveway of the Rifle Club. We have a bottle of Jack Daniels purchased and found at the scene.'

'When will we get the CCTV from them?'

'They promised it this afternoon.' Harris grabbed his ring finger. 'Four, I reckon it's Cole and his scaly mates.'

'Why aren't they all this easy?'

'These blokes are dumb. Who leaves evidence like this? It's just a nail in their coffin.'

'Shall we wait here for these guys to finish, or go see if we can find them?'

'How long will you boys be?' Harris asked no one in particular.

A white-overalls'd officer glanced up from his work. 'We'll finish before dark. We have a truck on its way to take it to the city depot for greater analysis for DNA and anything else we can find.'

'When can we expect a report?'

'Initial analysis within twenty-four hours. We should complete the bulk of it by the end of next week.'

'Okay, thanks. We'll leave you to it, unless you need anything from us.'

'Who called it in?' the officer asked.

'A farmer saw smoke and gave the local fireys a call.'

'We'll need to talk to him; do you have his details?' The forensic officer asked.

'I'll text them to you,' Harris said, as he strolled back to his car, working his phone.

Two hours later, the detectives were staking out a house in Newport that was reported to be the current residence of Michael Cole. They had been positioned for thirty minutes, searching for movement, seeing none.

'It's getting late. I reckon we should go have a chat. What do you think, partner?' Harris asked.

'If they're the gang, do you reckon we need backup?'

'Nope, we're just going to have a chat, nothing to get too excited about.'

'Should we go prepared?'

'You think they're going to come out blasting? A couple of scrawny kids starting a siege?'

'I prefer we call it in. Better safe than sorry.'

'Fair enough.'

After radioing for backup, the detectives went to the back of the car and released the boot, each grabbing a bullet-proof vest.

Sylvester struggled to strap his vest. 'These damn things are a nuisance,' he said, grappling to control the Velcro ties.

'It'll save your life one day.' Harris checked his standard issue .38 revolver, clipping it back into the holster. 'Let's go.'

The house was downhill from where they had parked their car. Sylvester twitched as they entered the front yard; Harris shrugged. Their breathing quickened with every step as they moved toward the verandah. No matter how long they trained, cautious anxiety always created a rush of adrenaline.

Harris stepped up to the front door and thudded his clenched fist into it with three loud thumps. 'Open up. Police.'

There was no response, but they could hear scurrying about the house.

Harris thumped again. 'Police! Open up.' He turned to Sylvester and shrugged.

'Let me try. Step away.'

Harris stepped back as Sylvester approached the door. With a solid kick, almost shattering the flimsy wooden door, he burst it open, rushed inside and screamed, 'Police!'

Sylvester searched through the front rooms. Harris danced down the hallway, drawing his pistol. He came to the lounge and pointed his gun at the startled boy cowering there. 'Get down! On the floor!

Do it!' Rocky Galatea complied, stretching his hands behind his head. 'Place your right hand behind you, son.'

Harris holstered his weapon, withdrawing handcuffs and snapping them on Galatea's wrist. 'Now your left.' Harris snapped the cuffs shut. 'Who else is here?'

'Micky and Tommy,' Galatea said. One minute he had been viewing cartoons on a blaring television, the next they planted his face into the sticky carpet.

Sylvester was now at the door.

'There are two more, Richie,' Harris said, standing over Galatea. 'Check the bedrooms; I'll go out back.'

'Take care, partner.'

Sylvester walked off and kicked open a bedroom door.

Harris moved through to the back of the house, crashing past strewn chairs in the kitchen and heading for the backyard. He stepped out into the unkempt plot as wailing police sirens approached. Drawing his weapon as he neared the corner of a shed, plants and overgrown grass creating hollows and dark places in the dusk light, circling the shed in a crouch, pistol pointing in a two-handed hold. He saw nothing, stepping closer to the fence to check that side of the shed, again, nothing.

Sylvester came out into the yard. 'Number two is secured.'

Harris raised a finger to his lips, flicking his pistol toward a rusty sheet of old corrugated iron leaning against the shed. Sylvester drew his weapon, covering Harris as he stretched toward one end, flipping the sheet away.

'Don't shoot. Don't shoot,' a frightened Mickey Cole pleaded, hands covering his face.

'Stand up, dipstick,' Sylvester commanded.

As he did, Harris went behind him, shackling him with handcuffs. 'Any reason you need to hide from the police, Mickey?'

'I ain't done nothin'.'

'You piss your pants in front of police when you're innocent, do you?' Sylvester chuckled, hauling him away. 'We need to have a chat, young man.'

Hanrahan found Ferguson resting on a bench by the main entrance of Alfred Hospital. Ferguson had informed ICU staff he was spending time outside to reflect on the important decision they required him to make. He also wanted to keep an eye out for Vikki's father, to avoid him for as long as he could.

'Mr Ferguson?' Hanrahan held out his hand. 'I'm Commander John Hanrahan. I'm overseeing your wife's investigation for the federal police. Can I have a word?'

Ferguson glanced up, took his hand and shook it, motioning him to sit.

'I just wanted to give you an update on the investigation.'

'Have you arrested anyone yet?'

'We have three men in custody and they're being interviewed.' Hanrahan studied Ferguson as he spoke. 'We believe we have enough evidence to charge them, and we expect to do that this evening.'

'Who are they?'

'Local lads. They run with a drug dealer called Ricardo Ortega. Do you know him?'

Ferguson hesitated enough for Hanrahan to notice.

'I've heard the name around the kids at school, but I wouldn't know him.'

'Perhaps you know these boys we arrested.'

'Why would I know them? I don't use or deal in drugs.'

'Not suggesting you do.' His response surprised Hanrahan. 'I'm thinking they may have gone to the school where you teach.'

'Sure, what are their names?'

Hanrahan tugged a sheet of paper from his jacket. 'Michael Cole, Thomas Haslam and Rocco Galatea.'

'I've heard the names, but they weren't my students.'

'Really? That surprises me.'

'Why is that?'

'I understand they were in in your remedial English class.'

'No, not mine. We have two, which could explain your query.'

'Fair enough.' Hanrahan stood to leave. 'How's your wife?'

'Holding on as best she can.' Ferguson glanced up. 'What're you going to charge them with?'

'At this stage, assault, so we can hold them, we may upgrade charges later.'

'If Vikki dies, would that mean murder, even though she was in hospital?'

'The injuries she sustained were from the brutal beating. If she dies, then we'll upgrade charges to murder. Why do you ask?'

Ferguson hesitated, turning away. 'I just want them punished.' As Hanrahan was stepping off he asked, 'Will Ortega be charged with murder as well?'

'If we can prove he was involved.'

'Thanks, Commander; I appreciate your advice.'

Ferguson waited until he was sure Hanrahan had gone. He stood, scanning around to detect any unwanted ears, listening. When he sat down, he swiped his way to Rikki Ortega's number and waited for the connection.

'It was you, you prick.'

Ortega didn't respond. 'Who is this?'

'The man who has your balls in his hand.'

'What d'ya want?'

'I'm told your partners in crime have been arrested and are to be charged later this evening with the assault on my wife.'

'Yeah, so?'

'I'm wondering how it plays out, when I tell them you threatened me.'

'Why? Let me think, coz ya owe me money? Yeah, that'll work, ya dumb prick.'

Ferguson hadn't expected this response but kept going. 'Yeah, well, what's the difference between assault and murder?'

'Youse're askin' the dumb questions, youse tell me.'

'I'm guessing twenty years.'

'Big problem with ya plan… she ain't dead.'

'Not yet.'

Ortega didn't respond for a moment, then said, 'Ya said she'll pull through.'

'Only if they operate, and only if I give permission.'

'Ya wouldn't do it. Not enough ticker.'

'Try me,' Ferguson sneered, responding to Ortega's anxiety. 'I'm guessing you're up to your neck in this either before or after the fact. With your track record, I reckon they could stitch murder into your charges.'

'What d'ya want?'

'I want you to credit me the twenty I owe you.'

'If I don't?'

'Then goodbye, little man,' Ferguson said. 'Enjoy your time behind bars.'

'What guarantee do I have she doesn't die?'

'None.'

Ortega didn't hesitate. 'Then no deal, moron. Ya think you can threaten me, then try to take cash from me? You better hope ya missus survives, otherwise you join her.'

'Bit hard to do anything when you're in jail.'

'Listen to ya. Ya think ya can threaten me? I've done time in jail, mate. I know what it's like. Youse don't. Believe me when I tell ya, unless ya keep me out of this shit, ya'll be doing time as well. Never think ya can threaten me. I love hurtin' people. I see you again, ya'll see what I mean.'

Ferguson was left checking his phone, thinking that the call hadn't gone to plan. He stifled a mirthless laugh, gazing across the forecourt and realising he might be in deeper trouble than he was before. He decided not to add to his anxiety by calling Bronte.

When Ferguson returned to the ICU, they directed him to a meeting room along the corridor. He entered gingerly to find assembled medical personnel discussing an issue around a long boardroom table, a white board with scrawled notations at the end, and Doctor Nguyen leading the conversation. Chatter stopped as Ferguson entered, and he was directed to a chair opposite Charlie Stevedore.

Nguyen updated Ferguson on why they were there, introducing the surgical team and the hospital legal officer. He glanced about the table, smiling and nodding as they introduced each face. When the doctor finished, he gazed at his father-in-law.

'We are working toward surgery tomorrow and we need your permission to proceed.' Nguyen finished her review.

All eyes settled on Ferguson as they waited. He tried to speak but needed to clear his throat, taking a glass of water offered. After gulping a mouthful of water, he said, 'I'm not sure Vikki would have wanted to go ahead with the operation.'

Stevedore dropped his hands to the table, looking as if he wanted to spring across it. 'You are kidding me. Just sign the permission so we can save her. You're wasting precious time.'

'Mr Ferguson, unless we act within the next twenty-four hours, we may struggle to save her,' emphasized Professor Thompson, who was sitting next to Doctor Nguyen.

Ferguson didn't respond, placing his elbows on the table and resting his chin in his interwoven hands, his eyes flicking around the faces as he tried to identify allies.

'You can't deny permission,' Stevedore insisted.

Ferguson breathed deep, filling his lungs. 'Yes I can, if I believe it's in her best interests to do so.'

'It's not, you moron,' Stevedore hollered, slapping the table.

'Minister, please calm down,' said the man introduced as the chief executive of the hospital. 'Mr Ferguson is within his rights to express what he has said; we just need to talk through the issues.'

'I'm her father, my rights override his.'

The legal officer sat forward and peered down the table to the attorney general. 'Actually, that is not the case. Precedence has always been to the closest next of kin to decide in terms of care.'

'Mr Ferguson, you are aware of the condition of Victoria,' Thompson mediated. 'What is troubling you?'

Ferguson breathed deep again, then flopped back into his chair. 'I just know my wife. I know she would not want to go through the pain of recovery and living her life mutilated as a reminder of her ordeal.'

'You don't know her,' Stevedore murmured, almost whispering. 'I know her better than you, I'd wager.'

No one responded.

'I can save her,' Thompson asserted.

'You cannot guarantee that. I asked you earlier, and you appeared flippant about the whole thing.'

'That's not true.' The comment surprised Thompson. 'I said, I could save them both if we move now.'

'Hang on,' Stevedore interrupted. 'You don't need to terminate the pregnancy?'

'Not if we respond soon,' Nguyen answered.

Ferguson waved away further discussion with a flick of his hand. 'I've made my decision.'

'You have no right to make this decision by yourself.' Stevedore changed to a conciliatory tone. 'Can we talk about it?'

Ferguson scoffed. 'Can we talk about it?' he smirked at his father-in-law. 'That's a good one.'

'Why is that so funny?' Thompson asked, encouraging discussion.

Ferguson eyed her. 'The irony is that this man before you is fighting for the right for families to have more say on the dignity of death. This is what I want for my wife, and now he asks if we can talk about it, as if to say, I have no rights in this matter.'

Stevedore stirred, sitting further forward in his seat. 'What does government policy on euthanasia have to do with operating on Vikki?'

'It has everything to do with it.'

'Please explain?' Thompson asked.

Ferguson did not release his glare from Stevedore. 'I want my wife to die with dignity. Her father agrees with this right and will legislate it, so all families can decide I have the right to make today.'

'You can't do this, Doug.' Tears welled in the attorney general's eyes. 'She's my daughter. She's all I have left, you can't do this to me.'

'You see, Charlie, this is your problem. You think this is about you, when it's about Vikki.' Ferguson glanced at the chief executive and the legal officer. 'I instruct you to turn the life support systems off and to do it this evening.'

The chief executive grimaced, gazing along the table to Thompson, who shrugged, pressed her palms together and slunk back into her chair. Doctor Nguyen responded. 'I'll make the preparations.'

Stevedore dropped his face into his hands, snivelling.

'Is that it?' Ferguson rapped his fingers on the table, then moved to the door. 'I have to make a call. I'll be back in thirty minutes for an update.'

After he closed the door, Nguyen carried a box of tissues to Stevedore, who snatched several, wiped his eyes and blew his nose.

He glanced up at Thompson. 'Is there nothing we can do?' She avoided his red-eyed gaze.

The chief executive responded. 'Nothing.'

The others were silent, avoiding gaping at the flustered father. 'Unless she survives,' Thompson offered.

Stevedore glanced up. 'What do you mean?'

'If she survives twenty-four hours, then we could operate as an emergency. We don't need permission.'

The legal officer considered the notion and nodded toward the chief executive.

'If she lives, you operate, what are her chances?' Stevedore asked.

'Ten percent,' Nguyen responded.

Thompson concurred. 'Better than nothing.'

'It would increase her chances if a court ordered us to act if she survives,' the legal officer added.

Stevedore searched the others for confirmation. 'So, if I cut it down from twenty-four hours to twelve, what are the odds?'

'Fifteen percent.'

Stevedore nodded, checking his watch. 'When will you turn off the resuscitator?'

'An hour,' Nguyen replied. 'There is no guarantee she will breathe, but she might.'

'If she does, we can operate in the morning?' Stevedore asked.

'Only if her signs are good,' Thompson said.

Nguyen added, 'Fact is, Minister, you may lose her any time once that machine is switched off.'

It was coming up to 9 p.m. when Ferguson reentered the ICU, almost ninety minutes after the meeting. 'Are we all set?' he asked the congregated medical staff.

They asked if he wanted to attend bedside. He responded he would prefer the viewing room. Once in the room, he noticed several medical personnel crowded around the bed. He saw Victoria's father holding her hand and smirked.

Ferguson turned to Doctor Nguyen. 'Let's do it.'

Nguyen tapped the glass, and Thompson glanced over, acknowledging the direction. She moved to Victoria and withdrew plastic respiratory tubes. Two came free easily; the third took a little more time, but then she was free of all breathing support.

Ferguson watched until the three tubes fell from the bed. Then he turned and departed, leaving others to grieve and provide support for her father.

An elevator was at that floor and he was out of the hospital within minutes, calling his girlfriend as he strode to his car.

'It's done,' Ferguson gushed. 'The future is ours.'

'Get your arse here as quick as you can. I need you, right now.'

The four steps up from the street into Punch Lane Brasserie often trapped the unwary, the landing providing little room to open the wooden-framed glass door. Cardinal Rosseau almost fell when he tripped on the top step. He collected himself, barging through the hard-to-manage door after regaining his feet, and startling the waiter by the cash register who offered support. Luckily, he had chosen not to wear his cassock, otherwise he would have fallen.

Rosseau brushed aside the waiter's offer, then confirmed his dinner appointment. He was shown to a table by the window and ordered a Campari and soda as an apéritif to enjoy while he waited for Parker Osborne.

Osborne had arranged to meet him, advising him that the iconic Melbourne bar and restaurant was a short walk from Saint Patrick's Cathedral, through a park and downhill from the Princess Theatre. He agreed to the dinner invitation when Osborne contacted him, confirming that he had flown to Melbourne that afternoon. Rosseau was keen to learn more about the progress of the referendum, and how the treasurer's covert crusade to stop the euthanasia legislation reaching the parliament was proceeding. He also fancied discussing strategies for dealing with sensitive material.

It was twenty minutes before Osborne appeared at the table, and Rosseau accepted his hand, returning the firm grip with a flimsy limp-wristed response. Osborne was a whippet-smart, younger man, but with dreadful manners and little respect for his title. Rosseau enjoyed time with him because of this abruptness.

'Morris, sorry I'm late.' Osborne was short of breath as he took the chair opposite. 'I caught up with our attorney general, who has had a dreadful few days.'

'What has happened?'

'It's the great paradox.' Osborne ordered an Italian beer from the attentive waiter. 'His daughter has been injured, life threatening, and he's in a dilemma about what to do.'

'What happened?'

'She's suffering with burns from a criminal assault and she's on life support… tragic, really. I know her, sort of, and she's a smart, attractive kid, doing well as a lawyer.'

'What's the dilemma?'

'Ah, you see, this is the paradox.' Osborne took a solid mouthful of beer once the waiter had placed the glass and small bottle of Peroni on the table. 'We give Charlie the authority to develop the euthanasia referendum legislation, and at the same time, he is struggling with life and death decisions about his daughter.'

'That's not a paradox, that's a tragedy.'

Osborne raised a doubtful eyebrow. 'It's no different to decisions a lot of folks make every day; but here we have the chief law officer raising his hand to bring in a bill which allows death by killing, and yet, and this is the paradox, he's fighting to save his daughter from a similar fate.'

Rosseau studied Osborne, who was taking another generous gulp of beer. 'You are the paradox, if you don't mind me saying.'

'Me? How so?'

'You fight hard for Christian values, but you battle your friends to get ahead.'

Osborne nodded. 'Ah, the great riddle of politics; unless you fight your friends, you will never be promoted. If you ever want to be a leader without fighting, then forget it.'

Rosseau smiled. 'This is why I like you, Parker; you're so ruthless in getting what you want, and so open about it.'

'Only to you, Morris,' Osborne grinned, 'I only confess to you.'

The cardinal laughed as he saluted his glass to finish his Campari. They then settled into ordering meals, with Osborne preferring pork loin and Rosseau ordering barramundi. Osborne ordered Rennie River's chardonnay, rationalising that it wasn't every day he could share an expensive bottle of wine with someone who could have been the Holy Father. After the waiter cleared the table of unnecessary cutlery and plates, Rosseau reflected upon Osborne.

'How is the campaign going now the prime minister has agreed to not force the referendum?'

Osborne smirked. 'That's a good question.'

'You have her commitment, don't you?'

'Yes, and no.'

'Is she changing her mind again?'

'Who the hell knows what her position is?' Osborne shook his head. 'Just a few short hours ago, on a radio programme, she stated, unequivocally, that she was going to progress the referendum.'

'She already agreed she wouldn't.' Rosseau shook his head.

'Yes, this is the problem with my erratic leader.'

'So, the referendum is back on?'

'Yes, one would assume so.' Osborne raised his eyebrow, pouting his lips at the cardinal. 'You have to understand, Morris, that is my preferred position.'

'It's not mine.' Rosseau sniffed, squeezing the tip of his nose. 'I disagree with your plan.'

'I want you to do nothing more than fight hard for the legislation to be terminated.' Osborne watched as the waiter poured the wine and after the tasting was waved away. 'Here's cheers.' He raised his glass, clinking it with Rosseau's. 'I'm playing the long game here. I want her to push the referendum to the electorate for a vote. I want you to put as much pressure as you can muster on her not to go ahead with it.'

'I'll continue to fight against it; you must know that.'

'I expect nothing less.'

'I don't understand, you're on the church's side on this issue. Like a good Catholic, you should follow what we say.'

'The church is not my master, it is my faith, but I'll do what I need to do.'

Rosseau panted a heavy sigh. 'How is this going to work?'

'I want to be prime minister.'

'She has already promised she will pass the baton to you.'

'Yes, but as I said, I want the job sooner than she is planning. Indeed, let me share a secret with you. I'm standing for the leadership within weeks, and you have an important role to play.'

'Why should I support someone who wants to support the referendum?'

'I don't advocate for a Yes vote, there is a big difference,' Osborne said, gazing over the rim of his glass. 'I want you to push her as hard as you can. She will then put the referendum forward, and after it has cleared the parliament, I will challenge her leadership.'

'That is no good. The referendum will still go forward, even if you are prime minister.'

'Exactly, and then as prime minister, I will campaign against it, as Howard did during the republic referendum.'

Rosseau sat back in his chair, glass in hand. 'I see the point you are making, but why not just kill it now?'

'If the euthanasia issue dies now, then you are the champion and we all get to celebrate. I will then run for the leadership because it has humiliated the prime minister.' Osborne's eyes and tone narrowed. 'But understand this: the issue won't die. The progressives, the rent-a-cause crowd and the atheists will come again, crying for the government to reconsider. I want to kill it outright, making sure it's cremated.'

Rosseau didn't understand and shook his head.

Osborne leaned in across the table. 'If I kill the bill with a No vote, it will never come back. If we don't take it to a referendum, we are only delaying it, not killing it.'

As the waiter arrived to serve, the cardinal observed, 'This is risky politics for you, and for us.'

'When I'm prime minister, politics will be different. The values and ideals of the church, which are the core values of Australia, will be revisited. Changes will come to the way this country is heading, and if that means repealing legislation, then so be it.'

'You think you can change decades of moral neglect?'

'Too right I can; the community is crying out for it.' Osborne grinned as he straightened. 'I will work hard to stop this ridiculous government spending on the lazy feckers in the community.' He checked himself, looking about him. 'Sure, I support helping those who can't help themselves. We need to show compassion. But we don't need to give them all the money. I reckon it's time for the community to step up and support their fellow man and not expect the government to do it. If folks want help, then it's the community who should help them, not government.'

'You're a cold, callous bastard, aren't you?' said Rosseau.

'In my business you have to be,' smirked Osborne, as he cut and then forked a large portion of pork into his mouth, and grinned at the cardinal, chewing.

Rosseau didn't respond, forking his way through his fish before sitting back for a moment, then asking, 'Do you provide political advice?'

'Depends who's asking,' Osborne said, cutting another piece of pork. 'Who's asking?'

Rosseau hesitated. 'A friend.'

'Oh, they're the best folks to give advice to, no repercussions.' Osborne laughed, shovelling food into his mouth.

'My friend has information that could destroy the career of a senior executive and maybe damage the brand.'

'Hmm, what's the senior executive done, bonked a staffer?'

'Something like that.'

'Very common in politics, I must say. Why jeopardise your career for sinful procreation is beyond me. Why can't colleagues just say no?'

'Precisely.'

'Politics is show business for ugly people. I just don't quite understand why rational people get excited talking to the morons they would not normally talk with, if they weren't a politician.'

'Power is the ultimate aphrodisiac.'

Osborne finished eating, placing his cutlery together on the plate. 'Who said that?'

'Henry Kissinger, if I recall.'

'Now that was one ugly operator, yet always seen with glamorous people.'

'Precisely.'

Osborne searched for a waiter as he picked at a tooth at the back of his mouth. 'What does your friend want to do?'

'He is unsure, expose the executive or use the information to get what he wants.'

'Interesting dilemma your friend has.' Osborne asked the waiter for a toothpick. 'Save the brand or become a criminal.'

'What do you mean, save the brand?'

'Getting rid of the executive will save the brand. Once executives cut corners, they always will. Nothing stops them, other than sacking them.'

'Interesting.' Rosseau stopped eating, still holding his cutlery.

'If your friend uses the information to blackmail, then they are no different and deserve to go down. This is how corrupt politicians get exposed.'

'Surely politicians are above all of that?'

'You're kidding me, aren't you?' Osborne attacked the crevice in his back tooth as soon as the waiter had delivered a tiny jar of wooden toothpicks, a hand covering his mouth. 'Once a politician takes a bribe, no matter the amount, could be a meal, then they are only ever negotiating price. Once politicians get what they want by using information against others, they become the problem and not the solution.'

Rosseau gawked at Osborne, somewhat perplexed. 'You are trying to shaft your prime minister, surely that is as bad?'

'I don't think so,' Osborne grinned. 'I'll expose her and her indiscretions to rid the brand of her, thus protecting the brand. If I were to blackmail her, then I would be as corrupt and not worthy of leading. If I accepted her terms for a leadership change, I would sell my soul, and then there would be no coming back.'

'You display very contradictory positions on these things, Parker.'

'Not really; I'm pretty consistent. I play the game hard. If my opponent is using different rules and being corrupted by the system, then it is incumbent upon me to act and stop them.'

'The prime minister is corrupt?'

'Yes, she is. Corrupt morally, because she drinks way too much, which affects her decision making. Politically corrupt, because she doesn't know what she stands for. No, wait… that's wrong. She does stand for something.'

'What might that be?'

'She's against everything the Catholics want.' Osborne laughed, then calmed to add, 'Her greatest weakness is the use of power to get the personal things she likes.'

'What should my friend do?'

'Morris, I think you should expose them and save the brand. Look what doing nothing did to the church in the sexual abuse cases. You're obligated to act, otherwise you are complicit.'

Rosseau wondered if the advice was what he wanted to hear. He thought he could use the information he had received to get what he wanted; now this was a more powerful approach. This was leadership, which he felt anxious displaying.

Osborne waited for a response, and when he didn't get one, added, 'Tell your priest or bishop to stop screwing the parishioners and leave the church.'

'If only it were that easy.'

'It doesn't matter who it is; if your evidence is conclusive, then disclose it to them, and encourage them to make the decision. If they are ethical and of sound mind, they will do the right thing.'

Over coffee, the cardinal asked if it would be appropriate for him to visit the attorney general.

'It would be sensational to our cause if you could, especially if you visit the hospital tonight when all the drama is transpiring. This will add to the pressure for Charlie to drop the legislation. The prime minster will be steaming once she learns you have been counselling him.'

'I will visit when I leave here. Can I get a taxi nearby?'

'Are you going looking like that?'

'Yes.' Rosseau raised an eyebrow. 'Why would you ask that?'

'I think the full regalia would have more influence at the hospital.'

'I'd rather go more for prayers and counsel. I would have thought this is not about me, but him. Subtlety not in your lexicon?'

'Trust me on this, Morris, go the whole hog on this one, if you want to influence Charlie.'

Ninety minutes later Cardinal Rosseau, in full religious regalia, stepped from a car to be swamped by photographers and flashes of light. Television microphones shoved in his way as he tried to push through the scrum of media. He didn't consider it a coincidence and remembered Osborne's parting words, *"Just tell the truth about why you are there"*.

'Cardinal Rosseau, are you here to talk to the attorney general?'

'Are you meeting to discuss the Kill Bill?'

'Do you support euthanasia, Cardinal Rosseau?'

'Why are you here?'

'What's the Pope's position on the legislation?'

Rosseau didn't bother with the truth; he just ignored all questions and brushed past the eager, baying journalists.

Once inside the hospital, he made his way to the ICU unit, heading for the elevator lobby. When the doors released, he was almost bowled over by a younger man in a hurry, more interested in his phone. On reaching the ICU floor, a duty nurse asked why he was attending, and he explained he needed to see the attorney general.

She directed him to a meeting room, outlining the difficult medical procedure the minister's daughter was going through.

Fifteen minutes later a distraught Charlie Stevedore, dressed in scrubs, knocked and entered the room. When he saw the cardinal, tears flowed, releasing the pent-up emotion. He stood shaking and sobbing, his head back, trying to breathe air. The cardinal moved to him, dragging a chair, encouraging Stevedore to sit. The distressed minister wept as he sat, the cardinal placing a comforting hand on the back of his head.

Rosseau tugged a chair close and sat, now stroking the minister's arm. Stevedore sat upright, wiping his face with the sleeve of his gown. Rosseau stretched to the centre of the table, dragging over a box of tissues, drawing out a number and handing them to Stevedore, who blew his nose.

'Sorry, Your Eminence. It's been a harrowing hour.'

'No need to apologise, my son. We need to react to crisis and stress the best way we can, and you are matching your mind and body's needs.'

Stevedore screwed his face and sobbed. 'I've just let my daughter go.'

Rosseau placed an arm across the weeping father's shoulders, waiting for him to rid himself of emotion. He then said, 'Jesus, at the cross, cried out to the Father, *"Why have you abandoned me?"*'

Stevedore didn't lift his head. 'She left me because her husband decided to let her go.' He wiped his eyes, then cleared his nose. 'She's a battler and hanging on. Now it's up to her and we must wait.'

'I imagine God, who is real, also weeps for us. That's why he gave us his Son: to wipe our tears and say, *"I know your pain and I shower you with mercy,"*' Rosseau offered. 'This tragedy is not God's plan, but God is here to grieve with us.'

'God can't help me at the moment, I'm afraid.' Stevedore stood, moving to the window and gazing out upon the buildings, leaning his hands on the sill. Rosseau followed, staying a short distance behind. 'I'm thankful for you coming; you humble me at this very stressful time, but you must have other important business to prosecute.'

'I'm here because several colleagues spoke of your crisis today. I've sought you out to bring you comfort during this troublesome time.'

'Eminence, I may be emotional right now.' Stevedore turned and gazed at him. 'Whilst I'm grateful for your prayers to a worried father, I'm also a politician and suspect there could be other motives.'

'I can assure you, there are not.' Rosseau clasped his hands before him. 'As you know, I'm in Australia for a reason, but that reason does not bring me here tonight.'

'That impresses me, no end,' Stevedore smiled.

'How is your daughter?'

'Her lousy husband had authority to turn the machines off, which we did around nine.' Stevedore relieved his burden, taking another seat at the table. 'They expected her to die but she didn't.'

'That must be a relief for you.'

'It is, but it places more stress on everyone. The plan is this: the hospital will treat her as an emergency patient, overriding all next of kin directions, if she survives the next twelve hours.'

'What happens then?'

'A court injunction stipulating that the hospital team take control of her care.'

'So, she just needs to get through the night?'

'That's it,' Stevedore replied.

'Would you mind if I wait with you?'

Stevedore grimaced. 'You don't have to do that.'

'I would like to.' Rosseau took a seat. 'It's not every day we at the top of the church provide pastoral care.'

'That's nice, and to have your prayer and blessings would be an honour for me.'

'Would you mind if I say a prayer now?'

'No, please.' Stevedore nodded, waving the cardinal on.

Rosseau stood and spoke in a hushed voice. 'Gentle Jesus, who cured the sick and laid a healing hand upon the lame, the blind and the handicapped, look with compassion upon Victoria in her suffering.' Rosseau marked the points of the cross as Stevedore crossed himself, head bowed. 'If it is not your will to cure her, then give us strength to bear her burden and offer it up to You. You suffered so much for us. Give us grace to offer our sufferings in union with

Your own, in reparation for our sins and those of others, for the needs of this troubled world, and for the release of the souls in purgatory. Mary, compassionate Mother, pray for your weary child. Health of the Sick, Comforter of the Afflicted, pray for Victoria. Amen.'

Stevedore kept his head bowed, wiping his eyes with the clutch of tissues still in his hand. 'Thank you, Eminence.'

'If we are to spend time together, then please call me Morris.'

Stevedore glimpsed up and smiled. 'Would you like a coffee? My preference is for something stronger, but I suspect they will only give us coffee.'

'Tea is preferable, but coffee will be fine.'

Stevedore stood and crossed to the phone on a sideboard, picking up the receiver and prodding numbers with his finger. 'Oh, hello. Sorry to disturb you, but Professor Thompson suggested that if I need a tea or coffee, then I was to call this number.' Stevedore made the order.

Rosseau smiled and nodded. 'Thank you.'

'No, it's a pleasure.' Stevedore returned to his seat, glanced at the cardinal, then after a few moments, asked, 'Do you want to talk about the legislation?'

'No.' Rosseau shook his head.

'What do you think we should do, drop it or push it to referendum?'

'I'm not here to talk about that.'

'Eminence, come on, play the game. What do you think we should do?'

Rosseau demurred, turning away, somewhat perplexed by the moment. He glanced back at Stevedore and said, 'You know my position and that of the church. We will always oppose a threat by the state to control life and death issues of policy.' He waited until Stevedore engaged him. 'Let me ask you this, and I mean no disrespect.'

'Please, go ahead.'

'Would you wish the same trauma you have been through today upon others?'

Stevedore thought for a moment. 'Not sure it's the same.'

'Again, with respect.'

Stevedore nodded, encouraging the cardinal to continue.

'Taking life and death decisions away from the medical clinicians and giving that responsibility to families may create similar challenges of dispute to those you are experiencing.'

'Euthanasia concerns a patient with a terminal illness; that's what I think it should be. Allowing them to decide about end of life on their terms.'

'Can you guarantee that the convenience of others won't become the norm, and we won't be left with decisions being made about the elderly that they don't agree with, but are fearful of saying anything about?'

'That's a little harsh.'

'Guarantee me it won't happen,' Rosseau challenged. 'We know medical staff push the limits now, so to suggest the limits won't be pushed if it becomes law is preposterous.'

'We will have adequate protections.'

'No matter what justifications it offers,' Rosseau altered his tone, 'it is a serious change to our approach to life and the irrevocable sanctity that should control our understanding of what it means to be human.'

'This bill is about compassion for those who are at the end of their life and terminally ill, no more.'

'You can't guarantee protection of the vulnerable, or the depressed, or even the poor,' Rosseau responded. 'It's unreasonable to suggest that patients who are nearing the end of their lives will not feel under pressure to choose termination.'

'And the terminally ill, how can we help them?'

'Through palliative care and increasing access for those needing support.'

'The hospice lobby group reckons they manage end of life and the pain of the terminally ill.' Stevedore leaned back in his chair and crossed his arms. 'What they cannot control is the loss of personal dignity. This bill will allow patients to determine that.'

'Minister, what we've witnessed in other countries is that euthanasia laws are driving economic policy. Instead of expensive treatment for the terminally ill, we have seen countries opting for termination, to save medical costs.'

'These are rather provocative statements.'

'They may be provocative, but they are true.'

Stevedore didn't respond, bringing his left forefinger to his mouth and gnawing on the nail. 'You make valid points and it seems there may be a need for further consideration.'

'I would hope you do.'

'My experience today hits home on the key point you make.'

'I do not want you to personalise this debate, Minister,' Rosseau said. 'I want you to make a judgment based on the sanctity of life. We don't need a situation when a radical husband's personal convenience can take the life of a loved one. Human life must be respected regardless of age, gender, race, religion, social status or potential for success.'

Stevedore paused for a moment and then whispered, 'Amen to that.'

Ferguson rolled over, stretching for his little bag of pleasure to prepare powdered lines for Bronte as part of their continuing celebration. He sat up, supported by an array of pillows, to ensure his preparation of the powder was in the right proportions, tugging his goodies from the bag.

'Will they let you know when she croaks?'

'She may be dead already.' Ferguson offered the mirrored plate to Mariner, who sniffed a line. 'Maybe they'll call me to come and work out details, I don't know.'

'Are you sad?' She sniffed another line. 'You'd better not be.'

'Sad? Hmm, maybe not sad. Maybe a tad sorry for her father, but sad for me? No.' Ferguson sniffed two lines, then snuggled down into her arms.

After a while, Mariner asked, 'We should rethink the plans for Ortega.'

Ferguson glanced up. 'How do you mean?'

'Given she's dead and they could implicate him, we should give him the money so there is no motive back to us.'

'I threatened him, kind of.'

'What do you mean, kind of? I told you to get the deal done.' Mariner sat up, leaning over Ferguson. 'What have you done?'

'I told him I wanted the credit as you suggested.' Ferguson slithered away, repositioning himself on the pillows.

'What did he say?'

'He said if Vikki dies then I will join her… so, it was no deal.'

'Why didn't you tell me?' she almost hollered at him, sitting up then flopping back, exasperated.

Ferguson thought through his options before replying. 'I was a tad anxious last night with all that was going on and didn't want to worry you.'

She ran a hand across his chest. 'I expect you to be honest with me all the time, baby, and not hide anything from me.' She drove her nails into him. 'Do you understand?'

Ferguson flinched. 'I was just trying to protect you.'

'I can look after myself, thanks very much.' Mariner rolled back into the pillows. 'We need to get the money to him. We should do it today.'

Ferguson's telephone sparked up and he reached for it on the side table. He didn't recognise the number, so he answered, 'Hello, Doug Ferguson.'

'Mr Ferguson, my name is Conan Stevens. I'm the duty nurse at the ICU where your wife is a patient.'

'Yes.' Ferguson was unsure why he was receiving the call and wiped his hand across his forehead. 'Is there paper work I failed to complete before leaving last night?'

'No, sir.' The nurse responded enthusiastically, increasing Ferguson's anxiety. 'I have been asked by Professor Thompson to suggest it might be a good idea for you to attend the hospital.'

Ferguson sat up, swinging his feet to the floor. 'Why would I do that?'

'The professor would like your further view on treatment.'

'On treatment?' Ferguson stood, wandering to the window. 'Treatment finished last night.'

'The resuscitation support finished last night, but the patient has survived the night and is showing signs of improvement.'

'You're kidding me,' exclaimed Ferguson.

Stevens increased his enthusiasm. 'It's good news, that's for sure.' He paused for just a moment. 'We need you to come in and help with the decision as to what we do now. The patient's father has sought an injunction to allow the surgeon to operate.'

Ferguson didn't respond.

After waiting for a moment, the nurse continued, 'Mr Ferguson… Mr Ferguson, are you there?'

Ferguson willed himself to speak. 'Yes, I'm here,' he croaked.

'What time can we expect you?' Stevens asked. 'We were thinking a nine o'clock meeting will be the best time.'

'Did you say she is improving, in what way?'

'In all ways, it's a significant result. We think we can operate this afternoon if we get the authority to do so. That's why we need you here.'

'I'm on my way.' Ferguson checked his phone and pressed the end call button, tossing it on the bed. He gazed out the window.

'What just happened?' Mariner asked.

Ferguson didn't reply; he just stared out onto the driveway and the street.

'Dougie, baby, what's happened?'

'The bitch survived.'

CHAPTER
37

The chill factor in the Canberra early morning breeze could sometimes be unbearable until the sun worked its charm. Osborne pulled his jacket together as he stepped from the white limousine, heaving his briefcase with him as he marched off toward the ministerial entrance of Parliament House.

'Good morning,' he smiled to security officers as he worked his way through the checkpoint, having his case scanned and a wand waved over his body. This was the same entrance the prime minister used, but her car always entered through the iron gates and she never had to walk through the security. One day soon he would have the same privilege, if his plans for further disruption were agreed at this morning's meeting.

Osborne headed through various heavy doors until he was on the grey blue carpet of the ministerial wing; he strolled along the corridor to the stairwell and its polished mahogany floor, crossing it to enter his office. There was no one at the reception desk, as his staff were stationed at his Sydney office, although a few advisers manned the parliamentary office during non-sitting weeks. His ever-present political adviser was already at her desk.

'Kaitlyn, you're early. I thought we agreed on the flight last night you would take the morning off.'

May glanced up from her computer and smiled. 'Yes, well, there is just too much to do and so little time.'

'I don't pay you to be at work all the time, you have to get a life.'

'Treasurer, if I didn't do the work I need to do, then I suspect you would be in opposition.'

Osborne smiled, admiring her retort.

'Yes, but if we were in opposition, then I would not be wasting my time sitting around this place.'

'That's true,' she smirked. 'I would be, though.'

'As a staffer or a member?'

'You know my plan is to replace you when you retire.'

Osborne chuckled. 'Is that so? Should I worry about my preselection?'

'Not if you keep doing your job,' May said, as he walked through to his own office.

Osborne dropped his briefcase on a visitor's chair, taking his seat at the desk to check emails and respond to urgent matters prior to meeting colleagues at 8.30. The increased number of emails from his electorate surprised him by commenting on the prime minister's interview with Sadler. Many complained about the aggressive nature of the commentator, but he could categorise most into three levels of disdain: those who thought Pasco out of her depth and needing replacing as leader; those who thought she was pathetic and should be replaced; and those who suggested the party would lose the next election if she remained leader. As a snapshot of the electorate it was biased, but the drums for change were sending an obvious message.

May interrupted his review at 8.25, encouraging him to leave. He picked up his briefcase, stepping out into the corridor for the short walk to a parliamentary committee room booked for the meeting with fifteen colleagues. He had ensured the room was internal with no windows, so inquisitive eyes could not see them. A covert meeting of politicians during a non-sitting week was bound to raise an eyebrow in the media.

Osborne entered the room to find almost full attendance, with a chair left vacant in the centre. He smiled, acknowledging his colleagues and tossing the usual banter and jokes back and forward before settling in, taking files from his case and preparing his notes.

'When did you blokes get here?'

'Most of us came into Sydney last night, meeting up in Campbelltown. Gerry organised a party function to justify the travel and accommodation. We hired a minibus leaving at sparrow's fart. We got here thirty minutes ago.'

'Nice one.' They impressed Osborne with the effort to conceal their travel. 'What about you?' He glanced at the others.

'Jim and I came up to Goulburn by train yesterday, and we hired a car.'

Osborne looked at the last colleague from Perth.

'I came in last night; I have a Public Accounts committee hearing this afternoon.'

'Nice one,' Osborne said again. 'Gentlemen, thank you for making the effort to get here this morning and keeping it under wraps. We are in perilous times and we must consider our options.'

The door opened, and everyone turned to see who entered.

Susie Ahmed, the local member for Canberra, skulked in, shrugging her shoulders. She mouthed an apology and took a chair at the end of the table.

'We had better lock the doors,' Osborne suggested. Two parliamentarians went to the doors in the four corners of the room, confirming they were secure.

'As I was saying, we are in a deep hole at the moment and we need to get out and turn around the public's view of us.'

'That won't happen whilst we have the leader we're saddled with,' a member opposite said.

'So,' Osborne challenged, reaching for a file. 'What do we intend to do about it?' He opened the file, quoting the latest party polling. 'The preferred prime minister ratings have the leader in dire unwinnable territory at eighteen percent. The poll indicates those figures would shift if we had a different leader.'

'What are they?' A question came from the group.

Osborne hesitated, then read, 'If Stevedore was leader, the figure would be forty-seven percent. If Susie was leader,' Osborne nodded to the end of the table, 'it would be fifty-four percent, both numbers would change the primary and second preference, getting us over the line.'

Ahmed had known Osborne for too long, way back to their student politics days, and asked, 'What are your numbers?'

Osborne picked up his glasses and turned a page, searching for a figure but already knowing it. 'It's... err, let me see... sixty-seven percent.' He turned and smirked at Ahmed, cupping his chin in his fingers with the forefinger resting on his cheek. There was no response as colleagues stole a glance at each other.

Osborne swung in the green leather chair, waiting for a response.

'Is the cardinal joining us?' a colleague asked.

'No, he's in Melbourne offering support to Charlie,' Osborne responded.

'Why? What's happened?' Ahmed asked.

'Charlie's daughter has been assaulted. Badly. So much so, they turned her life support off last night.'

'On no. Really? Have you heard from him?' Ahmed asked.

'I got a text this morning,' a colleague responded. 'He's in a dark place but working his way through it. His daughter survived the night and vital signs are improving.'

Osborne was taken aback by the information, considering it for a moment. 'It's a tragedy for Charlie and Victoria,' he said. 'This is remarkable news that his daughter is still managing without life support.'

'Why would you say it is remarkable?' a colleague asked.

Ahmed expected an opening and made a play. 'That's a little harsh, wouldn't you say, Parker? There is a family tragedy with a colleague and already you're looking for political advantage.'

Osborne spun his seat to look at her. 'I only make the point that if the AG is advocating euthanasia laws, and then virtually applying it to his daughter by switching off her machines, and then she survives, there is a compelling case for not giving the power to others, that's all.'

'You're shocking.' Ahmed fell back into her seat, her point made, trusting that colleagues would support her.

'Ozzie has a point, though,' a colleague said. 'If we take the personal emotion out of this tragedy and treat it as a case study, it stacks up, and maybe Charlie will have a change of mind toward what he is doing. He's the one pushing this damn legislation.'

'Under riding instructions from the prime minister,' Osborne added.

The group discussed the merits of the issue for thirty-five minutes, putting aside their absent colleague's obvious distress. As the discussion tailed off, two colleagues made last points.

'We have an obligation to our constituents to vote this down.'

'You mean we have an obligation to the church to vote it down.'

Osborne hadn't engaged in the discussion, preferring his colleagues to debate their views, and as they fell silent he sat forward, commanding the meeting. 'The bottom line is that these views do not overcome our problem, which is that, on current polling, we stand to lose the next election, no matter what we do on this referendum.'

'What would you have us do?' Ahmed asked.

'We kill two birds with just one stone.'

Ahmed grimaced. 'Oh, for heaven's sake, Parker, can you do away with the clichés for the moment?'

'If we kill the legislation, it will not solve the constant haranguing from the great unwashed who will continue to push for change.' Osborne ignored her. 'The only way to kill this bill is to have it voted No at the referendum.'

'If the prime minister supports it, it may get up,' Ahmed offered.

'That's true,' Osborne said. 'But, what happens if the prime minister doesn't support it and pushes for a No vote?'

A colleague chuckled. 'She'll never do it.'

Osborne dropped his head, and glaring through his brow at the colleague, said, 'What if she wasn't prime minister?'

The room fell silent, the second hand on the clock clicking its way up the dial.

One or two politicians averted their eyes, picking up a pen, feigning notes. Osborne waited for a moment longer.

'If we bring on the referendum and Pasco supports it, staking her leadership on it, then we kill the referendum and her leadership at the same time.'

Ahmed roused at the end of the table. 'Let me get this right... you want her to get the legislation through the parliament, then challenge her for the leadership, with the new prime minister campaigning against the referendum?'

'Yes, that's what I'm saying.'

'No doubt you think you should be prime minister,' Ahmed scoffed.

'No, I do not,' Osborne smirked, tapping his fingertips together in front of his face, his chin resting on his thumbs. 'That would be up to the party room, and there are three of us who could win the election instead of Nancy.' His eyes flicked about his colleagues to watch their response.

Ahmed fell silent, waiting for someone else to speak.

A colleague who had contributed little said, 'Crumbs, this is serious, isn't it?'

The politicians burst into laughter at the innocence of the remark, relieving the tension, and as they settled down, Osborne added, 'There are several things which have to happen.' He started counting off on his fingers. 'One, the cardinal needs to pressure the prime minister not to bring forward the legislation.'

'Why would he need to do that?' Ahmed asked.

'To make sure Nancy ignores his advocacy and goes against the church; that's what we want her to do.' Osborne linked his thumb and forefinger. 'Two, we create a covert operation of dissent backgrounding the media. Three, we begin a destabilisation campaign against Nancy.'

A colleague pondered, 'She's pretty clean; we have little on her.'

'I have plenty,' Osborne responded.

'Like what?' Ahmed asked.

'My files are fairly thick on everyone.'

'Yeah, I bet they are, you bastard,' a colleague interrupted.

'It's all part of the game, Mike, you know that.' Osborne grinned at him. 'Four, on the day the parliament provides the referendum's third reading, we initiate a leadership spill. The new prime minister then announces that the government will not support the Yes case.'

'That cuts Charlie from the election; he can't then vote against his legislation.'

'I suspect he may have other things on his mind than leadership,' Osborne suggested. 'So, this is the plan… are we agreed?'

They discussed the proposition for another twenty minutes, with most agreeing to tactics, before Osborne called an end to it. 'Right, folks, thanks for coming, and as agreed, I will keep you in the loop as we go about it.'

Ahmed asked, 'What have you got on the PM?'

Osborne had stood and was packing his files into his leather briefcase. 'There are travel entitlements associated with a staff member, and a rumour of a relationship.'

'That's old news.'

'There is a report of her buying property whilst travelling on government business, and I have a conflict of interest matter associated with the Americans.'

'Like what?'

'Nothing confirmed, yet.' Osborne straightened, glancing about his colleagues. 'There is a suggestion that a secret commission passed into her accounts over the decision on the armoured personnel carriers we're manufacturing.'

'Serious?' Ahmed stood by the door. 'Nancy would never do that sort of thing.'

'We are all human and sometimes, as you well know, Susie, temptation comes our way.'

'What's that supposed to mean?'

'All I'm saying is that temptation can come to us all, and Nancy is not a Christian.' Osborne glared at her, holding her eyes before reciting text. 'No temptation has overtaken you that is not common to man. God is faithful, and He will not let you be tempted beyond your ability, but with the temptation He will also provide the way of escape, that you may be able to endure it.'

Ahmed shook her head, bemused by Osborne's Machiavellian persona, then said, 'Just remember, Parker, the bible also says this: do not gloat when your enemy falls; when they stumble, do not let your heart rejoice. So, if you want this to happen, I would recommend you contain your enthusiasm.'

'I do not know what you mean.' Osborne walked past her, heading for his office.

CHAPTER

38

Cardinal Rosseau was in a funk; his muscles ached as he stretched them. It had been an uncomfortable night supporting Charlie Stevedore, but he suspected his subtle and careful counselling may have brought the man around to the orthodoxy of treating life as sacrosanct. The terrible fact Stevedore had no control over the life or death decision on his daughter helped weaken the impasse between them.

He had spent the night talking and quoting scriptures whenever Stevedore needed encouragement, and as it progressed, the miracle of knowing life was yet to leave his daughter. The pacing politician and the supportive cardinal had drunk coffee and laughed a few times, but were nervous about the next time a medical staffer would come to address them. Each time the door opened more positive news came, and as dawn approached, they were advised that the patient was coping well and it was time for a discussion about what to do next.

Stevedore knew he needed a court order to override his son-in-law's advice, and now he must do all he could to allow the surgical team to deliver on their promise of treating Vikki to repair the damage her body had suffered.

Rosseau believed he had done enough, and it was time for him to leave and allow the attorney general to do what he had to do to save his daughter. He said his goodbyes and promised to drop by later in the day. He blessed Stevedore and left for his accommodation, picking up a taxi at the Commercial Road rank. The cardinal directed the Indian driver to his accommodation, a room provided by the nearby Park Hyatt whenever a distinguished guest of the church was visiting St Patrick's Cathedral.

Once in his room, Rosseau kicked off his shoes, changing into his leisure outfit, then moved to the desk to check his emails. He then rang the Vatican to update progress, and when he mentioned to the Holy Father's assistant that developments were being made, he transferred him through to the Pope.

'I think we are making progress, Holy Father,' Rosseau said. 'I spent the night with the attorney general and he seems to be wavering on whether to bring forward the legislation.'

'This is good news, is it not?'

'I'm not sure; politics is played hard here. I'm uncertain whether the prime minister is supportive of our position.'

Caspian released a hollow laugh. 'Politics in the antipodes would not be as harsh or coarse as those in the home of Machiavelli, surely?'

'They would like us to apply greater pressure to the prime minister so that she responds in the opposite direction and brings on the vote.'

The Holy Father paused for a moment. 'How strange. If they legalise end of life killing, then the church's entire structure is under threat, as we no longer have a place in that policy discussion.'

'Holy Father; that talk is a little extreme, don't you think?'

'If we lose this debate, then the dominos will begin to fall elsewhere. Other western countries will follow the precedent for that, I'm positive. No doubt America will not be far behind. This thinking will then spread into the developing world, and they will question our presence as the moral leader in those countries. Our influence in most countries will then be jeopardised, and it will compromise our revenue model. We have to stop it, Morris.'

'The attorney general is coming back to our thinking.' Rosseau ran his fingers through his hair. 'His daughter is under medical care at the moment; he is battling over life and death decisions with his son-in-law. He now sees the connection between his own case and the unregulated use of the death wish, with families keen to end the life of a loved one.'

'You have a way with words, Morris; very floral this morning,' Caspian said. 'You just need to make sure it happens. When will you know?'

'Days, I would reckon. There is a political wave washing through the polity at the moment. It seems there may be significant changes to the shape of the government.'

'A change of leader?'

'Could very well be.' Rosseau paused. 'Have you considered what your plans will be for me when I get back?'

'No, why would I be considering your position?'

'You advised me before coming out that there would be opportunities for me in the future.'

'And there will be, but not right at this moment. Morris, you don't expect some sort of payoff for going to Australia?'

Rosseau considered the words before responding. 'Holy Father, you were at pains to tell me that this assignment was important and you held a positive outcome as the benchmark toward an appointment.'

'I don't recall making any promises.'

'Bertolli is retiring in six months.'

'He is younger than you.'

'Nevertheless, he is retiring from his position and I would like to be considered for it.' Caspian didn't respond as he considered the statement. 'Holy Father?'

'Yes, I'm here,' Caspian snapped. 'You don't expect to replace Bertolli as president, do you?'

'I only wish to serve, Holy Father.'

'You want to be second in charge?'

'There is a viable vacancy and I have the capability and experience to fill it.'

'They didn't pick you, Morris, when do you reckon you might get over it?'

'This has nothing to do with the election,' Rosseau said, the firmness in his tone deepening. 'It has a lot to do with ethics and keeping promises.'

'You are kidding me, are you not?' Caspian smiled the words. 'You cannot expect me to appoint you to the second highest position in the Vatican and not have you drooling for my job.'

Rosseau thought about this for a moment. 'I suppose you can do whatever you want; you are after all the Vicar of Christ, the pontiff of Rome, and the sovereign provided by our patrons Peter and Paul.'

'You know, Morris, when you say it like that, it seems to mean so much more.'

'I'm learning much from these politicians down here.'

'Oh yes, and what are they telling you?' Caspian sniffed.

'They tell me to be bold and forceful. They tell me to use whatever evidence I have to get what I want. Whatever it takes is the creed here.'

'Am I supposed to be concerned by this drivel?'

'Do you have anything to be concerned about?' Rosseau breathed into the phone.

There was no immediate response.

Caspian replied, 'Just get it done. Kill the bill, then we can talk about what might be an appropriate reward for you.'

'Holy Father, I will do what I have to do to get it done. I will then do whatever it takes to convince you of my ambitious plans for the organisation of the church.'

'We shall see.'

Caspian disconnected the phone before Rosseau had anything further to say.

The cardinal clicked through a few files and opened up the recording he had been sent. 'We shall see all right. Everyone will get to see this if I don't get what I want.'

CHAPTER

39

The meeting room table was was surrounded by various medical staff, invited to provide expert opinion if asked. Charlie Stevedore had been waiting for over thirty minutes and watched as they came into the room, chatting and laughing about the previous night's television programmes, their patient, or what they planned for the weekend. All seemed to carry plastic-lidded paper cups and didn't appear to care why the dishevelled man was sitting at the end of the table.

It was nearing nine o'clock when the well-dressed Vera Thompson entered, placing her files at a chair in the centre of the table, then advancing to Stevedore and grasping his hands in a warm welcome.

'I assume you are up-to-date with Vikki's condition? She has had a splendid night.'

'I know some things; a nurse has been keeping me informed.'

'They're good folks here and we support you. We will do what we can to save her and her baby,' Thompson said.

Stevedore felt uncomfortable under the intensity of her gaze, but reassured by her commitment.

'This meeting is to discuss the next steps, and hopefully we will have positive outcomes for you.'

'I appreciate your efforts,' Stevedore said.

As more personnel entered the room, Thompson resumed her seat, calling the meeting to order. 'It's nine o'clock so let's get started, is everyone here?'

'We are waiting on the husband, Mr Ferguson,' Chinh Nguyen advised, as she wheeled her chair into the table.

'All right, then. Okay, whilst we wait, can someone provide me with a bit of comfort regarding compliance with the Act if we are to ignore the husband's wishes?'

'I may help you with this issue,' Stevedore offered. All eyes switched to him.

Thompson responded with a smile, 'For those who don't know, this is Victoria's father, who just happens to be federal attorney general.' She laughed. 'If anyone should know the law, then it would have to be the chief law officer.'

A few colleagues whispered between each other and smiled as they took more interest in the man.

Stevedore opened a folder and flicked over several pages from a pad. 'While I was waiting for news earlier this morning, I researched the law surrounding these kinds of issues. According to the Medical Treatment Planning and Decisions Act, which I reckon passed in 2016, a medical team can respond to save a person's life, reduce pain or prevent serious damage to health.' Stevedore glanced up. 'I suspect that saving Vikki from dying comes into that category.' He gazed down at his notes again. 'The problem is that it provides a hierarchy of those who can give approval, and a spouse is ranked three places higher than a parent.'

'Is there anyone higher than a spouse?' Nguyen asked.

'Yes, an appointed decision maker or appointed guardian,' Stevedore responded. 'Both of which have to be court ordered to do so.'

'Are there any time limits before we have to decide?' Nguyen asked.

'None, just the time it takes to get a court order.'

Thompson leaned into the table. 'So, if the husband continues to withhold approval then the only thing we can do is get the patient's consent or a court order allowing us to act.'

'That's the way I interpret the Act.' Stevedore said.

'If we need a court order, how long would it take?' Thompson asked.

'I will seek an urgent sitting and have it by five this afternoon.'

'Hopefully, Mr Ferguson will provide approval.'

As if on cue, Ferguson knocked and entered the room, taking a chair at the table closest to the door. 'Sorry I'm late. I was held up.'

Stevedore checked his watch, then glowered at Ferguson at the opposite end of the table.

'Mr Ferguson.' Thompson formalised her voice. 'This meeting is to discuss the current state of your wife's health and to determine treatment. Are you in a position to make these decisions now?'

'Sure, how is Vikki?'

'After ceasing resuscitation last night, your wife has continued to breathe unassisted and is progressing well. In fact, well enough for tests and readiness for surgery.'

'Why would we be going into surgery?'

'Although Victoria remains critical, we consider her state to be good enough for surgery to help with recovery and ensure she continues responding to care,' Thompson advised.

'Why should that be an issue? My instructions were explicit. I asked you to manage her pain but allow her to die.'

Stevedore pushed his seat back and crossed his legs, not unnoticed by Ferguson.

'As a medical team, we believe we can save your wife. We also believe we have even-money odds on saving your unborn child.' Thompson said.

'I thought I made it clear last night, and indeed, I recall signing documents we should withhold treatment. Now, I'm a little surprised that my wishes are not being met.'

'Why do you want to kill Vikki?'

Stevedore's words hung like a black cloud over the meeting. Ferguson shifted in his chair and glanced at Thompson, who returned his gaze.

After a few moments, Ferguson cleared his throat and said, 'Vikki has always implied that if ever a situation eventuated where we face this very decision, she wanted to die with dignity.'

'That's bullshit,' Stevedore thundered, thrusting back into the table and slapping it.

'Mr Stevedore, please.' Thompson held up her hand and said, 'Let's remain civil during these discussions, out of respect for Victoria.'

'Why should you be concerned, anyway?' queried Ferguson, staring at Stevedore. 'This is what you want.'

'Don't verbal me, boy.'

'You are part of the government about to legislate euthanasia rights, and here we have the perfect case for doing so. Now you're ducking for cover.'

Stevedore stretched out his arms along the table, his hands seeking help. 'We have a chance to save her. Why are you not letting her live?' The impassioned father's plea touched most around the table, but not Ferguson.

'Because, she doesn't want it.'

'Mr Ferguson,' Thompson interrupted. 'There is a strong chance your wife can survive the operation and indeed recover to live a full and healthy life.'

'Possibility,' Ferguson responded.

'It provides challenges for us, but we're convinced we can give her a fighting chance.'

Ferguson sat back in his chair, and leaning on his left elbow, he rubbed his face, stroking his unshaven jaw, as if pondering the advice.

'Doug, please.' Stevedore interrupted his thinking. 'We have this chance, this open window of opportunity to save her. Surely, we should try everything we can.'

Ferguson glared back down the table and considered Stevedore's statement for a few moments. 'Nah, it's not what she wants.' He then glanced at Thompson. 'Are we done?'

Taken aback, Thompson straightened. 'Yes, we are.'

'Then I might go have a coffee.' He then pushed back his chair and left a stunned medical team.

A few moments after the glass door clattered closed, Stevedore broke the silence. 'Now you know why I can't stand that man.'

Thompson turned to him. 'It's not for us to pass judgment on anyone, Minister, but if you want to save your daughter, then I suspect you need a court order, pronto.'

'Best I get moving then.' Stevedore stood.

'Mr Stevedore.' Doctor Nguyen stood and faced him. 'I cannot overstate the importance of you getting this court order to us as quickly as possible. Your daughter's life depends on it, because without it we cannot provide treatment other than pain prevention.'

'I understand.' Stevedore offered his hand as he passed her, and she grasped it.

'Let me walk with you, please, if I may.' Thompson opened the door for him, then glanced over her shoulder at the rest of the staff. 'I'll be back in a few minutes to go over plans and after-surgery care.'

They strolled to the elevator and Thompson pushed the down button, opening the doors of an empty waiting elevator. 'I'll come down with you.'

Stevedore stood on the opposite side of the large elevator and considered the surgeon as they descended. 'You really think we can save her?'

'If we are in surgery this afternoon, then yes.'

Stevedore gazed to his feet and as the elevator bounced to a stop at the ground floor, he asked, 'This new treatment, will it work?'

'I have been dedicated to this procedure since being motivated by a surgeon many years ago. She was a burns specialist and took risks to not only save her patients but also allow healing that didn't scar as much as using skin grafts. This surgery for your daughter will work, I'm sure of it.'

As they left the elevator, others busy to get to their destination entered. They walked side by side toward the front entrance, where Stevedore asked, 'Is your team skilled enough?'

Thompson stopped and touched Stevedore's arm, stroking it as he also stopped and glanced at her. 'Let me quote my inspiration,

Fiona Wood, *"Do I think I'm a genius? No, I don't. Do I work in an environment where we have the capacity for genius? Yes, I do".* She taught me, mentored me, and inspired me to change lives. I will make sure your daughter recovers… believe me.'

Stevedore's eyes welled, and Thompson, recognising a father's distress, moved closer and hugged him. He accepted the warmth of her comfort, which allowed him to relax the tension from his body. After a few moments he straightened, recomposed, and she touched his face and smiled.

'Trust me… if you get my approval, I will ensure your daughter has a chance.' Stevedore took her hand from his face and kissed her fingers, then left.

On the street the rush of people confused Stevedore, and he wondered for a moment what he should be doing. Go home to freshen up or hit the office to get court approval? As he jumped into a waiting cab, he decided that acting to get approval for the medical team was his priority.

He prodded and swiped his phone until it connected, then issued instructions. 'Ensure there is an application for me to sign when I get to the office. I'm stuck in roadworks at the Domain, but I should be there in fifteen minutes.'

Stevedore tossed the phone aside and gazed out into the trees and traffic in St Kilda Road as the taxi stopped and started crawling its way to the city. The world was busy around him, yet he felt as if his own world had stopped, and he cared little for the bustle outside. His immediate concern was his daughter and doing what he could to save her.

The Sikh driver pulled away from the congestion and began trailing through side streets and lanes to escape the traffic. He emerged in South Melbourne and turned into Clarendon Street to take him to Bourke with his downcast passenger in the back.

As Stevedore laboured to leave the taxi, the driver transacted the fare on his credit card. His legs seemed too tired to swing from the car and he trapped foot under the front seat. He swayed back in and tugged his foot free, and then sat with legs out, waiting for his receipt. The taxi driver grasped his outstretched hand as he retrieved his credit card. 'In life and in death, peace lives with those who attain their guru.'

Stevedore left his hand in the soft clasp of the driver and gazed at his eyes, feeling comfort in their blackness. 'Thank you,' he said as he moved out.

'Go in peace, my brother.'

Stevedore closed the door and walked across the forecourt into the lobby, jumping into an empty elevator and taking the extended trip to his office on the fifty-first floor.

Smethers, already alerted by the security in the lobby that the minister was on his way, was waiting by the elevators, surprised to see the crumpled man step out.

'How are you feeling, boss?'

'I've had better days.' Stevedore brushed past, seeking the sanctuary of this office.

'We're just completing the application now, and I've instructed Debra Dally from Gamble Tate and Scholz to present it within the hour.'

'Do we know who will hear it?'

'No news, but Deb will get it through.'

Stevedore collapsed into his chair, pleased with the advice, and sighed as he dropped his head into a supporting fist, his elbow resting on the desk as he struggled to put his feet on the corner.

Smethers left him.

Stevedore gazed out the window to nothing in particular, reflecting on the last twenty-four hours, feeling bewildered by his son-in-law's attitude. He questioned his own thinking and wondered if he was doing the right thing. His gaze came back into the room and followed the line of his sideboard, settling on a white-framed photo of his wife. He looked at her and held his gaze on her smiling face and intense eyes. He loved the photo because it caught every aspect of her character, especially the lively nature of her eyes... he missed her.

'Am I doing it right, Steph?' Stevedore rasped. 'Should I fight or let her go?'

He dropped his feet off the desk and sat up in the chair, resting his elbows on his knees as he rolled his chair closer to the photograph.

'I know what you said, but this is different, surely. We can't let her go. It's different from what happened to you. We have a chance to help her. We can't let her go just because we suffered with you.' Stevedore knuckled a tear from his cheek. 'I mean, I tried my best. I've almost got the legislation up, but this catastrophe has changed my mind. That punk son-in-law wants to finish her. You were right about him and now he wants to kill our baby.'

He stretched and went to the window, crossing his arms, watching the traffic below.

'If I support euthanasia, then I'm allowing family like Ferguson to have a voice, but I can't… and I won't. This is different, and you would support me. I feel terrible about it. I'm conflicted about it all and wonder if I'm doing the right thing.'

Stevedore turned and sat on the windowsill, gazing at the photo.

'I know it was important to you I achieve legal euthanasia but, Stephanie, what has happened over the last few days has worried me and altered my thinking.'

He stretched over to the photograph, picked it up and drew it close.

'I hope you can forgive me.'

CHAPTER

40

Dennis Sadler met his producers every day, ninety minutes before his four o'clock nationwide syndicated radio show. Today did not differ from any other day.

Producers and production assistants were waiting for the celebrated star who commanded a significant lead in ratings after over twenty years behind the microphone. He was the feared talkback host sniffing out impropriety in politics and business. A call from Dennis Sadler sent chills up any spine.

Sadler was well read across most policy issues, a student of world affairs with an opinion on everything, and he was unafraid to provide it. The rakish loud-mouth treasured nothing more than bringing the ego blustering, self-important to their metaphorical knees with his questioning. He commanded a significant say in national politics, having changed the mood of the nation on many issues in the past.

He swung into the exclusive meeting room, reserved for his use. A large timber table and chairs stood at one end of the long room, a lounge and bar paraphernalia at the other. Tall lush plants separated the two areas of the room and a large wooden shelved divider displaying award trophies and statues. The bar had been installed so he could host his once legendary after-show drinks and raging late-night ratings success parties, which became less frequent as age caught up.

Staff stiffened as they saw the familiar figure swagger into the room, brushing past the greenery with a swathe of files and papers under his arm, just like any busy executive. His pink jacket, a startling contrast against his black shirt and trousers, added to his charismatic grooming; everything was in its place.

'What have we got today, are we bashing the wicked witch again?'

The executive producer cleared her throat. 'We are.' She smiled as if about to share a secret. 'We've had tremendous news fall into our lap this morning.'

'Oh, please, do tell.' Sadler dumped his files and papers, sitting at the head of the table in a gold leather chair made for him. He waved over a staff member who had followed him into the room with a small tray of peppermint tea and a variety of Turkish delight; he insisted that these helped prepare his voice.

The executive producer slid an envelope along the table to Sadler, who stopped it with a finger, then emptied the contents onto the table. Large black and white photos fell out, scattering around him, along with what appeared to be a typed report.

'The prime minister was in Bathurst five weeks ago. She visited a local irrigation scheme and announcing the government's new regional water policy.'

'Yeah, so what? So long as there's no fracking out that way, I couldn't care less.'

'It's not what she did,' the producer smiled, 'it's who she took with her.'

Sadler thanked the staffer for pouring his tea and took a quick sip as he studied the grainy black and white photographs, poking and prodding so he could see what they presented. As he reached the third photo he stopped, his cup of tea held in the air, as if stunned. 'Is that what I think it is?'

'We think it might be.'

'She could not be so stupid, surely?'

'We think she might be.' The producer was grinning even wider. 'Look at the next shot.'

They entranced Sadler, placing his cup back into its saucer, paying little attention to it. He slipped to the next photograph, his mouth falling agape. 'This is unbelievable. Where did you get them?'

'We've engaged a pap for three months, and this is the best he has done so far.'

'Why did it take so long to get them to me?' Sadler glanced up.

The producer shifted in her chair. 'We have been completing research and freedom of information requests.'

'Who is she?'

'Her chief of staff.'

'Really?' Sadler examined the other photos. 'How long has this been going on?'

'She came to her staff about three months ago, she's a journo from over in the west. She has an excellent reputation for writing on government policy and has helped to expose various scandals within the W.A. parliament. Ironically, around the misuse of travel allowances.'

'Did you link anything to the prime minister?'

'We believe we have.' The producer read from notes. 'Since joining the PM's staff as a media adviser, they promoted her to chief of staff. She now travels with the PM. What used to be the senior media adviser's role is now managed by the chief of staff.'

'So, what?'

'We've crossed referenced travelling with government business and we have discovered times when the PM and her chief travelled separately to a Queensland resort. We have them at the same place, but with only one expenditure item incurred for accommodation.'

'Nooo, really?' Sadler couldn't believe what he was hearing, shaking his head.

'Yes. A recent declaration on her parliamentary interests identifies the purchase of a new investment property in Trinity Beach, and when we checked the title, it's in two names.'

'Don't tell me,' Sadler chortled. 'The PM's and her chief of staff?'

'Exactly.'

Sadler leered at the photos again. 'Stuff me.'

'No other media outlet seems to have picked it up.'

'The husband must know?'

'Maybe he does.' The producer slid another page to Sadler. 'He's been living at Kirribilli in the guest wing for the last two months and has filed for divorce.'

'You're kidding me. Why doesn't anyone else know?'

'We picked it up from a source in Treasury.'

Sadler smirked, leaning on an elbow and running a finger across his lips as if satisfied after a moment of pleasure. He examined the photographs again.

'Why the car park?'

'It's outside. The thrill of being caught. Who hasn't wished to have sex on the bonnet of a car?'

'I could be so lucky.'

'Who knows? Maybe her staffer is a crazed sexual animal, or maybe the PM just likes younger women. What we know is that we have compelling evidence of her misusing government allowances, which in the past was a hanging offence.'

Sadler smiled. 'For a minister, maybe; a prime minister is a little different.'

'How do you want to use it?' The producer was keen to know if they needed to amend the run sheet for the programme.

Sadler collected the photographs, shuffling them together before going through them again, stalling on one rather explicit print.

'We can't use the photographs right now; maybe we can later if we need to. Whilst salacious, I don't think it fair we should expose her… excuse the pun.'

The producer was disappointed and glanced at a colleague who shrugged.

'We can use the travel allowance fraud. Once we expose her for that crime, and get her on record denying it, we can then tie in the property purchase. The last step, if we need it, is to threaten to reveal her relationship with her staffer, exposing her sham marriage.'

'Should we use our friends in the newspapers for an exclusive story, then go hard in the afternoon once they have denied the early media onslaught?'

'What's your preference?' Sadler asked.

'We screw her hard ourselves and ignore anyone else.'

Sadler laughed at the turn of phrase. 'Nothing she isn't already used to.' He leaned back in the chair, glancing at the ceiling. 'Let me talk to my contact in government and we shall hatch a plan. Well done, Lucy. This is terrific.'

CHAPTER

41

Stevedore's office door opened and Julia Smethers poked her head through to check on her boss and determine whether he could meet an unexpected caller.

'Minister?' she queried as she stepped into the office, swinging the door closed as she moved over to the desk. 'Are you okay?'

Stevedore glanced up from his thoughts, then rocked back in his chair, a shadow of his customary charismatic enthusiasm. 'I'm fine, what do you have for me?'

'I have Commander Hanrahan to see you, are you up for it?'

'Sure.' Stevedore straightened, washing over a return to formality. 'Show him in and perhaps offer him a cup of tea.'

'I already have and he didn't want one,' Smethers joked. 'Not sure I want to share my somewhat poor catering skills with the federal police.'

Stevedore smiled as he watched her disappear.

'Minister, thanks for seeing me without notice, but I thought I would speak to you about developments in the case.'

'You are very welcome, Commander. What can you tell me?'

'We have three boys in custody.'

'Already?' Stevedore was surprised and excited by the news.

'They're not the sharpest tools in the shed. We expect them to make full admissions.'

'What can you tell me about them?' Stevedore waved an offer to sit, but the police officer shook a decline.

'This is why I'm here.' Hanrahan opened his compendium and flicked through his legal pad. 'We have brought in for questioning a Ricardo Ortega, who we think may help us with our inquiries, and I was wondering if you would like to attend to observe the initial interview.'

'Why would I do that?'

'Ortega has a corporate structure in the wholesale distribution of various narcotics, and it seems he is the boss of these three thugs we suspect may be the offenders for your daughter's assault. How is she, by the way?'

'She is due for surgery later today… that is, if I get a judge to approve an intervention. I've been sitting around like a shag on a rock waiting for news.'

'Not sure what I can say about that news, Minister, other than to hope she does well.'

'Perhaps you can tell me then, if she dies before medical treatment, can we can upgrade the charge to murder?'

'We would consider it, sure.'

'What do you need to do to make it happen?'

'We would need to determine whether the assault caused the death or through the medical care.'

'She wouldn't be in hospital hanging on, like she is, without having been assaulted by these thugs.'

'As I said, we would need causation to make a murder change stick. Otherwise, we're looking at assault causing death.'

Stevedore turned away, got up from his chair and walked to the window, saying to no one, 'I want to hang the bastards.'

'Minister, the local boys will do what they can to get the outcomes we need, and they seem to be doing a magnificent job. We have Ortega in for questioning. It seems he has crossed the jurisdiction line on various drug matters, which means we're involved.'

'Why do you want me along?'

'There appears to be a connection to your family with the drugs.'

Stevedore spun, aroused by the statement. 'What do you mean?'

'I mean nothing other than that our initial investigations have linked him to a joint bank account your daughter has with her husband, which has been transferring money to him.' Hanrahan tightened his lips. 'It may mean nothing, as he buys and sells a lot of merchandise, but we thought you may like to observe when we talk to him.'

'Conflict of interest?'

'Sir, I considered that position, and yes, we could be accused of having some, but I believe there is none.'

'What do you want me to do?'

'Simply observe. I want to make sure you are aware of our process, and that it is transparent so there is no blow back on us, or indeed you.'

'Is he under arrest?'

'No. He is cooperating, and we have him in the Latrobe Street office waiting to be interviewed.'

'Should it not be state police handling this?'

'As I said, he's not under consideration in your daughter's case. This is a federal matter.'

'Sure, so when do you want to do it?'

'I'm thinking right now, if you have time.'

Stevedore checked his watch as he moved back to his desk, prodding a button and bringing Smethers on the line. 'Jules, I'm going out for an hour, or so, let me know when the injunction is available.'

'Yes, Minister.'

Stevedore grabbed his jacket and swung it on as he led Hanrahan out through the direct access security door into the elevator lobby, avoiding the primary office.

Twenty minutes later, after a brisk walk between buildings, they were standing behind a window in a darkened room watching Rikki Ortega casually cleaning his fingernails, unaware of who was behind the mirrored glass.

Stevedore declined the offer of coffee, taking a raised seat at the rear of the room behind seated police officers as he observed

Hanrahan enter the room, sitting opposite Ortega to begin questioning. An officer flicked a recording switch, engaging separate audio and videoed recordings.

'It's 3.37, on the twenty-eighth of November, and I am Commander Peter Hanrahan, badge number 5379, and I am accompanied by Detective Sergeant Owen Carmichael, badge number 9682. For the record, could you please state your name and address?'

'Ricardo Ortega and I live at eighty-five Electra Street in Williamstown.'

'Thank you, Mr Ortega. You have agreed to this interview after we contacted you requesting you to present yourself earlier today, is that correct?'

'I've no issue being here today to answer questions. I'd like to be outta here 4.30 if I can. I've a dinner date I can't miss, if ya know what I mean,' Ortega grinned.

'Please answer the question, Mr Ortega. You are here today, voluntarily, yes?'

'Yeah.'

'You have had your rights explained to you and you have waived your right to legal representation or having a support person present, is that correct?'

'I've nothin' to fear. I'm here to help youse.' Ortega glared at Hanrahan, then added, 'Ya believe that, don'tcha?'

'We thank you for your help on this matter, Mr Ortega.'

'Rikki, please.' Ortega leaned back with a swagger, still grinning. He slung his arm over the back of the chair, crossing his legs.

'Mr Ortega, we have statements from Michael Cole, Thomas Haslam and Rocco Galatea given to state police suggesting they work for you, is this correct?'

'I wouldn't say they work for me.'

'What would you say?'

'They hang around. I'm like an older brother.'

'Do they do anything for you, anything at all?'

'Like work, ya mean?'

'Yes.'

'Nah.'

'So, when they hang around a bit, what do they do?'

'Let's see,' Ortega gazed to the ceiling. 'They clean, they drive, they cook sometime, maybe, too often.'

'Do they do deliveries for you?'

'Depends.'

'On what?'

'What ya think they're deliverin'.'

'Does the name Victoria Stevedore mean anything to you?'

'Nah.'

Hanrahan studied the smirking criminal. 'Nothing at all?'

'Never heard of her.'

'Strange you would say that.' Hanrahan referred to his notes. 'It seems you have been taking money from her for around eighteen months now.'

'That's crap.' Ortega's demeanour tightened. 'I just told ya, I've never heard of her. Who is she?'

'Ms Stevedore is a victim of a serious criminal assault. State police are holding your mates on the allegation it involved them. They have made admissions about meeting her on a train.'

Ortega uncrossed his legs and sat forward, resting his elbows on the table. 'I know nothin' about that.'

'It seems you might know something. There is a financial link between you and the victim of this heinous crime.'

'Know nothin'.' He shook his head. 'Don't know whatcha talkin' about.'

'You know nothing about a car parked outside your house used in the crime that threatens the life of Ms Stevedore, which may proceed to murder charges?'

'No friggin' way.' Ortega fidgeted.

'You didn't direct your mates, who you say hang around, to dispose of the car and burn it?'

'Nah.'

'You know nothing of your mates having a few drinks and something to eat a few nights back in Yarraville?'

Ortega knew there would be CCTV footage at the Railway Hotel. 'I had a bite to eat and a few drinks with them the other night, yeah.'

'Are you aware your mates met Victoria Stevedore on the train to Williamstown that night?'

'Nah. Who they meet or talk to has nothin' to do with me.'

'Do you know a Douglas Ferguson?'

Stevedore leaned forward in his seat.

'Nah.'

'You don't know Douglas Ferguson?' Hanrahan's cynical tone gave away the fact that he might know the connection.

'Who?'

'Douglas Ferguson, of Aitken Street, Williamstown.'

'Ferguson… Ferguson… The name sounds familiar, but I don't know it.'

'I suspect you know Doug Ferguson.'

'Doug? I thought you said it was Douglas.'

'Douglas, Doug, Dougie… do you know him?'

'Dougie Ferguson? Yeah, I know Dougie. Everyone knows Dougie, a teacher, I think.'

'How well do you know him?'

Stevedore leaned his elbows on his knees as he watched.

'He's a teacher, I told ya.'

'Is he a client?'

Ortega didn't answer, turning away.

'It is our assertion that you know Douglas Ferguson, and you may have had a commercial relationship with him.'

'What? What's a commercial relationship?'

'He's your client. One of your dealers.'

'Hey look, I don't do drugs. Never have, never will.'

'Your mates say he owes you money.'

Ortega didn't respond.

Stevedore cupped his chin, fingers tapping his lips.

'Are you aware that Douglas Ferguson is the husband of Victoria Stevedore?'

Ortega's eyes widened, and he glanced up at Hanrahan. He licked his lips.

'Nah.'

Hanrahan didn't respond. Ortega was becoming more anxious, piecing together the information he had been told.

'I wanna leave now,' Ortega said. 'Are ya gonna charge me with anythin'?'

'You're free to go, Mr Ortega, but I must tell you, we consider you a prime suspect in this case, and we are close to confirming your involvement. I also advise you that Ms Stevedore is near to death. If she dies, you and your mates will face serious jail time.'

Stevedore whispered, 'Should be hanged.'

Ortega stood to leave. 'I had nothin' to do with what happened. Ferguson may owe me, but it's nothin' to do with her. Fact is, it's nothin' to do with youse.'

'Mr Ortega, you are implicated by virtue of your relationship with the boys in custody and Doug Ferguson. Anything that can mitigate your involvement would be helpful to our investigation and may help you.'

'What does mitigreat mean?'

'Mitigate, it means lessen your direct involvement.'

Ortega lingered by the door. 'That shithead Ferguson owes me money, but it has nothin' to do with what those morons did to the girl.'

'What do you know about it?'

'Nothin',' Ortega said. 'I've witnesses and it's nothin' to do with me.'

'We shall see.' Hanrahan nodded to his colleague to release the door. 'Stay around, Mr Ortega. You don't want me hunting you.'

Ortega glanced back at the commander, his bravado much feebler than it was. 'Ya got me number. Use it.'

'Interview ended.'

Stevedore sat back in his chair and considered what he'd witnessed, his thoughts scrambled and unsure. Was Vikki a victim of payback? Had this got anything to do with Ferguson's wish to turn her machines off? He sat reflecting until disturbed by Hanrahan, who switched on the overhead light as he entered the viewing room, taking a seat next to him.

'It's a tenuous link between Ortega and your daughter, but we almost have him implicating your son-in-law dealing drugs. He certainly owes him money. This could be the reason they assaulted her.'

'As payback?'

'Maybe, we just don't have enough to confirm motive.'

Stevedore didn't respond; he just shook his head, then asked, 'Will you investigate him?'

Hanrahan glanced at him. 'Yes, we'll be taking a specific interest in Ferguson and seek to learn more about this drug cell.'

'Do you think he might be connected to the assault against Vikki?'

'Not sure.' Hanrahan shrugged his shoulders. 'I'm thinking not. I suspect it could be a case of wrong place at the wrong time, and the rest is just coincidence.'

'Why then would he want to end her life?'

It surprised Hanrahan. 'Does he want to do that?'

'It seems he does. He has refused her medical treatment.'

'Lucky we don't have your euthanasia laws enacted, otherwise he might have tainted our inquiry with too much enthusiasm.' Hanrahan twisted his face, raising his eyebrows.

Stevedore gnawed at his bottom lip. 'Yeah, lucky.' His phone buzzed. Excusing himself, he looked at the message advising that the injunction was successful.

'I have to go… keep me in the loop.'

It was nearing four o'clock and Parker Osborne had his feet on the corner of his desk. He was working his way through a bag of English caramels, his go to sweet when he had ministerial briefings to read. Eight silver wrappings were strewn over his writing pad, with his jaw showing signs of wear from sucking and chewing. He was reading a confidential report on the use of parliamentary allowances by members of parliament, which he often reviewed to keep tabs on colleagues. He wasn't concerned about the opposition, although he monitored their leadership group's expenditure; no, he was more interested in the spending habits of his own party colleagues. Everyone had a blemish, some more than others. He wanted dirt on them so he could use the information to influence someone when he needed to.

'I have Dennis Sadler on line one for you, Treasurer,' a staffer's voice announced, and Osborne picked up the receiver.

'Cutting it fine, aren't you, Dennis? You're on air shortly.'

'Plenty of time; we have to get through the news first. I wanted to ask you a question.'

'Okay, go ahead.'

'We agreed to gain relevant negative information on the PM. I just wanted to know how that was going?'

'I'm working through travel allowances as we speak.'

'You'll need more than hotel bills to bring her down. Do you have any cabinet news?'

'What do you think will fly? The euthanasia thing is live.'

'That will not turn the polls, that's for your lot to work out between you. No, I need more than that. Are you having any energy policy discussions she is for or against?'

'We discussed fracking a few weeks back, but the cabinet didn't get to a decision.'

'Fracking is one of my issues. The topic is hot as hell out in the regions.'

Osborne kicked himself off the desk, swivelling his chair so that he could scribble notes. 'For or against?'

'Against, of course. I've got them jumping out in the regions. They will bring down the state government if it tries to approve licences.'

'There's nothing wrong with fracking. This water quality thing is a myth.'

'You know that, I know that, but I need to get them fired up over something, so when I began talking about soil and water degradation my ratings surged.'

'Why are ratings that important to you?'

'Treasurer, you know it's only ever about the money.' Osborne thought he could hear the cheesy grin. 'The higher my ratings, the greater the share of revenue.'

'Are you for or against on land gas extraction?'

'No different to offshore extraction, as far as I'm concerned, but I love the word fracking. When I say it, the cash registers ring for me.'

'What do you need?'

'Just the date of the meeting, who said what, and any decision made, that ought to do it.'

'There was no decision. We talked about it in September. The mining minister supported it, and so did the AG. The PM didn't have a view, which is her normal position on policy.'

'Thanks for that.' Sadler was winding up, wanting to get to why he rang. 'Look, just quickly, have you heard any scuttlebutt about the

PM and a new love in her life?'

Osborne flopped back into his chair, considering the question. 'I know she is having problems with her husband, something about needing a change.'

'I have photos of her in a loving embrace… well, no, that's wrong, I have her having sex in a car park.'

'You're kidding me?'

'No,' Sadler was firm. 'I want to know if you want me to use them?'

'What are they like?'

'Leaves nothing to the imagination, I can assure you.'

'Do you know who she's with?'

'Yes, but at this stage, I don't want to disclose who.'

'What do you want from me?'

'I want you to tell me if I should use them when the opportunity arises,' Sadler's voice smiled. 'Be aware, I'm recording your response.'

Osborne checked himself, thought through the options, then said, 'Hell, yes.'

'Said with the gusto and confidence of a genuine leader.'

Osborne smirked. 'Why, thank you, Dennis. Let's hope we get there soon.'

'We should get you there on the fracking issue. We won't need evidence of her misuse of travel claims. I'll use this new stuff on her to get rid of her, if I have to. Can I use you in about thirty minutes to talk about fracking policy?'

'Talk to me about the expense of the referendum, then toss in a throwaway line and I'll dither about it.'

'Excellent. My producer will call you soon.' Sadler's line went dead, leaving a beaming Osborne dangling the handset from his hand.

'It's beginning to look a lot like Christmas,' he sang as he replaced the phone, scooping his lolly papers into the bin. 'Kaitlyn?' he bellowed as he dropped the bin under his desk.

'Yes, boss?'

'The Sadler people will call soon; put them through to me when they do. In the meantime, can you put your hands on the cabinet briefing paper on land gas extraction? You had better send in Michael.'

'Will do. Cardinal Rosseau called, asking for you, when you were on the phone.'

'Can you get him for me?'

Osborne scribbled discussion prompts to prepare for his interview, as his political adviser joined him, sitting at the desk.

Osborne didn't look up. 'What should the key message be when talking with Sadler about the referendum funding?'

'It's very expensive, but necessary.' The adviser started reeling off points and Osborne wrote them down. 'The change in the constitution is necessary. Democracy is expensive. This is the prime minister's decision. There has been disagreement within cabinet about the expense. You can't reveal who supports, or who is against it, but… and always pause after the but, the PM requires you to do your job as directed.'

'That's a little close to the line, don't you think?' said Osborne, completing the notes.

'If you want a leadership spill, then you have to put it out there that you're against the referendum, and so are others, but not say so directly.'

'Okay. What do I say about fracking?'

'Why is that an issue? You favour it.'

'Yes, but Sadler will raise it, and I want to throw Pasco under the bus.'

'Then say nothing.'

Osborne glanced up, frowning. 'How does that hurt her?'

'Silence is golden. You don't want to attack her; you need to show you support her.'

'I don't.'

'You know that. I know that. Your colleagues know that. But the great unwashed don't, and they prefer loyalty.'

Osborne grinned as he chewed on his pen, gazing at his adviser. 'Nice one.'

Michael had been working with ministers and members of parliament for longer than Osborne had been in parliament, working his way through four leadership changes. He knew what the triggers were.

'We want the caucus to come to you when she is under siege and ask you to lead.' He tapped a pen on his pad. 'We want the media to report that you are a reluctant candidate and you support Pasco, as any loyal deputy does. We also need to confirm you will accept the leadership baton if they pass it to you. We do not want you to be seen taking it.'

May returned to the office, a red manila folder in her hand. 'The cardinal is on line three and this is the note you asked for.' She placed the file before him and departed.

'Thanks, Michael.'

'You know what to do. Be strong on finance and fumble over discussions about the PM,' Michael said, as he left the treasurer to his call.

'Morris, hello. How are you?'

'Rung out. I was up most of the night with Minister Stevedore; his daughter will go into surgery soon, in God's will.'

'That's nice. What did you want to talk to me about?'

'The Holy Father wants to get involved with the decision about the referendum.'

Osborne shook his head and straightened in his chair. 'He what? He doesn't get involved in laws of countries.'

'He wants to talk to the prime minister and convince her not to go ahead with the referendum.'

'That's not the deal,' Osborne snapped. 'You're to speak with the PM, not the Pope. That intervention could change our entire strategy.'

'You think the Holy Father will say something ill-considered?'

'Not at all. But as the head of the Catholic Church he is almost royalty, and to request our prime minister to act for him may have her do it.'

'You said she hated the church.'

'She does, with a passion, but speaking with the Pope may convince her delaying the referendum and obfuscating.' Osborne combed his fingers through his hair. 'We don't want that. She must act against the church and allow the referendum to happen. Then we campaign against it and we kill this euthanasia bill forever.'

'After speaking with Stevedore last night, I'm not even sure he supports the bill anymore.'

Osborne flopped back into his chair. 'Why would you say that?'

'This business that is going on with his daughter has affected him.'

'Crumbs, she only has a few burns. What is his problem?'

'It concerns his daughter's treatment plan and approvals for medical care.'

'Stop worrying about Stevedore. He is out of the leadership picture now. For this leadership change to work, we need the PM to want this referendum, no matter what Charlie recommends.'

'What happens if the voters approve the referendum?'

'It won't get a majority of the states, that's why we have to kill it now. If we don't have a referendum now, it might get the Yes vote in the future, don't you see?'

'I do, but if the referendum passes, what then?'

'It won't get the Yes vote if the prime minister of Australia campaigns against it. That's what I will do, even if Charlie Stevedore campaigns for it. As prime minister, I will make sure it doesn't get up.'

The cardinal didn't respond as he thought through Osborne's comments. 'What happens if you don't win the leadership?'

'That ain't going to happen, I can assure you. I have an ace up my sleeve.'

'Like what?'

'We have evidence of the PM caught with her pants down, literally.'

'You would use that against her?' the cardinal queried.

'I won't, but the media will. All I will do is threaten her with it. If she doesn't do what I ask, then I will launch release. Scandal in government is never well received by the punters.'

'I'm confused. You said you would never use information against a politician because it would make you a criminal.'

Osborne laughed. 'That's the theory, but sometimes, when you're close to the holy grail, then you must act in your best interests.'

Rosseau didn't reply for a moment, thinking through his own options. 'You think this type of blackmail, threatening exposure, works?'

'Every time. Everywhere.'

'No matter the organisation?'

'The more political the better.' Osborne prodded down the line. 'Politicians make their own future and can't wait for events to happen, otherwise their ambitions pass them by. Just look at what happened to you.'

May walked into the office. Osborne waved her further in, nodding as if understanding what she wanted.

'What do you mean?'

'If you want the top job, Morris, you would have a dirt file on your competitor and you would use it.'

'If I had such a file now?'

'Too late now, because the Holy Father will not resign; the church has dealt with scandal in high places before, they are expert at it.' Osborne stood, wanting to end the call. 'But you could use any information you have to get what you want. Morris, I have to go; but please, get onto the PM, make sure you tell her in no uncertain terms that you want her to stop the referendum, and under no circumstances should you have the Pope call her.'

'I shall heed your advice, take care, my son.'

Osborne smiled at the blessing. 'You too, Your Eminence.'

Thirty-five minutes later Osborne took a call from the prime minister's chief of staff, Donna Kellaway.

'Treasurer.' Her tone clipped. Osborne readied himself for what vitriol could be coming. 'Did you think to reach out with us before doing the Sadler show?'

'I wasn't aware I needed to seek approval.'

'Normally, you don't, but we issued a directive after the PM was last on Sadler, declaring that this office should approve any future government appearances.'

'I must have missed it, are you concerned?'

'Are we concerned?' Kellaway asked, then fell silent for a moment as Osborne smirked. 'we have considered your comments as a declaration of leadership ambition, which is contrary to the agreement the PM made with you.'

'I wasn't aware Nancy was in the habit of sharing secrets with her staff.'

'I'm across everything the PM does, and I'm not happy with your comments.'

'Which ones? I thought I provided support for the government?'

Kellaway sighed. 'Your comment that the decision to fund the referendum was the prime minister's decision.'

'It was.'

'Only after cabinet approved it. You made it sound as if you do not agree with the referendum and the PM is pushing it through as her own policy, not the government's.'

'She forced the plebiscite without cabinet agreement, and now she is pushing the referendum for an amendment to the constitution with little support in the electorate, which, as you no doubt know, will damage our election prospects.'

'You bastard. You know that's not right.'

'Watch your tone there, Donna,' Osborne snapped. 'Is there anything else you wanted to say?'

'Where did Sadler get the information about the PM's travel?'

'Complete surprise to me, and I responded. Has she bought a Queensland condo? I didn't know.'

'I don't know either, and it doesn't matter, but you could have done better.'

'I said, I supported the prime minister with everything she does.'

'Yes, and by doing so you implied she is not doing a good job.'

'Is she doing a good job?' Osborne joked. 'I support the prime minister, and I will continue to say that.'

'Can you just get your lines clearer?'

'What like?'

'Drop this concept of democracy isn't cheap for starters, that implies the PM doesn't care about taxpayers and links with the travel rort story.'

'You want me to lie when I'm asked such things?'

'We will come hard on this story and kill it. We don't want you commenting on it any further, is that understood?' Kellaway sounded as if she was standing, shouting into the phone.

Osborne held the phone aside until it was clear to speak. 'You worry too much about these things. It won't be news tomorrow. I have heard something that might be.'

'What might that be.'

'Is the PM having an affair?' Kellaway didn't respond. 'Are you there?' Osborne asked after a momentary pause.

'What have you heard?' The response was quiet and sullen.

'Just that she may be throwing the leg over someone and she may have been caught out.'

'She's as straight as an arrow, as far as I know.'

The turn of phrase confused Osborne. 'Scout around and see what might be happening.'

'There is nothing happening.'

'Sadler may have something.'

There was no immediate response.

'What's he got?'

'I don't know, but he is certain it will be a scandal if he ever releases it. You may want to talk to him.'

'Just do what we ask,' Kellaway said, as the phone clicked dead.

Osborne checked the hand piece, surprised by the sudden disconnection, and called for May to join him.

'Kellaway used a term which seemed out of context… I wonder what you might think she meant?'

'That doesn't surprise me; she has strange tastes, that one. What did she say?'

'I was advising her of a potential scandal with the PM's extracurricular activities, and she said Pasco was as straight as an arrow. What do you think she meant?'

'Pasco is straight.'

Osborne laughed. 'Of course she is. She's married, and it seems she may be having an affair.'

'You know Kellaway is gay, don't you?'

'Gay?' Osborne asked. 'I thought she was bonking someone in the gallery and that's why she moved here.'

'She was, but it was a girl.'

Osborne raised his eyebrows and shook his head. 'Nothing ever surprises me in politics, but that little snippet has.' He glanced out the window for a moment. 'Why would a gay staffer want to reaffirm that her boss was straight, when I mentioned she might be having an affair?'

'Interesting question, do you want me to get down to gossip central and ask around?'

'Why don't we both go? I could do with a drink.'

'I'll just finish up and maybe we can have dinner together.' May chanced the suggestion.

'Sure,' Osborne smiled. 'I have strategies we can talk about; get Michael to come along as well.'

May bit her lip momentarily, then left. 'Okay, let's leave in around thirty minutes.'

The stiff evening breeze chilled Stevedore as he strode across the forecourt to the hospital entrance. He shrugged his shoulders, holding his jacket in front, unsure whether it was the wind or the circumstances he found himself in. Drained emotionally, he could feel his body ache as if responding to a heavy dose of exercise. A huge yawn wracked him as he waited in the elevator lobby, feeling a flush of tiredness as he dropped his head to the side wall of the jam-packed elevator bouncing its way up, releasing passengers at various levels until his turn.

'Professor Thompson has been expecting you, sir. Please make your way to her office at the end of the corridor,' Conan Stevens said, pointing the way.

Stevedore shuffled along the corridor, tapping on the open door. It energised him to see a beaming Vera Thompson stand and move to welcome him.

'I've been looking forward to seeing you since I took the call from your office.' The professor pecked him on the cheek, leading him to a lounge chair at the other end of her office. 'It's so exciting how your daughter is fighting so hard.'

'It's been exhausting. Is Ferguson here?' Stevedore asked, taking a seat in the soft leather chair and sinking into its peaceful embrace of his weary body.

'He stepped out about an hour ago and is due back any minute. Would you like a drink? Tea? Coffee?' Thompson asked, hovering. 'Can't offer you anything stronger, I'm afraid. It's not a conducive workplace for that type of refreshment.'

'Not for me, thanks. I'll rain check the hard stuff if the surgery is successful.'

'Deal.' Thompson sat in a chair opposite. 'Now, tell me. Can we proceed?'

'My preference is not to use the court order. I'd still like Vikki's husband to provide the authority, but if he doesn't, then I will present the paperwork to get it done.'

'Excellent. Is there anything you need to know?'

Stevedore dropped his head back to think of any issues he might have unanswered, then straightened to face her. 'Your staff have been terrific, keeping me well informed.'

'She is doing very well and this decision to move to surgery is in her best interests.'

'Will she survive?'

Thompson released her positive face, looking more solemn. 'Surgery is always a risk; I won't deny it. But, since she is now stable off the machines, then I remain confident.' She paused a moment, then said in a hushed tone, 'I just want to make it clear, the team will do our very best, but I can't guarantee anything.'

'Understood.' Stevedore grimaced, turning away.

Thompson recognised the minister was struggling with the weight of worry and added, 'We should be in surgery for over six hours, that's my expectation. It could take longer, but I don't expect it to be any less.'

Stevedore brushed a tear from his left eye and nodded, chewing on his bottom lip.

'Will you have support people with you while you wait?'

'I have no other family. I wouldn't want to impose this stress on friends.'

'A colleague?'

Stevedore smirked as he grunted. 'They could not care less.'

'We'll set you up in a private room where you can sleep, rather than the lounge or an office.'

Stevedore nodded. 'What about the baby?'

Thompson tightened her lips and didn't respond as she gazed at Stevedore, then leaned her head before saying, 'Look, we'll do our best, no promises. Some of my colleagues have suggested we should terminate.' She waited for a response. 'What's your view?'

Stevedore eyed her, thinking through a reply.

'You know, I'm so conflicted by all of this, to be frank.' He turned away. 'I have been pro-life and argued that point in the parliament many times to the chagrin of feminists, including my daughter. Now I'm tasked with preparing legislation for the federal government to standardise national euthanasia laws, which is a polar opposite to pro-life.' He shook his head. 'It hasn't stopped the ratbags getting stuck into me.'

'What's your position with your daughter?'

'Do what you have to do to save her life. If that means terminating, then do so.'

'Excellent decision,' Thompson smiled. 'It doesn't matter; we think she is only two months.'

'Why doesn't that matter?'

'The medicos still consider it to be an embryo and not yet a fetus.'

'When does it become a baby?'

'A baby is a baby when it is outside the womb.'

'So, what is it before then?'

Thompson grinned, acknowledging that they were setting off into an area of discussion where no one wins.

'The only thing I can say is that science is settled on when the life of a human being begins, and that is at fertilisation.'

'No argument there,' Stevedore said.

'The ethical question for clinicians becomes: is it proper to reduce the moral status of an embryo, or indeed a fetus? There appears to be continued debate about this and who has the authority.'

'Who has the authority?'

'The male sperm determines fertilisation and provides a reason for a mix of the mother and the father chromosomes. I contend that there is more than one person charged with the responsibility to decide,' Thompson said.

'Interesting.'

'Don't get me wrong. I'm a feminist and believe the woman keeps the ultimate decision, but it seems to me the state is excluding more and more the rights of men on this issue. Nothing would happen in the first place if they had not taken part.'

'You don't mind us talking about this, do you, Professor?'

'Vera, please, Charles. I would prefer you used my name.'

'Sorry.' Stevedore said, flushing at being chastised.

Thompson smiled. 'I don't mind talking about these issues of ethics. It's good to talk about them, to reinforce the consciousness.'

'Sorry for raising it. It always seems to be a sensitive and provocative issue to raise, especially for a man.'

'Please, Charles, say what you want, what's troubling you?'

'I'm stressed by what's happening here and the parliamentary work I am supposed to be doing.'

'What concerns you about these matters?' Thompson encouraged him to clear his mind.

'The government funds over one hundred thousand termination treatments every year. I suspect we need to consider that statistic within a policy, but it opens up a polarised debate.'

'You want to legislate or criminalise termination?'

'You see, this is the polarisation. Policy, good policy, is damn hard to prepare, argue and then get enacted.'

'What? You would prefer to ignore it and hope it goes away, and shove desperate women back into the backyard hackers?'

'No, not at all.' Stevedore crossed his arms and thought for a moment. 'As a society, we don't seem to have the courage to discuss these things without the accusations of gender bias and increasing rancor. It seems we are incapable of having a good intelligent discussion without the barbs of emotion and political correctness.'

'Amen to that.' Thompson raised her eyebrows, then added, 'How does that impact your thinking on euthanasia legislation?'

'This thing with Vikki has thrown me. I was pro-euthanasia before her attack.'

Thompson grinned. 'Wait up. You're pro-life at the start of life, but pro-death at the end? How does that work?'

'Fascinating, isn't it? The challenges of being a politician.' Stevedore shrugged, prompting him to shift position. 'I watched my wife die without dignity and I don't want that to happen to anyone.'

'Palliative care should handle that.'

'It did, and she was well cared for, but she feared her future and didn't want to go through it.'

Thompson considered him. 'If you take those end-of-life decisions out of the hands of medical staff and patient carers and give the authority to others, how do you protect them? Your daughter's case as an example.'

'I understand the point you're making. I suppose this has placed an additional burden on me as I work through the issues of the legislation.'

'Why not just let the legislation die? Excuse the pun.'

'I suppose, I owe my wife.'

The discussion was disturbed by Conan Stevens knocking on the door and walking toward them. 'Professor, Mr Ferguson is here. It seems he may have had a few drinks whilst he was away.'

'You had better show him in.' Thompson stood, following the nurse to the door to wait for her patient's husband.

Stevedore remained seated, kneading his hands, and didn't bother looking at Ferguson when he entered the room, sitting opposite in Thompson's chair.

The professor sat in the three-seat lounge nearer to Stevedore. 'Thanks for coming to see me, Mr Ferguson. I appreciate it.'

'No problem.' Ferguson crossed his legs, leaning back in the chair.

'Have you been drinking?' Stevedore demanded.

Ferguson screwed his face with disdain. 'Not your concern, old man.'

'Let's just try to keep the meeting civil, if you don't mind,' Thompson ventured.

'I would have thought keeping off the booze would have been a good idea.'

'You are not my father, and no, I haven't been drinking.'

'Then, what's wrong with you?'

Ferguson didn't respond, glancing to the professor to take control.

'I think it's fair to say we are at the pointy end of discussion. I just wanted to make sure you had no issues you wanted to address before we continue our evaluation of the medical care for your wife.'

'As far as I am concerned, nothing has changed.' Ferguson's head wobbled. 'Vikki always said to me she didn't want the same thing to happen to her like the pain her mother went through. I'm just agreeing to her wishes.' No one responded. 'I mean, it's the right thing to do and only fair for her.'

'You haven't rethought the issues?'

'Like what?'

'Your wife's condition improving overnight and improving by the hour.'

'Well then, that's a good thing, isn't it?' Ferguson stifled a burp. 'So long as we follow my wishes, which are also hers by the way, and there is no medical support. Then who could complain?'

'We remain confident that surgery would improve her condition, and she may enjoy a healthy life.'

'If I've said this once, I have said it a thousand times.' Ferguson raised his voice, staccato-like. 'I do not want any further treatment. If you ignore my request, then I will take legal action and I will have zero hesitation in complaining to the medical board claiming deliberate malpractice.'

The room fell quiet and Ferguson struggled to keep his head erect. Thompson glanced over to Stevedore, who was sitting with his hands linked in front of his face, elbows resting on the arms of the chair. He fixed a menacing gaze over his fingers, trying to calm his need to hurt his son-in-law.

Stevedore asked, 'Do you know a Rikki Ortega?'

'Say what?' Ferguson flicked his head erect. 'I didn't hear you, Charlie. What did you say?'

Stevedore dropped his hands into his lap, squeezing them against each other. 'I asked if you know a Rikki Ortega?'

Ferguson squirmed, shifting in his seat. 'No. No, I don't. Why do you ask?'

'He seems to know you. He says he knows you very well.'

'Then he's lying.'

'He says he sells drugs to you.' Stevedore studied him. 'He says the thugs who attacked Vikki were part of his gang, and they know you.'

'Bullshit.' Ferguson dropped his hands to the arms of the chair, ready to lift himself.

'He says you owe him money, and you're refusing to pay him.'

'Crap, that's bullshit.' Ferguson drew himself forward, then asked Thompson, 'Are we done here?'

'The police want to know your connection with the assault; they're interested to know why you want Vikki to die.'

Ferguson flopped back into the chair, distraught. 'That's a terrible thing to say. How dare you?' His eyes welled. 'I love Vikki.' He turned to Thompson. 'I only want the best for her.'

Thompson nodded. 'Then approve the surgery.'

Ferguson didn't reply, regaining composure.

Stevedore leaned forward. 'If you agree to the surgery, I will help you with the police.'

Ferguson flicked his gaze to Stevedore, thinking about what to say. 'You can get stuffed, as far as I'm concerned.'

'Not the response I was expecting,' Thompson said.

Ferguson switched his gaze back to her. 'This bloke doesn't care for her, never has. Too busy solving the world's problems from Canberra. No time at all for his daughter, or his dying wife.'

Stevedore made a move to the edge of his seat, prompting Thompson to place a reassuring hand on his arm.

'That is a little unfair, don't you think?' she asked.

'It's his idea to legislate euthanasia laws, but only for everyone else, eh Charlie? Not for your own family, just the plebs out in the sticks.'

Stevedore breathed in, then snapped, 'You trumped up little prick.'

'Is that the best you can do?'

Stevedore began moving from the chair, but Thompson gripped his arm hard and he glanced at her, frowning, then changed his mind, relaxing back.

'You seem to think I'm bluffing when I say the federal police are interested in you,' Stevedore said. 'I was at their headquarters in the city and watched as they interviewed Ortega.'

Ferguson now seemed anxious.

'He was telling us he had a long relationship with you,' Stevedore lied. 'He told us you wanted to extend your market, and you were looking for a bigger slice of the pie. He suggested you said the only thing stopping you was your wife's insistence you give it all up.'

'That's bullshit. I never said that to him.'

'He told you he could fix it and you agreed,' Stevedore said.

'No way he would have said that, it didn't happen.'

'Whether or not it happened, the police think it did, so you are coming to their interest.'

'Nope, didn't happen.' Ferguson was convinced he was being fed lies.

Stevedore leaned forward. 'The point I want to make to you, is this: what happens if Vikki dies? It will implicate everyone involved in a conspiracy to murder.'

Ferguson gnawed on a fingertip as he weighed up what he was being told.

'Let's solve that by allowing the surgery,' Stevedore added. 'I can then help you and save you from further police action.'

Ferguson stood and towered over Stevedore.

'You're full of shit. You don't care about Vikki, you never have. This charade you're playing just shows how desperate and feeble you are. You do not know how Vikki feels about you, and I suspect you never will.'

Stevedore jumped to his feet, chesting Ferguson. This prompted Thompson to react, and she struggled to step between the men.

'Stop it, both of you.'

'Sign the approval forms,' Stevedore demanded.

Ferguson stood back, eyeing his father-in-law with disdain, before turning and storming off. 'Go fuck yourself.'

A moment after the door crashed closed, Thompson encouraged Stevedore to resume his place. 'Well, that was very interesting.'

'Don't suppose we can have that drink now?' Stevedore breathed, trying to regain control of his emotions.

'I should have a stash for moments like these, but I don't. Families don't respond to crisis like that. Mind you, there is plenty of emotion, but not like that.'

Stevedore turned and smirked. 'I always knew he was a dipstick, but Vikki saw something else in him.'

Thompson returned his grin. 'Well, Minister, what would you like to do?'

Stevedore pulled an envelope from his jacket, passing it to Thompson.

'This is a court order permitting you to do whatever you can to save my daughter's life.'

'This is a good thing.' She took it from Stevedore and flicked it open, unfolding the notice, then reading it. 'I have the CEO and our legal people on standby for this; I would suspect we will be in surgery within the hour, ninety minutes at the most.'

'It's a shame he didn't approve it, but it just goes to show who he is,' Stevedore said.

Thompson nodded as she finished reading the court order. 'Did he do a deal with the criminals as you say?'

'No, not really, I was exaggerating the story. The police don't have much on him. I just wanted to flush him out.'

'How did that work out for you?'

Stevedore glanced at her and grinned. 'Yeah, you're right, he called me on it, but there is a connection and he confirmed that. At least I think he did.'

'I suppose there will be fences to mend once your daughter recovers.'

'Just ensure she does,' Stevedore said.

'I'll do my best, but I can't guarantee it.'

'At least we're going to try.'

44

Cardinal Rosseau placed his knife and fork on the plate of his half-eaten fish meal, and dabbed his mouth. The draining influence of his trip, coupled with the stress of talking to politicians about legislation, was tiring him. His counselling and support for Charles Stevedore as the man awaited the potential death of his daughter was traumatic, and he was feeling it, stifling a yawn as the waitress cleared.

'Did you enjoy your meal?'

'Why would you ask? Do you ask everyone the same question?'

The waitress became flushed. 'Yes, I do.'

'Tell me…' Rosseau craned to see her name badge. 'Vanessa, do you care what my response is?'

'Of course, sir.' Vanessa smiled as she completed the clearing. 'I consider it nice to care. Now can I get you anything else? Perhaps I could interest you in dessert? We have a baked apple pie on the menu this evening.'

Rosseau perused her up and down, then settled on her smiling face.

'Thank you, but I think I've had quite enough. Can I sign the account, please?'

'Most certainly, you can.' Vanessa bowed. 'I can send a serving up to your room if you would like, maybe a late-night snack for you?'

Rosseau weakened his gruff, grumpy attitude and smiled. 'That's very kind of you, but I suspect my waistline doesn't need additional calories.'

'I could deliver it myself.' The bold response jolted him. 'Maybe receive a blessing?'

'I think not.'

Vanessa pouted a sultry disappointment, stepping away. 'Too bad. I'll get your bill.'

As Rosseau watched the woman saunter off, he wondered what embarrassments might have befallen him if he had wanted a pie in his room, then recited, 'Do not yield to temptation. It is no sin to be tempted; the sin lies in yielding.'

He followed the waitress until she leaned over the front reception, asking for the account. She kicked her foot back, her shoe dropping the heel.

Rosseau continued. 'While the sin exists only in Satan's solicitation, it is the devil's sin, not ours. When we yield, we make the devil's sin our own; then we enter temptation.'

Vanessa glanced over her shoulder and noticed that the cardinal was watching, so she tossed her head back, running her fingers through her long, dark, trussed hair.

'Resist the devil, and he will flee from you. Satan himself cannot force you to sin: till he wins over your will, he cannot bring you into subjection.'

Vanessa sashayed back to him, her gaze fixed on his eyes and a sultry smile on her lips.

'It may tempt you; but yield not to the temptation.'

'There you are, Your Eminence.' Rosseau took the leather bill folder. 'Is there anything else I can assist you with this evening?'

'No, thank you, Vanessa. You have been most helpful.'

'Enjoy the rest of your evening,' she said, as she left the table with the completed account.

'Bless you, my child.' Rosseau smirked as he also left the table and made his way to the elevator lobby, desperate for much needed sleep.

When he reached his door, he could hear his telephone. He had left it to recharge whilst he dined. He entered the room but didn't quite make it before the phone stopped ringing and pinged a missed call message. When he picked up the unit it surprised him to see that he had eleven missed calls: nine from one international number, one local and another international. He then checked his messages; there were only two.

He tapped his way to the first message and placed it on speakerphone so that he could get his shoes off his aching feet.

'Cardinal Rosseau, this is Nancy Pasco. I wonder if you could return my call when you can. I believe you have the number.'

Rosseau surmised what the prime minster may have wanted. She was under pressure and wanted the church to support her decision to move to a referendum rather than keep the recalcitrant stance he had asserted. He then let the next message play.

'Good evening, Your Eminence.' He recognised the voice as the Pope's personal assistant. 'The Holy Father would welcome a call from you at your earliest convenience to discuss an anonymous note he has received.'

Rosseau mused that the Holy Father had wasted little time in contacting him. He decided he would call in the morning, making the pretender wait a little longer. What had his interest was the incessant calling of a number from France? He prodded the recall tab and waited for a response.

'Bon après-midi, évêque Berneux parlant.'

'Good evening, Your Excellency. This is Cardinal Rosseau returning your many calls.'

'Eminence, thank you for calling.' The bishop seemed flustered. 'How is your trip progressing? Successful, I hope?'

'What do you want?'

There was an abrupt break in the conversation before the bishop spoke. 'It is my sad duty to advise you that your mother passed overnight.' Rosseau didn't respond. 'It was a gentle death, and she was well cared for.'

After another period of silence, Rosseau asked, 'I thought we were going to do this as soon as possible?'

'We did, Your Eminence, but your mother resisted the medication until we upped dosages, placing her into a final coma. We provided her support until she passed last night.'

'No suffering?'

'No. She was in very capable care.'

'I remain a little disappointed that this took so very long,' Rosseau said. 'Could it not have been much sooner?'

'We followed the protocols.'

'Yes, but why so slow?'

'Sometimes we're blessed with those who wish to savour life as much as possible. It may not be a conscious decision, but their bodies, and perhaps their souls, are hanging on for the right time.'

Rosseau didn't reply for a moment, then said, 'Thank you for letting me know.'

'How do we manage the final details?'

'Let my sisters earn their inheritance and have them make those decisions. You have advised me, and that is the end of it.'

'Will you be all right? Do you have support?'

'Excellency,' Rosseau sighed. 'You have done your duty, now let me be.' He dropped the phone and moved to the hotel's mini bar, cracked open a small miniature bottle of Chivas Regal and sculled the contents. It bit hard and he coughed. He then grabbed the white wine bottle and opened it, pouring a glass and moving back to the lounge where he flicked on the television. As he stretched his legs onto the coffee table, kicking off the magazines, he wondered what Vanessa might be doing.

Thirty minutes later and onto to his second glass, Rosseau's phone buzzed. 'Charles, it's late, what's up? Anything wrong?'

'Victoria has been in surgery for three hours; I've had little word of progress.'

'I'm on my way.'

Rosseau called for a car and was striding out of the hotel's lobby when it arrived. He hopped into the back seat for the twenty-minute trip, deciding to ring the prime minister who answered immediately.

'Good evening, Prime Minister. I apologise for the lateness of my call,' Rosseau said.

'Your Eminence, thank you for returning the call. How is your evening?'

'How can I help?'

The cardinal's brusqueness took Pasco aback. 'I just wanted to know if you, or the Holy Father, have changed your view on the proposed legislation.'

'Why is this so important now? We are weeks away from it progressing to parliament?' Rosseau queried, annoyed by the prime minister's intrusion.

'I'm planning on bringing the legislation into the parliament next week when we resume in Canberra. I would like your support.'

Rosseau didn't hesitate, 'You do not now, nor will you ever have, the support of His Holiness. I'm surprised you expected any other answer.'

'The church is being unreasonable on this issue.'

'You think?' Rosseau asked. 'We support the sanctity of life, we always have, but this is not only a moral issue for us, Prime Minister.'

'Oh yes?'

'The truth be known, this is also an economic issue for us.' The cardinal was a little too candid; perhaps the wine was loosening his tongue. 'This will affect our aged care model. I need to advise you, we will reconsider our position on what services we provide the community.'

'You cannot be serious?' Pasco snapped.

'There is no need to take that tone with me. Just remember who you are talking to.'

'I know who I'm talking to, and I know very well what the church does, and in return, the largesse governments provide it.'

'We value life, Prime Minister, and we will protect our right to provide for the living, be it hospitals, or our age care centres,' Rosseau snarled. 'You, on the other hand, do not espouse moral ethics, either personally or politically, as I'm informed.'

Pasco didn't respond immediately. 'We will bring forward the legislation next week. I will support the Yes campaign. I will do all in my power to expose the church to meddling in affairs of state by holding the nation back from providing a great social reform.'

'You think killing people is a social reform?'

'Euthanasia is death with dignity, as you very well know.'

'I would never support a threat to a life. The church will work to having this Kill Bill defeated.'

'This is the position of the Pope?'

'He is the church and the church will not support this referendum.'

'I'm sorry to hear that, cardinal. Good night.'

Rosseau didn't have a chance to respond. He gazed out the window as his car crossed the Yarra River on its way up Punt Road Hill to the Alfred and he sighed, dropping his phone into an inside pocket of his cassock.

Ten minutes later, the car pulled to a halt outside the main entrance. Rosseau strode through the elevator lobby, and soon after walked into a private patient room allocated to the attorney general for the evening.

'Would you like a drink, Your Eminence?' Stevedore was standing at a side table, pouring a handsome dram of whiskey into a plastic disposable cup. 'I went out and purchased a bottle, but I can't offer you any ice, I'm afraid.'

'That would be nice,' Rosseau said, as he made himself comfortable in one of the two lounge chairs relocated earlier by a ward orderly. 'How is the surgery going?'

'They have told me very little other than it's progressing as planned, whatever that means.' Stevedore passed over a cup for the cardinal, then carried his own to the other chair, flopping down, but making sure he didn't spill the whiskey. 'Here's to life and the living?' He raised his cup, taking a biting mouthful, numbing his senses.

'I wish you well, Minister, and for your daughter, I offer my blessings and prayers.' Rosseau followed the pattern with the same result, stifling a regurgitation.

'Do you have any family?' Stevedore enquired.

'I have two sisters in France.'

'Do they spend much time with you?'

'I seldom see or hear from them these days, not since I was a teenager.'

Stevedore cocked his head in surprise. 'You don't speak anymore?'

'We all had a falling out when I joined the church.' Rosseau dropped his head back on the chair, gazing at the ceiling. 'Something to do with providing for the family and my responsibility as the only male to do so.'

'Father died early?'

'No, ran off, who could blame him?' Rosseau flicked his head back for another swig. 'My mother wasn't the friendliest of people.'

'Whoever said parenting was easy was never a parent.'

'The bible says, *"Behold, children are a heritage from the lord, the fruit of the womb a reward."*'

'There haven't been too many rewards with mine, I can tell you,' Stevedore laughed, taking another swig.

'It's only ever hardship for parents, I suppose, mixed with joy, of course.'

'Spoken by someone who's not a parent.' Stevedore glanced at Rosseau. 'Oops, sorry, you aren't a parent, are you?'

Rosseau hooted out loud. 'No, not likely. Never had that opportunity.'

'Parenting is rewarding, but boy, it's darn hard work… even at my age.' The men sat for a time, swirling and sipping their whiskey.

Rosseau broke the silence.

'Would you mind if I ask you something?'

Stevedore dropped his head, glancing through his brow at the now serious Rosseau. 'Sure, what's up?'

'I had a chat with your prime minister on the way over. She tells me she will table the referendum legislation in parliament when you next sit, which I'm told is just over a week, is that correct?'

Stevedore didn't respond, trying to craft a political answer. 'The government promised legislation once the plebiscite result was known, and the prime minister would be responding to that promise.'

'I thought you had carriage of the legislation. Why are you pushing it through?'

'To be honest with you, the prime minister has her own people who can draw up legislation. My office would prefer to do it, which we are, but we can also review their efforts, cross-referencing any differences.'

Rosseau crossed his legs and leaned into Stevedore. 'I thought last night that you may equivocate on your decision.'

Stevedore finished his whiskey and crushed the cup.

'I've always supported the right for citizens to die with dignity. What I don't support is pressure applied to them to leave the world prematurely.'

'You are pro-life, right?'

'Yes. I understand the arguments for the woman to be in control, but I support the idea that once conceived, then there are other stakeholders within the decision-making process.'

'Stakeholders? You mean fathers, right?'

'I recognise there are mistakes made, forced pregnancies and cultural considerations, but I don't think termination should be a contraception method.'

'Then, if you are pro-life at the start of life, why then are you pro-death at the end?'

'I wouldn't say I'm pro-death, that's a little harsh.' Stevedore stood, moving to retrieve the whiskey and a small tower of plastic cups, placing them on the coffee table and pouring another handsome dram for himself. 'I watched my wife die with little dignity. I would like to resolve that pain for families.'

'Your daughter was almost a victim of an overzealous family member.'

Stevedore took the cardinal's point and considered the issue, turning away from him. 'I've reflected on that during the day. I suppose I could make sure that what happened here couldn't happen elsewhere.'

Rosseau studied the attorney general. 'It's difficult, these matters of family.'

A tear welled in Stevedore's eye. He cleared his throat as he tried to speak, then croaked, 'No.'

'Families shouldn't have to go to court to override an end-of-life decision.'

Stevedore took a sip of whiskey, rolling the plastic in his fingers, bending and buckling its shape. He queried, 'Have you ever had to make a decision about such things?'

'Luckily, no.' Rosseau ignored his mother's case. 'It's never easy for law-makers to do what is right.'

'Amen to that, Your Eminence.'

Rosseau grinned. 'What's your ultimate position going to be?'

'I made a promise to my wife. I told her I would make sure the referendum was successful. Now that I have seen what could happen, I don't know.'

'No one enjoys suffering,' Rosseau said, stretching for more whiskey. 'But that does not make it right to determine that a person should die.'

'What does God have to say on that?'

Rosseau harrumphed at the question, as he considered Stevedore to be more pragmatic than to rely on bible teachings. He thought about a response, then said, 'God cares about those who cry out for death and wish to end their suffering. God gives purpose in life even to the end.'

'That's not an answer.'

'Only God knows what is best. His timing, even in the matter of one's death, is perfect.'

'Just what exactly is the church's position?'

'We should never seek to prematurely end a life.' Rosseau took a sip then added, 'Neither must we go to extraordinary means to preserve a life.'

'It seems you are just as confounded on the issue as me.'

'To hasten death is wrong, to withhold treatment can also be wrong,' Rosseau said. 'To allow death to occur naturally for a terminally ill person is not wrong. Anyone facing this issue should pray to God for wisdom.'

'That's a total cop out, if you don't mind me saying.' Stevedore finished his whiskey, crumpling the cup. 'With these moral issues, the church seems to say nothing to progress debate. It just seems to want to hang onto its two thousand-year-old teachings.'

Rosseau was prickly at Stevedore's response. 'The practice of medicine cannot be both our healer and our killer.'

Stevedore ignored the comment, checking his watch. It was now four hours since his daughter went into surgery.

'I struggle with these legal propositions every day.' He poured a smaller dram of whisky. 'There are always two sides, and therefore, two solutions to any issue. It's just bunnies like me who have to decide what is right or wrong.'

'What teachings do you fall back on to help you?'

'It's difficult, very difficult. Morality has always been my considered position, and I always base this on a fact, or right and wrong.' Stevedore glanced at the cardinal. 'Who is the arbiter of right and wrong?'

'We think the church and its teachings are the determiner of such things.'

'Yes, but who gave you that privileged position?' Stevedore prodded. 'Culture is a set of rules we all abide by.'

'Brought to us by the church.'

'Not necessarily,' Stevedore smiled. 'Which church, for starters? What if there are no churches in a culture? What then?'

'The church has played a significant part in setting the rules. Moses, for starters.'

Stevedore snorted. 'That is an invention, and any person of rational intellect will subscribe to that notion. Religion is an invention.'

'Not sure I'm liking where you are taking this discussion, Charles.' Rosseau shifted in his chair, crossing his arms. Bleakness descended into his face.

'This is the exact challenge I have.' Stevedore sat up and back into his chair, then sipped from his plastic cup. 'We all have interests we want to pursue. They vary from individual to individual, but we want to avoid suffering and hardship. We pursue pleasure and fulfilling experiences.' He rested his cup on the arm of the chair. 'These days the great unwashed want government to solve their problems, and stuff the church's morality.'

'I suppose you're right. This is the reason the church must voice its view on these issues of life and death, otherwise we become barbarians.'

'I don't agree, for instance, we don't support capital punishment,' Stevedore said.

'History tells us we once did. Who's to say it won't come back? We see it happening in some western countries.'

'It'll never come back in Australia. Although, I must confess, I felt it should when I was told about the brutality perpetrated on Vikki.'

'Interesting. A politician making laws based on personal experiences, rather than considering the good for all?'

Stevedore turned, shamefaced. 'These are the challenges of which I speak. Politicians are human, yet we're placed under extraordinary pressure to manage the majority rather than react to our own feelings.'

'You came to politics as a volunteer.'

Stevedore leaned forward, annoyed. 'This is the damn argument everyone tosses at us when we try to explain the stresses.' He rested his forearms on his thighs. 'Community leaders are all volunteers; it doesn't mitigate the demands of the job.'

'Why invent new law rather than maintain the moral facts? In this case, to kill is wrong.'

Stevedore leaned back, crossing his arms, and shook his head. 'If only it were that easy.'

A sudden loud knock on the door interrupted them. The door was pushed open by a gowned Doctor Nguyen, bringing news.

Stevedore gazed at her and shuddered a sigh. He wept.

CHAPTER

45

Senator Richards was an angry man. Overweight and red-faced, he was loud and threatening when communicating with anyone, and had little respect for people's feelings. He had an opinion since his bullying days in school, but now remained an outspoken government critic, arguing that the need to replace the prime minister was imperative. He was considered amongst his colleagues to be just a loudmouth with little influence, and dismissed as a threat to the prime minister, but now he wanted action. He wanted to sack the prime minister.

'This dropkick has to go,' Richards said, as he sprawled in Parker Osborne's Sydney office. 'We will lose the election if she stays in the job.'

Osborne sat at his desk, swivelling his chair. His fingers were steepled before him, thumbs supporting his chin. 'She has promised to go within twelve months of the election.'

'Crap, who has she promised that to?'

'Me. I have a signed letter of her intention to retire.'

Richards scowled. 'And what? You think you're the man for the job?'

'I'll put my hand up.'

'If we don't bone her now, you will never be prime minister.'

'We'll win the election,' Osborne said.

'Mate, I can guarantee the punters will not vote for her.' Richards took a large drink of water from the glass he was holding. 'She is toxic in marginal seats, and if what I hear about her is correct, then scandal awaits her within days.'

'What do you know?'

'She has used government funds to travel to north Queensland to purchase an investment property. Yet to be confirmed, but she disclosed the purchase on her interests. I'm told she bought it with her chief of staff, who also travelled up there.'

'She rang me about it the other day.'

'Who, Pasco?'

'No, her chief of staff.' Osborne grinned, unblinking, staring at Richards. 'It seems I wasn't supportive enough with the euthanasia referendum. She questioned how the media were getting information about the prime minister's travel arrangements.'

'This euthanasia bill will be the death of us, excuse the pun.'

'What reason could I use to convince my colleagues to call a leadership spill?'

Richards scoffed. 'You don't need a bloody reason, she stinks in the electorate.'

'What would you say if I won the leadership and then campaigned against the referendum?'

'It's been done before, plenty of times. Leaders go where the votes are. You'd get no argument from my mob, that's for sure.'

'How many votes can you get me?'

'Forty percent,' Richards sniffed.

Osborne scoffed. 'Not fifty?'

'If you want to win the leadership, then you work for the other ten,' Richards smirked. 'Ahmed is your competitor. I reckon she has thirty locked in.'

'What about Stevedore?'

'He's useless.' Richards spat the words. 'Where has he been the last week, anyway?'

'Something to do with his daughter, I'm told.'

'Yeah, right, always an excuse to disappear from the front line. That guy has no balls. He shouldn't be in politics. He doesn't have the ticker.'

'What do you want?'

Richards spread his lips further. 'I want to be a minister, of course.'

'Do you have a portfolio in mind?'

'Nothing to do with the socialists or other beggars seeking government funds.' Richards pondered the question with a quizzical face. 'I want a job that gives me gravitas with the folks who have money. Defence materials, perhaps... trade, or maybe infrastructure.'

'Not social security?' Osborne joked.

'Heck no. What a dead-end job that is. Nothing but complainers in a thankless portfolio where the dregs of society linger.'

'You know politics too well, Stan. There are never any promises given or expected.'

'Of course, Parker, that's a given.' The senator leaned forward, placing his empty glass on the coffee table. 'Let me reassure you. I have the numbers, and if you want them, then you'll have to pay for them. It's a two-part deal, a ministry... plus, I want you to challenge her next week when we're back in Canberra.'

'Why so early?'

'If we leave it any longer, good news might come along, or she could change her mind on the euthanasia bill.'

Osborne gazed back at the smirking senator. The political code had only ever been about arithmetic. For an ambitious politician wanting to roll a sitting prime minister, it was best if he had the numbers to support him.

'Next week it is.' Osborne stood, walking toward the now departing senator. 'Thanks for dropping by and letting me know your thoughts.'

Richards grabbed the outstretched hand and squeezed, drawing Osborne closer. 'Give me what I want, son, and you'll be prime minister this time next week. Better to be prime minister for twelve months with a chance to win the election, than opposition leader with no chance of ever being in the chair.'

'I have a lunch meeting later with several colleagues. No doubt we will discuss your plan.'

'You Catholics,' Richards chortled. 'Don't you ever stop praying?'

'How do you know my colleagues are Catholics?'

'Parker, please.' Richards headed for the door. 'I know everything.'

As Osborne watched the door close, he thought about Richards' comment and considered that the senator was correct. Like salt and pepper, he was into everything.

Osborne turned, stepping to the window high above Bligh Street, gazing out into the harbour as ferries ploughed through the water, and sail boats played crazy games cutting across their bows. Citizens were going about their business, ignorant that a decision had just been made to sack their prime minister.

The door opened, and Kaitlyn May walked into the room with an arm full of files.

'These need to be signed before you leave for lunch, and Dennis Sadler's assistant has asked for you to return his call.'

Osborne didn't respond. His chief of staff stopped examining him for any sign she should worry about.

'Parker, are you okay?'

Osborne turned back into the room, his face unreadable. She circled as he made his way back to his desk.

'What's happened? Do you want to share with me? What did the senator tell you?'

'Richards gave me a math lesson.'

'Oh yes, what lesson was he teaching?'

'He believes the government is doomed; and, if I don't snatch the leadership next week, then I may never have another chance.'

'Did he say that?'

'He wants Pasco gone, that's for sure. I wouldn't put it past him. He has been setting her up for a fall for some time.'

'Wait up, I thought we held all the cards?'

'It seems he is playing himself into the game. His ultimatum is to be rewarded for the numbers he says he can bring.'

'How many?'

'Forty percent of the party room.'

May whistled through her teeth. 'That's gotta be good?'

Osborne shook off his brooding. 'Yeah, that's an excellent result, and it only cost me one ministry.'

May sat at the desk on a hard visitor's chair. 'That raises alarms and worries me a little. Why only one?'

'I don't know, politicians are only ever self-interested; Richards is no different.'

'It might mean he doesn't have the numbers he says he does. Otherwise, he would ask for more to payoff to his mates. I should be wary, if I were you.'

Osborne nodded, probing out his bottom lip, thinking through her suggestion. 'Would he be trying to set me up for Ahmed, do you think?'

'He could, but I don't think he's that shrewd. I just think he may not hold the votes he says he has, just be careful.'

'Do you think I should challenge?'

'Look, boss, the prime minister has promised you the job after the election; why would you want to move now?'

'What happens if we don't win the election?'

May shrugged, knowing that any chance of Osborne being prime minster would then disappear. Too many years in opposition would bring a younger contender, and the old ministry would have disappeared. The best he could hope for was a few years as opposition leader. She understood Osborne well enough to know that he would not be any good in that role.

'The way I'm thinking about it, is this; best to be prime minister for a few months rather than not at all. And who knows, I may deliver a victory for the true believers,' Osborne said.

'If the referendum goes down, and you made it happen, I would have thought you could win,' May said.

Osborne smiled and waited, then said, 'Dinner tonight?'

May stood, excited about the invitation, but yet again didn't show it, moving to the door. 'Get your chores done, then we can talk about your eating habits, since you are lunching with the cabal.'

'We never eat that much at these things. Way too much praying for my liking.'

'Get those files signed off, then call Sadler.'

'Yes, boss.' Osborne was yet to receive an acceptance to any of his invitations to his staffer over the years, but that didn't stop him from asking.

Nancy Pasco was far from pleased Treasurer Osborne had requested a formal meeting with her for the following day and would bring the government leader of the senate, Ann Gellibrand, with him. The dark art of politics was only ever about power, and she considered a small delegation of her leadership group a potential threat. She headed for the Lodge for a quiet lunch on the terrace, away from the never-ending demands of her parliamentary office.

The stones crunched her shoes as she walked to the front door which was swung open by her housekeeper as she arrived.

'I have set a place out on the terrace, Prime Minister. I thought a light meal of fish and salad may be nice out in the fresh air and sun.'

'Bring a bottle of Riesling out before you serve, will you please, Rennie?'

'I'll open a Pewsey Vale.'

'No, stuff that cheap South Australian crap. Bring up a bottle of Crawford River.'

'Yes, ma'am. You go make yourself comfortable. I'll bring you a glass straight away.'

'Has Mr Pasco called at all?'

'Not a whisper today. Will he be in Sydney for much longer?'

'Who knows, Rennie? Who the hell knows?'

Pasco dropped her oversized bag on a table as she walked through to the back of the house and out onto the terrace. There was a crispness in the air, but the sun was warm and relaxing. She decided to forgo the set table and relaxed on a pool lounge facing the sun, moved her sunglasses from the top of her head and lay down to soak in some energy.

Ten minutes later the housekeeper was walking toward her with an ice bucket and a large wine glass. 'Here you are, Prime Minister, a tasty wine for you to enjoy before lunch.'

Pasco didn't bother to respond. She waited for a poured glass to be handed to her before acknowledging her staffer. 'Thank you, and if anyone calls, I'm not available.'

'Understood.' Rennie moved off, but then stopped herself. 'If Miss Kellaway calls?'

Pasco glanced over at her, shading her eyes. 'Not even Miss Kellaway.'

The prime minister had almost finished her glass before she dropped her head back on the lounge, sighing. She closed her eyes, wishing the day would go away. The sun eased the tension, which had been building for many months. She was confused by the political events that seemed to grow further from her control every day. Her personal life was in disarray. She was now heading in a direction she would never had considered. It was exciting, but she remained confused by it all. Her political career was on the brink of collapse, with a leadership challenge likely. She was losing control of the political narrative and pondered that a career dedicated to serving the community could soon be over.

Ninety minutes later she was still sunning herself, almost asleep on the lounge with a half-eaten meal on the terracotta tiles below her, a second bottle of Riesling almost finished.

'Why are you ignoring me?'

The voice forced her to shade her eyes and see who was disturbing her slumber. 'What are you doing here?'

'You haven't been taking my calls.'

'I don't want to see or talk to anyone.'

'You can't just leave with no indication when you'll be back.' The prime minister's chief of staff sat on the lounge, obliging Pasco to move her feet and struggle to sit higher. 'I would have expected to speak to you.'

Pasco didn't want to open her eyes, but she shaded them, glaring at Kellaway. 'You are part of my problem.'

'What am I doing to be a problem?'

'Oh, I don't know, maybe because you are always at me to be more open about us.'

'I told you, I'm willing to give up my job and go back to journalism.'

'That's not the point.'

'We are together or we are not?'

Pasco dropped her hand, turning away. Kellaway caressed the prime minister's leg with her fingertips, running a nail deeper before holding Pasco's foot.

'Nan, I love you.'

'Please, don't say that,' Pasco snapped, tugging her legs closer, wrapping her arms around her knees. 'Just leave me alone for a while, please, Kell. I need to work this out by myself.'

'We know that will not work.' Kellaway turned away, gazing out onto the pool.

Pasco eyed Kellaway over her sunglasses. 'My world is collapsing, and everyone wants a piece of me, even you.'

Kellaway didn't respond. She glanced up into the sky, then turned back to face Pasco. 'You can't ignore what's in front of you. You lead the country, for heaven's sake.'

'I made a mistake when I pushed the plebiscite. I was thinking it would provide a definitive result.'

'That was never going to happen. I told you that,' Kellaway snapped.

'Yeah, yeah, but now what do I do?' Pasco reached for the Riesling bottle, emptying it into her glass and almost overflowing it. 'I have an AG who won't answer calls and now a treasurer moving against me.'

'I thought you gave him a commitment for a transition after the election.'

Pasco took a generous mouthful. 'He knows I would never agree to a leadership change; they are going to take me out in a coffin.' She spilt her wine as she returned the glass to the tiles.

'Why wouldn't you pass it to him?'

'Because he is a pompous moron, and the country doesn't need his Catholic politics.'

'Take him on, then. Your political nouse won you the job. The electorate is behind you.'

'He's coming with Gellibrand to see me tomorrow. Leadership delegations are never good news.'

'They want to stop the referendum, so why not kill it?'

'That's what the Catholics want, and I'll never give them that win.'

'Here's the thing, why not tell them you are going to kill it, then do the opposite?'

'That would not make sense. I would face a challenge if I did that.'

Kellaway turned to her, more enthused. 'No, listen, Osborne is coming to see you tomorrow seeking a leadership spill, right?'

'We assume that's why he's coming.'

'What reason would he be giving for a leadership spill?'

'Going ahead with the euthanasia legislation, I suppose.'

'Why not announce to them you'll kill the euthanasia bill?' Kellaway moved closer. 'Let them leak it to the media, then flush out Parker to speak either for or against you. It doesn't matter what he says, so long as he is out there.'

'Why would that be helpful?'

'Because next Tuesday, when the party room meets, you state you support the legislation, and you are prepared to test your leadership on it.'

'That's crazy. A stupid idea.'

'You need to take the initiative and have the leadership spill on your terms.'

'Why not announce the leadership spill tomorrow after they come see me? I can say they wanted me to reject the referendum. Then I can say I'm laying my leadership on the line to get the bill through the parliament.' Pasco finished her glass.

'That's a good idea. We can organise the media pack to wait in the courtyard, and you walk straight into a media conference before they background the press gallery.'

'I suppose we could do that.' Pasco smiled as the sun and wine lightened her head. 'Do I have the numbers?'

'I could check, but last week you did.'

'The Catholics wouldn't support me if they knew Parker was going to kill the bill.'

'Oh, I don't know. They might go to the electorate for a decision and have the voters kill it, rather than have Parker win the top job.'

'Where does Richards stand?'

'He wants a job, so he stands with who will give him one.'

'He hates me.'

'Look, Nan, he is a political pragmatist and will support self-interest. Osborne will offer him a job; you offer him a better one.'

'Yeah, you could be right.' Pasco drummed her fingernails against the empty glass. 'Do you want a drink?'

'No, I had better get back to the hill. I think you've had enough as well. You have a speech to deliver tonight.'

'You're probably right. I should go have a snooze,' Pasco said, smirking at Kellaway. 'You want to come tuck me in?'

Kellaway beamed a smile, stood and held out her hand to help Pasco, who staggered to her feet.

Charlie Stevedore sat by his daughter's bed holding her hand, the only part of her available to touch, and that Professor Thompson would allow. He was searching for any movement in the brief moments they allowed him. She had survived the eight-hour operation and now, under instructions, he was gowned head to toe in a sterile outfit to ensure unintended contamination did not infect her.

'Darling, Victoria,' he whispered. 'I'm so sorry for letting this happen. Fight it please, darling. I will see you soon.'

Doctor Nguyen placed a gentle hand on his shoulder, and he glanced up, knowing his precious time was at an end. As Stevedore left the isolation room, he saw Thompson behind the glass in the viewing section and walked around to the entrance to talk.

'Professor, I just wanted to…'

'Vera, please,' Thompson smiled.

The correction unsettled Stevedore and lost his train of thought. 'I just wanted to say…' He gulped, tugging his mask from his face. He struggled to control his voice. 'I just wanted to say thank you.'

'Your daughter is stronger than we give her credit for. Please take a seat.' Thompson ushered him to a chair, and she sat close. 'We closed the wounds, cleared out dead skin and tissue, and applied this new technology that my team are confident will turn her condition around.'

Stevedore wiped a tear from the corner of his eye. 'You are a miracle worker, honestly, you are magnificent.'

'I'm only as good as my training will allow. It's your daughter who should get your praise. We had no issue with her in theatre, and since coming here her signs are very encouraging.'

'When will we know?'

'That's the sixty-four-thousand-dollar question.' Thompson reached for his hand. 'We will know more in twelve hours if she continues to be stable and her body recovers. This time tomorrow we will do tests on the wounds to determine if they have begun a healing process. All her respiratory systems are recovering, but we will know further in a few hours whether we have managed to get her to a level where the chance of recovery becomes better than fifty percent.'

'I can't thank you enough.' Stevedore squeezed her hand.

Thompson caressed her thumb across the back of his hand. 'I keep telling you, the team did it, and we had enormous help from your daughter.'

Stevedore was yet to release the professor's hand, and he dropped his head into his other, fingers soothing his brow.

'She is in great care, Charles, so why don't you go home and rest? Get something to eat and have a shower.'

'No, I want to stay here, it's important.'

'Yes, it is, but so is not smelling.'

Stevedore glanced up at Thompson and scoffed. He then sniffed under his arms. 'I'm not that bad, am I?'

'I'm afraid you are; we've had complaints.' Thompson smiled, nodding, still holding his hand.

He stood, stretching, releasing her hand. 'I suppose you're right. It's been a few days.'

'Phew. We were all a tad worried how you would take the advice.'

'That bad?'

Thompson crossed her arms and nodded, beaming.

'Okay, I had better go.' Stevedore moved off. 'And just one other thing, Professor.'

'Yes, Charles?'

'Were you able to save the baby?'

Thompson frowned, a little annoyed with herself. 'Yes, we did; sorry, I should have told you earlier, all is good.'

Stevedore glanced back at the beaming surgeon and stepped toward her again, taking her in his arms. She responded, and the two held each other for a moment until Stevedore let go and stepped back.

'Thank you, I will never forget this.'

'It's what I do. Now do what you have to do.'

CHAPTER

48

Stevedore hadn't been lying on his bed long before the shrill of his phone startled him awake. He dozily answered, 'Hello?'

'It's Ozzie. Charlie, how are you?'

'I'm fine. Just resting at the moment.'

'That's great. Look, Ann Gellibrand and I are visiting the prime minister tomorrow to discuss various things, including a leadership spill.'

It overwhelmed Stevedore. 'What?'

'The polls are going south, and she has lost the support of the party room, so we are asking for a spill next week.'

Stevedore thought through the news. 'I won't be moving against her.'

'Of course you won't be; that's a given. You are doing an outstanding job as attorney. Why would you want to change?'

'I heard that Susie Ahmed was counting numbers.'

'She needs a calculator, because she can't count, that's for sure.'

'Who's going to stand?'

'That would be me, and I want your support.'

'Geezus, Oz, are you sure?'

'Please don't talk to me like that, Charlie. You know I'm sensitive to that sort of language.'

'You want to do over the prime minister of Australia, and you're worried about a mate saying Jesus?'

'Yeah, just that kinda guy, I suppose, do I have your support?'

'I'm not convinced Nancy needs to go. She should take us to the election, it's way too close to be changing leaders.'

'So, I don't have your support?' Parker quizzed.

'I'm not saying that. I'm asking you to consider the consequences if you don't have the numbers, and how it could affect the party.'

'Yeah, done that.' Osborne seemed bored in his response. 'Do I have your support?'

'I have a lot going on; I will need to think about it.'

'We all have something going on, Charlie. I'll put you down as a maybe,' Osborne replied. 'It's likely to be next week, so I'll see you then.'

Stevedore couldn't believe that the call had ended and checked his phone. He knew Osborne was self-obsessed, but to not ask about his predicament was a touch insensitive, he thought. He considered the call, then swiped his way to the prime minister's private number, pushing the button.

'Nancy's phone,' a hushed voice answered.

'Hello? I was expecting to speak to Nancy. Is she available?'

'Who's calling?'

'More the point, who are you?'

'I'm the prime minister's chief of staff.'

'It's Charlie Stevedore; is she available?'

'She's indisposed at the moment, Mr Stevedore.'

'What does that mean?'

'She's sleeping?'

'What, in the office?'

'No, she's at the Lodge. She needed rest before an event tonight.'

Stevedore shook his head, wondering why her chief of staff was answering the prime minister's private phone. 'Get her to call me as soon as she's available, please.'

'Anything I can help you with?'

'Not likely, goodbye.'

Stevedore gnawed at the corner of his phone as he pondered the call and then pushed the recall button.

'Hey, Charlie. What's up?'

'Ozzie, I am happy to support you if you decide to run.'

'What's brought this sudden change of heart?'

'I think we need different values in the Lodge. I would prefer to see someone with a strong ethical conviction leading Australia.'

'I'm very pleased, thank you.'

'Talk soon.' Stevedore tossed his phone aside and settled back into his pillow, hoping for the sleep that had eluded him over the last few days.

Cardinal Rosseau was disturbed by the incessant knocking on his door. He had switched off his phone and blocked all incoming calls from the hotel telephone, and had drawn the heavy drapes, seeking sleep after his shared vigil with the attorney general. His prayers had been answered and Victoria Stevedore was past the threat of death, achieving a solid foundation for recovery.

The knocking persisted, forcing Rosseau to attend to learn why he was being disturbed, even though the do not disturb door sign was in place. He stood behind the door and gazed through the security peephole, recognising a priest from the Archbishop of Melbourne's office.

'What do you want?' Rosseau asked from behind the door.

'I'm sorry for disturbing you, Your Eminence. The Holy Father has been calling and insisted we give you his message.'

Rosseau unlocked the door and cracked it open. 'Give it to me.'

The priest passed the sealed envelope through the doorway. Rosseau snatched at it, then slammed the door, leaving the priest to depart without thanks.

Rosseau crossed to the bed, tossed the envelope on the side table and fell back, dragging over the covers to regain blissful sleep. Despite his efforts to drop off, the message played on his mind and he realised he would have to read it if he were to get any sleep.

He stretched for the envelope, switching on the bedside lamp. Pushing back into the pillows, he tore open the envelope, unfolding the note and looking at the three words, then scrunched the paper and tossed it away. He was yet to contact the Pope after the message that had been left yesterday.

'Who the hell is he to be demanding urgency?' Rosseau asked himself out loud, then after a moment he answered, 'The Holy Father.'

Rosseau retrieved his charging phone and scrolled through contacts until he found the number he wanted and then tapped the call button.

'Cardinal Paas speaking,' a musical voice announced.

'John, it's Morris. Why would Papa be calling me?'

'Your Eminence, good morning.' The tone tightened. 'I would not know why he would call you. There is a suggestion of scandal within the Vatican, and la Repubblica has an editorial. Perhaps he wants to talk about that.'

'What scandal?' Rosseau asked, smiling.

'A sexual scandal and cover up,' Paas said, 'I have a copy here.'

'Does it implicate anyone?'

'No, Your Eminence, it does not. It suggests that a cover-up is being made at the highest echelons of the Vatican.'

'Has there been any more contact with the person who sent the link?'

'I have asked for further communication, but they are yet to contact me.'

'Wonderful work, John. Goodbye now.'

Rosseau laid back on the pillows, gazing at the ceiling and thinking through likely responses for Caspian. Should he raise the issue? What answer would soothe him? He swiped his contacts and tapped Papa's direct line.

'Holy Father, this is Morris Rosseau. How can I help?'

'What have you been up to, Your Eminence?'

'How do you mean?' Rosseau played his voice to sound confused. 'I think we are close to getting a result with the government.'

'How close?' Caspian sounded distracted.

'I spent the last couple of days with the attorney general. I believe he has altered his strategy and will campaign against the bill.'

'Will he kill it?'

'He now has a different view about it. Whether we see that in political action is yet to be seen. I'm very confident, though. Did you talk to the prime minister?'

'I haven't had time to consider that.' Caspian cut him short, taking control of the exchange. 'I received an anonymous note the other day suggesting there is footage of a senior Vatican official in a scandalous compromise.'

'Oh yes?' Rosseau smirked. 'Have you seen any evidence?'

'No, I have not, and I have asked all officers of the governorate if they have committed sinful acts which will compromise the Vatican.'

'I assume they all said no.' Rosseau grinned as he listened.

'So, I'm asking you.' Caspian paused. 'Have you been performing unsavoury acts that others may know?'

'Like what?'

'The note suggested a sexual incident involving a young person.'

'Boy or girl?'

'It didn't say, would it make a difference?'

'Yes, I believe it would.' Rosseau was enjoying himself as he lured Caspian into his web. 'I mean, I assume the person is teenage and therefore the media storm would not be as severe if it were a girl.'

'I can't believe you just said that,' Caspian snapped. 'You think sex with a young boy to be more sinful than with a girl?'

'What do you think, Holy Father?' Rosseau sat further up in his bed. 'Do you think having sex with a young boy is sinful?'

At first, Caspian didn't respond, then offered, 'It depends on the age of the person, I suppose.'

'Sex with a seventeen-year-old is okay?'

'Yes, I have married seventeen-year-olds.'

'Sixteen?'

'I don't want to play this stupid game with you. I just want to know if you have any dark secrets that could be out there to embarrass the church.'

'No, I don't, do you?'

'Of course I don't. I have passed the note to the gendarmerie and they will begin an investigation. We need to be open and transparent on this because the media will smell a scandal unless we do.'

Rosseau checked his phone, flicking to a recording app, and then asked, 'What do you expect to happen should the person be a high-ranking Vatican official?'

'If we have conclusive evidence, then there is no option other than to end their appointment in the church.'

'No matter the ranking?'

'Yes, of course; no matter the ranking.'

Rosseau smiled, tapping the record button off. 'Will you call the prime minister?' There was no immediate response.

'No, I'll leave that for you to manage.'

Rosseau flinched.

'Is there anything further you wish to discuss?'

Rosseau sighed. 'You may wish to get a copy of la Repubblica. I'm advised there may be an editorial that may interest you.'

'Peace be with you, my son.'

'And also with you, Holy Father.' Rosseau almost choked on the words as he ended the call. He didn't wish to have anything to do with the prime minister, and the instruction from Caspian had annoyed him a little more than he was expecting.

He tossed the phone aside and wriggled back into the bed for much needed sleep, but his mind could not rest as it raced through managing the many options before him. His priority was to resolve the Australian referendum issue. If that meant meeting with the prime minister, then so be it. Once done, he would return to Rome and plan a coup; well, at the very least, a promotion to the pontifical commission and the role of president.

Frustrated, he snatched at his phone, scrolling through his contacts yet again and tapping the entry he wanted.

'Hello, this is Cardinal Rosseau. I would like to arrange a meeting with the prime minister, if I may, for tomorrow.'

299

CHAPTER
50

Parliament House early morning was silent, the busyness of government yet to increase the hubbub. Parliamentary staff attended, preparing the house for the increased activity from six a.m.. Nancy Pasco walked to the house early, instructing her security detail to follow in the car rather than walk with her. She wanted the crispness of the Canberra air to clear her head after a day of slothful misery, drinking too much again, and missing an important speech she was to deliver to the Business Council of Australia.

It surprised the security team at the front entrance to see the prime minister enter through their station rather than the ministerial entrance at the other end of the building. She walked into the grand marble front foyer of the parliament, moving through the hall with its stunning staircases to even more security on the side entrance, off the hall. She wasn't carrying her security pass to wave over the scanner, and a smiling parliamentary security guard pushed a door release button to allow her entry.

She clomped her way along the polished wooden floors, gazing out onto the gardens beautifying the House of Representatives' wing. It was a long walk to her office, crossing over an atrium which opened up in the centre of the building. Pausing at the Pool of Reflection, a black marble water feature within the floor, she gawked up into the grand flagpole above her at the top of the building, the major feature of the parliament. She could see the flag fluttering and shook off a sudden chill as she set off toward her office.

She passed the newspaper library and rounded into the blue carpeted corridor leading to the cabinet room and her office. Waving to the security guard positioned behind security glass at the entry, she tugged on the large brass door handle and entered the office. In front of her was the doorway to the prime ministerial courtyard, where she delivered press conferences, and to the right were her staff offices. She headed to them to see if there were any early risers and found two media officers checking through the national press, identifying potential issues for the government.

'How long have you two been here?'

Taken aback to see the prime minister so early, they stumbled over a response. 'We were both in at four,' one smiled.

The other added, 'We get here every day to review the press.'

'Outstanding work and thank you for your efforts.' She couldn't remember their names.

Pasco turned back toward her office. She thought about a Bloody Mary to start the day, but resisted as she didn't have any tomato juice, settling instead for chilled water from her refrigerator within a cabinet along the side wall. She circled her desk, flopping into the chair and examining the daily schedule centred on her leather compendium. She noted that Cardinal Rosseau was due to meet her at ten. Osborne and Gellibrand were booked for a 'discussion' at eleven. The highlighted terminology made her smile. With those Machiavellian students, their meeting could only ever be about leadership.

A flustered Donna Kellaway marched into the room. 'Nan, what are you doing here so early?'

'Good morning to you, babe. Sleep well?'

'Like a baby until your security detail let me know you were walking to the house.' She dumped her bags and jacket on a chair at the desk, sitting on the other. 'What's up? Why are you here?'

'It seems I slept too long yesterday, so I came in early to catch up. Why are you here?'

'Doing my job, of course.'

'What will your job entail today?'

Kellaway didn't reply, surprised by the cantankerous snipe from Pasco. 'We have to prepare for a couple of important meetings this morning and perhaps plan our response for the party meeting next week.'

'Our response?' Pasco responded. 'Don't you mean my response?'

Kellaway stalled her reply. 'What's wrong?'

The prime minister stood and collected her glass of water, sipping as she moved to the large windows, gazing out into the courtyard, now brightening as the sun dawned. She crossed her arms, the glass resting on an elbow.

'Is it worth it?'

It confused Kellaway. 'What?'

'Everything. Is it worth it?'

'Of course. You're doing great things for the country.'

'I'm not so sure that is the case.' Pasco took more water. 'Otherwise, why are Gellibrand and Osborne coming to see me?'

'This is what we need to address this morning, before we see them.'

'What would life be like without all of this?'

Kellaway stood and moved to her, keeping a respectful distance. It conflicted her about her roles as staffer and lover, challenged by the mood of the prime minister. 'I don't understand, Nan. What are you saying?'

Pasco turned, arms still folded, contemplating her chief of staff. 'Would I have met you if I were not in politics? Indeed, would you find me attractive if I were not prime minister?'

Kellaway rubbed her nose, then cupped her cheek, her elbow tight to her hip, her brow furrowed. 'What are you saying, that I'm only in it for the status? That I'm some sort of doctor's wife who gets off on the power and privilege?'

The women glared at each other for a moment, then Pasco broke away, moving back to her desk and sitting. She settled her glass and took command, dragging her chair in and motioning Kellaway to sit.

'What are the plans for the day?'

'You're kidding me, right?' Kellaway placed her hands on her hips, motionless. 'You say something stupid like that and expect me not to react?'

'You're my chief of staff. I expect you to do your job, now what is planned?'

Kellaway regressed and sat at the desk, tugging a spiral notepad from her bag and flicking through pages until she came to a clean sheet. She poised her pen and glanced up with a snarky expression, waiting for the prime minister, then said, 'What do you want to do?'

'What is the cardinal coming to speak to me about?'

'I didn't speak to him last night. Cheryl advised he has a message from the Pope.'

'So, what? Why does he need to come see me?'

'He is departing for Rome this evening and wanted an audience with you.'

'Yeah, right,' Pasco sniffed. 'He no doubt has done his job and has the Catholics excited; so much so, they are planning a leadership coup.'

'Could be the case, I suppose, but for him to want to see you now could mean something else.'

'Like what? The Pope has made his position very clear, and the cardinal has been rendering succour to Stevedore, so why would he want to see me?'

'One last request to defer the legislation, I would imagine.'

Pasco rocked back in her chair and thought for a moment. 'You know, this could be good for us.'

'You mean good for you, don't you?' Kellaway smiled sassily.

Pasco curled a smirk in response. 'Don't be like that, otherwise momma will smack your bottom.'

Kellaway squirmed in her chair and fluttered her eyes. 'I do like it when you think I'm naughty.'

The two shared a look for just a moment.

'Now stay focused, Kell, please,' Pasco countered, reverting to the game of politics. 'If we can link his visit to the parliament today with Osborne, I think that may get us a few votes in the party room.'

'How would we do that?'

'Let the media know he's coming. Perhaps they can film him coming into the house, or better yet, leaving via the courtyard.' Pasco glanced out onto the now bright courtyard. 'I can make a meal of it, gushing over him.'

'Kiss his ring, perhaps.'

Pasco snorted. 'Yes, perhaps, even kiss his ring.'

'I don't get it. Why would that make a difference?'

'Because at midday, I will announce a leadership spill for next Tuesday. I then answer questions, implying that the Catholic Church is not only meddling in the referendum legislation, but they have conspired a leadership coup.'

Kellaway chewed on the end of her pen, thinking through the idea. 'You know, this is why I love you. You're a brilliant conniving politician, and this could set you up for a strong win on Tuesday.'

'Please don't say that.'

'What, that I love you?'

'Well, that as well; I'm not conniving.'

'Yes, you are, my queen, you know what you are doing all the time.'

'Once I did, but that was long ago.'

'You are the perfect Shakespearean character, you are conniving and cruel.'

Pasco harrumphed. 'I'm not cruel. Folks take advantage of me all the time.'

'To suggest I'm only attracted to you because of your status is very cruel.'

'Don't be ridiculous.'

'Would you like a drink?' The prime minister waved a brandy bottle at the cardinal as he took a seat on the lounge, as she had directed.

'A little early to be drinking, don't you think?' The request surprised Rosseau.

'It's midday in Auckland, and nip gets my heart pumping. And in this job, you need a good heart starter.'

'Not for me, thanks.' Rosseau dragged a file from his leather satchel as he settled in.

Pasco splashed a generous portion into a crystal tumbler and sculled it, before pouring another, taking a seat at a lounge chair opposite the cardinal.

'What can I help you with today, Your Eminence?'

'The Holy Father remains very concerned about the government's decision to continue with the legislation to enact euthanasia. He has requested that I attend today to present further our case for a deferment of the bill.'

'This is not possible. I have already expressed this view to you. Why aren't you listening?'

'All things are possible with God.' Rosseau smiled, crossing his legs, steepling his fingers before his face. 'I have spent time with your attorney general, and I believe, from our discussions, that he may have a different view on the government's policy.'

'Whatever Charles believes or says doesn't matter. He doesn't speak on behalf of my government.'

'There is an unwillingness within the community to embrace your government's position, you know that. You may lose the referendum, which would affect your leadership and therefore your government's standing in the community.'

Pasco slumped her head sideways into her hand, stroking her fingers through her hair, pondering a response. 'Why is this so important to the Vatican?'

'As I've advised, your referendum threatens core issues for us, in our teachings and our business model.'

'I get the teachings, thou shall not kill, blah, blah, blah.' Pasco spiralled her hand in a large gesture wave. 'Why do you think your business model is under threat?'

'This change to the laws will affect our aged care and hospice centres.' Rosseau tightened his lips as he spoke, suppressing his annoyance at the prime minister's alcohol-fuelled exuberance. 'We will never sanction euthanasia at our hospitals or other facilities and therefore we will have a drop in business.'

Pasco almost laughed. 'A drop in business? Is this how you see providing health services to the community?'

'Without the church, the government would struggle to meet the needs of the community.'

'Dare I say, Cardinal, that sounds a little sanctimonious, and might I suggest, coming from a religious leader, a tad pious?' Pasco pursed her lips, covering a smile that was trying to escape.

Rosseau bristled, straightened his legs and sat erect in the lounge. 'The government can ill afford to lose the support of the church in delivering services to the community, be it in health, education or other services we provide.'

'You do it tax free; thus it's a nice little earner for you.'

The comment unsettled Rosseau. 'You must be joking? You think the enormous number of services we offer the community are a nice little earner?'

'You know there are demands to bring you into the tax system. If you fight the government on this, then perhaps we should reconsider your privileged position.'

'You can't be serious?' Rosseau struggled to stand from the soft lounge. 'You are the first prime minister to threaten us like that. I will not stand for it.'

Pasco smiled. 'You just did.'

'You're expecting me not to report back to the Vatican about the nation's leader's very poor behaviour when discussing this important legislation?'

'You have already intruded far too much into the politics of this country and you deserve little support.'

Rosseau watched as Pasco struggled to her feet after finishing the contents of the tumbler, then asked, 'What are you suggesting?'

'You are working against me to change the leadership. You and your band of Catholic cronies within the government want one of yours to be the leader and do your bidding.'

'That is a ridiculous proposition.'

'Is it?' Pasco faced the cardinal, straightening her shoulders back with her hands fisted on her hips. 'Do you deny that your lackey, Parker Osborne, is about to confront me over the leadership?'

'I do not know what you are talking about.'

'You deny speaking with Osborne and his band of fellow travellers in Sydney?'

'We had a prayer meeting; of course we did.'

'Not what I heard.' Pasco tapped her nose. 'It seems Osborne has a rat in his ranks. I know that you and he have discussed changing leaders.'

'Whatever happens to you will have nothing to do with me.'

'I suspect you are wrong on that as well, Your Eminence.' Pasco seemed triumphant, and she waved open her arms as if giving a sermon. 'Whether I send the referendum to the Australian people will be my decision, not yours, and not your confederates like Parker Osborne.'

'Are you mad?'

Pasco tossed her head back, grinning. 'Maybe I am. The fact is, the church has little influence in Australia. I represent all Australians; you, on the other hand, represent a diminishing number of religious nuts.'

'Prime Minister, I think we have nothing more to say to each other.' Rosseau bowed.

'Finally, you get it.' Pasco nodded in return. 'We had nothing to say on this or any other issue.'

'Your foolishness will go unrewarded.'

'Cardinal, when I'm confronted by my political enemies I'm always reminded of Corinthians 16, 13: be on your guard; stand firm in the faith; be courageous; be strong.' Pasco smiled as she ushered the cardinal from the office. 'You would be best to remember that passage when you stand against my government, because my government applies it every day in every discussion.' She waved to the courtyard. 'My staff has a car waiting for you in the courtyard, ready to transfer you to the airport. Enjoy your travel home.'

'This will not end well for you.'

'To see your face right now is reward enough for me.'

Donna Kellaway was waiting to usher the cardinal to the car.

'I can't say it has been a pleasure, Prime Minister.' Rosseau strode off. 'Peace be with you.'

As the cardinal entered the courtyard and marched to the car, cameras began motoring. The smiling Pasco stood by the door, waving to the car as it began its journey. She hoped the photographs would picture her as a formidable leader.

At eleven o'clock, Kellaway entered the prime minister's office, announcing the leader of the senate, Ann Gellibrand, and the treasurer, Parker Osborne. Pasco remained seated at her desk, a foot on an opened lower drawer, a glass of wine in her resting hand, waiting.

As her colleagues settled, Kellaway taking a seat to the side, the prime minister spoke. 'It's never, ever good news when a small delegation of the leadership group comes visiting the leader. What do you want to tell me?'

'Good morning to you, Prime Minister.' Gellibrand was miffed at the immediate confrontation. 'How are you today?'

Osborne interrupted. 'She's not interested in any of that, Ann.'

'You're right, Parker. I'm not, so let's get to it.'

'Prime Minister, it is my melancholy duty to advise you that the party room has lost confidence in you. The issues surrounding the referendum, rumours that your personal life is falling off the rails, with your husband now living in Sydney, and suggestions that there has been a misuse of travel allowances,' Gellibrand announced, as if addressing the chamber.

'So, what?' Pasco snarled.

Osborne sighed, then added, 'Well, Prime Minister, it seems you're not doing your job, and the party wants to put an end to it. They want leadership and they aren't getting it from you at the moment.'

'No leadership?' Pasco laughed as she raised her glass in a salute.

'We believe the nation needs certainty. We think that since the result of the plebiscite was known we have been meandering, allowing the opposition to reposition itself and gain in the polls,' Gellibrand added.

'Is that it?'

Gellibrand and Osborne glanced at each other before nodding, then Osborne confirmed their thoughts. 'Pretty much.'

'The travel allowance issue is all within guidelines and therefore becomes irrelevant.' Pasco took a sip of wine and then wheeled into her desk. 'My personal life has nothing to do with my leadership. My husband is at Kirribilli House for a month whilst our daughter receives special needs treatment at a Sydney clinic. I suspect you didn't know that, as why else would you raise it?'

'Prime Minister, I'm sorry. I didn't know.' Gellibrand shifted in her seat, now uncomfortable at having agreed to attend the meeting. She was there because Senator Richards had threatened her health ministry appointment, and if she resisted speaking out, they also threatened her preselection.

'This is beside the point.' Osborne could sense his colleague weakening. 'The referendum is the real political issue you have failed to address. If we lose it, which is likely, the government will never recover.'

'You micks are all the same, aren't you, Parker?' Pasco glared at her treasurer. 'Any sign of trouble and you want to raise the white flag of peace.'

'This has nothing to do with my faith and I'm offended you've raised it.'

'You can be offended as much as you like,' Pasco mocked. 'I'm offended that you are sitting here discussing my leadership, but I've not said anything, now have I?'

'The church has nothing to do with this debate on euthanasia.' Osborne changed tact.

'You're kidding me?' Pasco bounced backwards in her chair. 'I've just had the Pope's emissary, your mate, here shooting the breeze and threatening my leadership.'

Osborne worked his tongue in his cheek at the news. 'I didn't know that.'

'Yes, it seems he doesn't want the referendum because of potential loss of funds to their business.'

'The referendum is about spiritual teachings,' Osborne emphasised.

'Not to the Vatican.' Pasco took a large mouthful of wine, draining the glass. 'Now unless you have other serious business for me, then I suggest you go do your numbers, because we will have a nice minor battle next Tuesday.'

'It shouldn't have to come to this, Prime Minister.' Gellibrand returned to the discussion. 'I think it's time to go, Nancy.'

'Are those your words or Senator Richards'?' Pasco sneered.

Gellibrand shrugged as Osborne rose from his seat.

'We would prefer you to resign, Prime Minister, but if you are going to fight, then let me just say...' Osborne glared at Pasco. 'Your legacy will never recover.'

'Oh, fuck off, Parker, you and this legacy bullshit.'

Pasco bounced out of her chair.

'You haven't got a candidate good enough to lead, and the mistake you are making is not knowing your numbers. Politics and leadership are about arithmetic, and I suspect my math is better than yours,' Pasco said.

Osborne paused for a moment before following Gellibrand from the room, then said over his shoulder, 'The government needs to change. We do that by replacing the leader next week.'

'By the way, Parker, that agreement we had? It no longer exists.'

Kellaway followed the delegation to the door, closing it behind them and turning the locking nib to secure the door from intrusion. She turned to Pasco, beaming with admiration.

'That was so awesome; that was such a display of power. I'm so proud of you.'

She crossed the room with open arms.

CHAPTER

51

The traffic report was finishing, and as the intro music to his show began, Dennis Sadler took a sip of his peppermint tea from his fine Wedgwood cup, cleared his throat and waited to begin his opening monologue. Today would be different; today he will kill the leadership of the prime minster.

The red light on his control panel meant he was live.

'It's the start of a new week, and tomorrow we could have a new prime minister. They say a week is a long time in politics. Well for me, twenty-four hours is a lifetime, because, dear listeners, I think we should encourage the government that a change of prime minister is in order for this nation. I believe the government to be rancid and in serious trouble, incapable of leading us. When we are crying out for leadership, we get the bumbling Nancy Pasco, trying to encourage cohesion, patriotism and pride in our country. We have an inept prime minister more interested in her next drink than policy.'

Sadler had been rehearsing the speech since Friday, when he had watched the shambles of the prime minister's media conference. She appeared flushed and slurred a few words, which to Sadler was telling, as although it was only midday, it seemed she might have had a drink. He shook his head as she blamed the Catholic Church for destabilising the government, admitting to meeting with the Pope's emissary in which the cardinal pressurised her to comply with their requests to stop the referendum.

'Listeners, you might remember that last Friday the prime minster, in a performance which is best described as classic pantomime, slated the Catholic Church, implicating them in a conspiracy to change the government of Australia. The prime minister suggested that the Pope's emissary had attended her that morning, insisting the government reject the Kill Bill, and if it didn't, then there would be a planned leadership coup.

'Frankly, this was the theatre of the absurd. No candidates have put their hands up to challenge her so far, and she is forcing a leadership spill upon them to test the party room's support. This is not leadership; this is madness.

'So, over the weekend, I did a little digging.' Sadler had done no digging. He was delivered a dirt sheet of information and added it to the information he already knew. 'What I've found is staggering and should concern every Australian, for I'm now of the firm opinion that we have a prime minister who is out of her mind. Nancy Pasco is not fit to even sit in the parliament, let alone lead the government, and the country.'

Parker Osborne was bunkered down in his Canberra office listening to Sadler's criticism of the prime minister and flinched at the abrasiveness of the words. Parliament was in session, its first day back after an extended four-week break; however, he wanted private time away from the business of the house after question time to listen to the programme. This rant and the subsequent follow up in the morning papers would add incredible incentive for his colleagues to end the prime minister's reign, in a subtle, yet lethal, coup de grâce at tomorrow's party meeting.

'I build my case against the prime minister on three fundamental principles.' Sadler was building a prosecutorial case. 'These are trust, judgment, and loyalty. If you are weak in these pillars of leadership and integrity, then I ask… how can you expect to keep the honour of serving as our prime minister?'

The producer of the radio programme had advised Nancy Pasco that there would be a monologue at the start of the Sadler Show and she rocked her desk chair as she listened, arms locked across her chest, Donna Kellaway sitting opposite.

'Let's look at the trust pillar, which I believe the prime minister has squandered over a period, leaving the electorate with little faith in her ability to lead the country. Just late last week, I was provided reams of files exposing various politicians in their misuse of travel allowances. Once my producers sifted through the data, there was one name that consistently came to the fore… Nancy Pasco, the prime minister.' Sadler's tone seemed quizzical and surprised as he read through the list. 'It seems the prime minister, after demanding ministers use domestic airlines instead of the RAAF fleet of VIP aircraft, such as the zippy little falcons, has been using them for her own travel.

'Now, I understand the prime minister needs to have flexibility in her travel arrangements, and of course there are security considerations, but why is she ghosting the VIP fleet for holidays and personal travel?' Sadler moved his mouth closer to the microphone, lowered his tone and said, 'I don't mind the PM travelling and doing her job, but when she orders flights to traipse around the country, then I get a little upset, and so should you, listeners.'

Osborne smiled when Sadler asked listeners to call in and record their displeasure.

'What do I mean by ghost flights? Well, these are flights that are empty. That's right, with no one, and that means no passengers on the flight, when they are sent to either pick up or drop off the PM and her staff. When I say the prime minister's staff, I only mean one staff member, not her media adviser, not her policy adviser, but on most occasions it's her chief of staff, Miss Donna Kellaway.'

Pasco winced.

'Now, I don't know if you have ever heard of Miss Kellaway. No one had heard of her until they pulled her from obscurity in Western Australia and added to the PM's staff. And, it seems from her resume she was a journo on some rag in Perth, with no apparent management experience; yet this woman has been thrust into the key position within the PM's office. This means that the prime minister of Australia's chief of staff has zero, let me repeat that, zero management experience.

'I don't know, Miss Kellaway. I hear she is attractive, not that that should make a difference in someone's capacity to do their job. I'm just saying that she is attractive, as an observation, this is what I'm told. Anyway, she may be skilled in policy, diplomacy, media, politics, economics and the essential management of the myriad of advisers and staff that the prime minister's office must have to run the nation, but her resume does not support those assumptions. She may be very experienced in all those areas, but I know she isn't. So, the question one has to ask is how, and why, did she get her job? For someone who has the enormous responsibility of running the prime minister of Australia's office, how did she get the job?

'Her resume states she spent two years in London on various assignments, which, as you would know, is the gap two years many young Australians succumb to, but in this case, these assignments aren't listed. In fact, it lists no British company as providing any work experience for her whilst she was in London.'

Pasco glanced at Kellaway, who avoided her glance with head bowed, listening to her history being broadcast.

'She spent twelve months at an ad agency and eighteen months on a rural newspaper. She worked in production at a radio station, but the resume doesn't identify whether she was a programme producer. It's hard to say from this resume, but I would place her at early to mid-thirties. So, we have a young chief of staff, with very little business and policy experience, appointed to manage the prime minister's office, yet she spends most of her time travelling with the PM… how come?

'The prime minister ghosted a flight to Townsville and back when she was there for three days earlier this year. Her official diary doesn't show any meetings or work completed. She went up there with her staffer, sent the VIP plane back to Canberra empty, then had the VIP plane return three days later… empty, to pick the holiday makers up, returning them to Canberra.

'Here's the rub. It cost twenty-two thousand dollars each way for the empty flights. That's a total cost of a staggering forty-four thousand taxpayer dollars spent on ghost flights to satisfy the flight demands of the prime minister, when a commercial flight could have been taken for far less than the amazing eighty-eight thousand dollars total cost for the three-day trip.' Sadler paused for a moment, then with menace, asked, 'What was she doing in Townsville that would warrant an eighty-eight thousand dollar use of the VIP fleet?

'There are others. A trip to Cairns soon after the Townsville trip. What for? No one knows. Except we learn from the members' interest disclosure documents that your prime minister bought an investment property at Trinity Beach. Coincidence? In my mind, not likely. She was there four days with, guess who, her chief of staff. The question I ask is this: who is looking after the prime minister's office when the PM and her chief of staff are away together on apparent government business? Or buying property?

'We have requested the PM's office to provide details on this trip, but we are yet to have a reply.'

Pasco looked over to Kellaway, who glanced up and nodded, before dropping her head.

'There is a ghost trip to Adelaide which cost you, dear listener, the taxpayer, eight thousand dollars, a trip to Darwin, one to Moree, another to Mildura. I could go on, and I confess, I am gob smacked by the list, but I think I have made my point.

'Who do you trust to manage your tax funds when we have a prime minister spending it on holidays and empty planes?'

Osborne clapped his hands, rubbing them briskly together with a broad smile as he listened.

'So for me, listeners, trust is dead with this prime minster. Dead as a carcass hanging from a tree swinging in the breeze, beset with a plague of flies.' Sadler waited for a few moments before continuing. 'The next pillar of leadership we are lacking with Nancy Pasco, is judgment. We want the person in charge to be making the right decisions on our behalf, and I suspect we have a dud in this prime minister with making decisions.

'Take, for example, the recent plebiscite, which cost us ninety million dollars. There is not one iota of support for having universal euthanasia laws. We have some states that have enacted death with dignity laws, but the prime minister, in her wisdom, if indeed she has any thought the people of Australia should determine if we need a new law. And what did they do? We told the government to do the job we elect them to do and make a decision.

'Now we are afflicted with this ludicrous idea of having a referendum to change the constitution to enact a death act. You see, dear listeners, to override state laws on this issue of life and death, we will need to add the idea to the constitution, therefore, we need a referendum.

'We just had a plebiscite and now we are being forced to have a referendum to enable the federal government to get involved in something so personal, and so private, in our lives. Why should the government tell us when we should die? This Kill Bill is a ridiculous proposition, showing a complete disregard for the states and the will of the people, who said no.

'Now the prime minister is seeking to reach a political outcome via a referendum, and almost fifty percent of citizens don't support it. Pasco will need a majority vote, in the majority of states, to get the constitution changed, and that listeners, will not happen. This is a ridiculous decision and a total waste of money, reflecting poorly on the judgment of anyone who supports this stupid waste of money.'

Kellaway got up and walked over to the side cabinet. She pulled a bottle of chardonnay from the stocked fridge, opened it and poured two generous glasses. She sidled back, handing one to a grateful Pasco, and squeezed her shoulder, reassuring her, before resuming her seat.

'That is a definite strike two for the pillars of leadership and adds to the reasons the government should act tomorrow and vote for a new prime minister.' Sadler dropped his tone again. 'Listeners, as you well know, I believe private lives are just that, private. We do not need to go down the English or American track, promoting the sleaze of public life in the media. What people do behind curtains is no business of mine, nor anyone else. The private lives of our politicians are their business and must remain private.' Sadler paused for a dramatic moment. 'Unless what they do is not private and in public.'

Osborne pursed his lips, sitting forward in his chair, as if making sure he didn't miss any of what was about to be said.

Pasco glanced over at Kellaway with a querying smirk. Kellaway shrugged, not knowing where Sadler could be heading.

'Listeners, it pains me to talk about this, but it goes to the pillar of loyalty. We demand loyalty from our leaders as they demand loyalty from us, fair enough. This is what we expect. What politicians do in private is their business, but we demand loyalty.

'Sadly, it has come to my attention that the prime minister has not been loyal, not to her family. Therefore, her disloyalty to them means she cannot be loyal to others, meaning us, the mob who votes for her. If you dump on your own family, then you'll dump on your country, as far as I'm concerned.'

Kellaway placed her glass on the desk, moving to the other side to be with Pasco. She knelt beside the chair holding Pasco's hand, gazing up into her blank, brooding face. Pasco didn't respond; it was if she was catatonic.

'Listeners, I have vivid photographic evidence of the prime minister in what I will politely say is a compromising position on the bonnet of a car in a public carpark. I'm sad to say that this series of photographs leaves nothing to the imagination. Now I don't want to comment on the person the prime minister is in this compromising position with, that is not my business. Let's just say it wasn't her husband. This is a public carpark, at the back of a hotel, around ten o'clock at night, in regional New South Wales; and, I'm told, they took these photographs just a few months ago.'

Osborne jumped from his chair, fist pumping during an almighty squeal. 'YES!'

'We shouldn't have to raise this issue, as I'm not sure the prime minister's family is aware of this incident. But the truth needs to be known before the vote tomorrow.

'Who is this prime minister, and can we trust her to do her job? I think not.'

Vera Thompson smiled when Charlie Stevedore appeared at the desk of intensive care reception. She smiled, opening her arms for a hug, and he complied.

'I wasn't expecting you back until tomorrow night. Aren't you supposed to be in Canberra?'

'I would not go up, but it seems there is a bit of a bun fight over the leadership, and they think I may be needed, so I'm off to the airport now, and thought I'd drop in and visit Vikki.'

'I heard the news a little while ago, is it true?'

'Is what true?'

'They have accused the prime minister of ripping off her travel allowance and using taxpayer funds.'

'There is always an explanation.' Stevedore leaned on the reception desk top. 'You always have to question these stories, who benefits from them the most? If you work that out, then you understand the reasons behind the story. I suspect one of my colleagues wants to make it difficult for the PM tomorrow, which is the reason they have asked me to go to Canberra.'

'You know, I studied and trained for fifteen years before I was confident to be a specialist at what I do, and yet, I can never work out how you do whatever it is you do.' Thompson thrust her hands into her white coat pockets. 'Politicians are all a bunch of crazy egotistical shysters as far as I'm concerned.'

'That would be me, I suppose,' Stevedore smiled.

'Oh, sorry.' It mortified Thompson. She cupped her mouth, reaching out an apologetic hand. 'I didn't mean you. Gee, I stuffed that up real bad.'

'Don't worry about it; I get it all the time, even from Vikki,' said Stevedore, reassuring her with a pat to her shoulder.

'Sorry, Charles… umm, anyway…' Thompson wanted to change the subject. 'The good news is, your daughter is awake, and you can go see her now if you like.'

'Fair dinkum?'

'Yes, Doctor Nguyen is just finishing tests. She should be done by the time you sterilise, so, let's go see her.'

'That's fantastic news.' Stevedore beamed, catching Thompson off guard by hugging her, then pecking her on the cheek as he stepped back from her. 'Brilliant, thank you.'

Thirty minutes later, Stevedore and Professor Thompson were standing amongst the machines, leaning over to look and speak to Vikki. When her eyes recognised Stevedore's, gleaming between a mask and cap, they crinkled into a smile as her face brightened.

'Hello, my darling,' Stevedore gushed. 'Welcome back.'

Vikki could barely speak, but squeezed out, 'Hi Daddy.'

'The medical team tell me you are on the mend.'

Vikki nodded slightly; she flicked her eyes to the professor and back to her father. 'Where's Dougie?'

Stevedore continued the veneer of smiling, thinking about what to say.

'We have informed him you're awake and he'll be here to see you tomorrow when you have rested,' Thompson interjected.

Vikki glanced at the professor, nodded and smiled. 'That's good.' She looked back at her father. 'How are you coping?'

Stevedore's eyes welled. 'Well, it's been a hell of a few days, I can tell you. I'm pleased to be talking to you.'

'I love you, Daddy.' Vikki struggled to get the words out, then added, 'I'm so sorry.'

'Nothing for you to be sorry about, honey; just trust in the medicos and you'll be home soon.' A tear dropped from the corner of Stevedore's eye. He turned to Thompson.

'I think that is enough of a visit for one day. We can do more tomorrow.' Thompson said.

Vikki's eyes drooped, and she nodded.

'I'm in Canberra tomorrow for a meeting, but I'll be back tomorrow night, so I shall see you then.'

Vikki smiled as she closed her eyes, prompting her visitors to step back and leave her.

'She's doing well,' Thompson said, as she placed her hand on Stevedore's shoulder, allowing him to pass through the sealed door first. 'Every day now she will improve, and we are monitoring the baby to ensure there are no problems.'

'Thank you, Professor; you have been magnificent.'

'Just doing my job, Charles,' Thompson said, as they headed into the corridor. 'Come, say goodbye on your way out.'

Stevedore smiled, bowed his head and moved off to the change room to rid himself of the garb. As he sat tying shoelaces, emotion flooded him. He first sniffed, then stifled a groan before a gush of shudders shrouded him, pushing him into a tearful breakdown. He supported his head as he sobbed into his hands. The relief, the stress, the anxiety and the worry rid itself from him as he thought about what could have been and how he had fought to save her.

Stevedore knocked on the professor's door twenty minutes later, more refreshed and with little evidence of his breakdown.

'Ah, there you are.' Thompson moved from behind her desk. 'Normally I would offer you a wine…'

'But you're a hospital.'

'Exactly.' Thompson stroked his arm and waved him to a seat. 'I just wanted to reassure you she's doing fine.'

'I know she's in quality care and I'm very appreciative,' Stevedore smiled.

'I wanted to say that we are yet to contact her husband. He hasn't responded to messages.'

Stevedore gnawed his bottom lip. 'Probably a good thing. Although Vikki seems keen to see him.'

'Yes, she would I expect. How do you want to handle telling her about the process we have been through?'

'Let me do that at the right time. I'll see how Ferguson responds before I talk to her. Who knows, she may never find out.'

'Love gets in the way sometimes.'

'Ferguson doesn't love her, that I'm sure of,' said Stevedore, almost snarling the words. 'I'll look to Vikki for cues and respond with the truth when she recovers.'

'Do you want anyone else to see her?'

'Not at this time, well, not until she is a little stronger. Who's asking?'

'We've taken a few calls; the police requested an interview.'

'Let's wait a few days before we do any of that.'

'Fair enough.' Thompson paused for a moment. 'What are your plans in Canberra?'

Stevedore rocked his head, 'Drums are beating for a change of leadership, but I'm not sure we should do that.'

'What about the referendum?'

'Not even sure I support it myself anymore. Not after seeing how it could be manipulated with Ferguson's attitude.'

'His behaviour is not a rare case,' Thompson said. 'I'm amazed at how family members insist on the manner of treatment for their supposed loved one. Some want them saved, no matter what, others want to end it as quick as they can, so they can get on with their lives.'

'I don't envy you.' Stevedore regarded her for a moment. 'Do you mind if I ask you a personal question?'

'Oh yes,' Thompson smiled and twisted in her chair. 'What could the attorney general be wanting to ask me? Have I killed anyone?'

'No.' Stevedore almost coughed the response.

'Then what do you want to ask me?'

Stevedore paused for a moment, hesitant whether he should ask. 'I've come to know you over the last week and I wonder… how does someone get on your dating roster?'

Thompson sat upright, a little stunned by the question. She glared at a now doubtful Stevedore, then smiled.

'You ask.'

CHAPTER

53

Doug Ferguson was feeling awkward. The light in the bedroom was increasing as the day beckoned. He needed to get home to change clothes and get off to the hospital. Mariner snuggled into his arm, her head resting on his chest and a leg draped over him. He gazed to the ceiling, thinking through his day and how he was going to manage his marriage.

'Can't you sleep?' Mariner croaked as she rolled away, still lying on his arm.

'I've been thinking.'

This sparked her attention, and she rolled back. 'What have you been thinking?'

'How I get out of this predicament with Vikki.'

She lowered her hand, cupping and gently squeezing him. 'There is no predicament.'

'Ow, be careful.' Ferguson tried to wriggle away from her hand, but she tightened her grip. 'Ouch, that hurts.'

Mariner frowned. 'Just remember who owns these two things and do what you've been told, understand?'

'Yes, let go, please,' Ferguson cried.

'I want you to tell her it's over, understand?'

Ferguson was taut, lifting himself away. 'Yes, I'll do it… I'll do it.'

She released her grip and wriggling down the bed, relaxing his tension.

Thirty minutes later Ferguson was sitting on the edge of the bed, slipping on his brogues and checking the five messages on his phone.

'It seems the hospital has been trying to get hold of me.'

'Nothing serious, I hope?'

'It might have to do with her condition, maybe she's woken up.'

'Once you find out, let me know. The sooner you let her know you are leaving her, the better it is for us.'

'I had better get going.'

Mariner rolled onto her stomach as she watched Ferguson leave the bedroom. 'Talk soon, darling, love you.'

Ferguson didn't respond, walking through the house, picking up his keys and pulling the front door closed. He stepped out onto the porch, breathing in the crisp morning air, filling his lungs. The sun was not yet up, shadowy shapes were forming, and he could hear the rubbish truck going about its collection further down the street, working its way toward him. He decided he had better get moving before the truck blocked him. He parked his car out front on the verge. He strode down the drive and out onto the street, checking the truck.

Ferguson didn't see him approach.

Rikki Ortega crossed the street from behind a row of parked cars. All Ferguson could feel was a gloved hand grabbing his mouth and a sharp pain in his back. It felt as if he was being punched in the kidneys. He resisted, trying to turn and identify who was punching him. Again and again the punches came to the same spot. Ferguson felt himself weaken, resistance failing.

Ortega thrust his hunting knife again, this time higher, letting Ferguson fall forward, limp, onto the car. Then, with a wielding arm from high, Ortega thrust the ten-inch blade into Ferguson's side to the hilt, piercing his ribs and plunging into his heart.

Air was expelled, and Ortega wrangled Ferguson's dead weight head-first into an almost empty roadside wheelie bin that he had set aside for this purpose.

Just ninety seconds after he had emerged, Ortega closed the lid and slunk off into the dense shrubbery that lined the street. He vaulted a fence, then peered back to ensure no curious neighbours were checking the blood streaked car or examining the bin.

The council truck arrived, its mechanical claw lifting the bin. It stopped during the process to assess weight, recording the overload against the residence. Then up it jerked above the truck, inverting the bin and banging its contents into the hopper to be squeezed further into the back of the truck.

As the truck squealed its brakes on the next residence, Ortega stepped out onto the path and strolled away.

Parker Osborne walked past the reception of Charlie Stevedore's Canberra ministerial office, heading through into his private room. Stevedore was behind his desk, working his way through a deep pile of files.

'Charlie,' Osborne announced as he hurried in, a bundle of morning papers under his arm. 'Nice to see you, ole son, when did you get in?'

'Late last night; I took a VIP up from Melbourne.'

'Naughty boy, according to the papers.'

'How do you mean? They wouldn't know my travel plans.'

'Not you, mate, the PM.' Osborne began tossing the papers one by one onto Stevedore's desk, displaying the headlines. 'It seems we have travel questions to be answered today whenever we see the press.'

Stevedore scanned the papers, each with a scathing headline about politicians being caught with their snouts in the travel trough; the biggest oinker was Prime Minister Pasco.

'Do they have to call us pigs?' Stevedore observed as he sifted through the collection.

'This will be the end of her,' Osborne stated. 'She can't survive this.'

'Did you need to do this to get the numbers?'

'I had nothing to do with this.' Osborne shook his head as he sprawled into a chair. 'I promise you.'

'How did they get their hands on this, who briefed them?' asked Stevedore as he waved at the newspapers.

'Where have you been, Charlie?' Osborne shook his head. 'Sadler knifed her yesterday in an editorial picked up by every news service.'

'What did he say?'

'She was not to be trusted; she was disloyal; and he called into question her decision about the referendum.' Osborne counted them off on his fingers. 'How's that going, anyway? Is this why you weren't here yesterday?'

Stevedore raised his eyebrows and bit his lower lip. 'I had personal things to do.'

'Anyway, she's toast. If she thought she had the numbers before the meeting, she won't have them now, no way.'

'If she doesn't have them, who does?'

Osborne smiled. 'I'm too modest to say.'

'Who's doing your numbers?'

'Stan Richards, and it'll cost me only one ministry.'

'Do you trust him?'

'He'll bring Queensland and New South Wales with him. I have the Catholics. And the West Australians, perhaps. Well...' Osborne scoffed. 'Who knows what they'll do? Flakes the lot of them.'

'Is Susie counting numbers?'

'Who cares, no one will vote for her.'

'What about an unknown?'

'Like who?' Osborne was now alert.

'A West Australian, for starters.'

'Mate, I only need fifty percent, plus one. I reckon I can get that with no favours.'

'What's your platform, your reason for change?'

'She's a pig not going to do it for you?'

'That ain't going to work for you. You'll need something to hang your hat on when you get questioned about it.'

'I suppose I'll talk about the economy and the need for a new direction.'

'You're the treasurer,' Stevedore laughed. 'Not sure that'll work.'

'The polls. We are lagging behind the other mob and we've lost the last thirty-three.'

'It'll only come back to haunt you if you use that. You know what happened years ago.'

'Yeah, that was a mistake.' Osborne displayed a nonchalance Stevedore considered pompous. 'Well, the news in the papers.'

'You'll need something else, I can assure you.'

'Christ, Charlie, why are you spoiling this for me?' His blasphemy startled Stevedore. 'Sorry, I shouldn't have said that, but you're rattling me.'

'What's Nancy's latest position on the referendum?'

'Oh, who the heck knows. She changes her view on it almost every day.'

Stevedore nodded. 'I think she's supporting it… well, that's what she told me she wanted to do.'

'Have you changed your view? You still support it, right?' Osborne wanted someone advocating it in the party room.

'Not sure any more.'

'Whoa there, big boy, not so fast.' Osborne sat forward, holding up his hand like a stop sign toward Stevedore. 'What do you mean you're changing your mind?'

Stevedore glared at his colleague and shook his head. 'The last few weeks have given me a fresh perspective.'

'Why? What's happened?'

'I don't believe you… really?' Stevedore fell back; his chair rocked.

'What?' Osborne asked.

'My daughter means nothing to you?'

'What's happened to her?' Osborne shook his head, gazing at Stevedore. 'I knew she wasn't well, but what has that got to do with the referendum?'

Stevedore paused for a moment.

'Nothing, I suppose. You're right; she has nothing to do with what we're talking about.'

'How is she, by the way?'

'She's fine and sends you her regards.' Stevedore cleared his throat. 'What time is the meeting?'

'It's been called for nine, before the joint party room meeting.' Osborne sat back, crossing his legs. 'Not sure what I'm going to say to those National Party blokes.'

'About what?'

'The referendum?' Osborne snapped.

Stevedore shook his head in disbelief. 'You're against it just like them, are you not?'

Osborne screwed his face, then smirked as he nodded his head. 'Yeah, nah, not really. I want us to do it, so I can then run a negative campaign as prime minister and kill it as an issue once and for all.'

'What happens to you if the referendum gets up?'

'It won't, and even if it does, then I tell the punters I accept their decision and we get on with it.'

'How magnanimous of you. How will the Vatican react?'

'Not well, I suspect, but I'll placate them; maybe, toss money at them, it's worked in the past.'

'Is this how you're going to run government?'

'How do you mean?'

'Tossing money at people?'

'How else do we get elected so we can do the things that need to be done?' Osborne said, shifting in his chair. 'Politics is only ever about two things, money and votes. We use the money to buy the votes.' He smiled like a used car salesman. 'It's the same at preselection, it's the same at the electorate level, and the same at government level, politics 101. Money means votes.'

'I'm more cynical about that. I prefer integrity, trust and giving folks something to dream about, and strive for.'

'You keep thinking that way, please.' Osborne scratched his cheek with a disdainful leer across his face. 'That's why you'll be a great attorney general for my government.' His tone sparked up. 'Unless, of course, you want to be a foreign minister. It's about time we got rid of Madeleine. The old duck is past her use by date.'

Stevedore rubbed his chin into the palm of his hand as he considered Osborne. 'Look, Ozzie, I have quite a few things to do before the party meeting. Could you give me some time?'

'Yes, of course, sorry.' Osborne sprung up, collected his newspapers and moved to the door. 'I have plenty of reading to do before the meeting. This will be fun, see you there.'

Stevedore picked at his teeth with his thumbnail as he considered the discussion, wondering what he should do. He reached for the phone, pushing the prime minister's button.

'Hello, Charles, I've just been thinking about you. How's Victoria?'

'She's good, Prime Minister. She was conscious yesterday, and I had the opportunity of speaking with her.'

'That's glorious news. Is she recovering okay? What do the medicos have to say?'

'She's doing very well, and the head surgeon, you may know her, Professor Thompson, believes she will recover with limited scarring.'

'That's amazing.' Pasco fell silent, waiting for Stevedore to raise the issue she was expecting.

'Prime Minister, are you sure about calling a spill this morning?'

It surprised Pasco. 'I thought you were going to tell me you couldn't support me.'

'I'm not sure I could support anyone else.'

'We all know who is coming after me.'

'Only if you call a spill, why do it?'

'I have to overcome this rubbish about me that's out there in the media.'

'You don't need to put your leadership on the line.'

'I hear you, Charles, but Sadler's show just confirmed that I should test my support,' Pasco said. 'If I don't kill the leadership speculation now, then it will hang around for months, killing our chances at the election.'

'I'm not sure Ozzie is the right alternative. I would prefer you to rethink it.'

'You're a solid colleague, Charles. I've appreciated your counsel in the past. I'm not sure I can survive in the electorate if I don't bring it on this morning.'

'Do you have the numbers?'

'I think I do.' Pasco sounded confident. 'I think I've nullified Richards. I offered him a better portfolio than what Parker offered.'

'You think he is solid?'

'I reckon he is. I also think I have the West Australians.'

'You can get the Catholics if you kill the referendum.'

'I've thought about it.' Pasco softened her voice. 'What's your advice?'

'I think I'm compromised with what happened to Victoria, but if I were you, I would stick to my guns and go for it.'

'You don't support it?'

'I don't know how I feel at the moment, it's too raw for me,' Stevedore said.

'Will you support it in the party room?'

'I'll support you, but don't ask me to speak, as I think I may lose it.'

'Fair enough.' Pasco lightened her tone. 'Have you seen the papers?'

Stevedore hesitated a moment. 'Yes, I have.'

'What did you think?'

'I think you should not spill the leadership.'

'You think the headlines might change votes?'

Stevedore didn't respond.

'Charles? What do you think?'

'I think it may affect the party vote, yes.'

'Thanks for your honesty; I appreciate it.'

'Are you okay, Nancy? Do you want me to come over?'

Pasco brightened. 'I'm okay; all is well. I'll see your smiling face in the party room at nine.'

'Take care, Nancy.'

'You too, Charles, and thank you for the years of friendship you have given me.'

'I've enjoyed working with you, Nancy; you're a good friend.' Stevedore's eyes welled.

'Bye now.' Pasco ended the call.

CHAPTER

55

The prime minister was scanning department papers when a staffer interrupted, reminding her it was 8.45 and time to leave for the party room. She stood, scooping up her leather compendium and three research books on euthanasia she wanted to return to the parliamentary library.

'Is Donna in?'

'She's called in sick, I'm afraid, Prime Minister.'

'Too hot for her, do you reckon?' Pasco smiled. 'I suppose she has seen the news and has a sudden headache.'

'I couldn't say,' the staffer replied.

'This is the trouble with politics, no one can say anything.' Pasco brushed past her, stepping out into the hall of the prime minister's suite. She left via the media room to find out if there was any news she should know.

She came across an adviser flicking through a newspaper, and as Pasco approached, the staffer covered the item she was reading.

'How are the polling figures?' Pasco asked.

The anxious staffer answered, and the prime minister scanned the room, catching heads dropping behind workstation screens to avoid contact.

'Keep up the outstanding work.' Tension was clear. Pasco didn't want to extend her presence, preferring staff not to feel stressed.

The embarrassed staffer mumbled, 'Good luck.'

The prime minister headed out into the corridor and glanced to her left, catching the social security minister, her greatest supporter in cabinet, walking out of her office toward her. She waited for her to catch up. When her colleague glimpsed the prime minister ahead, she waved an apology, retracing her steps back to her office.

'As I was saying, no one wants to speak today.'

Pasco strolled to the nearby elevator lobby and pushed a button. As the doors swished open, the laughing inside stopped as staff members noticed who was waiting.

'Good morning,' Pasco beamed.

The embarrassed staffers stepped from the elevator, mumbling a response and trying to avoid eye contact.

Pasco entered the elevator, pushing the button for the second floor, and within moments she was in the corridor leading to the parliamentary library, marching to the entrance, pushing open the glass door and strolling to the counter.

A startled librarian reacted when she saw who was in front of her. 'Prime Minister?'

'Good morning,' Pasco smiled. 'I just wanted to return these; I have no further use for them.'

'Thank you, Prime Minister. Anything else I can do for you?'

'No, you have been most kind.'

The librarian hesitated, before adding, 'I hope it goes well for you this morning, Prime Minister. You have been an honest leader, and it isn't fair what's happening to you. You deserve better.'

'Thank you; I appreciate it.' Pasco bowed her head as she left.

Rather than take the elevator, she walked past Mural Hall, the open function area overlooking the atrium at the centre of parliament house. As she passed, a business breakfast was in progress and it appeared the small business minister was coming to the end of his address. Pasco ventured closer, standing behind the tables and gaining his attention as he was concluding his remarks.

She pointed to her chest and nodded, showing a desire to speak, but the minister shook his head, passing the microphone back to a business leader who then began congratulating the minister on his speech and the manner in which he was supporting the franchise sector.

It disappointed Pasco not to have been acknowledged and moved off, walking to the balustrade surrounding the atrium and gazing over the edge down to the black marble water fountain two stories below. As she watched people stroll through the Members' Hall, the grandeur of the house captivated her. She gazed up through the glass roof, resting her compendium on a shelf and gripping the wooden rail with both hands to steady herself, and into the flagpole tower above. She then looked back down at the marble floor below before moving off.

As she headed away from the railing, she again glimpsed the social security minister, now crossing the marble floor below, heading for the party room. What surprised Pasco was that she was now walking with the treasurer, Parker Osborne. The two ministers paused at the water feature, animated in discussion. Pasco assumed her friend was giving the leadership conspirator a dressing down.

As Pasco was about to move off, she spotted Osborne lean in and kiss his colleague on the cheek, placing his arm around her shoulders as they strolled off together. Watching them go brought a devastating realisation to Pasco.

No matter the dedication she had given to win national elections over the years, bringing the party back into government; no matter the sacrifices she had made, the tough decisions she had to make: her political legacy to the nation now seemed to come down to a party room of self-interested colleagues.

The prime minister placed her compendium on the balustrade again and gripped the rail, anxiety flushing through her. A dizzy numbness worked over her, a need to sit and recover. She gripped the rail even tighter to ensure she didn't collapse or fall and waited for the wash of feeling to subside. Her head sank low and her eyes welled as she contemplated what to say if the votes didn't go her way. Would she break down and would they leak it to the media to humiliate her further?

She wished she had spoken to her husband earlier; perhaps he would have been a calming influence for her anxiety. Donna had been little support over the last few hours. After the Sadler show, Kellaway had left the office and had not been heard from since. Pasco harrumphed as she gazed toward the flag above the roof and thought about the love of her life stranded in bed with a headache. She even wondered if what was about to occur in the party room would threaten their relationship. Would there be a future with Donna when the glamour of office was stripped from her?

She started trembling as anxiety built within her, now embarrassed about the state she was deteriorating into. This would be no behaviour for any leader, let alone the prime minister. She began panting to calm herself.

She glanced up and spotted the small business minister rushing off. Another vote for or against, she mused as she watched him pass the atrium.

This was a time for strength and courage to face her accusers; a time to eliminate all obstacles before her as she had done in the past, and fight for her legacy and her future. She straightened, gazing up at the flag again, and beamed. The dizziness faded. The fog of her mind was clearing, now determined. Then with the deftness of a gymnast on a bar, she flicked herself over the railing, landing headfirst on the black marble below.

She never heard the screams.

CHAPTER

56

The stone cell-like room chilled Cardinal Rosseau as he entered; his meeting with the Holy Father arranged for a quiet place away from suspicious eyes and ears. His hands were icy, so he blew into them and gave them a vigorous rub after he placed his satchel on the bare desk. He sat in a hard wooden chair, which creaked as he eased himself into it.

A flurry of robes announced the Pope, who closed and latched the heavy wooden door. He made his way to the other side of the desk, leaning in like a raptor about to devour his prey, steam panting from him.

'Why did you want to meet with me so covertly, Morris?'

'We have much to discuss, and I didn't want curious staff undermining our meeting.'

'You want to confess you wasted your time in Australia?'

'You know very well there remains enormous uncertainty since the death of the prime minister. It has delayed the politics for a while, but they will sort it out. My man will make good and restore our hopes.'

'Then why do you want to see me?' The Pope rubbed his hands.

'What I learned in Australia is the ruthless manner in which they go about their politics. They taught me that expecting things to happen is wasted on the population; it is those who seize opportunity who win the battle for ideas.'

'Interesting.' the Pope leaned back. 'Luckily, we don't play these types of political games in the church.'

'You did in the conclave, you shafted me.'

'I didn't shaft you. I just used white privilege against you, that's all. It was time for a black Pope.'

Rosseau snorted. 'Yes, but we were thinking of someone from Africa, not Vegas.'

'I'm African.' the Pope shifted in his seat, upset by the suggestion. 'I have the confidence of the conclave, and judging by the manner I am building support, I shall be there for a long, long time but don't worry, I'll come to your funeral. I may not deliver your eulogy, though.' Caspian laughed, with a deep scoffing grunt.

'Oh, I'm very sure you'll be there, but you won't be sitting up front.'

Caspian's broad smile disappeared, turning into a scowl. 'What are you suggesting?'

'What am I suggesting?' Rosseau nodded, smirking at his nemesis. 'I'm suggesting it is time for you to retire.'

The Pope fell back, roaring with laughter.

'You are killing me,' he said through his guffaws. 'Why would I retire?'

'You are the sovereign of the Catholic Church, therefore you have to be above reproach.'

'Of course, and I am.'

'The church must have faith in you, we must trust you.'

'Of course.'

'We must have your loyalty, if you expect us to provide it.'

'Goes without saying.'

Rosseau was losing patience with the Holy Father's cockiness, but continued to plan.

'We expect our Pope to apply judgment in all decisions and actions.'

'I think I am wasting my time here; this is ridiculous.'

Rosseau reached into his satchel and withdrew a small notebook computer, flicking open the lid. 'I have something to show you, which may interest you.'

Caspian was restless, wanting to leave, impatient with the arrogance of Rosseau. 'This better be good, otherwise I suspect we will send you to the antipodes once again, but more permanently this time.'

Rosseau waited a moment for the device to warm up, then brought up a page with two URLs linked to it.

'This first video is a moment of lack of judgment.'

The recording started and showed a priest, his face pixilated, stopping at a café and sitting at an outside table. A few moments later a young man arrived and sat down, and the priest passed to him a shoe box which he tugged from a backpack. The young man opened the box, satisfied with the contents, left after depositing a small envelope.

'What is this, the latest blockbuster from Hollywood?'

'It's a payoff,' Rosseau said. 'Some weeks ago, they approached us with evidence that would hurt the church. Evidence we now know would damage the brand.' Rosseau air quoted. 'We then undertook negotiations to retrieve the evidence to safeguard the church, so under your name we delivered five hundred thousand euros to this person in return for the evidence.'

'Why would you involve me?'

'That is a good question. The answer is that the evidence we received was all to do with you.'

'This is rubbish, what are you suggesting?' Caspian licked his dry lips. 'There is nothing on me.'

'This is where trust comes into play, because we believe there is.'

Rosseau moved his fingers about the keyboard, opening the second link showing a black man and white youth in a passionate embrace.

'This is you, isn't it?'

Caspian didn't respond, spellbound by the images flashing before him. 'How did you get this?'

'I just told you; you paid for it.' The Pope wiped his face.

'As the Holy Father, you have lost trust by having relations with a young man. You then displayed poor judgment, paying hush money to him, and you have been disloyal to the teachings of the church. The many citizens who look to you for inspiration have been let down. You have stomped upon centuries of respect and responsibility.'

'It was only one time.'

'Once is more than enough, don't you think?'

It crushed the Pope, slouching back into the chair, the bravado tossed about just moments ago now washed from him.

'We have two options by our reckoning.'

'Who are we?'

'Senior members of the Vatican and conclave.'

'Others know?'

'Yes, of course, ribald actions as serious as this need to be shared, don't you think?' Rosseau sneered.

Caspian didn't respond as he considered his options.

Rosseau continued, 'You can resign and allow for the election of a new Pope, which, it seems, maybe me.'

Caspian glanced up but didn't acknowledge the hit.

'Or you can deny the evidence, open the church to months of unnecessary scandal, then be forced out by the conclave. Either way, it is the same result. Easy or hard… it's your choice.'

The Pope didn't reply.

'What we suggest is this: we make an announcement overnight that you have fallen ill with a virus, and you cannot continue with your official duties. You will appoint a Cardinal interregnum carmeriengo during this period of sede vacante.' Rosseau had rehearsed his lines. 'You will then resign in twelve months, allowing the conclave to elect a new Pope, one we can trust with loyalty.'

Defeated, the Pope asked, 'Will I have a future after the resignation?'

'You will live in the church's care and, who knows, you might enjoy a few years in the antipodes.'

'What title will I hold?'

'You cannot preach or provide any church services. You can live a life as a monk, but I suspect a Vegas chap like you would want to still surround yourself in the delights of others, so we shall ensure we meet your needs.'

'The boy?'

'Trust me; we will never hear from him again.'

'What do you want me to do?'

'I want you to sign these papers.' Rosseau withdrew them from his satchel. 'These confirm your impending resignation in twelve months. They also confirm the plan for your duties to be managed within the Vatican. There is also an agreement between you and the Vatican for you to allow, setting out the conditions of your retirement.'

'I shall take them to my chambers and consider them.'

'There is nothing to consider, you are done. Either sign them now or there is no deal and we will expose you as the awful person you are.'

Caspian said nothing, his head bowed, hands clasped across his chest. He crossed himself and leaned forward, taking Rosseau's proffered pen and signing the documents. Papa no more.

CHAPTER

57

It had been an emotional Christmas for the Stevedore family. They allowed Victoria home and her father insisted she decamp at his large, yet empty apartment while she continued to recover. The unknown whereabouts of her husband added to the emotion, as she was nearing her third trimester without his support.

The police clarified the suspicious circumstances in which Ferguson had disappeared. His car was found with blood smears on the driver's door and someone had ransacked their house. They weren't confident about finding him. Vikki had come to terms with the fact that her husband might have met foul play, never to be found.

The youths charged with her assault faced court in late December, pleaded guilty at their first court appearance and sentenced to a minimum term of ten years.

Ortega provided testimony for the crown; he never got his twenty thousand.

Vikki's life was piecing back together in the new year, then on Easter Monday she was rushed to hospital with the onset of her baby, eight weeks earlier than expected. The birthing suite was not only full of specialists for the premature birth, but was also attended by burns specialists, to ensure her skin and subsequent caesarean wound were meeting their high medical expectations. After a short birthing procedure, mother and baby were doing well and taking visitors.

A few weeks later, just before Anzac Day and she was visiting the Alfred for her fortnightly check and remedial exercise programme. As she pushed her daughter's pram onto the burns unit floor, she almost collided with Vera Thompson, who encouraged her to come to her office as she was about to watch the parliament for the announcement, or not, of the euthanasia referendum.

'We can do all of that later. Bring the bub to my office, so I can have a squeeze and a smell.'

'What is it about older women wanting to smell my baby?' Vikki said.

'Hey, wait up, I'm not old,' Thompson laughed. As they walked into her office she asked, 'Shall we do tea? I'll ring the café to bring up high tea, it shouldn't take long.'

'That will be lovely, thank you.'

Thompson ordered tea, sandwiches and cake from the café.

'Now, before I play with your baby, tell me, how are you? How is your skin recovering since the birth?'

'To be honest, I am not sure whether I'm feeling the caesar or it's still the skin recovering.'

'Are you still using the support bandages?'

'Yes, on my legs and arms.'

'Medications?'

'I'm trying not to take too much because of the baby.'

'Are you breast feeding?'

'Yes.'

'Excellent, is it sore?'

'I'm getting used to it. I don't think it's affecting my skin. I suppose I won't be able to see any stretch marks.'

'Yes, good one,' Thompson smiled. 'I'm expecting there to be some scarring around your breast, indeed most of your body, although your back may carry the most.'

'Good thing I can't see it then.'

'Now let's have a look at her; has she changed much?'

'Not since the last time you saw her.'

Thompson picked up the wrapped baby, snuggling her nose into its face, breathing deeply.

'Ah, I can't get enough of her.'

'What's this thing you are watching?' Vikki asked.

'They are telecasting a government statement concerning the euthanasia bill.'

'Will they go ahead with it?'

'Your father seems to think that if they do, it will be close.'

'Speaking of which, are you coming over tomorrow?' Vikki asked.

'I'm coming for the weekend.'

'Oh, really? Are you two getting serious?'

'I can never tell with your dad, but this will be our first sleepover.'

'You're kidding. You haven't done…'

'Done what?' Thompson smiled as she cuddled the baby.

'You know.'

'The answer to that question is… none of your business.'

Vikki took the baby off a reluctant Thompson when Stephie began noises suggesting a feed was in order. She secured the baby to suckle.

'What do you think the government will announce?' Vikki asked as she settled into her chair.

'Your father is a little worried about it, as you know.'

'He hasn't spoken about it with me, to be honest.' Vikki gazed down at her baby. 'Whenever I raise the referendum, he tries to avoid talking about it.'

'It stressed him out over you.'

'I'm sure he was, but we had a pact with Mum, so I hope he hasn't changed his mind.'

'Your circumstances were very difficult for your father, and he struggled to come to terms with that whole legal process it made us to go through. It had an enormous impact on him.'

'It's a straightforward decision to allow death with dignity. As a doctor, you'd have to agree?'

Thompson glanced at her and smiled. She remained hesitant whether it was time to explain the decisions made on her behalf during the first few days of the emergency care. A knock on her door interrupted her as a tray of tea and food was carried in.

Perhaps the weekend.

CHAPTER

58

The House of Representatives chamber was noisy as the politicians waited for the commencement of proceedings. Charlie Stevedore remained anxious about the announcement and sat sullen in his place. Parker Osborne was the opposite; he was excited to get on with the parliament, joking and laughing with colleagues sitting behind him.

'Honourable members: the speaker,' the sergeant at arms announced from the entrance adjoining Members Hall, and the procession of the sergeant, the speaker of the house and the attending clerks entered the chamber, parading to their positions. The house was silent as members stood during the formal procession.

When the speaker positioned herself at the throne-like chair above the clerks, gazing over the chamber, she waited for a moment, then read an acknowledgement of country and prayers. Members stood with heads bowed until the speaker sat at her chair, calling on the orders of the day.

'Clerk.'

Stevedore's anxiety grew, breathing deeply. He leaned across to Osborne, patting him on the arm for reassurance.

The clerk stood, and in the best monotone he could muster announced, 'Order of business: a bill to establish a fund for the eradication of feral cats.'

Stevedore interrupted proceedings by standing at the despatch box, gripping the sides to steady himself. He glanced toward the speaker and smiled, then looked up to the media gallery, which was full, all eyes watching the action below.

'Speaker, on indulgence, I seek leave to move a motion that standing orders and business of the day be suspended so that it will allow the government to move the first and second readings of urgent legislation.'

Stevedore stepped away, resuming his seat. Osborne glanced at him, nodding approval with a smile.

'Is leave granted?' The speaker glanced to the manager of opposition business, who nodded.

'Leave is granted.'

Osborne didn't move as he glanced at the speaker, then watched Stevedore stand at the despatch box and announce, 'I move the first reading of a bill, which provides for a referendum to be conducted to determine if the constitution can be amended to allow the establishment of laws for the federal government on the matters of euthanasia and abortion.'

'The question is that the bill be read a first time.' The speaker put the question to the chamber. 'All those in favour say aye, the contrary no. I think the ayes have it.'

Stevedore didn't hesitate.

'I move that the bill be now read a second time.'

Prime Minister Stevedore delivered a compelling speech, reflecting on his wife and the manner of her death, and his daughter's recent legal battles; he contrasted his angst and emotion with other families struggling through dense regulations and challenges.

Stevedore clarified that as a nation Australia could not have variable laws on life and death matters. He made the argument to have one law to cover abortion and euthanasia in a dignified manner. He argued that a referendum was necessary, as this decision was not for politicians who might play with the emotions and feelings of concerned groups, rather, he wanted a mature public debate, and a decision made by the people, for the people.

As he finished, Parker Osborne stood and shook his hand. The new foreign minister would now campaign for the No vote, but knew that with the support of a new prime minister, the referendum was now likely to succeed. His ambition for leadership now dampened.

Stevedore's daughter Vikki, viewing the broadcast, wiped away a tear.

ACKNOWLEDGEMENTS

In 1996 I spoke in the Commonwealth federal parliament on a Bill to override the Northern Territory's recently enacted legislation enabling euthanasia to be available for their citizens. I took the then unusual step of seeking advice from the community I represented, seeking the opinions of many groups within the electorate, including churches. I provided the details of the Bill and provided the second reading speeches of speakers for and against the legislation. I then facilitated public meetings to determine if the community was for or against; firstly the issue of states' rights to determine their own laws; and second, whether euthanasia should be legislated. The overwhelming response was to vote for the Bill and against legalised euthanasia.

What I learned during my research was the manner euthanasia was managed by medical teams caring for a patient; the inadequacy of palliative care; and the potential for greedy and impatient family members wishing the death of a family member. This later issue still concerns me with the growing support for end-of-life legislation, hence the book. Death should be ours to determine without the influence of others.

The process of publishing is long, and there are many players.

Patty Kavadias, Trish Stewart, and Anne and Michael Keaney have again provided valuable feedback as has Phil and Cate Barresi, and Deborah Daly. Michael Tate provided insight regarding geographic consistencies, and Greg and Anthea Pelgrave provide continued support. Denise and Paul Tyrrell also provide substantial support, and I remain grateful for their promotional efforts.

I thank my colleagues at Yarraville writer's group for their willingness to provide suggestions and support. I also acknowledge the splendid work the Australian Society of Authors do to support novelists needing a kindly word. Their Literary Speed dating allowed me to present the full manuscript read by several publishers. I encourage you to join your local writers' group and even join your representative body to increase the voice of authors.

I also acknowledge the good folk of Williamstown who make the village the best kept secret in Melbourne and remain interested in the work I am doing. I named most of the characters in this story using the village's street names.

I thank the many folks who contact me to discuss my work, and I appreciate their feedback.

I want to thank 852 Press for the effort in providing support to an author wanting to get the story onto bookshelves and their strong support for Australian authors.

The support I receive from my extended family and friends is terrific, and I look forward to discussing politics with you all whenever we meet. Julia, Anthony, Kaitlyn and Taylor provide many laughs, good times and support my writing, thank you.

Finally, I wish to thank my brother Peter and his wife Jan for the support and care they provided our mother during her last days and helped the sad end come with dignity to a woman who lived, loved and mattered.

ABOUT THE AUTHOR

As a political insider, Richard Evans served as a federal member of parliament for Cowan in Western Australia during the turbulent 1990s. He now specialises in writing political thrillers, writing about the exotic characters in the mysterious world of the Australian Parliament. He lives above a pub, opposite a church in the historic bayside village of Williamstown, overlooking the grand international city of Melbourne.

For more information about his other books,
or to contact Richard please visit:
www.richardevans-author.com

FORGOTTEN PEOPLE

She wants her culture and country back. Independence was never ceded, and she will do whatever it takes to get it back, including the ultimate sacrifice. When government peace talks stop, revolution begins.

Should a government be obliged to negotiate a treaty with First Nations, ending decades of discrimination and disrespect for the Forgotten People, or will it defeat the revolutionaries fighting for justice in this gripping Australian political thriller?

Revolutionary leader, Nellie Millergoorra, campaigns for an aboriginal homeland to preserve indigenous culture by advocating the prohibition of mining in Arnhem Land using a United Nations declaration to convince a disrespectful government to sign a treaty. Nellie will do whatever it takes to finally gain independence and end government regulation over her people.

When there is no agreement, she recruits mercenary special forces to inflame community chaos establishing an explosive aboriginal revolutionary movement. Using high-tech intervention, the mercenaries destablise the national energy grid starting a fanatical revolution with chaos on the streets. Their secret intent is to embezzle money when security systems are disabled.

A contemptuous government is forced to the negotiation table to agree on a peace agreement putting an end to the escalating hostile revolution. Millergoorra wants more and demands sovereignty for First Nations, proclaiming a partitioned homeland is non-negotiable.

In a surprising confrontation with a reluctant prime minister, who is threatened with an ultimatum he can't ignore, Millergoorra negotiates a treaty whilst facing her own battle for survival.

Forgotten People is gripping political thriller featuring surprising plot twists, compelling characters, and a kick-arse female heroine.

DUPLICITY

The Mercantiles, a long-established, clandestine group of high-taxpaying business owners have grown frustrated by Prime Minister Andrew Gerrard's failure to meet promises, and decide the nation needs a change of government at the upcoming election. They call upon experienced and ruthless political operative Jonathan Wolff to organise their election campaign, and defeat the prime minister.

Realising he cannot win the election his way, Wolff initiates an explosive campaign designed to remove the prime minister by defeating him in his own electorate using an independent candidate. Tapping into the communities' latent anxiety over immigration policy, the community is subjected to violent demonstrations, triggering increased racist attacks. Ironically, the candidate Wolff supports — and manipulates to drive the campaign against the prime minister — is Indian immigrant and university professor, Jaya Rukhmani.

Investigative journalist Anita Devlin is appointed by her editor to promote the Stanley campaign as the publishing owner, unknown to her, is a member of the Mercantiles. She discovers the nefarious Wolff strategically working the campaign, and endeavours to expose his influence and manipulation.

DOOMED

Three years after the change of government, the nation is facing huge social, policy, and environmental-related disasters yet the Australian government seems paralyzed on how to proceed. Two senior ministers resolve that a change of prime minister is essential for Australia's future, and begin to lay the foundations for his dismissal.

Meanwhile, the parliament is held in a balance of power by the independent, Jaya Rukhmani, who can decide at any time if government legislation will be approved. Upon hearing the news that former prime minister Andrew Gerrard wishes to re-enter parliament, Jaya turns to Barton Messenger as an ally.

Doomed takes us behind the scenes of a parliament unaware of how their ambitions and political manipulations affect the everyday Australian. When the environment and economy are brought into the mix, which will be the one to flourish, and which one is doomed?

www.ingramcontent.com/pod-product-compliance
Lightning Source LLC
Chambersburg PA
CBHW021955130726
47903CB00014B/1459